HIDDEN ONES
A VEIL OF MEMORIES

OTHER NOVELS BY MARCIA FINE

Historical Fiction

Paper Children—An Immigrant's Legacy

The Blind Eye—A Sephardic Journey

Paris Lamb

Satire

Stressed In Scottsdale

Boomerang—When Life Comes Back To Bite You

Gossip.com

HIDDEN ONES
A VEIL OF MEMORIES

HISTORICAL FICTION

MARCIA FINE

L'IMAGE LP PRESS

Historical fiction | Sephardic Jews | Mexico 1650s | Inquisition in Mexico | Mexican Jews | Crypto Jews | Southwest Territories

ISBN Paperback: 978-0-9826952-5-8

Printed in the United States of America

With gratitude for those who carry this family history.

AN ACT OF FAITH
LORD INQUISITOR DR. JUAN SAENZ
DE MAÑZOCA

13 de abril 1649
Ciudad de México
Auto-de-fé

Two *barrenderos* swept their brooms across cobblestones, arms swinging, cotton pants swaying in the slight breeze under a grey sky. The first signs of spring appeared with buds on trees and unpredictable weather; however, the unclean air, gloomy with smoke, lingered, singeing the men's nostrils.

They were witnesses to the orchestrated exhibition that began two days earlier with an all-night vigil of prayer followed by a solemn Mass for the devout at daybreak and a sumptuous breakfast feast of mangoes, pineapple, oranges and ham for our priests. They dressed in their finest gold-trimmed robes, and two processions—one, a parade of *familiares* that included 500 officers of the Inquisition, nobility dressed in velvet jewel tones, knights in clinking armor, the consul in a squashed hat, university staff in formal attire and municipal authorities of the Tribunal of the Inquisition in uniforms, all on horseback. The viceroy, wearing the elaborate clothes of Spanish nobility, rode in their midst, smiling and waving.

I, as an inquisitor, rode in this group, my head held high, a black cloak with a peek of red lining covering my head and most of my face. The church felt it best that we not be easily identified by the public. After all, we did not choose the punishments. We merely accused, investigated and turned the guilty over to the civil authorities with the admonition to treat them with mercy. The church never killed anyone.

After us came another procession of penitents in conical hats who were to be reconciled or relaxed. They followed the authorities through narrow streets, some with heads hanging in shame and others staring with defiance. Those who agreed to be reconciled would be welcomed back to the bosom of the church—after the appropriate punishments, of course. Still, all of the thirteen men and women had two confessors who never left their side, anticipating a last-minute change of heart. Those who were to be relaxed— our term for the finality of fire—still had an opportunity to save themselves from the flames. If they confessed and were willing to be with the one true faith in death, our charity allowed us to garrote them before their feet felt flames. Only one stubborn man refused. Tomás Treviño de Sobremonte, whose thirteen year-old-son testified against him. The Church in its glory encouraged public shame as the best way to transform behavior.

When the hundred and nine convicts, all but one a Judaizer, reached the main plaza, many doll-like effigies of those accused and absent were placed at the highest level of stairs leading to the stage while the penitents, hunched with humiliation, were guided to the lower steps. Our church brethren were seated under a black velvet canopy trimmed with gold fringe. It has been estimated that almost twenty thousand people watched from wooden bleachers, although the square in front of the Viceregal Palace swelled with another twenty thousand souls that stretched to the horizon. Hundreds of candles illuminated the stage, our reminder to the populace that light scares the devil, unless they follow our God-given rules.

Evil lurks everywhere.

The viceroy stood behind a pulpit after repeating his oath, while the secretary of the Inquisition stood behind another pulpit. I, as the prosecutor, was seated behind both of them so I heard every word. The roar of the crowd gathered for a spectacle quieted when the viceroy lifted his arms for silence. His voice, sonorous with authority, finger pointing across the expanse of people, stated the declaration of faith.

Afterward, he said, I close by swearing to defend the Catholic Church and the Inquisition against heretics, ones who would annihilate our way of life in the New World. I persuade all to confess today to be cleansed of sin. Let us proceed.

I could see people near the front were moved by this. Women wiped tears with the hems of their dresses, men slugged back more wine, and children played among the blankets. Many had come from smaller cities and rural ranches, dressed in their finest for a carnival. An old man with a sun-wizened face yelled out, We are setting a good example with this impressive celebration!

For this Act of Faith we have cleared our prisons of the worst offenders. Many have been with us for a decade or more. Others are so petrified they cannot stop trembling. More women than men this time, many who came to us after the church distributed a leaflet of what to look for when identifying those who still clung to their rituals and traditions. They gave themselves away by clean clothes or a tablecloth on the Sabbath, or draining meat of blood, or fasting on certain days. Neighbors or servants noticed. These stiff-necked people deserved to be punished for not accepting the Trinity into their hearts.

After thousands of the faithful had gathered the night before, the plaza was now deserted except for scavengers. Children brushed away ashes that caught on their eyelashes and coated their tongues, oily grey reminders of a successful fiesta day. The ribaldry of the crowd's screams and laughter echoed; however, there was little mirth as the workers stacked lumber, nails, stairs and awnings to be stored for future use.

Men set about deconstructing the thirty-seven wooden stages, viewing platforms and scaffoldings erected so that elite merchants who supported us and our church officials could watch with ease from wooden benches, plush pillows cushioning their spines.

Following the laboring men were boys dragging straw baskets attached to bands of woven fabric strapped across their foreheads to fill with rubbish. They hoped for sweets by collecting debris, small hands gathering fruit and bread left behind. Discarded goat bladders enticed the boys to throw back their heads for a few drops of wine; a sin, but not a bad one for thirsty children.

With a game of push and shove, the foragers also harvested snippets of yellow sackcloth torn from *sanbenitos*, the garment of shame worn by those paraded through the streets. If the accused were not in yellow with a red cross signed across their bodies, others who were not willing to be forgiven, the impenitents, wore black with flames and devils dancing around the hem. The accused, their sanbenitos falling to their ankles in the front and back, shuffled with dread. We carried little sympathy for those who did not follow the tenets of the church.

Vestiges of incense still hung in the air with the putrid smell of wicked deeds, our critics would say. I accepted all that the church decreed; others felt a little sympathy for the indicted, perhaps because some of our priests were exposed to that other faith in childhood. Younger boys squatted to scrape green wax from cobblestones with broken shells that sliced their pliable fingers. They sucked blood from the tips until thunder collided in the heavens. Lightning followed with an errant thundershower that cleared the space, quashing the last hot embers that still glowed. The boys scattered under scaffolding until the rain stopped. Others searched through the embers for treasures with sticks. I stayed dry from my vantage point on the higher floor of a nearby building where I lived, sitting on a chair near the window. The short walk to work pleased me.

By the end of the day the plaza was empty except for the smells that tainted the air. Children ran home, candies clutched in sweaty palms. A few found teeth in the detritus of the fires, proud to have found a viable souvenir. I am sure their mothers greeted them with honor for being of service to the Church. Few children grasped the spectacle that their parents found entertaining. For the adults it was a day of religious performance, the Last Judgment in full review, an act of faith. It was done to remind them to be more devout, that the church was all-powerful, that we were doing the work of the Father, the Son and the Holy Ghost.

My attention was drawn to the two sweeping barrenderos who worked in silence. I imagined their conversation as they strolled home. After all, as Dr. Juan Saenz de Mañzoca, the Lord Inquisitor and prosecutor for the royal court of Spain, I have not made many friends. The job of an inquisitor is lonely, although I have found a concubine to give me solace after a difficult day.

I imagine these two common men saying:

Were you here last night? asks the first man, tamping tobacco into the bowl of a small clay pipe.

Yes. He hesitates. In the back. I saw the flames leaping, licking the sky. I heard the screams. His voice catches. Judaizers all.

What was the total?

Twenty-one men and five women reconciled. Seven women and six men relaxed.

Did anyone survive? A puff of smoke curls around his head as he exhales.

Only the reconciled who transformed themselves in the last fateful minutes.

Lashes? He taps the pipe on the ground to clean it of burned tobacco.

Only ninety-four, but they exhumed dozens of bones to burn in effigy, almost sixty I think. A great achievement for the Grand Day of Faith!

BOOK ONE
1650–1665

CHAPTER ONE

CELENDARIA

4 de julio 1650
Ciudad de México

Vague sounds capture me, caught in the web of my dreams—birds flying, the lift of freedom in their wings, a rhythm of liberty, they sail the skies of my mind with abandon. I stir in the early morning hour to wake myself. My grandmother, downstairs to prepare our morning coffee, moves with her steady pace as she opens the back door to bring in firewood, unfastens a canister for our blend prepared by my father's traders, tinkles a spoon against a pot, clicks shut a case where bread is hidden from critters.

I want to see her. I roll away quietly from my snoring sisters to land my feet on the floor. I slip them into felt slippers and stand, my white gown billowing from an open shutter. With a crocheted shawl wrapped around my shoulders, I make my way down the stairs with the stealth of a stalking cat.

I do not want to startle her so I sit on the bottom step, elbows on knees, waiting until she finishes her tasks so I can make myself known. She is busy arranging sticks for the tops of the logs to ignite in our hearth. The coffee pot, placed with care, begins to percolate, bubbles of aroma that will awaken everyone soon. I inhale a dreamy reverie about the birds in flight, winging their way to somewhere else, able to escape on a whim.

My grandfather dozes in his sleeping chair, my grandmother's bustle not disturbing his steady pattern of rest, his breath inhaled with a halt and then released with a whoosh.

A knock at the door interrupts my reverie, so soft I am not sure I heard it. I wrap my shawl tighter around me in the silvery light to listen again. Another knock. Who would come at this early hour? I call out, Who is it?

My grandmother reacts before I can, leaving her post at the hearth and shuffling to the door. Who is it? She calls in the stillness of morning. Perhaps it is a friend saying goodbye. Many leave in the stealth of darkness, the *auto-de-fé* of 1649 still fresh in our minds.

I do not hear a response. I am too afraid to run back up to my room. My grandmother, *mi abuela*, unlatches the door to open it a sliver. I cannot see who is there until a hand pushes it back with a slam that awakens my grandfather. Unable to make out what has happened, he is confused without his glasses, blinking in bewilderment.

Three monks in brown robes have come before the first light of dawn to stand in our living space. They are outlined in the light of the fire. I watch my grandmother's face as they offer soothing words. Do not worry. We are not here to harm you. Merely a brief inquiry, Doña Clara. It is nothing. Do not be anxious.

My grandmother's expression shifts from one of calm acceptance to ferocious protest. She knows this is not a social visit. She assumes they have come for her. It has happened to many before her, gossip buzzing through our community, swarms of bees ready to sting those under suspicion. No, I will not go! I have done nothing wrong, she says backing up to a wall. Our small quarters do not make it easy to escape out back to our donkey in its small shelter or through our courtyard, past our wall to the street.

I am shocked to see these men frightening my grandmother. I stand, self-conscious in my nightclothes, the shawl pulled across me. My mother slips by me to confront them. I feel her body heat. What do you want of her? She is an old woman who rises early to start a fire and boil water for our morning coffee. Is that a crime?

Señora, we do not mean to alarm anyone, but our Lord has called us to this home. She must accompany us. The authorities have questions. We are only here to pray for her safe return.

My mother clenches her fists. Two of the men lead her to the door as more men in uniforms enter. The monks slip away in the opalescent light of dawn.

Obstreperous voices shout at my meek grandmother. Come with us now! No delays!

My grandfather, alert to what is happening, begins a desperate wail.

My mother responds, her voice choking. Take me instead. Whatever you accuse her of is a lie. She is a good, observant woman, devoted to her family.

I survey the room as my father rushes past me, pulling on his shirt. My young sisters, their bodies warm from sleep, creep behind me to watch from the stairs too. The household has awakened. Mi abuela, my lovely grandmother. Where are they taking her?

The man with a large mustache speaks, addressing mi abuela directly. Doña Clara, we understand your chickens lay the best *blanquillos* in our area. And your preparation of them with vegetables from your garden is rumored to be exceptional.

Their flattery disgusts me. How do they do know what we are eating in our home? I never doubt the elongated arms of the church and the ears of their many spies. I am imbued with suspicions. I have been brought up with caution.

Mi abuela does not care about their flattery. My mother sobs. My father stands with his face to the wall, head bent in submission. I am a child without power. The authorities are finished with us.

The chief constable stands on one side of mi abuela, a commissary on the other, the last man, carrying a musket, waits behind her. The men grab her arms on each side to hold her, as if she could run away. Her face twists in anguish but no sounds erupt.

My father rushes to her, pulling at the hands of the constable, trying to save his mother-in-law. An elbow flies out to my father's stomach and he doubles over in agony, rolling to the floor. The man with the musket stands over him, pointing it at him.

Do not resist us. We are here under orders from the Church's inquisitors.

My father lifts his hands in supplication and crawls to the corner of the room. It could be worse. What if they shot him before us for his resistance, his blood spilling in our home?

Mi abuelo chokes on his tears, bowing his head, his slippered feet soundless across the tiles. He collapses into his sleeping chair, hands trembling on his lap. He is older than my grandmother and frail, his eyes milky in the diffused light. Take me, he says, offering himself to the unknown.

His foot jerks, knocking over a small table. My grandmother's sewing basket tumbles to the floor, the colored threads chasing across the floor. The embroidered quilt done by her hand falls around my grandpa's shivering legs. He grabs it and rises, the reds and blues illuminated by the rising sun spilling through the open door, jewels at the feet of terror.

The chill in the morning air makes mi abuela shudder. As my grandfather places the quilt around her shoulders, he smells her neck and hair, the usual freshness of flowers transformed into a stink of fright. The hand of the constable pushes him back to his chair. And then they are gone. Gone from Calle Santo Domingo.

I cry out, Where are they taking her? When will she be back? The answers to my questions remain unanswered.

Celendaria, my mother says with a guarded voice, your grandmother has been taken for questioning. She stuffs her knuckles into her mouth to stifle a sob.

My grandfather leans in to speak to us, his voice softening. The ones who came did not come to inquire about her cooking skills. For a moment, I had the idea that perhaps a bribery of our exceptional textiles might be a distraction, but I dismissed it. If they come for the matriarch of a home, an established pious member of our community, then the accusations must be very serious.

What is she guilty of? I knew the answer to my own question. I had been prepared many times, not unlike the demands of cooking our meals—catching the chicken, slaughtering it with a quick slice of knife across the throat, draining the blood outside, plucking the feathers to the pimply skin, washing and rubbing it with spices. I stop my recitation. We are secret Jews who follow the traditions of the centuries. I am not allowed to breathe the words of our faith except in our home.

My mother puts her finger to her lips. Silence. Another secret. In a small dwelling, we are aware of what transpires—secrets, gossip, unorthodox meetings. The Church searches for many of our kind.

Where should I say she is if the neighbors ask? I am practical in a crisis.

Say she went to visit cousins in Puebla, says my mother.

No one will believe me.

Gabriela! My father admonishes my mother. Don't make her tell more lies. By the time the sun is overhead, the whole city will know our matriarch has been arrested.

My brother, Aruh, bursts through the back door. Has she been charged?

How did you hear with such haste? my father asks.

Señor Behar heard her screams as they got close to the jail. What is she accused of? asks Aruh.

My incensed grandfather spits out, They do not tell us. We do not have a system of justice, a reason for fairness. He sits with a straight spine in his chair demanding answers we cannot give.

Maybe they will release her, I say with the naiveté of my ten years. I observe much of what is said and done in our family with curiosity, a trait my mother has warned me could be my undoing.

My father turns to address us, bitter words spewing from his lips. How many of our people have been arrested and held without charges? How many innocents have been indicted? For what? So they can impose their beliefs on us, confiscate our goods? Later, some may be released on the street, broken, confused or worse—sent to the fires. And our neighbors enjoy the spectacle of an *auto-de-fé*. For them it is a holiday. He sputters with outrage, spraying drops of spittle on his garment.

Tears well in my eyes. My father is defeated. He is not angry at me but grieving for the intrusion of the Church in our lives. Why do they persecute us? We follow their rules, worship their Savior, tithe at the cathedral. What do they want?

My grandfather, disconsolate, asks, Who could have made an accusation? We are guarded. His posture collapses as he blinks without his glasses. He mourns for his wife of over thirty years, mi abuela.

Aruh, watching our discourse, enters the fray in a hoarse whisper. We must do something to release her. The longer she stays, the farther into the bowels of secret cells she will be taken. We may never hear from her again.

My grandfather has been passive, inconsolable until now. What?! You cannot utter such profanity. She must come home. He slams his hand on his knee.

Aruh heaves a sigh, perhaps in an effort to calm himself. His fingers run through his thick hair, his arms muscular from farm work. My brother offers a suggestion. We must seek assistance of our parish priest. Or someone else. But who?

My grandfather responds, leaning forward. I had been dozing in my chair, dreaming of water seeping through our walls from unstoppable rain, fleeing the collapse of our home. He halts. Maybe the realization of what he was saying stuns him. He continues. My dear wife, her eyes, wide with fear, begged me. But what could I do as she scanned the room for an escape? Oh, the panic she must have felt, her heart fluttering like mine. The monks were an apparition, fading into the shadows of the wall, slipping out the door.

My mother says, Maybe our friend's son who is part of them now. Ach, an absurd suggestion.

My father, pulling at his chin, says, Ridiculous. They never give a gift. They only accept them. Besides, Señora Lopez's son is besieged with requests. He has become the harshest of all, turning away the most desperate of us without a flash of recognition.

Yes, when I followed them outside the chief constable demanded money. I gave him silver coins from my pocket.

Bah, this is not enough, the commissary told me when I placed them in his open palm. I had no more. I did not want to plead. I showed strength and dignity, but they insisted, harassing me with the threat of confiscations. Why are you taking her? What has she done? They remained silent as a monolith.

What do they want with my wife? Inside, my heart howled as though wounded with an arrow. My grandfather breaks down, his face covered with his hands, shoulders rocking.

My mother crosses the room to be near him. He lifts his head, wiping tears with the back of his hand and starts anew.

They dragged her with force out the door, her legs no longer able to support her. She glanced at me from the donkey cart, terrified, her face distorted, tears spooling down her face onto her shawl.

Mi abuelo cannot continue. He closes his eyes, perhaps to block out the pain.

My father must feel the anguish of his mother disappearing into the dark hole. Why do they want her? He asks no one in particular. Someone has accused her of Judaizing. We must find out who did this to our family.

My indignant mother asks, Who would do such a thing? To tear at the fabric of our family like this? We are so secretive our neighbors have no idea of our customs.

I have been unnoticed in my favorite place near the bottom of the stairs against the wall. Not so long ago, my mother and grandmother shared with me that we follow the Law of Moses in secret, despite appearing as Sunday Catholics, never missing Mass.

Our family speaks over one another. I cannot discern all the voices after my other brother, León, shows up. Can we find out the charges? What do they want from us? Why must we obey their cruel rules? My grandfather calms the family with words from Ladino, a language his ancestors spoke in Spain and Portugal. He speaks with resolve.

I repeat with my family, *La sensya y la pasensya abaten al enimgo.* Wisdom and patience beat the enemy. We repeat the words again to calm ourselves. I have interest in learning this tongue of Spanish and Hebrew. Could this saying be true?

I notice mi abuelo straightens his spine, finding strength in his faith. He claps his hands together. Enough. The accusers will not reveal anything. We have seen this before with others. Doña Clara remains a brave soul, loyal to God. Her faith gives her strength. We must all pray.

And so, we lower our heads.

CHAPTER TWO

CLARA

10 de julio 1650, in the morning
Ciudad de México
Santa Oficina de la Inquisición

We, the Inquisitors, who stand against Heretical Depravity and Apostasy in the City of Mexico, the provinces of New Spain, the Maya territory of Verapaz in Guatemala, Nicaragua, Yucatán, Honduras, islands of the Philippines, Cartegena in Columbia and regions of Lima, Peru, state that the enemies of religion are also the enemies of the state. You have been brought to the Audience chamber to repeat your life story. State your name and place of birth.

I am Doña Clara Henriquez de Crespin, born *el primero* de mayo, 1606, in this city. My parents died when I was six years of age. First my mother and then my father passed into eternity. My maiden aunt, Maria Luz, raised me. She enrolled me at the Poor Clares Convent of the Ascension when I was ten years old so I would be educated in the faith. I learned how to read and write. At the age of sixteen, my aunt arranged a marriage for me. Please do not judge that I did not stay in the boundaries of the Church. A certain kind of woman is meant for that life. I desired to have a family and educate my children in the ways of the Church. I was married in the cathedral in the smaller chapel to my husband, Esteban Rubén Crespin, in 1622. He was the owner of a small stall in the marketplace that sold lace veils and velvet cloth for the aristocracy. I am the mother of four daughters.

I inhale a breath to give myself a moment to put my thoughts in order. Nerves pound like my pestle when I grind corn. The restiveness has long been with me, amplifying my heartbeat to a drum level.

Please name them.

Maria, the eldest, after our Holy Mother, Gabriela, Rosa and Oliva. Two others passed in infancy.

What they do not know is that the names of our daughters have been chosen with tradition—our oldest chosen to honor my husband's grandmother, the second daughter after my deceased mother, the third after my father, and the fourth after my aunt, the one who took me in when there was no hope. It was our way of honoring the generations, the *Toledot*, so their time on earth would live on in our memories. My husband had many regrets that I did not give birth to a son so he could honor his grandfather, a rabbi of the highest order descended from the tribe of Abraham.

My husband and I followed the tradition of giving the girls first names for their spiritual identity with the hope that someday they could practice their faith without complication. For them not to have a bad destiny, we chose the names of our children with deliberation.

Can you confirm you are a baptized Christian who has heard the Mass, confessed and taken part in the Eucharist?

I bow my head and then regard the eyes of the four inquisitors with feigned interest. I cross myself, nerves coursing through my body. After the *gran* auto-de-fé of 1649, a friend from our secret *sinagoga* warned me I might be under suspicion. I lived in fear of all who approached me. Señora Lopez, whose son joined a holy order, grieved at losing another one to the Church. For a time, she wept with consternation. Later she embraced the extra knowledge available to her through surreptitious sources as well as certain privileges.

I did my best to remain calm, although my inquisitor's eyes bored through me with evil and sinister coldness. I remembered some of the catechism from my early life, but had lost much of it. With a rumor that I may be watched, my two eldest daughters, Maria and Rosa, came to the house so we could pack our minds, not unlike the sausage casings that hung in the market from the intestines of pigs, ones we did not eat. We memorized the Law of the Church and the twelve Articles of the Faith until we could rattle them to each other in a half-dozed state, a guarantee in case I was accused. If I was, they might be too. Maria stayed upstairs with sick twins. We studied in the basement where we learned clandestine lessons by candlelight, my granddaughter, Celendaria, nearby, with her mother, Gabriela.

My third daughter was not invited. Why would we not include Oliva? It was not her slow-witted manner, or the lazy eye that followed one's mobility after she finished gazing upon you, or the malady of hysteria, one to fell her at unexpected times of despair, a melancholia that afflicted so many of our kind. No. It was as she saw it, an uncountable firmness in the story of Jesus, the Virgin Mary and the Immaculate Conception, the Resurrection of the Savior. It stirred within her a passion that I could see from the earliest age, one whose beliefs were heresy for me and our kind.

Do I feel guilt that I had to teach them all the ways of the Catholics? It caused me great anguish; however, my husband, a most learned man, assured me it was essential for our survival. I did it in the most dispassionate way, with only the obligatory knowledge necessary. I did not want them to unlearn what I taught them when I broached our one true faith in their adolescence with a storm of secrecy. Her sisters were like me, a believer in one God, but Oliva was different, *reconciliada,* one who returned to the Church without regret to embrace the pageantry of the Mass, as many of us did in the glory of safety. Of course as a New Christian we would always be suspect, so much so that the church did not allow us to sit with Old Christians. What better way to prove loyalty than to renounce another?

But they did not come for me back then.

An imperceptible shudder shook my body. It could not have been observed by my conquerors under this loose sanbenito. My faith that I could defeat them reverberated within me. I recited the seven mortal sins when asked—wrath, avarice, sloth, pride, lust, envy, gluttony—with an ardent desire to impress. A heavy sigh could expose my hidden secrets so I swallowed it. I paused to look deep into their dead eyes. I knew one of my interrogators, Lord Inquisitor Juan Saenz de Mañzoca, an intimidating prosecutor for the royal court sent to New Spain to ferret out heretics and criminals. In their eyes I was worse than a thief or a murderer. Once, when my husband had a dispute about lace with a merchant who cheated us, he favored the wealthy nobleman who refused to pay us for our goods. Another time he sent another hidden one, our neighbor, to the fires for evidence that never materialized. But, he could not admit he made a wrong accusation.

I am asked to state the prayers. I begin with Our Father, the Ave Maria, the Creed and the Salve Regina. I recite this without feeling in my heart. I am aware of breaching my faith by telling lies that causes me great pain. Tiny pearls of sweat bead above my lip.

I recite another prayer with conviction. It is more important for me to survive, to tell the story of a people faithful to one God the way we were taught in our Torah. It is a sacred document for the ages, an ethical system of six hundred and thirteen commandments we have carried for thousands of years. We have been good stewards by keeping the Sabbath, observing the holidays, learning Hebrew to read the Book, staying clean, following our customs. A flame burns within me that future generations must know about our people. Even if none of us lives, someone will remember our greatest admonition—*bind them as a sign on your hand and write them on the doorposts of your house, teach them to your children when you lie down and when you rise up*, all written in Deuteronomy 11:19. I am commanded to cheat death.

I commence with the Law of the Church, the Articles of General Confession and the sacraments, a beatific smile dancing around my mouth. They did not think I would know so much. It is an ability of our people to memorize, especially after confiscation of all our books. Why would the Church allow followers to read? The danger is they might learn and question the infinite power of the Pope.

I pause, my back stiff from the heavy chains binding my hands and ankles, as if I could escape. The carpus of my right wrist and the ligaments of my ankles throb, distracting me from flashing pain in the part of my neck I know to be the clavicle. It is as persistent as the onerous buzzing of street flies around excrement.

I know these facts because my husband, a learned man, taught me all the parts of the anatomy as he knows them. An admirer of Moses Maimonides, an esteemed man revered as a philosopher, astronomer, rabbi, scholar and physician, Esteban studied his words with zeal, especially the Thirteen Principles of Faith.

Finally, after I recite a few more prayers of the Christian doctrine, I bow my head with finality. What more could they ask of me? I am a true Christian in that moment, begging for mercy.

Doña Clara Henriquez de Crespin is dismissed. Take her back to her cell.

The inquisitor I recognize stares at me without shame.

Nods are exchanged among the men, the guard included. When my arms are held on either side, their fingers crush through the rough yellow linen of my sanbenito, the penitent tunic that brings my family and me shame. The *coroza*, a conical hat of pressed paper, has been left in my cell. I am led away, repeating the watchwords of the One True Faith in my mind: *Shema Yisroel Adonai*…Hear, O Israel…

It comforts my damaged soul.

CHAPTER THREE

CELENDARIA

23 de julio 1650
Ciudad de México

No, I do not want it, I tell Elena, our servant's daughter as she urges her palm toward me with a mangled piece of bread. I refuse the offering not because of her grimy nails but because I do not know its origins. It might have been prepared with lard or a street vendor's unclean grill. Or found among the abandoned *basura* that lines our streets with offensive odors. Cleanliness is paramount in our preparation of food, recipes and remedies that my mother learned from her mother, who repeated them from previous generations before her in Spain, then Portugal.

My mother prepares petite loaves in a frying pan flooded with olive oil, an ancient Andalusian recipe blended with semolina and cinnamon. I do my best to help stir the mixture as she folds and rolls it into individual rounds with a rhythm that belies my clumsy manner. We plunge them into a vegetable broth that cooks on our open hearth, unable to mix dairy and meat. She spoons them out; I wave my hand over the breads to hasten the cooling. The first bite is heavenly, but must be consumed with haste before it turns gummy.

Celendaria, no? Elena asks, thrusting the crust of bread toward me again, picking small pieces off with two fingers and placing them in her mouth. A small girl of *mestizo* heritage with a nut-brown face, she wears a loose dress that hangs to her knees, grey from washings, and roughshod shoes, not as fine as my leather *chapines*. My stomach growls, a dog after another's bone. It is hard for me to resist, but I know it could cause me illness. My father's voice in my head admonishes me that we must wait to eat on fast days until God grants permission with the final slice of sun, an orange rind in the sky.

I seal my lips. At ten years, I am two years older than Elena. We are friends who play together when her mother comes to help with cleaning and laundry. We chase chickens in our yard, play with straw dolls made from scraps and lift water from the well in front. Unlike my family who has enough to eat, hers is poor. She is kind to offer bread, but I know she needs it more than I.

You must be as hungry as starving wolves after fasting for Lent, says Elena. We can eat now. It's dusk.

Her head motions up to the pearlescent sky.

I shrug my shoulders to express disinterest and turn toward the heavens washed with vestiges of fading light, dim clouds staining the glorious landscape to illuminate our faces. Hunger can thrust me into drowsiness when I am without nourishment.

Outside the back door of our kitchen, the soul of our home, I twirl away from the reddish-brown stains that discolor the ground near the rock wall. It is where the blood from goats, lambs and chickens splashes out of a pan used to slaughter animals. My mother wields a sacred sharp knife for our Sabbath and holiday feasts. I have watched her slice struggling fowl in the soft space of their necks, blood stealing across the place that sustains them, their desperate scramble for freedom. Finally, their limp bodies collapse as she cradles them. Only the chickens squawk resisting their fate, flailing, fluttering, agitating their useless wings against her stout, aproned body until they, too, flop over without breath.

Elena stuffs the bread into her mouth in one piece without the refined manners I have been taught. I watch as she savors it, my gut rumbling with envy.

Why did I refuse? It is not time for our Sabbath to begin, when we can take our meal with prayers to the Almighty. Dusk does not signal the beginning of our sacred time. We wait for three stars.

What are the stains on the ground? Elena asks me, making my heart beat faster.

With a swift motion I sidestep along the wall, swirling the dirt with the toe of my shoe.

Nothing. They are nothing. I do not want to raise suspicion about our customs that are different from our neighbors. I lean into the wall scuffling my feet back and forth, knowing she is at times dim with confusion. It is long past the hour for her mother to leave.

A river of sadness sweeps over me as I think about the animals I have fed and cared for hanging upside down by a rope under the eaves, their lifeblood draining from their faintly warm carcasses. The murky melancholy subsides when the juice in my mouth tastes the roasted lamb or crackled chicken skin my mother prepares served with purple *berenjenas*, speckled tomatoes and yellow *calabaza*, a favorite squash my mother purchases from the ancient widow at the market.

My mother sticks her head outside the back door looking for me. Celendaria, the time is now. Elena, your mother waits for you in the front. She nods and follows me inside.

I am relieved Elena is gone. Arousing suspicions has killed many since the Church absolves all who make confessions, their encouragement of salvation a danger to us. My mother has warned me many times to watch what I say, especially since mi abuela was taken.

I know the difference between dusk and the sunset that our household observes. Catholics resume nourishment after fasting when the sky spurts its dusky colors, a purple tincture on the hazy edges. We note different sanctions in the privacy of our home; servants dismissed, drapes drawn over wood shutters, candles ready for lighting. Mi abuelo, the father of my father, says we have to wait until three stars appear in the sky before we consume God's gifts. We begin at sundown when the fading painter's brush sweeps away any vestige of light.

But first I help my mother roll a wooden barrel into the kitchen from a small storage area nearby, fill it with steaming water sprinkled with rosemary for our bath. The aroma seeps into the corners of the room, tickling my nose. We strip to our thin white undergarments made from cotton that my father has native women create, techniques he learned from his father who no longer makes lace with his fading eyesight. These are soft and do not scratch the skin. The women go first—my mother, me, my two younger sisters who dip together, and then we change the water for the men—my grandfather, father and two older brothers, weary from traveling the roads as common cloth peddlers—after we empty most of the liquid, hand-carried in pots to another cistern outside for our vegetable greens to grow. I miss my grandmother. How will she bathe in that terrible place? We are commanded to keep clean.

Our neighbors do not bathe once a week as is our custom. Our laws require that we cleanse our bodies before presenting ourselves to God, dressed in holy white as we gather around the mantled table, the men's heads covered with skullcaps, my mother's draped with lace curtaining the sides of her cheeks, cupped hands motioning toward herself to welcome our Sabbath bride. I look forward to the illuminated faces from the candles while we recite the Shema together, the prayer of our people—*Shema Yis'ra'eil Adonai Eloheinu Adonai echad.* Hear, Israel, the Lord is our God, the Lord is One.

I anticipate this special day each week. The story that I have been told is that our brethren journeyed from the affluence of Burgos in Spain as textile merchants of the highest quality on the second of Ab, 5252, or as it is now known, 4 de agosto 1492, exiled by the evil Queen Isabella of Castile and her insipid husband, King Ferdinand of Aragon. After they confiscated all the goods and gold of the believers who followed the Law of Moses, most entered Portugal, some by boat, others by land in mule-driven carts. King John II of Portugal granted us asylum for one hundred *cruzados,* but we were thwarted by his death two years later.

The blot of the hundreds of children kidnapped in 1493 in Lisbon, ripped from their mothers' arms and later deported to the island colony of São Tomé near Africa to be raised as Catholics, stigmatized his reign forever. Many say they were treated as slaves, dying under harsh conditions.

My mother keeps a close eye on me and my sisters because of these stories that hang over us, threatening our well-being. I do not fully understand why the Church pulled babies from their mothers' breasts. Many mysteries confound me, igniting fears that taunt me in my dreams.

CHAPTER FOUR

CLARA

26 de julio 1650
Santa Oficina de la Inquisición

I have missed another Shabbat with my family, a quiet time of prayers and candles. I know they continue without me. Our faith, embedded for centuries, stays with us. I wait in my cell, praying in silence to be rescued. What could they want with an old woman of forty-four? Who would do this to me?

I understand there must be five witnesses to testify, but the Church designs its own rules. It can be one accusation that can damn me for life. Our workshop, a small factory on the outskirts of the city, has brought us modest success. We have done our best not to be noticed, invisible to their jealousies. But someone else may have noticed our ability to create finery. After all, we produce textiles for the court, a pale copy of what transpires in Spain, but still a court with the viceroy, marquees and marquises and ladies-in-waiting. They arrive in elaborate carriages with footmen to palaces where they are entertained, their hair piled high, decorated with precious stones. It is a farce in this land of barbaric conquerors where they slaughtered the native people, tricking them with beads, murdering them with cannons and disease.

My trivial life means little to them, except to drain the resources of my family.

CHAPTER FIVE

CELENDARIA

1 de agosto 1650
Ciudad de México

My grandfather and I bring another blanket, a clean sheet, linen napkins, loaves of bread, and jam made from fresh berries to where mi abuela is held. We have been told about the freezing temperatures, the scarcity of food and that the poorer prisoners dwell in the damp basement where dirt floors transform into muddy rivers under their feet. I do not know if she receives what we bring. We were not allowed to see her.

My grandfather went to the side of the building where a few barred windows on high look over a courtyard. The prisoners are charged for all that they use. He calls her name. Clara. Doña Clara. Come to me. He repeats this with exhaustion until he falls in a heap, the sun beating down on his back. He cries out. Take me instead! She is innocent of whatever you are charging her with!

I help him up, dusting debris from his pants. I am almost eleven and feel older.

Finally, a mop of dark hair and a thin, pale face appears between the bars. It is not her. Hush, Señor Crespin. Your wife is fine. She is only being questioned. Your inquiries will make it worse. Go. Go.

She waves us away.

When we return, mi abuelo explains to my mother that he did not see his beloved wife. All doors were closed to us, he says. A futile trip with gifts that may not reach her. I pleaded with Father Medina. He knows me well because I provide the finest silks for his concubine. Even he refused to see me.

My grandfather returns to his chair with a sigh.

My mother consoles herself with an offer. Let us continue as before, as though she is an innocent. Perhaps they will release her in a few days. We do not want to arouse suspicion. Maybe your network of Freemasons can assist, she says to console my grandfather. They have long arms that reach inside the highest institutions, from the Old World to the new.

He shrugs his shoulders.

Mi abuelo gets up and crosses the room to sit with a straight back in a kitchen chair. He reflects, telling a story I have not heard before. I was accepted into this society with your father. The Church has great hostility toward the symbols of Solomon's Temple, religious freedom, the immortality of the soul. The Church does not encourage education. A populace who reads will ask questions. If they ask questions, they will doubt the sources of their faith.

He continues, The Church opposes Freemasons. What makes you think they have any influence? Over eight hundred cases were pursued from 1574 until 1600 here in Ciudad de México, most murdered for their wealth. Spain did not want to support this tribunal so they twisted their own confiscations and fines to their advantage.

Is it because some of ours were accepted into the higher ranks of the Church? asks my mother.

My grandfather slumps forward. Who can we trust? A question could be a death sentence. We must be accomplished liars to survive.

Angry, his body straightens and his chair falls backward to the wall as he pulls himself to his full height. I am going to her. They must let me see her. Ach, it started with the evil queen. An air of hopelessness streams over him.

It has been going on almost two hundred years, says my mother as she tries to placate him.

My grandfather knows he cannot return so soon. He appears wistful as he says to my mother, I have heard they write down everything that transpires in their malevolent penitentiary. They have large books that list the names and families of those they interrogate and the ones they torment and murder.

Who told you this? She asks as she turns to stir a pot in the open hearth. Señora Lopez's son will no longer reveal any information, even to his mother. He is a priest who apprises them of what happens behind the walls of detention.

Can she find out anything? Where are they holding her? What does she need? My grandfather sounds so desperate, his questions not waiting for answers.

My mother tries to calm him. We must go about our business with our customary activities so they do not monitor us. We are seen as a cultured race that draws the attention of our predators, almost like wolves observing prey before pouncing.

My grandfather searches for answers that we do not have. Do you think our superior textiles caught their eye? We have been making more than clothing. We produce wool rugs, serapes, embroidered *huipiles.* The women sew the flowers by hand, something Celendaria should learn to do, he says eyeing me. When we set up the small workshop on the outskirts of town with spindles and looms, I told my son it might arouse suspicion. So many of the native women are needed to clean, gin, card and spin the raw cotton. But I doubt they would jeopardize their positions. Maybe it was the farmers we purchased the goods from to make *manta* who said something.

I pinch my mother's leg to get her attention. I was not supposed to be in the room. I was a tall girl with the legs of a new colt. I blended in with women, not my little sisters. With the seriousness of the arrest, I was ignored.

We have had enough days without work. Worrying does not bring money, says my father who enters the room of sad faces. A large man with a thick beard, he dominates our small space.

His voice, naturally loud, lowers a few octaves, aware that spies can be anywhere. We are textile merchants brokering serapes—wool shawls of red, yellow and blue, the dyes crafted from plants and bugs. The native women use back-strap looms in the country, but we have modernized. An adequate business that feeds us, but we will never be the wealthy patrons we once were in Spain. What do they want from us?

In the evenings we repeat our ancestor's stories, our history read from parchment pages like our sacred Torahs, all hidden in false walls or below streets where we build cellars and passages of escape. My grandfather repeats the one about the Castillo at the top of a hill in Burgos where the authorities lived, allowing the Jews to live inside the walls. When jealousy erupted from those below, the Jews escaped to the countryside through an underground tunnel. He reminds us, We are survivors. Then he dozes.

We savor the names of our ancestors, those who embraced mysticism and the Kabbalah based on secret teachings of our rabbis. Our family names, repetitious over hundreds of years, followed a pattern of naming firstborn sons after their paternal grandfather, the second male child after the maternal grandfather, the first daughter after the paternal grandmother and so on, a mélange of designations that tied us together. We are still here.

My father continues. Ach, it is difficult to obtain manta from the fibers of the yucca plant. Now the raw fiber can be grown in the lowlands near the ocean. Your brothers earn money transporting it to us in the mountains, but our business diminishes. As much as our Spanish overlords like to wear cotton, they prefer wool. It is cheaper to produce because the sheep are nearby.

My father paces across the small floor with a few steps. He does not miss an opportunity to chastise the Spanish. With a bitter note he adds, The *conquistadores* took away the Mayan natives back-strap looms because the cloth was not wide enough to make fabric for a civilized mode of dress. They imported the foot treadle machines we use today.

My grandfather is bored with textile talk. What do we do about my Doña Clara locked up, possibly without food or water?

We wait. We simply wait, says my mother. But in the meantime, we can inquire of Señora Lopez about her son, Miguel, a priest. She brags about having one of her children, a part of those that track us, as an ear to the inside.

I forbid it, says my father. It will arouse suspicion.

I will, I offer. I have met her at the market with *Mama*.

My father says, No, do not let the curious child out of the house!

CHAPTER SIX

CLARA

18 de agosto 1650, in the afternoon
Santa Oficina de la Inquisición

Intimidated by my second interrogation, I have at least learned my captors' purpose. This time I study the richness of the room between silences, the parquet floors that my leg chains drag against, a chamber adorned with the finest tapestries I have seen. Many columns across the room are draped with damask silk in autumn colors of russet, brown and deep red, the color of blood. I have handled textiles this exquisite and know the value. To my right stands an elaborate altar I have noticed before but avoided examining until now.

In a corner is the secretary sitting at a desk writing down all that is said. He is the most frightening person in the room, his identity hidden by a cloak covering his head. In the center is a saint accepting the chasuble of their Virgin Mother. Moses warned us not to make graven images.

We order you to answer our questions. Are you a Christian?

Yes, of course.

I am brought back to what is in front of me: three inquisitors on a platform framed by an intricate tapestry emblazoned with the Royal Coat of Arms, sitting on high-backed chairs covered in crimson velvet, trimmed in gold, their vestments heavy against the chilled air and an ever-present dampness. Two wear tri-cornered hats and the other, a priest in a fur collar, displays a skullcap on his baldhead. The table draped in brocade separates us as I sit on a low wooden chair.

You seem well versed in the Catholic faith.

I do not make eye contact. I was educated in the convent. The nuns prescribed what I know.

How did your husband arrive here?

My husband came in the early1600s with General Fernando de Sosa's flotilla. Some family members drowned, but he survived.

I pause, not wanting to offer more information than I have to. I study the large silver crucifix of their savior hanging on a cross to the side, angels with banners and swords protecting him.

Which port?

He arrived in Veracruz and then traveled to Mexico City.

Have you been here this entire time?

Yes. We only left during the great floods, but our family returned soon thereafter. I know they are asking this to see if we have relatives they can pursue in other places. I have heard of their devious ways to build a case from other's secrets.

Were they Christians?

Oh yes, sir. All in our family are Old Christians from Burgos, good Catholics including my godparents.

Why did you come here?

I was raised here by my aunt. I met my husband when I was fourteen.

Why did he come at that time?

Most honored sirs; I do not know the motivations of his heart. Perhaps to find a better life in the New World. *They waited for me to continue, obviously not satisfied with my response.* My husband's family is all deceased.

Tell us the story of your life again.

And so I repeated in what I thought was word for word my tale of displacement from the last interview. They would try to catch me in something if the facts did not match. I took my time. After all, at least I was out of the cramped cell and the air was clearer in here.

I was exhausted from the recitation of my life and those who came before me. How could I possibly know what my ancestors were thinking, except to acknowledge that fear and restlessness played their part.

Have you ever celebrated Christ's Last Supper?

Ah, this is about Judaizing. I wipe away thoughts of our beautiful Seders after hours of preparation, unleavened bread, the retelling of the story of Moses and the exodus from Egypt to contemplate Easter, a holiday I dread. Thoughts of their savior drooped on the cross, their celebration of pain, the flagellants crowding the streets plague me. It never got better, especially after the last auto-de-fé where we lost so many. It stretches me into a despair that resides in my soul.

No. Of course not. Why would I?

Many celebrate this meal to honor our Lord.

A trap. I must consider this.

Most Honored, we only celebrate the Crucifixion and the Resurrection at Easter, a time of reflection. My family and I attend Mass with the auspicious notion that He may rise again.

And do you know when Easter occurs?

My mind dips low. I feel my stomach turn like the secret tops the children spin for the Festival of Lights. My fearful voice carries my answer an octave higher. I pause before I speak.

I do not know. I rely on the priests to inform us which Sunday it transpires in the month of April. We are a devout family who follow the rules of the church.

Are you aware of the first Sunday after Paschal with a full moon? Do you acknowledge the Jews killed our Lord?

A nod of the head was not sufficient so I speak up. Yes.

Their neutral expressions shift to gloomy bleak ones, the corners of their mouths turned down, eyes into crooked slits. We do not arrest someone without sufficient information of the deeds that have been committed.

May I know what they are?

Out of reverence to our Virgin Mother, the Lord, Jesus Christ, the Holy Office of the Inquisition, you may not. We ask you to tell the truth without embellishment.

The truth is I am an ignorant woman who only wants to serve the Church and my family. I think that I must make my plea count, but I doubt anything I say will dissolve their suspicions. Whatever I have done, I am not aware and beg your forgiveness, Inquisitors General.

The sincerity of your beliefs is in question. A mallet hits the desk and startles me. You are dismissed to reconsider.

CHAPTER SEVEN

CELENDARIA

11 de noviembre 1650

Months have passed since my grandmother's incarceration with her absence noted for Rosh Hashanah, the New Year, and Yom Kippur, the Day of Atonement, our most sacred of days we call el Gran Día, the day of the year. Without her, it was inconceivable. The rainy season when she was arrested has meandered toward colder, drier weather. A gloom layered our home, one balancing on top of another until they crashed upon us as we impelled ourselves through our home with silent sighs.

Elena wants to play, but I have taken over responsibilities in our home, with meals assigned to my mother, Gabriela, and our servant, Teresa, Elena's mother. Often my aunts, Maria and Rosa, come over to cook with us. I love the rich smell of stew when everyone contributes ingredients from their garden, sharing spices traded or bought.

We all miss our loving abuela, worry over her absence, pray for her safe return, but mi abuelo is the most disconsolate, refusing to eat for days at a time. I think he looks bonier, his silver hair losing its gloss and thinning too. We whisper among ourselves any gossip we might have heard at the market so he does not hear.

What is the point in upsetting the old man? My mother asks.

On the days Elena comes with her mother, we carry water from the well in front of the house, the heavy pail used for cooking as well as to water the animals in the back—a stubborn donkey, three merino sheep my mother shears in season, a sad-eyed lamb destined for our Passover feast, a dozen squawking hens that peck my feet and a few goats. We do not raise cattle or horses or trap for fur like others. We remain city people, raising food for our own use, sharing summer squash, ripe tomatoes and eggplants with our family and neighbors.

When the chores are complete, Elena and I play in the front room. She is an illiterate, often shoeless, her dirty feet unwashed except for brief trips to the river. My mother has told me not to speak of our baths on Friday, an extravagance common people would not understand. She is closer in age to my younger sisters, the twins, Yael and Yonah, but they are not interested in her. They have each other, speaking a secret language that only they share. They ignore me except at bedtime when they like to brush my hair. Elena has a sweet temperament. Sometimes she picks wildflowers in the washes, arriving with a spray of colors—crystal blue stalks, golden cardrops and vivid red blossoms she calls *chuparosas,* a favorite of hummingbirds. I am fascinated by the miniature birds with trembling wings. I express my delight by sharing some sweet grapes with her.

Once, only once, I followed her outside of our neighborhood to the dry riverbed to see the miraculous tiny creatures I had only viewed on rare occasions. I was terrified, glancing over my shoulder repeatedly as we walked. I had been warned of many evils, but I loved God's creatures with their magical flutterings, similar to my heart. After the declivity of a hill, we arrived in a field of *chuparosas.* Dozens of hummingbirds darted into blossoms, sucking nectar through their needle noses. Their throats and bellies were the colors of jewels that the Evil Queen wore—sapphire blues, emerald glossy greens and ruby red paintbrushes. Mi abuelo told me the Queen took the treasures from our people. I stood in awe as the landscape unfolded before me, a vibrant vision with the perfume of bouquets prickling my nose. We gathered many flowers that we brought to my home. I lied to my mother and told her Elena brought them.

I cannot reveal to Elena that I have learned to read Hebrew and Spanish in secret lessons with mi abuelo. I would love to share some of the stories from our ancient Bible that I have learned, but I am forbidden. The church she attends with her mother does not allow them to read, only listen and view the splendorous idols that decorate the altar made from minerals found in the mines. My father says it is a sacrilege to worship idols, but I like the shiny silver decorations and the plaster Virgin Mother holding her Son.

Elena calls her *Our White Pure Lady.*

Sometimes mi abuelo and I huddle in the attic with a lantern—my mother cautions us about fire—before I go to bed, the languages soaring from my mouth as he teaches me Hebrew letters and Ladino, the language of exile. I am familiar with the Spanish and Portuguese that flows in our household, but Ladino, a language that started in Spain, unites Hebrew and Spanish and maintains my grandfather's interest.

Abuelo, why do we not speak more Ladino?

My grandfather's expression shifts from a serious scholar with glasses perched on his nose to a lover, his eyes pooling with tears.

Because Ladino is a remnant of our rich culture, an exodus of an interminable journey where fear traveled in our ancestor's blood with false hope that our fate would improve, only to encounter more oppression, loss and uncertainty.

But we could speak it more among ourselves, I offer.

We do speak Ladino among ourselves when your father and uncles and I travel on business, but the Church sees it as an affront to their authority, a challenge of power, so we use it with caution in the city. It identifies us as heretics in the eyes of the Church. The melodious language resonates with poetic phrases like the psalms. It is better to learn Judah Halevi's writings from the eleventh century. He wrote three hundred poems about our longing for Jerusalem and respect for the Sabbath.

With a wistful voice he recites,

On Friday doth my cup o'erflow,
What blissful rest the night shall know,
When, in thine arms, my toil and woe are all forgot, Sabbath my love!
'Tis dusk, with sudden light, distilled from one sweet face, the world is filled; The tumult of my heart is stilled—For thou art come, Sabbath my love!

Bring fruits and wine and sing a gladsome lay, Cry, "come in peace, O restful Seventh day!"

On this particular Shabbat, our lesson has gone well. He takes two books wrapped in heavy cotton tied with sisal from a small trunk, repeating almost the same words every time. I move closer to him. He has taken these books out for me before in secrecy. A musty smell encircles us as he turns the pages with care.

Mi cariño, these books are my prizes. This one is from Ferrara in Italy, put into print shortly after the Expulsion. It has prayers for the whole year, including Rosh Hashanah and el Gran Día. It has been saved from the fires many times. His dry lips kiss the cover with its square Hebrew characters. He repeats the origins of books as though they have a history similar to our Sepher Toledot that defines our family.

Next, he unwraps a small, wine-colored book with gold embossed lettering on the pimpled cover, a gift from Señor Abulafia in Peru, a great danger to himself and his family. He strokes its cover.

I have not seen this one before and I notice how he treasures it. The light from the lantern comes from over his shoulder, casting a shadow on half his face.

Obtained from my brother in Salonika, he tells me, smuggled through the Caribbean where the Inquisition's eyes are blocked by the sun. It is recent, written by Isaac de Moises de Pas. But, if we must flee and only one book can travel with me, it will be the *Espejo de Consolación*.

What is it about? I ask questions so I can stay with him in this quiet setting, both of us hunched over, straining our eyes to decipher letters from foreign languages. I want to learn them with fluency.

It is a religious manual of Moses Maimonides, one of our greatest rabbis born in Córdoba in the twelfth century. It contains the Thirteen Articles of Faith and Ten Commandments, and our feast and fast days.

He passes it to me. I know he regards them as precious and requires me to rinse my hands in clean water before we climb the ladder to get up here. The cover is stiff and the pages stick a bit in their newness. It is valuable—as all books are—because it is written in our ancient languages of Hebrew and Ladino, our mother tongue.

I cannot read the Ladino. My grandfather knows this.

You are from a rich, well-educated culture. Someday you must teach all this to your children.

Abuelo, I am only eleven.

Yes, a smart eleven. Perhaps someday we will live among people who allow us to read and learn with the flush of freedom. If we must flee again, this small trunk is what will travel with me.

Are we going to leave Mexico?

Hush, *mi nieta*, enough for today. He smiles at me, a rare occurrence in recent times.

I am grateful to learn the words of our ancestors, I tell mi abuela.

He leans forward to kiss my cheek, places the books in their hidden place, pushing the small chest behind a pile of serape scraps. Then he blows out the candle in the lantern, lowers the rope ladder and assists me in starting my backward descent.

CHAPTER EIGHT

CLARA

2 de diciembre 1651
Santa Oficina de la Inquisición

I am back before my inquisitors, after so much time has passed I cannot keep the dates but more than a year must have passed. Ay, my children, my grandchildren have grown so that I can no longer visualize them wih their sweet faces. I have great anxiety, but relish the change of scenery from my cold, stone cell. At least here I can gaze at fine tapestries.

Doña Clara, we have sent you to your cell to search your memory. Do you remember any names of those who taught you the Law of Moses?

No, I do not. I make an effort not to answer with the tediousness I feel. This is my first time in this room. It is similar to the other I have been interrogated in, but larger. The notary writes down every word I utter.

We are not making progress here. Repeat your life story once more.

I am weary but I go through the litany of my ordinary birth, upbringing and marriage once more, the names of my children.

Repeat the Sacraments.

I do so.

Name others whom you know to be Judaizers.

Sirs, I know no one who speaks blasphemy.

Then how did you come to be educated in these ways?

The wife of my doctor told them to me.

Where is she now?

I have been asked this question before and I have sworn to God that I will not give up a living soul. I respond with confidence. She is dead.

Where is she buried?

I do not know.

And her husband, the doctor?

He was elderly. He has also passed.

In these situations, we exhume the body and burn the remains. A heretic does not belong among good Catholics. The doctor's wife is in Hell with Satan.

The one in the middle speaks to me today. Until now, it has been the same man interrogating me; however, they change positions so I am confused. It is dim in the room and the secretary writes down what transpires, dipping his pen into a bottle of ink. The quill scratches the parchment. Often I am asked to repeat my answers so an accurate record is kept. At the end of each session, they guide me forward to a desk to sign my name. I must swear that what I have said is true.

It is all lies.

Do you understand we must have details? What is the name of the doctor's wife?

Señora Rosa Malka de Silva. I have made this name up with trepidation. There is so much time between interviews that maybe they are sending their priests and missionaries to look for these poor souls who do not exist. I am anxious, panicky. I should not have told such a bold lie.

When did you last speak to Rosa Malka de Silva?

It was many years ago.

What did she say to you?

I do not remember what she said.

You realize we have detained you so you could improve your memory. It does not seem to have helped.

Sirs, I am past forty years of age. My memory is failing.

Perhaps you will remember more when we burn Señora de Silva in effigy since we cannot dig up her grave.

The idea of burning people in effigy appalls me. When they find the grave, they dig it up, parading the bones on fire with the penitents. It is their way of showing that sinners will be pursued past death. There is never freedom from this Church.

Have you performed any other rites or ceremonies that are contrary to Our Lord Jesus Christ?

No.

I am beginning to sweat profusely under my arms, between my breasts and where I sit. I understand their symbolic gesture to intimidate me.

We will bring you materials to make a small doll of Señora Rosa Malka de Silva in her likeness. Bailiff, remove her.

CHAPTER NINE

CELENDARIA

14 de diciembre 1651

Often mi abuelo is the only male at home. I keep him company. While my father and brothers work or travel, we become a household of women, stifled in our domesticity. Today everyone is present, a rarity. I help with food preparation, chopping vegetables, taking the shells off pistachios (a task that breaks my nails), and setting the table for our supper.

After our meal of chicken with rice, chopped chilies and sliced jicama roots, we consume avocados, *aguacate* to the Spanish, who adore the sweet mushiness. My mother serves the soft fruit on *bolillos*, a crusty roll learned from the French. We spread it like butter, dressing it with lime juice.

The men gather to discuss business while the women clear the table. Food that has not been consumed, a rarity with so many hungry appetites, is set aside. I bring a tub of water from the barrel in the back yard to wash the plates. I take a moment to look at the stars while I am outside, a comfort to me. I dawdle, spinning around a few times until the donkey starts to bray. I hurry inside with my *cazuela* of water, the same one we use for stew, trying not to splash any over the sides.

What has happened to the last shipment of cotton cloth? My brother León wants to know. It is long overdue at the factory.

The thinker and natural learner among our siblings, his voice rings with fury. As a man of short stature with small hands and feet, he bellows to be heard. His fine features gleaned from the women in our family make him appear as a man of quality with his aquiline nose, a wide mouth and our signature curly, midnight hair that falls forward onto his brow. He reads books surreptitiously, his eyesight poor like my grandfather. He refuses to wear glasses so his dark eyes squint in the dim light.

Aruh, taller and not as fine looking, picks his teeth with a splinter in a casual manner. Are you accusing the church again? You blame them for everything.

León's voice is annoyed and loud. You are a fool! The church steals all we have, even our souls. I wanted to hire a guard to guide them safe passage. You are the one who was not interested in safety precautions. We could have hired a bounty hunter from the north. They share few loyalties except to those that pay them.

My grandfather slaps his hand on the table. We jump at the noise. Enough! We must get this shipment of goods back. Do they want a ransom? Who has them? Renegade priests? Apaches reaching into the depths of Mexico? Where are these criminals coming from?

The women are busy with the aftermath of the meal. We are not involved in the family business, but I am a questioning girl who wants to know all so I lag behind while clearing the table. Sometimes I steal a sip of wine left in the ceramic cups before washing.

My father places his elbows on the wood table and folds his hand under his chin. This is his sternest pose. Then his hands sweep through his curls as he makes a strange noise. Ach, our goods have been waylaid by bandits. Or at least that is what the son of Señor Galanos sent us in a message. We cannot fight amongst ourselves.

Aruh has been silent and moody during dinner, eating with haste. He asks, What was in the order?

He is probably sullen because he and León have many conflicts, ones my father and grandfather try to ignore.

My father speaks. Our caravan of six donkeys, loaded with inventory for a few months, is gone. I cannot run the workshop without cotton for the women to spin, sew and fashion into simple shirts for the ranchers. We have orders for quilted cotton that can be used as armor against bows and arrows, spears and knives to protect themselves from the natives to the north. And, I had a special order of velvets and silks in rainbow colors from the Philippines, plus skeins of gold embroidery thread. We will be ruined if we don't deliver.

Why is what I want to know but I cannot ask. My brother Aruh does. Why? Who are the clients?

My father says, It does not matter. People willing to pay for quality. The Spanish landowners have many opportunities to invest in finer things for themselves and their homes. They think they're replicating the Spanish court in Mexico. No matter.

He dismisses our circumstances with a wave of his hand. I must take our donkey to search for them.

Aruh, my stronger brother, a young man of twenty without trepidation, is ready for any confrontation. He offers to assist. I will go with you. I have a knife for slaughtering. Where were they last seen?

I can tell he is angry, his impulsive nature one that I fear.

León knows. Near the Royal Road that trails through Querétaro to Zacatecas from Mexico City. They have a slow cart pulled by oxen as well as the donkeys.

My grandfather interrupts. You cannot go there. Bandits lie in wait for the silver mine shipments. Only idiots think we can get our merchandise back.

He closes his eyes, weary of life.

We can retrieve our merchandise, says Aruh. We must buy a gun like the bandits. That stops them when they are shot through the heart.

My father protests. The next sentence is spit out with force as droplets of water fall on the table. These people kill rather than ask a question! It is a foolish venture to try to catch them. We know they are well guarded. How will you protect yourself? Do you think they will hand over our stolen goods even if you can find them? You are both fools.

Grandfather, who has passed the business to my father, speaks. We have to do something. I cannot watch our livelihood destroyed so many times. Enough that they slaughter us like the paschal lamb for our beliefs. We have to eat.

Leon offers another idea with good will. We sent shipments in the past by canoe. It takes longer than land but if we disguise the wrapped fabrics with *chayotes* or *nopales*, they might make it through.

I think it is a feasible idea with my child's mind because I love the pale-green, wrinkled, potato vegetable and the de-spined cactus paddles that my mother cooks until tender, soaking them in kosher salt.

Aruh becomes angry. When you want to take action to retrieve our goods, let me know. I am leaving. He pushes back his chair, retrieves his hat and cloak and slams the door.

My mother enters the room, wiping her hands on a small kitchen cloth. Stop! She pleads. There must be a solution in the light of day. For tonight, no one else goes anywhere. I will inquire of Señor Behar's wife. They have many connections.

Ach. A waste of time, mutters my grandfather.

Those seated lean back in their chairs with a collective sigh, their spines rounded with doubt. With Aruh's hasty exit, the dinner is concluded. The incarceration of our matriarch has put us all on edge. I hear my father and grandfather exchange heated words. After I set down the cazuela in the kitchen, I linger near the doorway to the other room. I am a child in the middle of the five of us without compatriots. Alone in our birth order, I like to spy on the grown-ups. I have nothing in common with my silly younger sisters, and my older brothers only acknowledge me with a nod.

I want to go to her, says my grandfather, his eyes welling with tears. Some fall into his tea-stained, white beard.

You were just there, says my father.

I go almost every day.

My father responds with strength, confronting his own father-in-law. No, you must stop this. It does no good. You think wailing in front of their grand palace will change anything? You draw attention to us, arousing suspicion. We have tried every means, even bribing officials, but it is not adequate to buy our beloved mother's freedom. At least they take our goods to bring to her, although I cannot swear she receives them. And the rest of us? Would she want you to sacrifice all of us? It is more important we remember this story of intolerance, the unjust judgment of men upon a peaceful people. Our perseverance brought us to this point in time. We must pray for God's guidance to overcome these monsters.

My grandfather elevates his voice. I have to go to her. They must allow me to see her. I have put up with their accusations for so long. When will it end? Let them take me!

I wonder if they will arrest us too, a chill shivering up my spine with the thought of the imposing jail where she is held. Mi abuelo's adamantine will frustrates my father.

My father, usually a reflective man, often sits in a melancholy pose at the end of the day, his eyes closed, his breaths labored. I know he's not sleeping as I tiptoe around him because sometimes he grabs my arm as I pass, to pull me toward him for a kiss on the top of my head. Now he explodes in rage, his voice inflated.

We cannot expose ourselves. She must not have revealed much because they have not interrogated us. He pauses to calm himself. What if we moved north? There are fewer hazards in those territories.

My grandfather's response erupts to fill the room. What? Leave her behind? Out of the question. How would we live without commerce? No! Their damned church has chased us halfway around the world after the expulsion in 1492, to the golden shores of Portugal with its olives and wine in abundance. What a land. We stayed while others fled, worshipping in secret, remembering our traditions, pretending to be Catholic, all the while preserving our beliefs, our customs, our precious prayers to one God.

My grandfather continues in his agitation. We lived like that until Hernán Cortes, the explorer, came with sailors of our persuasion to Mexico. Many were doctors, scholars and merchants willing to risk everything. Our ancestors came to this place with only their faith. After the Spanish destroyed the native population, they stayed to build this country with bloodstained hands, bringing my great grandmother many times removed to begin a family. The Crespins have a long history of survival. I will not let that stop. He removes himself from the table and moves to his sleeping chair to recline. His fury has worn him out.

A chill shivers up my spine to the back of my neck. I wonder if they will arrest us too. A vision of the imposing prison and palace, a monolithic building on the square where my dear grandmother, mi abuela *dulce*, is held, remains a terrifying mystery.

My father shifts in his chair with a sigh. He looks worn, the bags under his eyes dark with shame and anger. Our ancestors came as hidden ones, their faith buried in their minds. We had a good life here until this trouble. I will not give them the satisfaction of flight. Yet, I feel shame that I cannot protect my family.

Mi abuelo leans his head back into a pillow, his mouth a rictus of tension. Anger and shame will not help us one whit. We must find a way to get her out. He closes his eyes and recites a story we have heard numerous times without any tone in his voice. Out of respect, we listen to our patriarch, a learned man who reminds us where we came from and why.

We are in this place because our ancestors followed Hernando Alonso, who came from Cuba in 1519 with Hernán Cortés, the conqueror of the Aztecs. Hernando, whose family left Spain and Portugal, was a man of faith with carpentry skills. He built the fine brigantine Hernán Cortés sailed on to Nueva España. He was trusted and used his skills to build the city for Cortés. He was rewarded with land for a cattle and hog ranch. It is strange one of ours chose to deal with what is forbidden, but he saw demand for the filthy pigs.

Soon Hernando Alonso was one of the most successful men in the area. He brought a wife, the origins of the Crespins and friends from Cuba to make our community. Ah, we were happy here, prospering by hard work, praying together, marrying among ourselves. Unfortunately, the church noticed. It did not take long for them to open their tribunal of torture in 1571. Hernando Alonso was accused by a Dominican friar and became the first *converso* to be prosecuted and burned here. The fate of our relative sinks in my soul every day when I think of my wife, my Clara. Please, dear God, not that fate.

Tears glisten on my grandfather's cheeks. No one has shooed me away so I stay to listen as he continues. Ay, we are a stubborn lot. In the past, those who chose to leave carved our ancient Hebrew letters of dedication into the stone walls of our abandoned homes. Many took their keys with them thinking they might return someday. His eyes become watery again and he removes his glasses.

The caterpillar indentations on their doorposts contained mezuzahs with a tiny piece of parchment inside that hid the Shema, our sacred prayer that affirms our faith in God. Those remained behind with our goods, wealth, books and a sadness that permeated the soul. It stays with us until this day.

I think about where the mezuzah is concealed in the front of our dwelling, carved into the interior of the brick well where I draw water. I am afraid to acknowledge it with a touch of the fingers and a kiss to the lips unless no one is around. The one for the back door is hidden under the eaves, a reminder to sweep debris into the center of the room, never past the door that holds the daily reminder of our identity.

The strain of reiterating the chronicle of our family depletes mi abuelo. He shrinks into a smaller version of himself, his eyes closing for the evening. The other adults begin to stir.

My father is explosive. What is the point of retelling if we are still persecuted? Maybe the inquisitors are behind our stolen goods. We can trust no one.

Esteban, lower your voice, my mother tells him. We do not want to arouse suspicion at this hour. She rises, twisting the hem of her skirt, crumpling the fabric in her hand, and lowers her eyes.

My father sits in silence with a countenance of anger.

My mother taps me on the back to go upstairs where my sisters slumber, a light snoring filling the stairwell. I scurry like a pantry mouse into the shadows.

CHAPTER TEN

CLARA

16 de febrero 1652
Santa Oficina de la Inquisición

I have another penitent in my cell, a comely young woman with light-colored hair and green eyes, a European from first glance. She is tossed in without regard to her injury, clothes filthy with the streets. At least the shameful robe I wear is clean, even if a black stripe, half of Saint Andrew's cross, goes from my shoulder to the hem. It means I am under moderate suspicion of heresy. Ha! As if there is any fairness or justice to these proceedings.

She smells of garbage, her left eye purple with the penumbra of damaged skin. A blanket is thrown in after her. She wails incoherent noises and a strange language until I am fearful she will draw attention. She eyes me with suspicion, wrapping the worn blanket around her shoulders as she curls herself inside it. She finds a space in the corner of our cell. I am not chained in confinement. I creep toward her with caution, touching her arm with the gentleness I used to handle my babies. I sit down next to this dirty creature.

I ask, what is your name?

Go away.

The ones who can harm you are outside, not in here.

Go away.

Tell me your name.

No.

I will learn it soon enough. I reach over to a pan on the floor meant for a dog, dip the tin cup into the water and bring it to her lips. I see they are swollen, bloody around the gums. Her jade eyes look at me. I can tell she would like not to trust me but who else is here? She cups her hand around my offering, slurping it all at once. This is one of their cruelties, a lack of water to parch our throats. She slumps over to the side and sleeps, emitting guttural sounds.

I cannot decide whether it is better to have hostile company or be alone with my own grief. She sleeps for many hours and finally awakens in a stupor of confusion, her eyes blinking.

Why are you here? I ask.

Her hand pushes back her mane of hair, the lightest I have seen among the Iberian peoples. Her eyes survey our cell. There is not much to see—a small table, a broken chair, a few dishes, some utensils. She scrambles to the dish filled with water, splashing her face, slurping, her damp hands sliding the mop away from her face. Her eye is more swollen today.

What is your name?

She is not responsive. I sit against the wall, the cold stone cooling my back. I have nothing else to do but wait. I am afraid to sing because the wrong language might reveal me so I make faces at her. I smile, I frown, I pretend to cry. I try everything to gain her attention.

Time passes. I cannot tell how long but I know my stomach rumbles with hunger. My family must be preparing supper, my granddaughter Celendaria—oh, how I miss her!—the most intelligent and helpful of *mis nietos* and a companion to my husband. I do not allow my mind to dwell on his loving nature, my blessing in this life. He is the one who absorbs the abundant knowledge of our people.

We are not fed on a regular basis. The chief dispenser who controls the food my family sends does not give me my portions. A guard passes food underneath the steel bars with a sneer, leading me to believe this may be my last meal each time. At this point, the cravings of nourishment do not hound me. I have been here so long I no longer care. A year. Maybe more, with infrequent visitors.

I have been told my husband comes many days to howl my name outside the prison walls. A few times I have been able to shout to him, standing on the unsteady chair, my head bobbing above the window sill.

At least I have light as long as my family keeps paying. I can only imagine what they have sold and sacrificed to grant me a vista of sky. The food is slop I would not feed to my animals, but I must eat it for sustenance. I still harbor hope someone will figure out a way to release me, unlikely as it seems. I am sure the swill that is left is *treife,* forbidden by our God, but what can I do? Our great provider wants me to survive. I know this.

Days pass in silence with the bottle-green eyes watching me as though I am the perpetrator of her misery. I can see she is healing because she paces our small space, lips pressed, her eye normal, fingers working the knots in her hair through the ends. Then they take her away.

CHAPTER ELEVEN

CALENDARIA

25 de octubre 1652

Celendaria, what are you doing?

My mother's voice catches me as I wash my undergarments with lye soap in a cazuela in the back yard. I am afraid to tell her of the blood. At first I was petrified to feel the wetness, but I am not afraid now. I have seen many animals that have been slaughtered then hung to drain their fluids, their life force leaving them. My mother wants me to observe so I can learn to do this for my family someday. With an expedient motion of my mother's wrist, her knife slays the chicken, lamb or goat according to our *kashrut* laws, the blade cleansed after each butchering and concealed in a safe space under the tiles of our kitchen floor.

Celendaria, tell me what is going on.

I cannot speak. It is unusual for mi madre to speak to me in anger. Our eyes meet. With her womanly presentiments, she understands what is happening.

Is this the first time?

I nod in the affirmative.

Stay here.

She returns with rolled cotton and a few yards of linen in the crook of her arm. She motions me to her. I stop my scrubbing, hands wet and raw from the soap.

She holds me to her. You are a woman now.

What does this mean? I want to know.

It is the cycle of the moon that makes you fertile to bear children.

Will this happen again?

Yes, every month.

Forever?

I am astonished. I do not comprehend what is happening to my body.

First, my flat chest, the same as my younger sisters, began to hurt. Small, unwanted bumps appeared until they grew like mushrooms sprouting from moist soil under the steps. Now, enlarged to the size of oranges, rigid and problematic, my mother commented about them at my bath on Shabbat. Afterward, she brought me bandages of gauzy cotton to wrap them in so they cannot move when I swing my arms at play with Elena. Something else has taken over.

Is it their devil? I ask. The hens roust around my legs searching for corn kernels.

She stifles a laugh. No. We do not believe in such nonsense. It is part of the life process. God's will. Maybe I should have told you what to expect. It is different for all women.

I am flushed with embarrassment that a male might know.

Do my brothers have this?

She holds me away from her. She smiles with the joy I have seen when my father arrives home from a long trip.

No. Only women. Let me know when you finish. I will take you to the *mikvah* seven days later. Until then, you are unclean and cannot touch anything.

Why? I do not want this. Will the water of the mikvah cleanse me?

Yes, the women in our family go together.

I am puzzled.

My mother explains to me that I need to cleanse in clear waters, a time to be grateful to God.

You will like the time alone for reflection, but you must go under the clear water and purify your face and hair too. It is not possible to change anything. You are growing up. At fifteen, we can search for your husband.

What a terrifying idea! I want to live with my family forever.

Where will you find him?

The thought of a dark-haired stranger sharing my space, or worse yet, taking me away to live with his family staggers me. Is it possible I will not see mine again?

We will find him through appropriate channels. Perhaps one of your cousins.

The ones I know are younger and insipid.

Those are your first cousins. We have second, third and fourth ones to search.

In Mexico?

In Mexico, Peru, maybe Colombia. Your grandfather received correspondence from some who have relocated to the north, away from the madness.

Where? Abuelo says the native peoples attack settlers and remove their scalps. I am afraid to go there.

San Miguel el Grande. Or Zacatecas where there is a silver mine. Or into the southwest territories.

Is that far?

Everything is far when you walk or ride a burro. Enough questions. Finish your washing and hang it to dry. She turns to go back inside.

Mama, how long will this last?

Not so long. But you must watch the cycles of the moon so you know when it will return at the same time next month.

Again, this idea distresses me. It must show on my face.

Celendaria, this is not a cycle to dread. It is a good one, God's way of giving life.

I do not comprehend how my bleeding has anything to do with life. Will I lose my life force this way, like the animals we drain?

CHAPTER TWELVE

CLARA

10 de diciembre 1652
Santa Oficina de la Inquisición

The freezing air chills me to my bones. Any fat padding nestled on my body has long disappeared. Inside these walls, they ready themselves for the savior's birthday, a time of reflection. Nuns come to the bars of my cell offering small breads made by prisoners sentenced to knead dough for the rest of their lives. I cannot touch it. To eat from the hand of an indentured slave must be a sacrilege.

I worry like a motherless child while my cellmate is gone. Although she has not said anything to me, I feel her presence, the warmth of another body. It has crossed my mind that she may be a spy sent to learn my secrets, but somehow this seems implausible.

The assistant of the chief jailer, the hideous man I saw when I first entered this abominable place, brings me detritus from other prisoners with instructions to make a likeness of la señora I have accused of Judaizing. I fashion my imaginary señora from straw with a few threads of wool and bits of cloth I tear from the hem of

65

my sanbenito, this garment I despise with its rough hewn cotton, so unlike what I am used to wearing. I fashion hair from feathers in my mattress. It occupies me and I think of how I might gain more materials to make dolls for mis nietos. It will not happen. I fall asleep, my neck bent with the inflexibility of anguish.

I hear the guard's keys and sit up with terror. Have they come for me again? No, my cellmate is roughly pushed inside. The doll is confiscated from my bosom where I clutch it. What does this mean?

I wait until her hands stop twitching, her shaking head tossing her hair side to side. It has been a while since my last appearance in front of the court. I want to know what transpired. Are the same three inquisitors there? Or terrifying new ones?

I whisper, What is your name?

I do not expect an answer because she has not spoken before, but this time she tells me in a whisper.

Amber. Her voice is soft and feathery like the down that envelops my kitchen when I pluck birds.

A suspicion that she is not one of us pierces me. We do not give our children such names. But what is she?

I am Clara, I offer, my advanced years apparent. I have been incarcerated a long time in this perpetual prison.

She nods with acknowledgement, hugging her knees to her chest.

What transpired?

She ignores my question.

What do they accuse you of?

She looks at me as though I am endangering her.

Finally, she speaks. How long have you been here?

I do not know. Almost two years. My family brings me supplies for which they are charged exorbitant prices. Do you have someone who will bring you food, come to see you?

She shakes her head.

I cannot trust anyone, but I want to know if she understands what this place is. Maybe I am wrong about her origins. I want to know where she came from. What are her memories? My mind wanders to the ripe strawberries my daughters and I gathered from the vines in a valley near us, their juice dribbling down our chins in the evanescent summer light. I share that memory with her.

She is not moved by my explanation, the strawberries a signal to other hidden Jews that we are of the same tribe. I try another tack.

Have you ever raised peacocks? They are ornery birds, shrieking in their vain prancing, plumage exposing a fan of elegance. We had a pair brought from India on one of the boats that chased away all the other birds in our front yard, but the female laid three eggs.

I watch Amber's face as I tell her about our unusual pets for a sign of recognition. When I meet a new person on the outside and desire to know if they are amenable to the Law of Moses, I wait for a positive response to strawberries or peacocks. Her expression remains blank, an unwritten page in one of our books.

Amber, we are in serious detainment. Will you speak to me? There was no point forcing myself on her if she was not willing to communicate.

What do you want to know? She asks in her breathy voice, taking all of me in with a glance.

What are you accused of?

She does not respond, staring at me with clear eyes, an ocean of mistrust.

Do you have any relatives who can help you? Her intent look is not one of darting eyes I have seen in fear. No reaction.

I turn away to lie down, close my eyes to these unspeakable surroundings, conjure thoughts of my family, what they must be doing now. My husband, my poor husband. He needs me for solace. We carry the memories of our people fleeing, the story of our family ingrained since birth, the trauma of displacement never erased. We do not believe in their Trinity or Original Sin, but the past haunts our souls anyway. We give birth and the children appear as we do. How are we so different from others? Is it possible we are born with mental characteristics too? Like the way my daughters fear rodents or are particular about their cleanliness?

I am a Protestant. Her words cut the silence.

What? This surprises me. I know little of Martin Luther and his proclamations, except they were nailed to church doors and trees, his booklet passed from one hand to another without signing his name.

I ask, Where are you from?

I am Dutch.

Her Spanish is rudimentary, but I understand.

My family emigrated from the north of Spain, near the border of France to Holland.

But the Dutch are tolerant.

Sometimes. My family took a ship to Veracruz with the hope we could convert the Indians before all of the country turned Catholic. She halts to bite her bottom lip.

Perhaps she realizes she has said too much. It is difficult to fake Catholicism.

She has no hope.

And you?

I am reluctant to share anything. I am a Catholic. I state this with the rigid necessity of conviction, my spine straight.

So why are you here?

I lower my head in shame.

If I do not state a shred of truth, she will learn from the prison gossip. My faith is in doubt. I can tell from her expression she is not cognizant of the ways of the Inquisition.

CHAPTER THIRTEEN

CELENDARIA

30 de abril 1653

Celendaria, take the heavier blanket. The cold from those stone walls freezes the bones. Bring a goatskin of wine.

Abuelo, they will not allow us to bring that to her.

Try. I have heard some have a glass of spirits. She must be hungry. Pack extra bread around your hips. He is jumpy with suggestions. What about clean garments?

They will confiscate them. We have been told to arrive with empty hands save our basket of linens.

At last, we have received a message that women are allowed to visit my grandmother. My mother, nervous with preparations, organizes us. Her older sisters, my *tía* Maria, a stout woman with a sweet demeanor, and my tía Rosa, my favorite because she smiles often and prepares the most delicious honey cakes at the New Year, have come to our home. Oliva, the youngest aunt, comes too. She has always been strange to me; I cannot follow her gaze. Impatient, she often scolds her young children and me. She is also the most devout.

I am uneasy about seeing my grandmother after such a long time. Another Pesach has passed without her presence at our table. Mi abuelo has urged me to whisper in her ear that he loves her. I am sure she knows this, but I have committed. At last we can observe with our own eyes her condition. It is a long time to be detained.

We arrive at the Palace of the Inquisition on the square and stand at the entrance built into the corner so no one can escape. We are a throng of women eager to see our loved one. The receptor accepts us. We are led down many stairs through a long, damp hallway to my abuela Clara's cell, the door clanking behind us. As the youngest, I am filled with dread that they may not let us leave when it is time. A hollow sound echoes in the hall behind us. What if we are locked in here forever? I am frightened of confinement in small spaces. I know this because when Elena and I hide from one another, I never choose under the bed.

We rush around her, the aroma of bodies and fragrances rising from our tight circle. We breathe in each other's air, touching mi abuela's hair. She holds our faces in her hands, tears spilling, kissing each of our cheeks. When she gets to me, she says, Celendaria, I can tell you are a woman now, one of great beauty who will carry on our family name.

We all glance at each other. Her words are code for us to keep the faith. I am besieged with sadness, but I do not let it show on my face.

When I step back I can see my grandmother has aged, spiders of grey dancing through her former black hair that was the color of the darkest onyx, a precious commodity used for jewelry or carvings. Her cheeks have fallen, composing lines on either side of her lips. Outside of these walls mi abuela was magnificent, sauntering the streets near our home, bags filled with goods for our table and home, her posture that of noble heritage.

We are silent for a moment, reverent in her presence. She is our Madre, the one who has given us life, not their Virgin Mother that has become a cult of worship, but our own sacred being in the flesh. In the hush, I scrutinize her meager surroundings. I am shocked to detect a pair of grass-colored eyes piercing the muted light.

Who is she? I ask pointing to a mass huddled in a corner hugging her knees, tangled hair a sign of neglect.

Mi abuela looks to where I have thrust my interest and responds with a shrug as she leans in. She is silent. She will not bother us. Speak with caution.

We all start to speak at once, our words tumbling out with reports of children, spouses, the textile business, what is happening in the community.

She brings our exuberance to a halt. She speaks in measured, soft tones. I do not know how much time we have, but it is short. It brings my heart joy to see you, to know you are thriving.

My mother turns her back to the guard and reaches under her skirts for the bread wrapped in a cloth. My grandmother is very hungry and tears off a piece to share with the woman hunched in the corner, tossing it to her. Mi abuela eats it quickly only to vomit minutes later, embarrassed by the stench. A rag appears from under one of the aunt's skirts to wipe it up, pushing it through the bars so we can avoid the sour odor, the action so swift I hardly notice. The woman in the corner with her illuminated hair ignores us.

Mama, my mother asks, What do you need?

I need nothing except to know you are well.

Would you like more food? Water? my tía Maria asks.

I need nothing. I am treated with respect, she announces so the guard can hear. He shifts his feet and slides away from our cage.

Who is she? Asks Aunt Rosa.

We know the guard is still listening and our disposition is not to reveal anything of importance.

Ah, she is a confused person who knows nothing of strawberries or peacocks.

Even I understand this message.

Until now, my Aunt Oliva has held back. Peculiar in her demeanor, she wears a large cross with the hanging one to demonstrate her dedication to their orthodoxy. Or perhaps to make us all look more devout. Her head shifts from side to side as she addresses my grandmother and clears her throat. Madre, have you prayed to Jesus to forgive your sins? We can arrange a priest to come for a confession.

We are all silent. Confessions are made under great duress. We are able to communicate directly to our Holy One without an intermediary. An agonizing chore at best. Forgive me, Father, for I have sinned. Then what? We make things up. For the sin of not speaking well of my sisters. Or for the sin of taking a larger portion of food for myself. Or for coveting my neighbor's ring. Something, anything to draw attention away from our one true faith. We are often given the same number of Hail Mary's. I have been taught to kneel in the back of the church in case I am being observed. It is important to appear pious.

I do not know if Oliva is devout or a good pretender. Her performance is credible as a devout Catholic. I was very young when her marriage was arranged, but I remember the difficulty in finding a match, someone who would not detect her slow eye and strange mannerisms. With a larger dowry offered than for her sisters, a match was made with a childless, middle-aged widower who knew my grandfather from travels in the north of Mexico. As is our tradition, the two viewed each other twice, once at the fall festival of Succoth, a time of harvest when the leaves change to mystical colors of reds, oranges and yellows. The other was at Pesach in the spring. I remember sitting on the floor as mi abuela and aunts dressed the bride in heavy veils. As has transpired, my Uncle Berto, a man of commerce with a brick business, has been pleased with his choice. Tía Oliva's fertile womb has given him four healthy sons, a blessing in any family.

My grandmother responds in a low voice. I have confessed many times in the past. I do not need to do it again.

Oliva persists. But Madre, we all have sins, her good eye wandering toward me.

My mother and aunts look away. I can tell no one wants to bring up the church. It is a painful topic fraught with innuendoes.

My grandmother breaks the silence. My dearest daughter Oliva, I am in a righteous place with the Father, the Son and the Holy Ghost.

We all know Oliva is the most ardent with their trinity. She is also a bit simple, unable to read and memorize with rapidity like the rest of us. It is especially difficult at Pesach when we read the Haggadah, a guide that retells the Exodus and answers the questions of our history. However, as my grandmother has reminded us in the past, Oliva is of our blood and we must love her.

The jailer rattles his keys with menace. We know it is time to depart. We each take our turn hugging and kissing our matriarch, smoothing her hair, making an effort not to shed tears. When she comes to me, I whisper mi abuelo's message close to her ear. She smiles. I have given her a moment of happiness.

CHAPTER FOURTEEN

CLARA

7 de mayo 1653, late afternoon
Santa Oficina de la Inquisición

I am dragged back to the tribunal a week after my daughters' and granddaughter's visit. It was strange to see them. We had kept our voices low because we knew the guard listened to every word. After they departed, when I was alone in my cell, save for the quiet one, I reviewed the moments we spent together, especially Celendaria's last words of my husband's love. It is a relief that all is well with them.

A joy flows over me as I wrap the extra blanket around my body. The scents of my family fill me with sweet dreams as I doze. I regret I was not allowed to clean myself. I am used to washing every week. I miss that ritual the most.

I am in the presence of men with unchanging agate expressions. Yet, I am grateful for my family's visit. I miss my husband. Instead of being ebullient with happiness, the visit plunged me into despair for the next few days. Would I ever be free again?

Señora. Doña. A title of respect I have earned, has evaporated.

Señora Crespin.

Their eyes are fixated on me. I must pay attention. I do not know what they intend to question me about today. I have so little to tell them.

Did you make this? The effigy I made is held up to me.

Yes, sirs.

Is this an accurate likeness of Señora de Silva? Yes, my inquisitors.

Defense Attorney, bring her to the window. This small, hunched man has been named as my protector. For much of the time I thought he was a silent partner of the tribunal, an observer of the Notary, but instead I learned he is a joke, a sham to show the fairness of the court. He has not said a word in my favor.

My heart leaps at a vision of the outside world. It is of the courtyard I know well, a view of the nunnery across the plaza, a few trees. People move about with ease. Tears roll down my face. I have forgotten what freedom looks like.

From the corner of my eye I see the inquisition officers hand a guard, one of their dour African slaves, the doll.

I stand at the window, waiting. I do not know why I am allowed to view blue sky, the verdant trees, the serapes of the Mexican men pulling mules, their carts loaded with goods, bottles, food. I lick my lips. It has been so long since I have tasted anything that is juicy, salty and delectable with flavors that hit the roof of my mouth. I watch a mother dragging a small child by the hand across the plaza.

I hear the guard exit the doors behind me.

After a time I am ready to sit but it is not possible. I am tired but I do not want to waste this view by blinking for a moment. Suddenly, I spot the African with other guards in front of the church across the plaza, calling onlookers. I cannot hear the directives. Sticks are gathered by children—oh please do not let mis nietos, the children of my heart, be among them. A small fire is started. Is this for me? I begin to sweat profusely, my sanbenito damp in many places.

A tall priest exits from the church, his black cappa worn over a white habit with a large cross, visible from afar. He carries a book with him. I cannot hear his words but he garners the attention of a crowd that gathers. Whatever he says frightens me, a panic racing from my feet to my head. I begin to tremble without control.

The priest enhances the fire by igniting more flames from the bottom. He reads from the open book he has brought with him, lifting his head to look at the crowd from time to time. The flames reach waist high. More people gather, children dancing to the rhythm of the blaze as it stretches higher. The crowd enjoys the spectacle of fire, adding small branches and bits of garbage to the bottom of the flames.

Why am I made to watch this? I turn to the inquisitors.

Do not move, Señora.

When I turn my gaze back across the plaza, the priest throws my doll into the flames. The crowd cheers, a few fists pumping the air.

I cry, not for the doll, or the imaginary doctor's wife I have condemned, but for all those who have come before me and met this fate.

CHAPTER FIFTEEN

CELENDARIA

8 de octubre 1653
Erev Sukkot

Time moves slowly without my grandmother's presence, especially the space between holidays. Tonight we make preparations for Sukkot, a holiday that occurs five days after Yom Kippur, el Gran Día, our holiest day of the year. We go from the most solemn of days to one of the most joyous when we are commanded to dwell in temporary shelters and celebrate the harvest.

Our ancestors built open structures to eat outside under a roof of date palm leaves to catch a glimpse of the stars and commemorate our biblical wanderings for forty years. But it is too dangerous for us. We do not have a lulav to wave, a fan of palm, willow and myrtle; however, citrons and late summer squash decorate our mantel.

Instead, we make preparations to eat inside. The twins make a dessert of cactus pears and pomegranate seeds, my favorite for their refreshing taste. I prepare *adafina,* a dish of onions, garlic and eggplant from ancient recipes, while my mother cooks *mujadara,* a

78

dish of Arabic influence with lentils, spices and rice piled high with wedges of fried onions. Afterward, she fries a slab of meat in olive oil. We do not use lard from a pig. She worries the smell of meat frying will alert our neighbors.

She says, Close the shutters, Yael. Then to the rest of us she says, Many of these recipes are from a time when Jews, Moslems and Christians lived in La Convivencia, a time of mutual agreement that lasted until the fifteenth century. As she speaks of the time of peace, her voice is filled with longing.

Mi abuelo interrupts us. Gabriela, La Convivencia is a myth, not a time of goodwill. We will not know peace until the Messiah comes.

Mi abuelo has become cranky with the absence of my grandmother, impatient with Yael and Yonah, cantankerous with all of us, his irritation with the incarceration of mi abuela a tumor on his soul.

Soon my father arrives. He is silent while he washes his hands. When the food is prepared, we sit and bow our heads in prayer around the table.

Blessed are You, Lord our God, King of the Universe, who has sanctified us with His commandments and has commanded us concerning the waving of the lulav.

We have had many family conferences about our situation, tentative bonds that leave excruciating memories of when our family was whole.

My grandfather mourns his wife every day even though she is not dead, just gone, absent from us. There have been two more visits where I was allowed to accompany him to see her. The first time we were permitted to meet in a room with wooden benches under the guards' watchful eyes. My grandfather held her hands, her wrists chained, and wept. She too could not share her thoughts, only her desire to leave the vile place.

The second time we were permitted to enter at night only after we passed a bribe of silks, a rare commodity, brought from the Philippines to Señor Lopez's mother; her son, Miguel, is the priest who had previously refused to assist us. We had to appear at her dwelling after midnight with the package wrapped like meat.

Our offering, gathered at great risk through secret channels, took months of preparation. Mi abuelo could not see well in the darkness without a moon. I held his arm to steady him since I knew the streets to la señora's home. She and mi madre often shared spices from their gardens—nutmeg used for medicinal purposes, cumin and ginger for cooking, and cinnamon, a fragrant addition to the smells of the body and clothing. We kept to the shadows of the walls as we crossed to another neighborhood. It would arouse suspicion to be out at this late hour when most were safely tucked in their beds. Finally, when we reached our destination, we crept along the side of her house and rapped on the shutters. A dog began to bark. I shivered. What would happen to us if we were caught?

La señora opened the shutters to us. The fear among our people was so great she did not invite us inside her home, uncustomary for the hospitality that was common. The package was propped on the windowsill. She peeled back the corner of the plain cotton wrapping to reveal a panoply of colors unlike those I had ever seen before—something my father called turquoise, a blend of blue and green together that looked like the sea, and pink, the lightest rose that reminded me of a baby's skin, and midnight blue, a plum hue close to the color of the berenjenas that grow in our yard.

As la señora exclaimed over the luscious tints in candlelight, I looked behind her into the room. I saw a young man with a comely face in the doorway, a distinct collar framing his face, his cheekbones illuminated. Her son. He looked like us with his dark hair and full lips. A change of heart did not change a face. He was still from a family of *conversos* like us. Our eyes met. What would he do with the valuable pieces of silk? I glanced down, aware of the danger for mi abuelo, who often mentioned that he wished he could change places with his wife.

La señora whispered, Wait a few days before you return to your wife. He will arrange a longer visit in private. His parish has changed. He is in a better position now. Please show no recognition if he materializes in the church near you. Mi abuelo grabbed my hand. It was time to go.

So that is how we were able to be with mi abuela alone in a small, walled garden designed so other prisoners could not observe us. We sat on a bench under a tree, her chains visible. I treasured their privacy and moved to the side so they could have a few intimate moments, a couple who had been together for more than three decades. The silks bought him access and had given them hope. She was revived with the gifts we were allowed to bring—quinces, cherries, late for the season, peaches conserved in sweet syrup, clean, soft cotton undergarments, a comb for her hair, a bit of cow oil for her parched lips.

We returned ebullient with hope, repeating every interaction to my mother and father, savoring the parts of her smile. We dined in celebration knowing that we had a channel inside the offices of the Inquisition. Maybe we could change mi abuela's fate.

That evening as my mother got the younger girls ready for bed, we murmured in soft tones about the happiness of my grandfather. While my sisters slept, my mother reached for me, guiding us into a small space at the top of the stairs. She faced me and stroked my hair. It is almost time for you to marry and start a family of your own.

My eyes widened in surprise. I cannot imagine such an occurrence. I feel like a child inside, although I am about to reach my fifteenth year. No. I do not want this. I scramble for an excuse, my alarm causing me to feel faint. I lean back against the wall, my breath coming in short gasps. No, mi madre, por favor. I can live here and take care of you, grandfather, my sisters' children when they appear. What if grandmother is not released? Who will assist all of you?

She takes my face in her hands and brings it close to hers, kissing my forehead. *Mi hija*, do not worry. We will make a good match.

I am not ready.

Celendaria, there is no time to be ready. We will set two meetings for this coming Pesach and next Sukkot. All will be different in a year.

I can only think of my Aunt Oliva's hairy, middle-aged husband. Madre, please, no.

It is not possible. Our people must go forward. You are meant to have babies.

I pull from her grasp and turn to the wall to hide my tears.

CHAPTER SIXTEEN

CLARA

10 de marzo 1654, late at night
Santa Oficina de la Inquisición

We, the Inquisitors, who stand against Heretical Depravity and Apostasy in the City of Mexico, the provinces of New Spain, the Maya territory of Verapaz in Guatemala, Nicaragua, Yucatán, Honduras, islands of the Philippines, Cartegena in Columbia and regions of Lima, Peru, state that the enemies of religion are also the enemies of the state. You have committed sins and crimes.

I have heard all of this before. I do not understand why they are keeping an old woman imprisoned for this many years. Why has this persecution continued for so long?

What about your daughters?

I have been awakened from a deep sleep, stumbling in my chains to stand before these wicked men. My heart beats with rapid movement. I must think with clarity to protect my family. My knees lock in tension. I gather myself to say, my daughters are all baptized as good Catholics and have been taught the ways of the Church.

Along with the Law of Moses?

No, sirs. They are pure. I kept them to myself.

They are not well versed in the feasts and holidays your kind celebrates, especially the youngest one of beauty, who goes by the name…? They murmur among themselves. Celendaria?

Oh, I am terrified. Celendaria, my most precious granddaughter! It cannot be. We are all in danger. How could the Seders that we have celebrated for the Jews exiting out of Egypt, the treats we have prepared for a sweet new year at Rosh Hashanah, the recitation of our sins at Yom Kippur cause us harm? Especially my amiable Celendaria. Most honored Sirs, I do not know of what you speak.

Señora, we have kept you incarcerated all this time so that you could remember your transgressions. The burning in effigy of Señora de Silva was to remind you of your inevitable fate.

I take an audible breath. The faces of my daughters flicker, their progeny tainted and tied to me. I must protect them at all costs.

Are you aware, Señora that once we make clear your lapses into the Law of Moses, your descendants for three generations will be tainted by your disobedience to the Church?

I have heard this before, but to hear it from the tribunal causes me great distress. No matter what I do my family will suffer. We are all Jews born to other Jews. We cannot change this. A pang grips my stomach and I bend in pain. It is of no interest to my inquisitors.

Señora, I will read to you what the penalties are to your family by their association with you. Your children, your grandchildren and their children will not be able to hold office, wear luxury items, ride horses or carry firearms.

What does it matter to me? But to my family it will cause inconveniences. It will destine them to the poorest classes in a country that, without these bogus investigations, could be a land of plenty like the Jerusalem in the Bible.

Tell us again about the doctor's wife burned in effigy.

I was fooled by her. I am an ignorant woman who knows little.

A woman who can read.

My heart quivers with trepidation. How could they know?

You realize it is a travesty to read words without the benefit of a priest's interpretation.

Yes, señor.

What did she tell you that you were so fooled?

Maybe this is my time to confess. If they are going to set me aflame anyway, it may be better to acknowledge and apologize for my offenses to the Church. She explained to me that according to the Bible we are to take a day of rest. I do not go on. Maybe this will be enough.

Why is this important?

I do not know. Maybe my ignorance will save me.

Are there preparations for this day of rest? I remind you to not censor your replies. We have familiarity with your customs as well as ways to obtain the truth.

A shiver travels from the bottom of my spine to the back of my neck. The dread of their intimidation is what I fear the most. Others have been brave, some returning to our community, their broken bones causing me horror and fright, but not enough for me to discontinue my faith. That is why I have blamed the nonexistent señora rather than jeopardize my family. For the first time I break down in tears in front of my inquisitors. I fall apart for a few minutes, gather myself and bend over to wipe my tears on the hem of the sanbenito.

Señora, are you prepared to continue?

In a small voice I say, She explained to me that there were preparations for the day of rest.

What were they?

To bathe.

Speak up. We cannot hear you.

I clear my throat. To bathe in clean water, to prepare food before sundown so there would be no use of fire for cooking, to change the linens on our beds. I feel a great sense of relief to get this out. I want it to satisfy them.

How did you prepare the food?

Ay, I do not want to say this, but I must. She taught me how to kill an animal with a knife.

Why is that?

Because it is more humane than twisting their necks.

As if they could understand the meaning of the word humane. The flicker of Shabbat candles sears my mind, the way we gathered once a week to forgive each other, to love the Lord, to celebrate life itself.

Is there anything else you want to confess?

No, sirs.

Take her away.

I am returned to my cell in a sad state, mostly dragged because my feet and ankles have become mush, similar to what we are fed. Amber is standing, stretching her arms. She raises her eyebrows in question. I quake with terror, my hands uncontrollable.

CHAPTER SEVENTEEN

CELENDARIA

1 de abril 1654

I am in dread of a marriage arranged by my parents. It is our custom to choose among our community of conversos. Most likely my father will be the one to pick out my future husband from his complex set of contacts in many places, perhaps among his Freemasons or textile merchants. I have begged him to choose among those in Ciudad de México, even a cousin, rather than someone far away where I would be required to follow. It occupies my mind every day. I cannot leave my family.

I no longer play with Elena. It has hurt her feelings that I am not available, but now that I am a woman, my mother has explained to me that our romps are undignified. She trusts me to do the shopping in the market on my own, my head covered with a scarf so no man except my future husband will see my hair.

Today I venture out to deliver goods and stop at the market, a basket over my arm. My mother kisses me on each cheek as I depart.

Celendaria, be wise. We are under suspicion. Stop into the church in case neighbors are watching.

My first stop is to deliver ground chili peppers and allspice to Señora Lopez. Mi madre has informed me I am to pick up ginger and cloves, inquiring as to her son's influence with our situation. It is simple to find the way to her neighborhood in the light of day, the sun bright overhead. Many stay indoors at this hour for siesta and return to work later in the day, but I am not deterred. I want to bring back information about mi abuela.

Señora Lopez answers the door at the sound of my rapping knuckles. Since this is a legitimate visit, I do not have to sneak to the side window.

Ah, Celendaria, come in. Would you like a refreshment to cool your throat?

I have not been to her home alone in the daylight. I glance around the room, sunlight streaming across her kitchen table. She places a tin cup of water in front of me. *¿Como está tu madre?*

I answer that she is fine while I examine a large silver cross hanging on the wall next to me. On her mantle is a statue of Jesus in Mother Mary's lap. She also has a larger hearth to prepare food and keep the house warm on chillier nights. When I have taken in as much as I can without being rude, I look her in the eye. She is wearing a scarf made from the rose-pink silk my grandfather and I delivered at great risk. I am stunned, as if a deadly snakebite staggered me. The precious textiles were supposed to go to her son who claimed influence with the inquisitors.

And you, Celendaria, are they finding a match for you?

I am infuriated. I nod so as not to reveal my anger. How can I broach this subject? Then I remember the charms of mi abuela when

I accompanied her on errands, enchanting male vendors with her eyes, lowering her eyelashes for a better price.

Ah, señor, these are beautiful oranges. Yes, señora, imported from Spain.

But the price is too high. Can it be lowered?

For you, Doña Crespin, I can make an exception.

Señora Lopez, my voice sweet with sugar, do you have any news for me?

She shifts in her chair, her expression one of embarrassment. Did your mother send the spices I need?

It is bold of me to speak this way, but I am seething inside. Por favor, Señora Lopez, do you have information about mi abuela?

She glances around the room as though someone might be listening. She hisses at me, You cannot bring this up.

I may only be fifteen but I am not stupid. I understand that she is evading her part of the bargain, a piece of exquisite silk draped around her neck. I ask, Why not?

Because too many of us will be endangered.

Then why did you accept the goods that my grandfather risked his life for?

You are an insolent girl.

No, I am a woman. What has your son done to assist us?

You may not speak to me this way. Out. Out of my home.

My stomach clutches. My mother will not be pleased I have not made the exchange of spices. And started a confrontation. I calm myself with a deep breath, something I have been taught to do before I say the Shema. Please, Señora, let us not be angry. I reach into my basket on the floor next to me and hand her the carefully wrapped package.

She stares at it. If she doesn't take it, it means I will return home empty-handed. She sighs, places her hands on the table to lift herself and goes to the shelves near the Hanging One. She hands me a similarly swathed package without returning to her seat. She wants me to leave, her arm opened toward the door.

I exit, petrified that I may have done more harm than good. Her son who could assist us can also destroy us. Ay, my heart is heavy. The streets are deserted at this hour, the sun intense on my back as I squint into the bright light. I walk with heavy steps, not anxious to return with no news, worse yet, a disagreement to repeat. Mi madre will be angry, worried, teary. What can I do? I repeat the scene in my head. A man with a recalcitrant donkey rides too close to me, the animal's head twisting, rebelling at his load. Mud splashes the bottom of my skirt. I am upset with his carelessness, trying to brush away the filth. When I right myself, I realize I have lost my way.

I look for church spires so I can guide myself back to the correct streets. I recognize the Iglesia de Santo Domingo and head toward it. Most of us live within a small area between the grand Catedral Metropolitana de la Asunción de María and the Iglesia de Santo Domingo, a stone's throw from the offices of the Inquisition. Priests are always helpful with directions or any verbal exchange, an opportunity to empty our spirits of heresy. I pass the side of the church. There is little shade at this hour, but priests are lined up at a small table where a scribe writes legal documents, important messages and love letters for those who are illiterate. I will not know anyone here who can vouch for me.

I enter the coolness of the sanctuary, my eyes blinking after the bright, high sun. I am familiar with the grandeur of all the cathedrals built by the Church after the conversion of the Indians, sometimes rumored to be four thousand souls a day. After a time, the Church gave up on the native population because their religion would not be erased. So the church folded teachings into theirs. What a shame they did not give us any room for other choices.

Quiet gives me comfort after an unpleasant confrontation with mi madre's friend. From the back, I see a few widows in the front pews, their black scarves a symbol of eternal grief. Two of them kneel together, facing the illuminated altar covered with candles. I have not entered this sanctuary before, our family preferring to attend the grand cathedral so neighbors can identify us.

I stand at the back studying a statue of the Apostle Thomas, whose story the Church has refashioned from the Aztecs' Quetzalcoatl, a feathered serpent related to the gods. They did not want to give up their faith either. Soon the women retreat up the aisle. Perhaps someone saw me enter so that it can be mentioned to a neighbor that I was in the Iglesia de Santo Domingo.

I pause before going up the aisle to light a candle, the incense making my eyes itch. If my mother were with me, she would insist I cannot rub my eyes like a common girl. Then I dip my fingers in a basin of water and make the sign of the cross.

I go forward to genuflect in front of the altar. I do not like their confessionals, the priest tucked inside the darkness, my bench hard with only a lattice of wood separating me from them. It is only in recent times the screen has been sanctioned by the Church. My mother said priests' hands could wander where they wanted in previous times. But maybe today is the day I need to come forward, tell a half-truth for not obeying my mother, an opportunity to appear pious and clear my thoughts. I enter and wait. Usually the priest is already there or comes soon after, although I have not done this many times. My family warns me to do as little as possible so I do not have to take their hard cracker and wine symbolizing the flesh and blood of their Savior.

I wait, my thumbs twirling. I hear soft voices, muffled. They are not inside this small space with me. They must be outside. Another minute passes and it is silent. Where is the priest? Then I hear a moan. It is unlike what I have heard before. A person in pain? In trouble? In distress? With a cautious motion, I open the door and tiptoe toward the sound. With steady paces, I follow the noise behind the confessional. In the darkness I discern two figures pressed to one another, a white hand lifted to the face of the other, an ecclesiastical ring on the third finger of the left hand.

It is an intimate moment I have encountered. My body is hidden by the confessional, but my eyes see what transpires. They have adjusted to the darkness. The two faces kiss, their lips hungry, a passion I only know from my Aunt Maria's fervent words about why I will like to be married. Their heads part and I see one is a woman, her scarf fallen to her shoulders, and the other a man, a priest, from the ring and his white collar close to his face. I am fearful when he thrusts her back to the wall, the scraping of fabric on her dress like the sound of mice in the walls. He elevates her higher than his head. She groans. The silhouette of his lower body shifts with steady rhythm, a musical theme of back and forth. I inhale a breath with the recognition of what is happening. The woman's face turns to the sanctuary candlelight, mouth open, eyes closed. When her head drops, I see she has a distinctive nose and chin with a crease, one that reminds me of someone. But I know not whom.

The man moans, his head falling back, neck stretched like the lambs my mother slaughters. I must leave. But I cannot. I am transfixed, repulsed, fascinated at the same time. The recognition of their illicit behavior stuns me. The animals do this from behind, not face to face.

They are making a child. And it is the priest who participates, forbidden from this activity, although rumors persist. I can distinguish his cassock pulled up with one arm, steadying himself on the wall behind her with the other. He lets out a sound I have never heard before, a wounded animal that howls with longing. His head falls forward to her bosom. I view her naked breasts that have burst from the top of her blouse. He puts his mouth to her nipple, like a baby for sustenance, at first tender and then as if to consume her. When he lifts his head for breath, I glimpse his face, eyes closed in an ecstasy reserved for God, pale alabaster stretched over his cheekbones, angular in the shadows. Her breast glows, white, firm, luscious as a peach at harvest. It is a thing of beauty. I am unable to move. My feet are planted here. If I make a sound I will be discovered. The thrusting begins again. She must be aroused in terror because she cries out, louder than him, with such agony that he places his hand across her mouth.

I cannot eavesdrop more. My feet fly me out of there, a bird of prey that takes off from the ground to escape a predator. I am shocked by the light that hits my face. I blink. Tears fill my eyes. Where should I go? I am breathing too hard to keep running. I turn the corner where the men write letters, the tables empty now in the heat of day, and lean against a wall in the shade, heaving. My head begins to clear.

Whoever it was must have heard my departure as my shoes slapped against tiles. I wait a few moments to clear my head, gazing into the empty Plaza de Santo Domingo save a few lost dogs. It is time for me to leave for the safety of my home.

Before I venture from my shady spot, a comely woman dashes by me. I am unnoticed. She is in a great hurry. Ah, the same profile I saw inside. But who is she? I glance toward the church. The priest is standing in the open doorway, surveying the empty plaza. He does not see me, but I recognize him. And now I remember her. Señor Behar's beautiful daughter, the one with the flawless skin, the one whose body has no markings from harsh weather, the one with thick, wavy hair.

I have forgotten the package of ginger and cloves for my mother inside the confessional.

CHAPTER EIGHTEEN

CLARA

7 de abril 1654, evening
Santa Oficina de la Inquisición

This is my ninth audience with the court. I place my feet apart for better balance, waiting for their pointed, repetitive questions. I never dreamed I would be kept alive this long. It is almost five years since my arrest. Many times I pray for this to end so my family can be at peace. But according to our Portuguese friends, the Inquisition's pace reveals itself more slowly ever since the Mexican tribunal became bankrupt in May of 1642. The viceroy, Juan de Palafox, started arresting people again to fill the treasury. It continues to this day. Why else would an old woman be a target? My mind that dreams and thinks wonders who put me here. My neighbors? Other hidden Jews? My loyal servant, Teresa? Her silly child, Elena? Elena? Could it be?

Señora, are you prepared to give us the names of other Judaizers?

I do arrange my thoughts before I come before these monstrous men who represent an ecclesiastical mountain of dogma, but today

I am weary of keeping my lies straight. They do not believe me anyway. They merely untwine a piece of the thread each time, its own form of torture.

Sirs, I know of no one else.

Take her away. We know how to make her remember.

Terrified, I begin to weep as I am led away.

In my cell, Amber is at rest. She speaks a few words to me now. I am grateful she is not hostile. A kind, lost soul far from her family, I think of her as one of my daughters. She sits up, staring at me.

I am afraid, I tell her.

Why?

The men are warning me.

About what?

Of the torment that awaits me. They have done this to others. We keep ourselves apprised of what the Church does. Many Protestants and Calvinists have suffered, not only pirates captured and charged from the coastal areas of the Yucatán, but women too—witches, visionaries, astrologers, sorcerers, anyone they deem an intruder, especially the French. And bigamists, those that leave families on the other side of the ocean and start another in Nueva España. Ha! The irony of their so called morality, brotherhood and charity discharged by the Holy Office.

I break down again. I am petrified of the torture. Bravery is not a possibility for a woman of weak will like me.

Shh, I warn Amber. Do not speak. I have seen their guards stalk the halls in slippered feet to spy on us.

I understand spies. I sit back with resignation. Of course. They are all powerful. It is another way to build their suspicions.

I remind her, You must be careful what you say. That is why I speak little. It is not to your benefit for them to know what you fear. We are all being watched all the time. There is no hope for me.

I turn away, distraught.

I was picked up with others, Amber whispers. I was found with a book. Our leader teaches that our salvation and Heaven are not earned by good deeds. The book is a gift of God. She smiles, her small, even teeth like polished stones.

I nod. I have heard this before. I do not want to reveal anymore about myself.

Amber gives me a serious look, her eyes askance as if in warning. If you do not believe in Jesus, you will burn in hell.

You are a Lutheran? I have surprised her. Her eyebrows shoot up in dismay. It has been our task to discover what others believe. Our Judaism is the origin of it all.

Yes, Martin Luther's. He insisted we all be called Christians, the only acceptable name for us.

I am a New Christian.

It is not the same, she says, her voice rising with indoctrination. Jews do not deserve their homes, synagogues or money. It is all to be confiscated, destroyed, their liberties curtailed.

This pains me. The Protestant menace, as it is called, is against us too. Why do so many hate us? Martin Luther has started a movement in defiance of the Church. I reach out to touch her hand.

Do you believe this? We are lost souls in this incarceration. We may never be free.

That is not true. I have others on the outside assisting me with my freedom. I have not been called so many times before the tribunal.

Yes, but only because the Holy Office has tired of concentrating on big problems to focus on little ones. They do not want any other faith to take hold in New Spain.

She gazes at me with sadness that crumbles her face. They have confiscated my book. I am lost without it.

I reflect on my relationship with the books in my home, a sin according to the church. Ah, this is something I understand. I have begged my husband to destroy books hidden in many places—buried in the spice garden, inside the secret wall of the basement, under the kitchen floor, a library in the attic. I know about the heretical literature. I beg them to dispose of anything that offends their monolithic religion, like the two banned books smuggled from Italy, one that declares the story of Jesus Christ is a mystical allegory, and the other, a newer, true love poem called *Eloisa and Abelard*, which I will not allow my daughters to read.

I drift away into a restless sleep.

CHAPTER NINETEEN

CELENDARIA

8 de abril 1654
Pesach

I have told no one about what I saw in the Iglesia de Santo Domingo a few days ago. It skulks into my days and haunts me at night, an indistinct monster. I cannot confide in mi madre. She was angry I lost the spices, ones we needed for Pesach. I did not make up a story. I told her they were forgotten in the confessional. Even this is questioned. She gave me her squinty-eyed look, knowing I have few sins and we do not follow the tradition of professing them except on el Gran Día. She wanted me to go back to look for them but the hour was late.

Señora Behar, mi madre's closest friend, visits early in the morning as we prepare for our festival of Passover. It is not the first or second evening of the eight-day festival as customary because we do not want to arouse suspicion of the authorities. We put ourselves at great risk reading from a precious Haggadah that tells the story of the Israelites' enslavement to the Exodus with Moses, asking why this night is different. Poignant, especially with a family member imprisoned with a mistrust of Judaizing, and the fact that mi abuela has never been formally charged. The Inquisition is known to take years to build a case against someone, scouring for witnesses, exacting revenge against those who do not cooperate.

I am anxious, finding it difficult to relax while I start my chore of cleaning any crumbs left from bread or cakes from our house. Our home must be uncontaminated of leavened bread. I am sweeping toward the middle of the floor when Señora Behar arrives.

My mother, schooled in the manners of the Spanish, greets her friend. Maybe she is practicing to welcome the young man, intended for me, and his family. Beatriz, please come in. I will decant tea for us.

I finish my chore, scraping the debris into a paper and take it out to the back of the house. I dawdle to give them time alone. All I can think of is the man meant for me. He is not old. At least my mother has shared this. When I return to the hearth, I sit on a wooden bench to watch from the side and embroider, mending tablecloths and napkins that have been washed too many times, a basket of thread and scissors beside me. I lower my head, pulling thread and needle through a stain that I cover with a small flower. I can think of nothing else save the naked breast of Señora Behar's daughter exposed to Father Lopez. Warmth rises from my collarbone to my neck, ascending my face. Will I do this with my husband?

They speak of family while mi madre bustles with hot water, a china cup, a piece of *pan de afflición,* the hard cracker we eat on Pesach, and a small bowl of berries that have been sugared and boiled into jam. La señora glances at me, then around the room at the copper pots hanging on one wall, plates and utensils on shelves fashioned by my brothers. It is a plain, functional room, unlike those of our compatriots who have carried their antiquities across the sea.

To what do we owe this visit? Mi madre asks, handing her a cup of tea poured from a large pot. She settles in near her friend, her hand smoothing her skirt.

Gabriela, this is delicious. Where did you find pan de afflición? There are few ovens not contaminated with bread. I have a few pieces but it is not enough.

I will give you some to take with you. One baker has a horno, a clay oven outside of town hidden beneath a stand of trees. He stores his supplies to bake the unleavened bread in a nearby cave. He rushes so as not to be caught, not unlike our ancestors who could not wait for it to rise. He brings it to us in his cart underneath a woolen blanket.

A cave? I have not heard of this.

Yes, ancient caverns that the Aztecs knew about and never shared with their Spanish conquerors. The city was called Tenochtitlan then. It is said some of the rooms are so large we used it to gather Sephardim to pray together for Rosh Hashanah.

I am amazed at your knowledge.

My mother lowers her eyes, pleased with the compliment.

I am here for two reasons. One, I want to say blessings for Celendaria that she will meet her intended tonight with an open heart. I only wish we can be as fortunate with our lovely Mariel. Without a substantial dowry, there are not many choices. Besides, she shows little interest in anything. We have done our best to educate her. It is considered desirable among our kind to have a woman who reads and writes so she can teach her children, but she is lazy, staring outside for hours. In fact, I am concerned with her new interest in the Church.

No, this cannot be. Our people have struggled to keep our faith alive. Are we going to lose another one? Is she attending regularly?

Please, dear God, no. Her father will not allow that and would be inconsolable if something happened to her. We must find her a mate. Soon.

I am fascinated with this discussion about the moods of Mariel. A shiver goes up my spine. I stop my embroidery and revisit the passion on her face. She is doomed to a marriage without love or respect if she has experienced an ardor as I have witnessed. Will I know such fervor?

My thoughts are interrupted by Señora Behar's second reason for coming.

Some of the women—Aracelia, Delfina, Consuelo—are planning to soak in a large cistern at a home near the edge of town before the next Shabbat. It is safe. It will be an uncommon pleasure. Bring your white clothes under a wrap. Celendaria and the girls are invited too.

But what about the men? They are using it earlier. Diego will speak to Esteban.

My ears have pricked up. Will I see Mariel in her splendor once again?

I am flush with warmth and excuse myself so the ladies can speak in private, leaving my mending on the bench. I retire to an old chair in the backyard under a tree. So much is blooming with the recent rains and the animals seem content. A slight breeze rustles my hair.

The preparations for Passover are monumental, not only because of our Seder meal, but also I am to meet my intended for the first time. I am nervous, fearful, anticipating the worst. What if he has bad breath? Or is squat with duck feet that slap the floor? Or shorter than me so that I am a bell tower over him? I am not anticipating this with enthusiasm.

This morning the twins teased me when we awakened. He will be old and have bad teeth! Yael shrieked with laughter. No, he will be fat and waddle, said Yonah. What if he cannot grow a beard? What if his clothes smell?

Stop! At least I will not be in a bed with children anymore. For a while anyway.

I crawled from under the covers to stand, lifted my chin in defiance and glided out of our bedroom, as if they have not made me feel small, insecure and anxious. I know little about him except that my father and grandfather have chosen him from among their network of Freemasons, some relationships that antecede our Diaspora from the Old World. The bloodlines my father and grandfather recite into the night prompt long dialogues. Last week while I spied on them from the stairs, I fell asleep and tumbled down to the bottom. They never heard me.

The next night I overheard mi abuelo converse about the Sepher Toledot, handling it with care, researching the lines of families. He tells mi padre that the young man they are focused on might be a cousin because the family name, Rebozo, originated in Spain. When they migrated to Portugal, it appears again with the Mendozas in Jamaica in the 1600s.

Young? Thanks to God. He is not an old, hard-boiled egg.

My father says, We have no one in Jamaica. They cannot be part of our bloodline.

Mi abuelo is the authority in these matters. His impatience confirms his frustration with my father. I have checked, he says. These are not the same Rebozos.

When a slurp ensues, I know they must be drinking Jerez sherry, perhaps in celebration of finding a mate for me.

Yes, some of the Mendozas married Rebozos and Crespins, continues mi abuelo. They traded in cowhides and sugar, but were expelled in 1643.

Where did they go? Mi padre asks.

I am curious too. Our history remains a long, complicated one.

They sailed to Cape Saint Anthony in Cuba. Cuba was good to us for a while. I wish we could have stayed, mi abuelo says with a wistful voice.

If this is so, how did they get to Mexico?

My grandfather starts to exude impatience. A few became captains and pilots of ships, especially from Nevis and Barbados. We are resourceful if nothing else. These conversos were part of the silent trade, our networks protecting us because so many prohibitions were placed on us. Ah, we are still outcasts of the New World.

Mi madre's voice alerts me. How do you know they were not slave traders from this area of the world? I do not want my eldest daughter mixed up with a sordid business.

It is true some of our kind were involved, says mi padre. We took opportunities because we were abandoned by the world, marooned like seamen to fend for ourselves.

My mother is upset. I will not have it! My sons have married into respectable families. I want my daughter to do the same.

Yes, and they did not need a dowry. Shush, Gabriela. We will find her a suitable match within our own kind. It is the only choice we have.

My father is not enthused; however, he knows when I leave, it will be one less mouth to feed.

My grandfather adds, Slavery is an abhorrent act for a people seeking justice.

My father says, These people are not slave traders. Leave that to the Spanish and the people to the north. It is not an issue. These people have few possessions and are willing to accept our meager dowry.

I am thinking the question as my mother asks it.

What's wrong with the boy?

Nothing. He is studious, learned in our ways.

This is dangerous. Does this mean he does not have a profession? He cannot be a furrier or a man of merchandise. If he is part of the lowly tailoring trades like us, we will never enhance our status.

Gabriela, forget your ambitions, interjects mi abuelo. Our heritage is vital to our survival.

It can also be the death of us. What will he do with this knowledge? Become a secret rabbi?

It is a possibility. We need them.

No! I will not have it. Your wife is locked up never to be seen again and you want us to perpetuate this nonsense of *limpieza de sangre*. Our blood can never be pure again.

My father shouts, Enough! We will make a match and Celendaria will marry.

I want my eldest daughter to have a decent life, says my mother, one of ease. How will this studious young man support a family?

My mother cares for my destiny.

Like many of us, he participates in a family business with his father and uncles, offers mi abuelo.

What is it?

It is as though I am sitting on my mother's lap asking the same questions.

They are settled in the north promoting trade as merchants, working sometimes as *fiadores*.

My mother does not know this word. Nor do I. I am straining to hear every word.

Bondsmen. They catch criminals to turn over to the authorities for a fee.

My mother is furious. No! This cannot be possible. These are the people who chase us like criminals. Scandalous! I do not want my daughter to be part of this. This is not a refined vocation.

She begins to cry, murmuring to herself.

I peek around the wall and thwart my impulse to rush to her. Mi padre calms himself with another sip of sherry and calmly explains. Gabriela, his family is trying to ease themselves out of this. It is a way to learn the area around San Miguel and other outposts in the territories. They desire another life across the Rio Grande River to escape the Inquisition in Mexico. We cannot be so picky. Let us pray Celendaria feels welcoming to this young man. Her life will be one of cooking, cleaning and children no matter where she lives.

Are you telling me I will lose my daughter to a farther destination? You must ask him about his business practices. What happens when a converso strays into his path? Will he arrest people like us, perhaps moving toward a more stable life?

My father slams his hand to his knee. Gabriela, you are impossible! We have no control over who is arrested. Better that Celendaria is married. What am I to do with three daughters?

I hear Mama weep, sniffling.

We have few options, says my father in a resigned voice.

Up until now mi abuelo has been quiet. He must have left the room for a time. When he returns, he says, I have found a few copies of the Haggadah for Pesach printed in Amsterdam in 1622. Maybe some rare books can be part of the dowry.

His offer is met with silence. I creep up the stairs, my feet light, to collapse into bed, stirring my sisters. I pull the sheet close to my face. It smells fresh, clean air after a downpour.

Hearing my parents argue saddens me behind the closed door through thin walls. I feel adrift, lost at sea without sight of a shore. I want to go far away from the threats to our freedom, to practice our faith in peace. Do I want a man whose family chases criminals? I still have no idea what my intended will look like.

* * *

Soon enough I meet my future husband, his father and three brothers—maybe the twins can find a mate among them—as we gather around our long table set with fine linens, china and glassware mi abuela saved in hidden trunks.

I glance at Francisco de Mendoza Rebozo. He is not the shriveled studious boy I expected. He is older, maybe twenty-four or twenty-five, with broad shoulders that fill the doorway, his clothes respectable, with a hat perched on his head and a fine face—wide, fig-colored eyes with heavy brows, a trimmed beard, and a thick head of hair combed back from his forehead. He stares straight at me in a bold manner when we are introduced. I am not prepared for this. I expected him to be shy, reticent to communicate. He takes my hand and kisses the back of it, his lips supple. Celendaria. The way he says my name is seductive. I am in a dream.

After we are settled at the table, his younger brothers placed at the end with my silly sisters, I am seated with Francisco across from me.

Where is his mother? My mother inquires after her.

Francisco's father replies, My charming wife, Devorah, has passed. We are in need of a woman's touch at our home. I am afraid these boys may be a bit rough, especially because of our business.

How could we not have known this? Am I to be a slave cooking and cleaning for all these men? I am hardly old enough to take care of myself. A panic courses through my body. My leg rattles back and forth. The dread of marriage and what transpires on a wedding night grips me.

Mi abuelo begins the story of Passover.

Francisco's eyes take me in. I return the gaze with defiance. I am betrothed to a man who has not smiled at me. Maybe because he chases lawbreakers into the new territory he appears more daring. I cast my glance downward. My grandfather's resonant voice begins to read from the Haggadah.

Blessed are You, Lord, our God, King of the Universe, who creates fruit of the vine.

Blessed are You, God, our God, King of the Universe, who has chosen us from among all people, raised us above all tongues, and made us holy through His commandments. And You, God, our God, have given us love, Shabbats for rest and festivals for happiness, feasts and seasons for rejoicing…to commemorate the departure from Egypt.

I am familiar with the story and enjoy the recitations. Since I am betrothed, I am allowed to have a glass of wine to sip. We stare at each other across the table until the Haggadah is finished, the elaborate meal we have prepared is served and the men retire to the corners of the room, taking their chairs away from the table. We are not permitted to be alone. He is not what I expected, but I am not disappointed either.

Señora Crespin, many compliments to you and your family for serving my sons and me such a delicious meal. I am afraid we have been neglectful of some celebrations since my wife passed away three years ago.

Our daughter is well versed in keeping our traditions.

I am sleepy from the wine, but get up with Yael and Yonah to clear the table.

My father's voice dominates the conversation. Now the matter of the dowry. Please understand it cannot be much—some fine linens, sheaths of watermarked silk, Sabbath candlesticks of heavy silver that have been in my father's family since Spain, a little livestock, some rare books. We do not have much. Most of our wealth has been used to feed my mother in prison. Maybe a few goats. We are saving the lamb for a feast.

And so it goes into the night. If I do not see Francisco de Mendoza Rebozo at Succoth, the engagement is off.

CHAPTER TWENTY

CLARA

abril 1654
Santa Oficina de la Inquisición

So much time has passed since I have seen anyone from my family. I do not know the days of the week or how long I have been incarcerated. It must be near the time of Pesach because the guard handed me the pan de afflición wrapped in a linen handkerchief. I pretended not to know what it was for and he smirked at me. When I heard his footsteps fade away, I turned my back and ate the dry cracker. Was it a trick? Or did someone send it to me from the outside? The evidence is gone save a mouse nibbling on a piece I dropped.

Amber and I speak every day, her motivation to bring me to her Lutheran beliefs and mine, to hear the sound of my own voice so I can practice speaking. She has been called before the tribunal half a dozen times, but they do not seem to have taken action against her. Many of us are held for a long time, sometimes years, while the Inquisition builds a case against us. If there is a case.

Amber and I communicate in soft tones so that we cannot be heard. This conversation centers on the difference of the sacraments between the two faiths.

The Catholics believe God grants grace through seven sacraments—baptism, Holy Communion and the Eucharist, reconciliation, confirmation, holy orders, matrimony and anointing of the sick. I know this because I memorized them to prove to my inquisitors I am a good Catholic.

I nod, although I am bored with her lecture because I have heard it many times. Why do others think their religion is better? As Jews, some of us feel an advantage because of our appreciation of the written word, but mostly we want to be left alone. My mind crosses to the glory of Medieval Spain when the Jews were the most populous of all Europe, at the highest level of intellectual prowess. What did the Evil Queen gain by sending us all away? I sigh in frustration.

And the Lutherans believe only in two sacraments, drones Amber, baptism and the Eucharist.

I feel sleepy and stretch out my legs. I do not want to hear about any religion and the anguish they have caused millions, including the indigenous people slaughtered in this country we call home. Why do we all have to believe the same way? Before I sleep, I review the faces of my family, my sweet husband, my four daughters, the grandchildren. I cannot review food and the meals I have cooked because it inflames my hunger.

Without the usual warning call of our names, keys rattle against the iron bars, a silent force releases our door. Me? Again? Two guards pull Amber to her feet, dragging her away as she screams, No, no! No!

I do not know where they are taking her until many hours pass. I await her return, but I will never see her again. I will only hear the sound of her voice, once soft and pleasant, filled with ardor, now the unbridled shrieks of an animal caught in a trap. They continue for hours until I am almost dead with fear, disconsolate with gloom. I have heard screams before behind locked doors but this time I know who they belong to.

It is over. We are coming to the end.

CHAPTER TWENTY-ONE

CELENDARIA

17 de abril 1654, afternoon

On Friday, a new moon awaits us. Long before we will view the three stars in the sky, my mother, sisters and I set off to the bathing house, straw baskets over our arms with clean white undergarments, simple white dresses and small bags of cloves and flower petals, our contribution to the holy admonition to be unsoiled for the Sabbath. The baskets are covered with scraps of serapes from the workshop, a jumble of colors made to look as though we are delivering goods to a client. Mi madre leads the way and I follow behind with Yael and Yonah who hold hands, skipping over stones until I admonish them to not draw attention to us.

After we have passed the cathedral, we turn away from our neighborhood. Mi madre hesitates at a corner to recognize the street that will lead us to a rare, intimate afternoon among women, our work halted for the week. I follow her erect back as she proceeds with confidence, the basket swinging from her arm, her hair tucked underneath the hood of a light cape, the hem of her dress feathering in the breeze.

I feel more of a woman now that I have met my intended, Francisco, although we exchanged nary a word. With a husband, I will need to bathe often, observe the rules of cleanliness. I cannot decide if I am attracted to him with his solid body and fine-looking face, or repelled by his scandalous occupation of chasing criminals. Maybe they are not criminals. Maybe they are people like me who want to escape to a safer place, a place where people worship in peace.

Unfortunately, we lose our way. Mi madre searches the spires, frantic as she scurries from one corner to another. She counts streets on her fingers. I wait under a shade tree with the girls who are tired and whining. I have no patience for them. I look away. I understand the danger of not finding your way in a big city. Never answer too many questions is what I have been taught.

Mi madre, can I help? I call out. She waves me away with her hand. I cannot sit down on the ground because the girls will do the same and roll like dirty dogs scratching their backs. Madre, are we lost? Now she is blocking the sun with her hands across her eyes. I scuff my new *chapines* back and forth in the dust. Yael wears one of my old pairs, shiny with cow fat, because as everything with my body, my feet have grown larger.

Celendaria, *muchachas*, follow me, she calls as she takes off in a different direction. I am frustrated because I do not believe she knows where she is going.

Finally, we reach our destination, a bit late, our throats parched from the sun and dry air. It is a small adobe structure on an empty street of warehouses used for storage. Others have come before us.

The girls greet the daughters of Delfina, a converso whose family we have known for three generations, and her widowed mother. After our greetings, which sound similar to the green Caribbean parrots traded in the market, we gather in the next room around a massive spruce wood container with metal brackets to hold hands and say prayers. The shutters are closed to the light outside. Candles perched on small shelves around the room illuminate us. We close our eyes and take a breath together, a communal sigh that the week has ended. We can be in a state of reverence to our God. I do not know if the owner is among us, but I feel safe in this peaceful moment.

When we open our eyes, the moment breaks. Now it is time to take turns soaking. No one speaks. There seems to be a natural order as the women hang their clothes on hooks.

As the aroma of cloves and cinnamon sticks perfume the air from the steaming tub, I catch sight through the vapor wings of Señora Behar and her exquisite daughter, Mariel, standing next to her. It is a shock. I had forgotten I would see her here. She smiles at me and I cannot return one. Although we have met through the years as children, she has always intimidated me with her sea-green eyes and her self-assurance. We may be close in age but we are a world apart in our ripeness of womanhood, she, the fleshy, sweet insides of a mango and me, the tough skin of the outside before it ripens. I know this because I saw her body, the fervor for the flesh of another, her cries of obsession, the fixation, at great risk, which my grandfather has for books.

A new feeling surges through me in these short moments, an envy of another experience, a resentment of Mariel's beauty, a distrust of her nature to entice others. I covet her secret with knowledge of her passion. Yet, I know the situation is wrong. It is wrong for her to be with any man, especially a priest. It is also wrong for him, one who has left our ranks to be with the enemy. Yet, my petty judgments leave me on the day the Sabbath bride arrives to share a renewal. Yet, I am as captivated by Mariel as she is of her paramour. I glance again to look at her, the untamed wildness of her hair. It reminds me of horse manes rippling in the wind as *vaqueros* round them up.

And then I am thrust into the moment as mi madre and her friends repeat a centuries-old prayer in Portuguese, a language of respect to those who came before us. It is a fragment from a hidden one, a doctor from Portugal denounced in the 1580s by the same Inquisition that pursues us, the deep-seated yearning for our messiah to appear, to collect us in Jerusalem, to find everlasting peace.

O meus Deus, quem ja se vira
N'aquela santa cidade
Chamada Jerusalem.
Jerusalem está esperando
cada hora e cada dia…
O alto Deus d'Israel,
Cumpri vossas profecias…

O my God, pray one would be so fortunate / to reside in that holy city / called Jerusalem. / Waiting for Jerusalem, / every hour and every day…/O exalted God of Israel, / accomplish your prophecies…

Since we will light candles with our families at home, we save those prayers and recite the Shema together. Hear, O Israel, the Lord is Our God, the Lord is One. Afterward, we separate to dip in groups, my sisters squeezing each other in delight because mi madre and I will bathe together.

Covered with towels, we wait our turn on benches around the room; small sticks from an orange tree are passed to clean under our nails. A few of the women have brought small scissors to clip their nails starting with the ring finger of the left hand. A small child comes to each of us to collect the parings in a cloth bag. They must be burned since nothing from us can be swept away. All is sacred.

Some older women wait in the room we entered as we climb short steps into the mist of condensation. We do not speak. I push aside petals of flowers, orange blossoms and spice sticks gathered on top, my hands undulating through the water until I clear a space for me to sink myself below the water line, my head, and hair, all of me descending below the surface.

After our family has had our turns and we are dressed in clean garments, we comb each other's hair, loosening stray flower petals. We are prepared to leave. As we wish a Shabbat shalóm to our friends, I realize I have forgotten my basket in the other room. Others have gone after us, the water being changed and heated by a trusted servant. Mi madre is insistent we must hurry. I knock on the wall next to the drape that shields the tub as my sisters dance on their toes. I thrust the drape aside, rushed by my mother's impatience to head back.

There, in the glossy candlelight, droplets of water kissing her skin, stands Mariel, the grandeur of her body a wonder. Her breasts, more voluptuous than I remember, remain elevated, the hair below as luxurious as the fur collars of the elite. Only a second passes before she reaches for a cloth to cover herself from a hook on the wall. In that instance I see the curvature of her belly. She clutches it to her as her mother's shadow emerges from the darkened corner.

Oh, Celendaria, it is you. We are almost finished.

I-I fo-forgot my basket, I say, reaching down to collect it.

Mariel's emerald eyes catch mine, her lashes lowering to her cheeks.

The feeling I had earlier of envy returns, but with a new knowledge of trouble ahead.

CHAPTER TWENTY-TWO

CLARA

30 de abril 1654
Santa Oficina de la Inquisición

I am before the three men in their black cloaks and white tunics once again. I am not as fearful as I have been in the past. A solace has swathed me in acceptance of my inevitable fate. The one I recognize, Lord Inquisitor Juan Saenz de Mañzoca, speaks to me. His hair hangs in greasy strands from under his hat. This man, who brags in our community of his close relationship with the bishop, dominates the outcome of my destiny.

Señora Crespin, we have waited for a confession from you, an acknowledgement of your sins. You have missed your opportunity for a light penance that is given to those who come forward.

I do not know what I am guilty of, Your Honor.

You are accused of Judaizing.

I do not know who would use such a word about me. I am a good Catholic.

One who spreads heresy. Have you taught others about your ways?

118

Your Honor, I do not know of what you speak.

There will be no mercy for you.

Sirs, I have done nothing wrong.

Señora, I do not know if you can be rehabilitated and reconciled to the bosom of the Church, but as of now, you are unnamed in the Book of Life.

I am willing to do what is necessary to be returned to freedom.

Señora, you speak well for yourself today. If a lawyer could speak for you, he would say the same, but alas, lawyers are not given permission to interrupt the proceedings. His warped smile appears amused. Your family claims they cannot afford someone to represent you any longer.

Sirs, I am an innocent grandmother who does not wish to remain here to the end of my days. I want to see my family.

I feel brave today so I speak with the bold yet insane pleasure that they will relent.

Señora, you do not accept the gravity of your condition. We are here to show you love and charity. The Church does not encourage killing or bloodshed; however, we do admonish our civil authorities to set the parameters of punishment with zeal.

I am silent. My courage has waned. Once more, I dread what can be done to my body. They can never own my mind.

We are losing patience with your stubbornness.

Take her away.

CHAPTER TWENTY-THREE

CELENDARIA

19 de mayo 1654, afternoon

While mi abuelo dozes in his chair and my mother slumbers upstairs with Yael and Yonah, I contemplate how much I miss mi abuela: her strong presence in this house, her husky voice calling my name, her innate intelligence about all matters and her patience with my questions about our fate. She has taught me about herbs. She knows the best ones to bring out flavor in our meals as well as those for relief and healing.

I consider her destiny. A fly buzzes near me. I slap it away in boredom. I miss Elena even though I am too old to play. I think about the hummingbirds and flowers, something to cheer me. I tiptoe to the door holding my breath. I must get out of here. I cannot linger in a limbo any longer, their feared place between Heaven and Hell. The door squeaks on its hinge. I am cautious to make myself small and slip through the open space.

I move with haste to a stand of spruce trees nearby, the kind the Indians use to make canoes. My father has told me when the boards are cut they remain straight without knots, useful for ceiling beams too. I wait to ensure no one has seen me, and then I move to the next street toward the grand cathedral that tolls one of its many bells. I fold into the shadows of the afternoon light to sit on a low stool someone has left behind from a market. I do not want to be observed and pull my headscarf closer to my face like the Moslem women I have seen in pictures in one of mi abuelo's forbidden books about the history of Spain. The Evil Queen booted us all out, but she was afraid of the Moors' armies and let them be while scattering and hounding us to the ends of the earth.

Without warning, I detect Señora Lopez rushing by me, clutching a bundle to her chest, her broad bottom tossing up and down as she passes me, a worried look on her face. I observe a glint of rose color on her head. Ah, she has made a scarf from the silks we have sent to bribe her son! And what has he done for us?

As she disappears around a corner, I contemplate this and reflect on what I have learned in lessons from mi abuelo. With his eyesight dimming since mi abuela's arrest, I read to him from his secret books, some that he has acquired at great risk through smuggled trade among our kind. We are thirsty for knowledge, he says, as he turns pages with reverence. We are not allowed any books except those approved by the Church, which hold no interest. He teaches me to deliberate, consider possibilities, to make a plan, not to move with impulse. This is how we have survived to see this day, he tells me often.

Señora Lopez's son, Father Miguel, has been asked to aid us, relieve our family of worry, find out the status of our abuela. Will he do this? So far no report of her well-being has reached us. *El cárcel de secreta*, the jail of secrets, reveals little. No accusation, no testimony, no trial. If a witness makes a statement, no one knows.

The accused cannot defend herself. Who could say anything about mi abuela? Last night my father cursed the priest under his breath: After I gave him my best silks, he gives us nothing.

Then he made a spitting sound.

I linger in the fresh air, a slight breeze soothing my face. I listen to a mob of chachalacas bandy their raucous calls from the church eaves. They have freedom to pick up and fly away, their chicken-like brown bodies, small and sturdy, bare red necks vulnerable. Church bells shatter my silence.

I have an idea. A dangerous one. It is known the Church is having difficulty controlling their priests in New Spain, an ocean voyage away from the seat of honor, a treacherous one at that. So many die in the storms. A few renegades ignore the religious hierarchy and its rules of celibacy to dwell with parishioners, even living openly with their concubines and children, ones not only without parentage but of ill-conceived origin, part white, and part *mestizo*. I have seen these children and my mother jostles me away from them. No one accepts them. Last year a priest was sent into a ten-year exile for ignoring the laws to remain chaste. I have seen his children begging on the streets.

I scuttle away, a ravenous dog looking for scraps, to enact a plan. I am angry that our goods have been received and we have been offered no relief. I head back to our home refreshed from my freedom. I do not like being in a house all day. I do not know how my grandmother can stand the unbearable. Yet, sometimes, I feel trapped too. When I enter, my grandfather groans from his chair. His dreams are all nightmares and when he awakens, the grief rolls over him once again.

Once our supper of stew is over, no one has anything to say. I assist with the chores to tidy up after our meal.

Yael and Yonah bring water from the well, then retire to coil their limbs around one another in the bed we share, a feather mattress set upon a wooden frame. They are slithering snakes that entwine under a rock ledge. Once they cease moving, their rhythmic breathing a union of flutters, I think about the scene I observed with Señor Behar's daughter and Señora Lopez's son.

I see the illicit lovers again in my mind, their milky faces pressing into one another's lips. I brush two of my fingers across my own mouth. Again. It is soft to the touch. One finger impels its way into my parted lips and dangles back and forth across my bottom lip. This is forbidden. I know this from both faiths. I cannot help myself. A breath forces its way out of me. My other hand drifts to my chest, across the soft cotton undergarments as smooth as a lamb's belly. I see his lips on her nipple and hear her moan. I squeeze mine between my thumb and forefinger after a long stroke. I gasp, panting like a stray dog.

I stop. I am afraid my sounds will awaken the girls next to me. They are such tellers of tales, their illicit stories whispered behind my back. I have difficulty telling them apart if I cannot see their birth blemishes, distinctive blue stains almost faded to light smudges below where their delicate necks bend. Common to our kind, these marks at birth leave a trail from Portugal across the world. Madre, says one, curling a piece of hair around her finger, Celendaria refuses to help make our bed. The other looks down, hands folded, waiting with her complaint. I am too old to be sleeping in a bed with children.

I have roused new feelings in myself, unfamiliar experiences as I take a breath in and let it out slowly to steady myself. I caress my breasts with both hands. I cannot think of anything else save the look on Mariel's face when she reached the summit of the mountain she was scaling, one of pleasure and pain at the same time. More. Wetness. I turn to my side. One of the twins shifts her body with a sigh. My breath is faster. My hand slips between my thighs. Warm. Velvety to the touch, the down of baby chicks, the hairs more coarse in dampness. I compress two of my fingers into the gash, my hips arcing like the gauchos I have seen in the saddle. A wave rolls over me with force, sweeping away everything in its path. I shudder, an uncontrollable moan from my lips. One of the girls flops to her back.

Celendaria? What are you doing, Celendaria? She says lifting herself onto her elbow.

A dream, only a dream.

CHAPTER TWENTY-FOUR

CLARA

27 de mayo 1654
Santa Oficina de la Inquisición

It is lonely without my cellmate, even with her Protestant chatter. I do not know where they have taken Amber but she is gone, a flower frozen in time like her namesake. Her screams disturb my sleep. I fling back and forth, waking myself. Will this be my fate?

A terror consumes me, one that causes me to shake. I can no longer eat the slop they bring to my cell. My trepidation sinks me, a stone tossed into a bottomless well. My aunt who raised me said our people became dispirited with melancholia, a black bile that invades the mind like the conquistadores destroying the indigenous peoples with diseases. Many of those afflicted sat for hours without food or water, unable to move when the hopelessness invaded their minds, their souls. She said it was part of our nature, a result of the expulsions, a lingering sadness.

As a young woman I did not understand her explanation of our ancestors transporting this disheartening disease to other shores, but now that it has swept over me, I feel the zeal of its fever. The anguish of banishment from Spain, Portugal, Brazil, to this vanquished Mexican land can only turn its survivors into flowing seasons of mistrust. We start over so many times without homes, possessions, family, friends, all seized, lost forever, except for the thread of our faith. This melancholia trails us across continents unless we drown in the sea. I am one of them.

We can only depend on one another.

Señora. I hear a voice and the rattle of keys and see the outline of my jailer.

Come with me.

CHAPTER TWENTY-FIVE

CELENDARIA

12 de junio 1654

It happens on a Shabbat morning while mi abuelo is teaching me in our common area. It is too hot to be in the attic. The girls play in the back while they feed the chickens our leftovers. With a resonant voice he begins.

When the Portuguese King Manuel came to power decreeing all had to convert—or leave the country without our children, my family took the Christian vows again to be safe.

He glances down, his expression one of shame, lips pressed together, repeating that we gave in. Ach, what was a little water sprinkled on our heads and a sultry look at their hanging one on the cross?

My mother sighs audibly, her hands folded across her lap. She does not initiate our meal preparation as we wait for the three stars to appear in the sky to repeat the havdalah blessings. The end of the Sabbath, a time of contemplation, means we smell cloves and cinnamon that we pass in a small box. I rest on a woven rug at her feet, my head settled against her. I have heard these recitations before and know their importance. I must memorize them to teach my children someday.

Mi abuelo enjoys the recitation of our history. He repeats the stories in a cadence so he will not lose them to the dusk of age. His failing eyes no longer able to read long passages, he launches into the narrative of the massacre at Rossio Square in Portugal in April of 1506, one I am familiar with, a heartrending event.

At the convent of São Domingos de Lisboa, starts mi abuelo, where many gathered to pray for the end of a drought, a zealot swore he saw the illuminated face of Christ on the altar, which could only be a miracle of the Messiah. My great ancestor, Emanuel Mendoza, objected and pointed out that it had only been the reflection of a candle.

Tears come to my grandfather's eyes before he can continue.

Dragged to the street by his hair, Mendoza was murdered by the mob and burned on the spot. It became the Easter Slaughter of two thousand other souls, or by some reports four thousand in the name of justice for Christ. All the Jews had someone murdered that was related to them. Emanuel Mendoza was murdered with an undeniable belief in God. The Dominican friars incited a mob of five hundred by promising absolution from sins to those who killed more heretics. When the massacre began, it frightened us underground, especially since it took place thirty years before the Inquisition established itself in Portugal. We had much to fear.

It was told to me, continues mi abuelo, that our clandestine Rabbi said Kaddish, the prayer for the dead, in the basement of our home behind a private sliding door that housed a small room with artifacts of our faith: a menorah to celebrate the Festival of Lights, heavy silver candlesticks and books, some holy, others about medicine and science. Besides the Old Testament, the one tome deemed precious to us, one that came with us if we had to flee—was the Sepher Toledot.

His story ceased. Sometimes the painful memories overwhelm mi abuelo. It was not necessary for me to inquire about the Sepher Toledot. He shifts in his chair, adjusting a pillow behind his back.

The chronicle of our generations that carried the names of our kin, mi abuelo goes on, that unbroken ancestry from when we first settled on the Iberian Coast and the unfortunate exiles that brought us to this point in time, remains precious. It is peppered with the names of our cousins—Mendoza, Rosales, Marcus, Rebozo and Crespin—all with whom we intermarried to preserve our faith, customs and blood lines. Although, I must add, since we were living as Catholics, when two first cousins wanted to marry, it required special dispensation from the Church. He snorts at the hypocrisy. They bend their rules with ease as long as we follow the doctrine and pay money.

I had heard mi abuelo recite the account many times. He rocked back and forth in his chair as if at prayer, a narration of great magnitude to our people. Yet, in all the sadness we found joy in our prayers, in God, in natural beauty, our love of each other.

A knock at the door interrupts us. We are alarmed, glancing around the room for the trappings of our faith, but there is nothing. All is hidden in the floorboards underneath a trap door in the kitchen, or covered with a rug or in a secret room in the basement behind a phony bookcase filled with their books that we do not touch.

The knock is louder. Señora Crespin, Gabriela, open the door.

Mi madre gets up, her eyes wide with fear, and opens the door a crack.

Oh, Señora Behar, come in. Is everyone in good health? What are you doing here on Shabbat?

My mother's friend has ropey lines between her brows. What can it be? Has she discovered her daughter and the Lopez priest?

May I speak to you in privacy? She motions her head toward me.

I am not surprised. Often the two of them engage in conversation about food preparation, their children, even husbands. They trust one another. But why is she here on a holy day?

Mi abuelo, perhaps tired from his recitation, senses it is time for a siesta and goes upstairs with the girls, who are delighted to be dismissed. I follow to tuck the girls in our bed, small beans in a pod spooned together.

I get up to head toward the stairs, but curiosity overcomes me. I only climb a few to be out of sight.

Gabriela.

I peek and see mi madre's friend lean over to touch her knee. A rumor. Maybe it is nothing.

What is it?

She begins to cry, hands hiding her face. Gossip from the marketplace.

I pull back so I am not seen. With an intake of breath, I listen with caution as my mother speaks.

Tell me, Beatriz. Is everything all right with Diego?

Yes, he is fine.

Mariel?

A sob initiates itself in the back of Beatriz's throat. I hear it catch, the final click of an iron key in a lock.

I must peek again. The name of her daughter, the one that I know has an unfathomable secret, tows me forward, a caravel cutting through waves. Silence follows. Maybe they have spotted me. I steal another look. Señora Behar has covered her face with a handkerchief.

My mother bends toward her friend, a hand placed with care upon her knee.

Tell me, Beatriz.

The pause echoes in my head. I cannot imagine what she is going to say. Unless she has discovered the truth about her daughter, Mariel. What is worse? To keep the company of a committed Catholic? A priest no less. Or to be with child unwed? A sin for all. My mind rotates, a wheel spinning through sludge, splashing me with images of the illicit lovers, an orphaned baby, the anger of men, muck covering my skirts.

I regret to bring you sad news on Shabbat, Gabriela. Perhaps Our Father has planned it this way. Silence fills the room until she begins again.

They are coming for Celendaria.

What? My mother cries.

Shh, Gabriela.

I am flat against the wall, blood rushing to my head. I must get out of here. I tiptoe up the rest of the stairs. The girls are lying in bed giggling, playing with hair ribbons. I look in my parents' space where mi abuelo snores, chin dropped to his chest. I lie down next to the girls and make them move closer to one another with a slight nudge of my elbow. This news cannot be possible. A mistake, an aberration, confusion with someone else. What would the Inquisition want with me? A girl? Peril suffuses through my body causing me to tremble. Is the Inquisition casting me into its net? Has Señora Lopez's son pointed a finger at me? It is not unusual for some to be two-faced, promising one thing and delivering another while one prays for protection. Forces can work against us as well as them. Why not? Maybe his words have caused our family to be a target of their attention instead of a distraction from it. Has he learned I know of his indiscretion with Señor Behar's daughter? It cannot be possible. I have told no one.

Worry pervades our home. Many discussions take place in the evening after mi madre shares the perilous news from the market. In the beginning they exclude me, but soon it is not possible. We examine every option.

First, my father's solution is to contact Francisco and his father to spirit me away.

What? You would have your most virtuous daughter go with men who apprehend criminals? Mi madre does not like this idea. What about a wedding? Her voice squeaks with anguish. We cannot lose another one, she says. Tears pour from her eyes. How can we send her away? She wrings her hands in anguish, tugging a linen handkerchief.

Where else could she go? asks mi abuelo. She is still a child. He peers at the ceiling. What do they want with a child?

A hush of silence envelops the room, a complete absence of sound, the void in an abandoned cave where all noise is smothered.

I bow my head in prayer. Please save me, dear God. I am not courageous or valiant. I am a fool. A deceitful fool.

Finally, mi padre speaks with great effort, his voice uneven in tone. She must go to her betrothed in San Miguel.

No, it is not far away enough. Too close to Ciudad de México, offers my grandfather.

My mother is concerned with my virtue. Alas, I am too, but now that I have knowledge of the exquisite pleasures that my body can produce, I feel bold.

How would we get her there? Mi abuelo asks, his eyes watery and shifting. He would miss his most interested, loyal student.

A pang navigates my chest at the thought of separation from my family, what I know to be true. We suffer a devastating hole among us without mi abuela, and now I might sink below the depths, too, an opaque ocean floor, deeper than I can stand.

Ha! You think they would not notice this trickery? Mi madre cries once again. We are being watched. That is how Señora Behar heard this terrifying news in the market. They destroy all that we have.

My father, the sensible one, controlling his voice with fury, says, We must draw attention away from Celendaria. We must flee with haste.

I sink into myself, a desire to collapse inside, to be small, unknowing. This cannot happen. I must think of another plan.

What? My mother cries out.

The Church is looking for more heretics so they can confiscate our goods, adds my father.

But we have nothing left, my mother wails, pulling a shawl around her shoulders to cocoon herself. Celendaria, it is time for bed. We must talk in private.

My mother gathers us, a hen herding chicks, upstairs into our room with a bed and dressers, linen curtains covering the window. My grandfather often sleeps in his chair, his neck propped with a pillow, until the dawn when he gets up to nap in one of our beds as we greet the morning with chores. He is not a good sleeper in the absence of his wife.

After I awaken my narcoleptic sisters by moving the bedclothes in the morning, I slither down the steps into the shadow of the doorway to catch snippets of men's conversation. I recognize Mariel's father's voice. I can see where they all sit—my mother and father on a bench against the wall, mi abuelo in his chair and Señor Behar in another.

Where did you hear this? Asks my father, his voice filled with anxiety.

My mother interjects, Another son of a neighbor is training with the Jesuits. He gave us warning that arrests will be made soon. But we have nothing. There is no more to take! my mother cries.

Ah, they do not have your soul, Señora, says Señor Behar, his eyes pooling with tears.

My grandfather, more thoughtful than his furious son, settles back into his chair.

Why do they pursue us with such zeal? Asks my mother. We are already at the ends of the earth.

Her question is met with silence. We knew the answer. They pursued us no matter how we tried to observe their rules. I knew the reasons. Yael begins to whimper softly as I clutch her to my breast without explanation, laying her gently into the down where she sinks in slumber.

I return to the doorway to observe my mother's face, her eyes tired with lines after cooking. She knows we are doomed unless decisions are made. Once they charge you—

With what? My father bellows. She is an innocent girl.

Señor Behar says, It is of no matter. A neighbor or a servant makes an accusation. It only takes one person to level an accusation, a suspicion. Not even an eyewitness is necessary. You are considered a criminal and a sinner at that moment. Their church trades in superstitions and lies. You must prepare. A few families are gathering tomorrow night—I pray we have one more day—so we can travel together. Do you have a cart?

My father's voice sounds low in tone. Yes, a cart and a donkey.

Pack all you can. Once you are accused, they confiscate all your goods to pay for your trial and incarceration. It is a perpetual prison where you will never see light.

Bu-but we have done nothing wrong. His voice stutters in protest.

None of us have except to believe the Law of Moses, says our friend, his head falling forward.

We will not do this again. My father sounds disconsolate.

Think of your family, your father, your wife, your grown sons and little girls. The Jesuits have a school in Ciudad de México to train more priests, their pathway to heaven, says Señor Behar. There will only be more to trap us.

My father's shadow reveals his head dropping into his hands. It will never end. How far can we go? We have converted three times or more. How many times can I wash their baptismal chrism of oil from the heads of my children? The aroma nauseates me!

Then my grandfather perks up, his chin wobbly with defiance. How do you know they come for us?

Señor Behar says, Because your neighbors, the Sandovals, were arrested yesterday when the parish priest saw no smoke from their chimney. But we think in the far north they will not bother us. Such a dry, remote area filled with cactus.

They will chase us down to the last one. Will you come with us? my father asks.

My mother notices me listening. She taps my shoulder as she moves past me to approach my father.

Esteban, we must go. I will pack in the morning. We will be long gone before they come for Celendaria.

Ha. That is all that gives me satisfaction. The priests, with their concubines who make bastards, will arrive to find our place empty. Nothing for them. They are fat and wealthy enough.

I have never heard my father speak with such bitterness, his mouth like mine when I taste horseradish on Passover.

My grandfather says, I cannot leave. It is too far away from Clara.

But, Mama, where are we going? I plead.

She pulls me toward her, smoothing my wild hair, the curls that pass through our family that gives us the name Crespin. Even the twins and my older brothers have unruly hair, a source of teasing by others.

North, farther north.

I express my fear. Madre, Padre, the Comanche roam and kill people. I have heard the stories that the churches are built like fortresses to ward off attacks.

Señor Behar stands to leave. Meet at the muleteer's barn outside of town at sunset. Watch for the three stars. Believe nothing they tell you.

CHAPTER TWENTY-SIX

CLARA

22 de junio 1654
Santa Oficina de la Inquisición

I am alone in the darkness, an inky midnight that prevents me from seeing the details and shapes of where I am. But the images when I was brought in sear my brain, a brand stamped on a cow's flank. I fought them as they dragged me into this torture chamber, the guards and a surgeon holding candles, a priest in robes behind them. I was so overcome with fear I bled tears from my eyes and drool from my mouth, my face stained with snot. I am petrified of pain. I have seen the marks they leave on innocent bodies, hands crippled, limps pronounced, joints distorted.

The guards placed slop and water against the wall. I saw their instruments of torture, too terrible to describe because then I would have to think about them again. My eyes took it all in. I wanted to close them so my brain would not chronicle their devices, an evil beyond all measure, but I could not. I revisit this—it is large chamber with many leather straps hanging from irons in the rough stone walls. Tables and other bizarre devices fill the space.

I could not control my fear, collapsing on my hands and knees, vomiting bile. I am not a brave woman. I am a coward. I knew not what would come next. I waited, heaving.

And then they were gone. And so was the light. They blew out their candles and left me in darkness, a solitude that became a blessing for a time so I did not have to look at what they had devised. I trembled, my body shaking like the stray dogs that bathed in the river, drying themselves with shivers.

It is not over. They will be back. I know this. I fall to my side in exhaustion.

CHAPTER TWENTY-SEVEN

CELENDARIA

23 de junio 1654

We do not leave. Nor do the Behars. The rains do not stop. I feel liquid myself lacking potency in my bones, muscles or skin. I am a marionette without strings. Hours of endless rains that when they cease, the ground sponges water and my rope-soled shoes sink, stained with mud, mud that carries away dead animals, garbage and waste from our bodies. They are unsanitary rivers of filth. Bugs, leeches, others that slither along the ground appear in our yard. Where are the birds to pluck them away? And the trees, their woody bark peeling to the nude skin underneath, lose branches that litter the ground as the sky continues leaking, seeping.

I do not sleep, tossing, my legs moving as if I am running in a dream, hunted, the rabbit without a chance. I do not comb my hair. Nor wash. Or clean my teeth with a splayed root. The girls do not want to be near me in the bed. I find them rolled into rugs and blankets on the floor, a jumble of colors, their pale limbs twisted together.

Days pass. Nothing. It is obvious no one is fleeing—no packing, goodbyes, food preparation for a journey. Mi madre y mi padre work through channels to gain more information. Are we under siege, among the last holdouts against the Romans in Biblical times? Or is there a path to sanity?

Mi padre pursues secret meetings with men whose identities he does not share with us, perhaps seeking a better match for me. One time I follow him to the other side of the city, a place unfamiliar, to a store below a grand home. I watch and wait for hours. He does not reappear and I find my way home alone. Later, I ask mi abuelo where my father went.

He explains that in Europe there are salons that promote scientific thought. When I interrupt for an explanation of a salon, he waves me away. What good is it all now? He murmurs under his breath.

Discussions of bribery last into the night for many days. Who can be bought? For how much? Will it implicate them? My father bangs his hand into a wall. We can bribe and then they will take everything anyway. Maybe I have to close the workshop, let the women go back to their villages.

Then mi madre yells through tears, what do they want with a child? Where does the cruelty lie in their hearts? No, you cannot do this. How will we live? Eat?

What are you talking about? Cruelty? They can never be trusted, says mi abuelo. Remember what they did to the Carvajal family in 1596? They burned him, a governor, his mother and three sisters here in Ciudad de México, the first time a woman was set afire. Who is to say they will not do it again? A family destroyed, all for uttering the words, May God be with you, a heretical phrase according to the Church. This group of zealots will not change their behavior after so much time.

I know my history. That was almost sixty years ago.

Did my mother in her naiveté, her mist of hope, think the Church forgot?

Mi abuelo spits out his words. What does it matter? They will not rest until every one of us is dead. Carvajal's brothers escaped to España, the seat of all our trouble. Mexico is not safe. I say we abandon it and go north.

Then his voice softens. I can barely hear him say as his voice catches.

They cannot take my Celendaria.

My father challenges his father. Where? San Miguel, an outpost? How will we earn a living there? Join the bondsmen? You can be killed in a job that requires guns. And you would leave your wife locked way in a prison? His question causes tears in mi abuelo's eyes. Where should we go? To defend a settlement with Indians waiting to attack?

Mi abuelo leaves the room.

Our household remains uneasy, a footfall near the door a reason for dread. I worry every moment, anticipating the guard's arrival early in the morning, when a family is rising, unlikely to object in their sleepiness. I can eat only small amounts. Yael and Yonah want to know the source of our short tempers, our tears, the upsets, the desperate kisses as mi padre leaves to associate with other conversos, anyone who has a connection through the desperate back alley of our society. Some shun him. Our community wants no association with the Crespins who are under investigation with their matriarch shuttered away.

Our days plod by, changeless with inactivity. We make an attempt to appear normal in our activities—mi padre at the factory, the threads of serapes clinging to his clothes when he returns at day's end, mi madre at the market, pausing to chat—but everyone knows I am bolted away in our home, staying out of sight, as if the Inquisition will forget me. As if.

And what of Celendaria's match? The neighbors ask. Hah! Hardly a match.

The subject of Father Lopez comes up again one evening after dinner, a meal of chard, breadcrumbs and cheese in a casserole, thinly sliced cucumbers from the garden drizzled with olive oil and eggs prepared a special way. I took off the shells after I hardboiled them to separate yolks, stirring in thyme, pepper, a mite of ginger and kosher salt. I packed the mixture with gentleness into the hollow whites. They were devoured in minutes.

Let us go back to his mother, Señora Lopez, my father suggests. Perhaps a gift of rare lace I have imported from Belgium will impress her. She is still one of us, even if her son is another.

My mother objects, No, we must offer more. The silks were to save your mother. Now it is our daughter.

Yes, and she took them without results, says mi abuelo, his face creased with torment.

I think of Señora Lopez scuttling by me, the flash of silk on her head.

Mi abuelo offers a suggestion. I will travel to Zacatecas with its steep slopes and deep valley. It is rich in silver and has a major road that passes through San Miguel de Grande with two fresh springs. I will take our rare books.

My father has disgust in his voice. What good will this do? They watch us. You will be robbed. Or worse, arrested. We might as well all walk to the Inquisition offices and turn ourselves in. We have no power. What influence does a half-blind old man have?

My mother says the obvious. We all know it is not possible for an old man to travel alone. Two men together with bundles will arouse suspicion.

I will go on foot instead of the cart and donkey. Besides, I have contacts in the area.

Who? my mother wants to know. She is pulling yarn into a ball, her fingers gliding over the fibers, separating colors without looking.

Mi abuelo with his weak voice offers, Acquaintances from business, others who believe as we do. One man belongs to a wealthy clan of hidden Jews here in the city. He administers control over an extended family that decides where and how they live, religious ceremonies, marriages, burials—

Nonsense! A waste of our precious resources. My mother, impatient with her father-in-law, a man who has aged in a short time, fumes with anger. I have never heard her raise her voice to him before.

We are running out of merchandise for the secretary of sequestered goods, she goes on. Nothing can satisfy him. We have used almost everything to keep Clara alive. What do we have for Celendaria? They confiscate everything.

My father's head falls into his hands. I feel his grief. With a muted voice he says, Our faith recognizes the obligation to provide for our family before all other rules of law. I must do this.

Ach, this is a foolish idea, says mi abuelo, the mention of his precious books a travesty. Better Celendaria declares herself an indigent. The poorest in their prisons are not tortured because there is nothing for the secretary to add to his list of expenses. They have bled us dry.

Stop! I place my hands over my ears so I do not have to hear their ridiculous plans. No one escapes, I say aloud.

143

They all look at me, my emotions melting like beeswax in the afternoon sun.

You cannot bribe Señora Lopez with textiles. I saw her wearing one of the unusual silks you had me deliver. She will betray us again.

Then I reveal a bold statement.

Mariel Behar is pregnant.

What? The voices respond in unison. Who? How do you know this?

I wait for them to reach a calm place. Listen. I saw her at the baths. She is round, I say to their incredulous faces.

How could this be? My mother screams at me. It is an impossibility!

Then I am accused of telling lies.

You cannot say this about a pure young woman in our community!

The verbal attack stuns me and I retreat inside my clothes, wanting to be a desert turtle, pulling myself inside so only a hard case reveals itself to the world.

My father's voice is the loudest. You cannot defame others to save yourself! The Behars are our dearest friends. Our families have been side by side for a hundred years. Shame on your soul for making such accusations. Pray that God will forgive you. Leave! I do not want to see your face.

CHAPTER TWENTY-EIGHT

CLARA

5 de julio 1654
Santa Oficina de la Inquisición

I wait with false hope. Maybe I am losing my mind. I speak with the vision of my husband often. I talk to myself so I can hear a voice. Now I wear the sanbenito with a cross across the front. I am a marked woman.

Once, the doctor and guards returned to examine me. I quaked with fear. What do they want with me? What more suffering can they impose? My family took good care of me in the beginning but now I have been here so long, the provisions are in short supply. Who knows if I will ever be returned to my cell, to dim light, with my meager belongings?

The doctor, a surgeon, is employed by the Church. He is not a learned man like our Sephardic doctors. He is a hack, another sham to let us think good care is uppermost in the minds of the Inquisition. The barber earns a higher salary. But what does it matter? The Church has many employees to keep intimidation at the highest echelon. His only service to me was the candle he gripped in his fat fingers to radiate the room, an opportunity for me to see where the machines of torment are placed so I do not trip.

In the darkness I found my way to the table, an instrument of agony, climbed on top and slept for one night without the mice tracking across my body. But I could not do it again. What if they found me there? I do not know how this strange act would be interpreted. The distress of their cruelty leaves me little rest. I am racked with a cough, one that assails my body with spasms, echoing into this hollow space. I lie on the cold floor, curling myself into a ball for warmth. Maybe it will kill me, preferable to whatever ghouls wait for me in these monstrous machines.

CHAPTER TWENTY-NINE

CELENDARIA

8 de julio 1654

Days of silence. I am a pariah in my home. But I know what I have said is true. When my mother hangs wet clothes and bedding from a line in the back, I sidle up to her. She is lost in thought, startled when I appear next to her. The chickens swarm my legs looking for feed.

Mama, what I have said is true. I do not want to hurt the Behars or Mariel. She does not stop draping wet garments across the thin rope strung from the eaves above the back door to the shed for the animals near the back fence.

Your father does not want me to speak to you. She continues with her task, ignoring me.

Mama, please listen. I can no longer hold it inside of me. I blurt out with the force of a waterfall: I saw Mariel with Señor Lopez's son, the priest, behind the confessional.

Now she ceases her activity of reaching into the bin of wet clothes, back bent, her face upturned. Her expression is one of complete shock. I am relieved not to be saying this about myself.

I repeat my revelation. Her body absorbs the words.

Mama, maybe this information can assist me or abuelita.

I am begging, my plea a grasp for sympathy.

How long have you known this?

I lower my head. Too long, I say in a meek voice.

But then I am encouraged by the light in her eyes.

Mariel must be revealing her belly by now.

Was she at the mikvah last week? I ask.

No. She hesitates, thinking. She has not visited it for a while. Beatriz said she was not well. We do not inquire of each other's cycles.

My mother straightens her back, immobile, the wet laundry at her feet, puzzling over what I have told her. Then her face crumbles into sobs.

Beatriz, my poor Beatriz. This will bring such shame to their family. Irreparable shame.

Mama, we must seize the moment. We cannot change anything. I have a plan.

She is not paying attention to me. She leaves the laundry and rushes inside. I pick up the dripping pieces and stretch them across the rope, missing a time when we had a servant to help with chores.

After dinner, my father asks to speak to me alone. We take two wooden chairs from the kitchen and place them side by side under the eaves outside the back door while the twins assist my mother with the dishes. No one will hear our conversation with the rain that splashes drops around our feet. I am afraid of another condemnation. He has not spoken to me since I revealed Mariel was pregnant, accused of telling untruths.

Celendaria, are you telling the truth about Mariel Behar? Do you understand the consequence if this is untrue?

Yes. I would not invent such a lie to save myself. But, papa, it holds possibilities. I lean toward him in an effort to make him comprehend. Maybe we can use the information about the priest who did this to bribe someone inside the walls. She is not responsible for her condition. The priest is to blame. Perhaps her family knows already. How can I cause these good people more pain? But maybe it will save me.

He exhales with a groan, the noise lost in the rain clattering into the nearby cistern.

How will this help us? He asks, his voice cheerless.

I speak with passion. Because the Church looks for priests that have strayed. Spain is losing control of what happens here. We know this from so many abuses. We can make an accusation, perhaps with the Behars, bribe the officials to send him away and distract them from me.

He stares at me, eyes poignant with aching. My daughter, this is not a plan. It is a death sentence. Do you understand their trickery? They will arrest both families in hours. More goods for their coffers. As it is, they have almost bled us dry.

What can we do? There must be something. I feel a bleak despair.

No. There is nothing. I have spoken to the Behars. Diego does not have the heart to cast out his own daughter to the streets and Beatriz will not allow Mariel to be a concubine of this priest. They are doomed. He looks away from me. Bastard children, the words lost in a clap of thunder, but I hear them. Bastard children. A shame on an entire family.

He gets up to go inside, taking his chair with him.

I sit watching the rain.

CHAPTER THIRTY

CLARA

23 de julio 1654
Santa Oficina de la Inquisición

Fleas bite my skin under the tattered sanbenito I have worn too long. I scratch, then cough, a hacking that makes me think my innards will fall on the floor. I hold my hand around one wrist. It is so thin it feels like it could snap a damaged twig in a breeze. I no longer walk. I crawl to the dishes they leave me with water and slop, sucking from the bowls like a scurrilous dog. I am dehumanized. I sit, my back against the wall, my eyes closed so I see my own darkness, where I can paint portraits of my family, their faces, the soft skin of grandchildren.

I am broken.

CHAPTER THIRTY-ONE

CELENDARIA

6 de agosto 1654

We have no other hope, no ideas. All we do is wait. No one can run from them. The Church, all powerful, smashes us like bugs under their feet.

It is too late to implement a plan of blackmail with the Lopez priest. My mother visits Beatriz and sees Mariel.

She reports to us that she is large with child and cannot leave the house. Her father rages against her—sex before marriage, a priest no less, although we know they intend to seek out girls but sometimes approach boys. I am horrified at this abomination.

What are they going to do? My father asks.

It is done. He has been transferred to another parish. The Behars are leaving.

What? Where can they go?

As soon as they baby is born, they will place it in an orphanage with the nuns. Beatriz cries every day about the loss of a grandchild.

No! This sounds unbearable to me. Have I caused this? I cry, guilt swelling inside my chest. This sensuous girl, ripe as a succulent pear,

151

invaded my dreams with her passion. These sensations of culpability strike me, a brilliant light that blazes across murky heavens with thunder, a drama of nature. Or God's angry voice. I am filled with remorse.

Celendaria, stop thinking only of yourself, my father reprimands me while I sob. The Behars knew long before we said anything. It is too late.

I am not privy to other conversations. I do not know when the baby is due or where the Behars will go, but I am sad to the bottom of my soul, unless I dwell on my own situation. I wait in this undefined state, a shapeless cloud that plummets me from on high to a cavern of despair. I sit in a chair by the window waiting for my adversaries, my skirts layered for warmth. It is very cold in the cells. My mother coaches me in Catholic liturgy, forbidding me to leave the house. I will be questioned. My mind wanders. Will I see mi abuela? Will she be the same? Or so greatly changed, like others I have seen, that I will not recognize her? I cannot keep their saints straight. I cannot remember anything in my fear—the catechism, the date of my baptism, the Apostle's Creed. The liturgy jumbles in my head.

The family, melancholy, realizes they are picking us off one by one. My father laments our limited resources. We persuade him not to venture to Zacatecas with mi abuelo. The danger is too great.

The last of the rains visit us with the frequency of birds checking their nests, a never-ending deluge of downpours that cause leaks in our roof and seepage through our walls. The street in front of our house becomes a stream of sludge and death—a bloated dog, hair matted, feet in the air, food rubbish, human waste—the steamy odor risesing from the moving refuse to grasp our nostrils as rats scamper through it. There is little relief from the pounding. Everything is damp, sweating.

The explorers built our city on an island in a shallow lake. We have flooding with frequency, many having lost their homes in the major flood of 1645. I am grateful we are on higher ground. The livestock has been moved to the barn of Señor Gonzalez in exchange for textiles.

My mother hurries to place pans below the worst spots. She has difficulty lighting a fire.

CHAPTER THIRTY-TWO

CLARA

24 de agosto 1654
Santa Oficina de la Inquisición

I am in darkness. I feel nothing. Maybe I am weak enough to die. A blessing. I remember the grand bed my aunt and I slept in. I smile at her kindness. The words in my head do not come easily. I struggle to think of them. *Gente de nação*, the Portuguese phrase for people of the nation. My first language was Portuguese; then I learned Ladino and Spanish. We attended a synagogue in the basement of a friend after she taught me the Law of Moses for the holy days. Prayer books lined the walls, some with our daily rituals, others of holidays, essays of Jewish history, commentaries on the Law, mystical treaties I did not understand, pieces of scorched parchments snatched from the fires, a palimpsest parchment scrubbed, new Hebrew text added. Such documents were a danger yet we could not part with them.

I want to see my husband, my life companion, his proud stature from a noble Spanish heritage. When we met, he was gentle, his brown eyes flecked with gold, full of intelligence, his black beard a sky without stars, the top curl of his lip ready with a quip. After we married, he allowed me to trim his hair with iron scissors instead of going to the barber. I caught the curls of our name in a sheet to throw in the fire. I gave shape to his eyebrows, the stray hairs like a recalcitrant goat that wanders off.

Now grey as a stormy day, he is as withered as I am, eyes near blind, with crevices on his face that remind me of a deep river until they fold into his mouth. He stands before me, a vision to be sure. I stand with my back to the wall and reach for him. Vapor. I stumble and fall. I cannot stop crying loud sobs of agony.

Clara, mi Clarita. Please, calm yourself. You must be strong, certain, unforgiving.

I hear him, although my sobs are never-ending, his voice soft, like our whispers under the covers at night. He can be loud, accusatory, inviolate, especially with our grandsons, Aruh and León, about the textiles, but now he is seductive, enticing.

Clara, mi *bella* Clara, mi *amor*—I think of you every moment the sun is up. I am diminished without you. We must go on. We are all well except for Celendaria. And then he sings to me—*la esposa de mi corazon*, until he evaporates, fading away into the mist after a heavy rain. Ah, the wife of my heart.

Where is Celendaria? She is my heart, the smart one by my side. Such joy. Does she need care? Is something wrong? I have not seen a face that loves me in a long time. I do not know whether they try to visit and are turned away or maybe I am forgotten.

It is important for me to keep my mind acute. I hear scratching noises. Mice. I am petrified of them more than the objects of torture surrounding me. They represent the unclean. I am sad inside my soul, the deepest part, mourning for what I am missing in my family's life.

Slumber is my safe place except if nightmares rule. When I awake, I am calling his name, Esteban, mi amor. I think that I cannot feel anymore sadness but it is possible when I think my husband was here to visit me and I could not see him. Why is he not allowed to visit me? I was told he has been to this coffin many times. The inquisitors have stringent rules, unbreakable. He must come to sign after I give testimony because my signature is no good. As a woman, I am worthless. Ah, but maybe this is how they trick him because they know he can read and write.

I am scratching. The lice are eating me. The filth.

I cannot go on. Where is he?

CHAPTER THIRTY-THREE

CELENDARIA

14 de septiembre 1654

A sadness pervades our home that we cannot celebrate Rosh Hashanah, the New Year, in a place of solitude. The Feast of the Trumpets is a quiet day with only a few blasts of the ram's horn in the cellar. Mi abuelo is mostly silent. He no longer wishes to communicate.

It may be my last Rosh Hashanah among the bosom of my family.

I hardly think of Francisco. Bad enough I have a small dowry but locked up in the prison palace of the Inquisition will not impress him. I mourn, not for him, but what could be—a marriage, physicality, and the most important, babies, the clean smell of a newborn suckling my breast.

I do not know when they are coming. I cannot concentrate. What of Mariel and her priest? Will he be at her side when she labors? It is not possible. Who will be? Her mother? A midwife? A cousin? No man will be waiting, overjoyed to hear the news. Sometimes they smother the bastards, in particular when the father wants no part of it, declaring to those who wait it was stillborn, cold and blue.

I have heard the screams from my own mother when she delivered the twins after hours of agony, only to see my father's disappointment that both were girls. Boys. They always want boys to work in the family, not pay dowries for weddings.

Poor Mariel. So much pain for nothing. Who will accept her? No one. I feel badly, although it was not my error except for guilt that I was so ready to give her up. God has punished me for the suggestion that revealed her plight, assuming it could help me.

CHAPTER THIRTY-FOUR

CLARA

15 de septiembre 1654
Santa Oficina de la Inquisición

I have no words as I crawl inside my melancholia, my mind tripping over the stories of our Diaspora, secret prayers murmured in basements or forgotten rooms. Have I done my duty to God by bringing children into this world of dangerous, religious conviction? I could have simplified our lives by endorsing only Catholicism, although the Church would not accept us anymore than they do now. They will not allow New Christians to sit with them in church. They see our Judaism as a stain that will never go away, no matter how many times we convert. I would not be here if I was not compelled to reject their trinity. My family might have avoided the menace of the Inquisition. Who stands up for us?

It does not matter if they torture me. I feel nothing.

CHAPTER THIRTY-FIVE

CELENDARIA

16 de septiembre 1654, early morning

Thank God I have eaten bread and taken tea! The chief constable comes to our door from the offices of the Inquisition. He is dressed in a long, dark robe and tri-cornered hat, the kind the prosecutors wear in court and on the street, strutting with pride, the power of their position intimidating the rest of us. My father is not home, mi abuelo still sleeps, so mi madre answers their knocks.

We are here to arrest Celendaria Mendoza de Crespin, age sixteen.

I cannot stand up from the bench in the kitchen. Or move. It is not unexpected, yet I am not prepared for the intimidation of their uniforms, sturdy boots, weapons strapped to their sides, hats shading their eyes and dour faces, the looks of those who make incarcerating others their trade.

My mother asks, frantic, rushing to gather supplies, What do you want with a child? A good Catholic? An innocent? Unable to keep calm, she reminds me of doves trapped inside cages in the market, their wings flapping for freedom. Her hands flutter to her forehead and chest, twisting her garments with needle fingers. Please. Do not take her. Take me.

She pleads without consolation.

My sisters have been instructed to hide when strangers come to the door. We are all at risk.

Mi abuelo's face appears on the stairs, disturbed by loud voices, fearful for his own arrest. He flees back to bed.

Who was that? A guard asks, as he unscrolls a piece of paper to show an authorization of my arrest to my mother.

Daring, despite her panic, she asks, What do you want with an old man?

The same reason they want an old woman, I think with irony. I am frozen as though time has ceased to move forward, unfolding dream-like. Rain continues to pour through crevices in our roof. The sound of leaking reminds me of their torture I have heard about where hot wax is dripped on the victim's chest in the sign of the cross. I will not be able to bear this. My bravado has escaped. I am frightened. What do they want with me? I may appear a woman but I am a girl on the inside.

The guards stand at my side lifting me up by each arm, propelling me toward the front of the house. I glance back to see my mother, her eyes covered with her arm, crying into the wall where she has re-hung the crucifixion.

I am led away.

CHAPTER THIRTY-SIX

CELENDARIA

19 de septiembre 1654
Santa Oficina de la Inquisición

My extra layers of skirts keep me warmer. I am grateful they have not taken my clothes and made me wear a sanbenito. I have had no contact with a human for three days except for a hand that shoves mush in a bowl and a tin cup of water beneath my door. I hear sounds from others who are detained—cries, moans, hysterical, pitted screams—but no one speaks.

A chilly dampness pervades the walls, the floors. I suffer shock that I am here even though I was warned. The clanging of doors, the jangle of keys, and the reverberations of cries echo around me. There are no happy souls here. The clever ecclesiastical hierarchy does not reveal why I have been arrested. They seek to intimidate, create fear. My family has little left of valuable possessions, save my grandfather's hidden books, which are considered heretical. They cannot be mentioned. The thought of his exquisite tomes, some embossed with gold leaf and decorated by ancient scribes, chill me.

When I turn the pages in my mind, I try to calm myself, to remember what I am supposed to know and what I am destined to forget.

And then I vomit in the corner of the room. The smell sickens me. Will my family be allowed to see me? Bring me some comforts? The mattress is stained with the liquids of the body—urine, pus, snot. I am used to cleanliness, the fresh sheets of Shabbat. The basket my mother packed with care has been confiscated.

I am determined I will track the days, recite the Shema, maintain the integrity of my soul.

I do not want to be a hysteric who loses sense of reality, of what is true and not true. I must stay anchored to my God, one I can speak to with direct intention.

Does my grandmother know I am here? Where is she?

CHAPTER THIRTY-SEVEN

CLARA

22 de septiembre 1654
Kol Nidre, the night before el Gran Día
Santa Oficina de la Inquisición

Although I have lost track of days, months, years in my incarceration, my intuition, the inner knowing I receive from Our Heavenly Father, guides me toward a sensitivity that we are approaching the holy day of Yom Kippur. In my mind it is Kol Nidre, the evening before the most sacred day, a time of introspection, repentance and to ask God's forgiveness. On the eve of this Sabbath of Sabbaths, I envision our family consuming their final meal before the fast. I see each one's countenance around the table.

I review the names of my grandchildren, their ages, the ones I can remember, how they appear, each a precious gem with a divine spark. How could the innocents be imbued with Original Sin? They are pure.

My eldest daughter, Maria, was the first to marry. One Friday morning as we tucked corners of clean sheets into our bed, she expressed trepidation about her wedding night that was fast approaching.

Mi madre, I dread the force of the consummation. Will it hurt? What if I cry out? Will blood stain the sheets? Her eyes filled with dread spilled with tears.

I came to her side of the bed to hold her in my arms. *Mi hija*, I have not done a good job of explaining what will transpire. The primary purpose of this act is to reinforce the marital bond, a loving attachment that offers companionship during a time of joy. Yes, we hope for children, but this is not the only reason to engage in *yod-dalet-ayin*, according to our Torah.

She asked me in such a small voice, embarrassed at my frankness, that I could barely hear her. What does that mean?

It means "*to know.*" She was puzzled so I had to clarify that the experience involved both the heart and mind, not just the body. I held her away from me for a moment to look in her deep, olive green eyes.

A husband has a duty to ensure that sex is pleasurable for his wife. It is your right written into the *ketubah*, the marriage contract, along with the provision of food and clothing.

Madre, I am still dreading it.

I stroked her dark hair. You will enjoy this. I promise. He can never force you. Be patient with him and yourself. It takes time to adjust to your new circumstances. I must have conveyed enough consolation that I never had to share with the others. Maria taught them.

Now Rosa, only a year younger and my reticent, quiet one, would sing under her breath. She could barely lift her head to answer a question. Her curiosity was lacking but she was a diligent worker who sewed or stirred pots for me. At the time, we had servants who lent a hand for some of the harder chores of washing and scrubbing, but to keep our privacy they were dismissed before we began preparations for Shabbat or feasts. It aroused some suspicion but I treated them like family, always paying a bit extra and sharing vegetables from our garden. Rosa gave me no problems and married a man as quiet as she is. Esteban and I joked that they had not spoken since the wedding although they gave us four fine grandchildren.

Gabriela, my third, is the smartest, her mind racing with ideas. I could not keep her contained when she was younger so I enlisted my husband to teach her to study his books, a habit she passed on to my feisty granddaughter, Celendaria, also a clever girl. Our son-in-law is a good match for Gabriela. No need for me to explain the wedding night to her. She was pregnant with their first son nine months after a small wedding and an exchange of brief vows. Although it is not of great importance, she was also the most beautiful, her face erupting into a smile with fine white teeth when she was pleased.

Last, I envision my Oliva, a most difficult birth. My husband wanted a boy, a son to carry our knowledge forward. I labored many hours with this delivery because she wanted to enter the world feet first. Did the midwife pull too hard on one of those tiny feet and dislodge a hip? I blame myself for her limp. My inner knowing whispered something was incomplete when the midwife bundled her into my arms. No flashing of hands or the wail of entry into a new world. I saw other differences later. I kept her close because she cried more than the others. She walked later than most, stumbling unaware, off balance.

My fears for her centered around the river. She was born without caution, the profound experience remaining with me. Children could be washed away in a torrent or pulled beneath without warning. How would I know?

Later, we could observe that one eye shifts, following who knows what, birds flying, the other eye firm. I thought she could not see or learn, but soon this was proven not to be true. She comprehends at the pace of her walk: slowly yet with deliberation. With a bent carriage listing to one side, she reminds me of a wagon with three wheels as my heart breaks. I do not know what caused this. In the beginning I was bereft, my husband praying into the night with the other men, but then she smiled. I love my daughters the same, although the last one challenged me. I had much to do with four girls.

One evening as I lay in exhaustion, Esteban said to me, Clara, there will be no more children.

Why?

Because this last one gives you too much work.

What about a son?

It is not meant to be.

But how will I stop it? I am fertile now. I knew this because I counted my days to the moon's cycle.

I will use something that offers protection made of lambskin.

Does Adonai approve?

Adonai wants us to be a family of bliss.

Of course the priests were drawn to Oliva and her affliction. They halted me in the street. Please Señora Crespin, bring her to church. She needs the power, the grandeur of the Holy Spirit. I brought her for their blessings. What could it hurt?

I taught the older girls about the Law of Moses. Of course I delayed until after their menses so they would not be confused. They learned about our generations of devotion, quickly repeating to me, One God, only One. I lied to keep them away from the priests and their liturgy, appearing pious when questioned. I covered my head to teach the girls blessings for the wine and bread, the significance of the holidays from biblical times, the sacredness of our Torah, their eyes wide with the mystery of thousands of us teaching these rituals to the next generation and the next one, the unending string that takes us to our Adonai.

Amen.

CHAPTER THIRTY-EIGHT

CELENDARIA

12 de octubre 1654
Santa Oficina de la Inquisición

I have tracked many days without contact from anyone. The boredom is overwhelming. How I would love to clean, feed animals, change linens! Even take our garbage away from the house. No one has visited me yet. I have counted five days passing. I cannot see other prisoners but sometimes I hear them. Or maybe its rats scratching with their rodent claws. I shiver with chills. I must survive this.

I am in the basement with indigent prisoners, the poorest of the poor. Rumors passed outside say this is for the bigamists, of which I am not one. True, some women want to escape appalling husbands so they abandon them and find a new one. Others see visions, or say they do, especially the mestizo women confused by the replacement of their native religions and tongues with Catholicism. I am not one of them. Still others use sorcery, magic potions, peyote to bring spells, and charge for their services, which is all forbidden.

I hear the scraping again. I get close to the wall and listen. No! I cannot tolerate a rat in my space. I will strangle it with my bare hands. I will smother it under the filthy mattress that my head had not touched. It cannot be.

But the chaffing continues with a rhythm. What can it be? I touch the cool adobe wall with my hands. I feel a vibration, a continual rasping. A tremor sings under my fingers. I am pulsating with fear. I have no shoes to kill the beast. I will have to be resourceful. But with what?

I have a tin cup for water. I gulp down what is left and sit across from the throbbing noise, my hands around my knees, prepared to spring and smash the head with my only weapon. I tap it against my leg, impatient.

And then, a sliver of light appears in a hole where the sounds have come from as I shudder with anticipation. I can kill. I have watched my mother slaughter chickens, lambs, a goat. I can kill.

And then the sliver grows into a small hole. I know mice can flatten their bodies to creep under a door. Can rats do the same? My heart hammers inside of me. I see a glint of metal pulsating through the gap, a miniscule tear in the wall. I get up to move closer, sweat pouring from my body despite the chill. I do not allow my eyes to waver from the puncture, my hands gripping the cup with such force my fingers go numb.

It is a needle, a needle that has eaten away the adobe by consistent repetition.

Someone on the other side has made a hole with a sewing needle.

Then it goes black.

Hello? Hello? It is a woman's voice. Hello? Are you new?

A mouth waits for me in the cavity.

I can barely speak. Yes, new.

What is your name?

Celendaria.

Why are you here?

I am caught off guard with this question. Why are *you* here?

We are not told our offenses.

I gather my thoughts. Do you know my grandmother? Clara Crespin?

Momentary silence.

She waits in the torture room upstairs.

I am overcome. No!

She must be. There have been no screams. Yet.

Hush. The guard comes.

CHAPTER THIRTY-NINE

CLARA

20 de octubre 1654
Santa Oficina de la Inquisición

The guards have removed me from the torture chamber. Are they preparing to burn me at the stake without retribution? What have I been charged with? What is the evidence against me? I open and close my eyes. I cannot speak of visions. It is another crime. Why have they returned me to my cell? Is this where I was before? Nothing is familiar—not the mattress or the stool or the bucket. A mouse scampers away from me. Ah, the lice-ridden mice are familiar.

Mi abuela.

The voice, supple as lamb's wool, envelops the space. I do not understand why I have been brought back to my original cell. The light from the window assaults my eyes. How have the inquisitors conjured a ghost? I do not have a habit of visions, but my mind no longer remains whole.

Abuela?

Hello? I look to the ceiling. Is that where angels appear? Has my mind been engaged by their Holy Ghost? A young woman seems to lounge under the window, light spilling onto her head, her dark hair flowing to her shoulders. An apparition?

Mi abuela, I have missed you.

I move away, closer to the bars and my jailers who sometimes reach through to torment me. It speaks to me. This happens in my dreams. When I awakened in the total darkness of the torture cell, without knowing day from night, I saw my husband, heard his voice. Clara. Clara, I love you.

Mi abuela, I want to hold you, stroke your hair.

A hallucination. I know of these. Some go mad in these chambers, seeing visions, unlikely entities that make them bawl like babies, sniveling for hours, or howl like the coyotes that roam the desert.

The ghoul propels itself toward me, arms outstretched. I shriek in terror, cowering near the bars.

Mi abuela, do not be afraid. I will not harm you. It is your Celendaria.

I am limp with trepidation, cowering on the floor, my hands covering my eyes. If I will not be pulled apart by their rack, they have devised another method to render me useless. My fear is so great I cannot look at what transpires next. Arms wrap themselves around my back, holding me tight. I smell hair freshened with orange blossoms and night-blooming jasmine, the aroma of clean water before Shabbat. My rational mind has taken flight and left me with a strange lunacy.

CHAPTER FORTY

CELENDARIA

23 de noviembre 1654, late afternoon
Santa Oficina de la Inquisición

I have been incarcerated for over two months according to the calendar I scratch on the wall. At least I have been permitted to keep a comb. No charges have been weighed against me. That is their way—to intimidate with fear. I have not been called to testify. I am afraid I will melt into a puddle. Another upset bridles my mind. What of my engagement? If I do not see Francisco at Sukkot, the commitment is void. He will find another. No one will want a woman who has the taint of the Inquisition on her. How long will I be here? Forever?

This causes me to cry, something I have not indulged in often, the dread of my unacceptable future consuming all my tears. I think about this man with a handsome face, educated in our ways, who agreed to a meager dowry by arrangement. He may be riding into strange territories to capture thieves or merely detain a bigamist, but I believed in his ambition to provide for me. Until now. Will my fruitfulness dry up like a summer monsoon? I do not want to be without children, the smell of babies, the experience of a man. I will ask mi abuela about the relationship between a man and woman.

I know nothing.

My grandmother and I now share her original cell with the window. The fact that they have kept it empty for her is not a good sign. I long for my freedom. I do not understand why I am here, except to be accused of Judaizing, which happens infrequently in these times, or to glean information that will convict my beloved abuela.

Time passes before I convince her I was not an apparition; that the arms that held her were real, that my breath lingers with truth. She spends hours in disbelief stroking my hair, arms, knees, until she finally utters a hoarse whisper of my name. Celendaria. Celendaria, an incantation to the one on most high. She holds my hand for hours.

More than three years have passed since she has experienced freedom, the joy of walking outside, listening to birds sing near me, reciting prayers with family. She has shrunken to nothing, a wisp in a ragged sanbenito, her face stretched with lines, her grey hair in patches, I would not know her if we passed each other in Santo Domingo Plaza. The stunning Doña Clara, whose skirts swooshed on the streets fashioned from the finest velvet, has disappeared. In her place remains a genuine ghost.

In the beginning, I spoke with her at length about our family, mi abuelo who is also a shadow of himself, his undying love, of their four daughters: Maria, a mother of four, grandmother of two, her excellent cooking skills treasured by all; Rosa with three children who work in the textile factory, meeting the demand for cotton velvet and lace embellishments demanded by the Mexican court, a pallid imitation of Spanish royalty, who remains close to my mother,

Gabriela, a strong woman who guides us, and Oliva, the youngest, a passionate follower of the church. I am cautious with my words, guiding her to the corners of our cell when we communicate. Spies bloom here. After all, a scrap of information, a new accusation may free another soul. They foment us to turn upon each another.

I spend my time thinking about why I have been brought here. I have not been taken to the tribunal; no accusations have been launched against me, although I am prepared. It can only be to entrap mi abuela further into their lair of lies. It has been a relief that her body was not harmed, but her mind remains fragile. The wicked conduct of the Church and their diabolical Inquisition lingers as the rest of the world forges ahead to create a new reality.

Do you have news of the outside world? It is my grandmother's way of asking what letters we have received and avoiding talk of the family in case someone is listening.

Yes, Oliver Cromwell of England is invading Spanish territory. The Spanish are in great debt after years of war. She raises her eyebrows and shakes her head in disbelief. Our cousin, Pedro (a name I invent) sent a missive that dogs are persecuted in Poland and Persia, my secret way of letting mi abuela know our fate was not turning in our favor anywhere in the world.

And to the north? she asks.

I whisper, It is rumored our compatriots from Brazil have made their way to the shores far north.

What of the Indians?

The Spanish support them in Florida.

Is there hope for a place of freedom?

Yes, in the north near the Rio Grande River there are stories of religious freedom if people can escape the natives.

Would it be possible for us to go?

I shake my head to the negative, although mi abuelo has taught me to believe in change, in the good will of God. I cannot lose expectations.

CHAPTER FORTY-ONE

CLARA

10 de diciembre 1654, early morning
Palacio de la Santa Inquisición

The surprise of my granddaughter's visit elates and flabbergasts me at the same time. What kind of entrapment is this? Both Celendaria and I are dozing against the wall, shivering in the chilled air, when Oliva appears in our cell, her entry silent as flower petals wafting in a wind gust.

Oliva, what are you doing here? I ask, afraid my apparitions may have returned.

She leans over to kiss my papery cheek, her cross dangling near my face. Mi madre, I am filled with joy to see you. You have lost weight, but otherwise appear healthy.

I am here too, tía, says Celendaria, sidling out of the shadows to greet her aunt.

Oh, Celendaria, are you well?

Oliva's strange eye wanders to the iron door where the guard gave her entry. She does not greet my granddaughter with amiability, but then Oliva has always been my peculiar child.

Yes, tía, I am as well as can be expected in these circumstances. I do not feel as close to Oliva as I do to my other aunts.

Pleasantries are exchanged with brief news of our family. I only want to know of my husband, his health and well-being.

Is he well? Does he miss me? I ask.

Oliva limps to the broken chair, her gait unsteady.

I have brought you a basket of items that the inquisitors in their grace and glory have allowed me to share.

She pulls back a white linen napkin to reveal two red-green apples, almonds wrapped in paper, and a small cask of wine. Underneath are unblemished, folded sheets, blanched white, sparkling with cleanliness.

I seize an apple and press it to my lips while Celendaria snatches a sheet to hold next to her face, inhaling the freshness.

I see you both are hungry for the comforts of home. Please have some wine.

Oliva pours some from the cask into our metal cups. Even though it is an early hour to drink, I take sips between savoring the apple, but Celendaria looks at her aunt with suspicion.

My niece, have some spirits from the finest grapes.

She offers a cup that Celendaria accepts with caution, sipping, munching the nuts, quiet until Oliva speaks again.

Your families want to save you from the fate of death. I have been sent to convince you of your sins of Judaizing. The court awaits a confession from you, mi madre.

Celendaria's expression changes to one of anger, her eyebrows arched as she raises her voice. So this is why you have come? To elicit a confession? Enticing us with gifts? You have come to ensnare your own mother!

Shh, Celendaria. Oliva means no harm.

Celendaria folds her arms across her chest, her back turned away from us. I hear her mutter, Damn you to hell, Oliva.

My daughter does not hear her. Her afflictions include a slight loss of hearing, an excuse as a child to ignore my requests.

I have come to persuade you to take Jesus Christ into your hearts. Until then, you can never be truly free. I can bring a priest for a confession. Once you have done this, a trial can proceed and then the court can rule on whether—

Oliva, stop it! Celendaria turns to face us, standing on her feet. My grandmother, your mother, has nothing to confess. She is an innocent. You came to entrap her with the taste of fresh fruit, clean linens and a little wine to loosen her tongue.

Oliva lowers her head. She speaks through pursed lips. We are all tainted with Original Sin from Adam.

Who sent you to deceive her, to lure her into a confession? Does your mother have to believe in this hereditary stain? She suckled you, gave you life, allowed you to breathe.

I came on my own out of concern for the fires, says Oliva, shifting her weight on the unbalanced chair, self-conscious with confrontation.

Which ones? Challenges Celendaria, her voice heavy with sarcasm. The ones in the courtyard for heretics and banned books, or the ones in hell?

No, please stop, both of you! I cannot bear arguing.

I am bereft with tears that stream down my face. I thought I had no more, that my finite pools of water were desiccated as dried apricots, shriveled and waterless.

Ach! Call the guards to take her away, says Celendaria.

I am reluctant to see my youngest daughter leave when we are at odds. She knows my heart lies with One God, not the trinity, yet she has come to save me. From what? I will die anyway, fulfilling the prophecy of our leaders that we perish in a foreign land.

Oliva limps toward the steel bars. Guard! Guard! I am ready.

I stand to hold her in my arms, kissing both of her cheeks. Stay well, my child.

Oliva speaks to me in a serious tone. Mama, consider ending this nightmare, free your soul, and release your family from pain. It is for the best. You have been here a long time without purpose. Embrace the trinity.

Her final words land in the air. And then she is gone with her empty basket. My apple rolls across the floor.

Celendaria, eat the apple before the rats get it, I tell her as I smooth the clean sheet onto our mattress on the floor.

CHAPTER FORTY-TWO

CLARA

22 de diciembre 1654
Santa Oficina de la Inquisición

Celendaria and I wonder about the world outside. It is close to the time for a celebration of their Lord. My husband and sons would be busy with Advent, which begins the fourth Sunday before Christmas Eve, celebrated with balls and banquets, a boon for our textile business. The ladies in the court—an imitation of the Spanish one that will never be as grand—require new dresses, and the men, gentleman's finery. I remember a deep purple velvet my grandsons created with their blade-sharp eyes, a liturgical color worn by the priests different from the red-violet shade used for Lent robes. We made promises of exclusivity so others would not appear in the same colors, my husband supervising the mixture of dyes made from dead beetles in vats far from town. I once asked a neighbor about Advent, in an innocent way of course.

It is a way of looking forward to Christ's birth when he will appear again.

Of course, I nodded in agreement. And may it be so.

Celendaria sleeps for hours, her head nestled into the clean sheet, a way of escape. I do not know what to make of this. We whisper many conversations. I think the visit from Oliva and the arrest of Celendaria are to get me to confess. I consider this at great length. To do so would endanger everyone in my family.

CHAPTER FORTY-THREE

CELENDARIA

1 de enero 1655

Without warning, I am set free. The guards take me away, my grandmother clinging to me until the one with a bulbous nose and rotted teeth shoves her away with a rough slap. I cannot bear to see her sobbing in a heap on the floor, but I have no options. They remove me to the tribunal. I face the terrible men mi abuela has told me about as a young jailer steers me into a hard chair. Chains prevent me from touching my face to push away a strand of hair in my eyes. I am still in the clothes I wore when they arrested me. I have been handled roughly but I am not hurt. I worry for mi abuela who needs my help. Will she ever be free?

We, the Inquisitors against Heretical Depravity and Apostasy in the City of México and provinces of New Spain, Guatemala, Honduras, Nicaragua, Yucatán, Verapaz and the Islands of the Philippines have ordered you, Celendaria Mendoza Crespin, before the court.

A pause ensues and I am not sure whether an accusation will be made. Do they know I can read and write? My heart beats at a frantic pace. The man in the middle I know to be among the cruelest speaks to me.

Although we have doubts about your belief in the perpetual virginity of Mary and are aware of your avoidance of pork products, we find little evidence to hold you. Our witness has recanted their accusation. Therefore, the court has scheduled you for release.

My ears must be deceiving me. Release? A witness? I cast my eyes downward to quell my panic. A mistake?

We have found no cause to keep you, although suspicion will continue to suspend itself over you and your home. Move with caution and be reverent. The Lord Jesus Christ and the brethren of this Inquisition watch over you.

How can this be? Did their plan for mi abuela fail? I want to ask about her, but my lips tremble. I am afraid to speak, that tears will flow. A knob of hard wood inhabits the center of my throat. I am incapable of uttering a sound.

Your name is placed in the records of our tribunal. In testimony, we sign our names and seal this document with the seal of the Holy Office, signed by Secretaries of the Holy Secret. Chief Jailer, release the prisoner. Notary, her father waits outside to sign the papers.

I am shocked. The chains are removed from my ankles and wrists, both raw with fleabites.

In moments there are lights as I am led into an elaborate chamber, a library with hundreds of books, tomes of the Church that justify the charity they show to others. A swell of anger rises in me as I smooth my hair and brush my skirts. My father appears older, his hair flecked with grey. I too am older in many ways. We embrace, holding each other until the guard says we must stop. How many scenes of joy have occurred in this room? A rare occurrence I am sure.

With formality, he signs papers that I am discharged. The receptor, who is in charge of confiscated goods, stands by as a witness with the notary.

We exit with contrition. I run to the enormous wooden doors toward my freedom, the cold air smacking against my face. My father places a wool shawl around my shoulders. Out of earshot, I turn to my father.

Padre, what did you give up to get me out?

Celendaria, I do not want to speak of this.

Please. I tug his sleeve. I beg with my eyes. I must know.

His head drops. Never speak to me of this again. Your grandfather gave up the silver candlesticks from his family.

What? After so many generations? No. It occurs to me to ask, Why not for his wife?

We offered through channels but they were not accepted. There is a stubborn witness against your grandmother. We do not know who it is and they will not reveal the person's name. It gives them reason to hold her indefinitely in their perpetual jail. Bribery is no longer a choice for us. The subject is finished.

But who took them? Mi padre does not respond. You sold them? To whom?

Celendaria, enough with your questions. We had to make a decision. He touches my arm. It has been discussed at length in our community ... that it is unlikely Francisco has waited for you, or that we will find another suitor even though your incarceration was brief. Let us say we traded the candlesticks to a wealthy benefactor for silver coins.

Abuelo gave them up for me?

My father nods with resolution.

I do not want to cry so I swallow to repress the emotion. Oh, but the thought that mi abuelo lost his precious possessions for me reinforces our family history, one of sacrifice. What love he has expressed!

Soon we are home where my mother and sisters cry with happiness that I am free, but it is bittersweet. Mi abuela is not with me.

I am offered wine before I speak. Mi abuelo is the most attentive, sitting close to my elbow, his face filled with emotion about my return. Yael and Yonah have grown inches since I left, small breasts beneath their blouses. They too are happy to see me, teasing about all of us in the same bed again. I share what news I have about our beloved grandmother until mi madre calls us for a supper of egg-and-cheese casserole she has spiced with cumin, cinnamon and cloves. I lick the spices from my lips with joy.

But I cannot forget mi abuela, alone in a cell.

CHAPTER FORTY-FOUR

CELENDARIA

10 de enero 1655, dawn

I do not sleep well since my return. Nightmares of mi abuela haunt me through the early hours. Why am I free and she is trapped? Instead of waking my sisters, I creep down stairs in my gown and felt slippers for a glass of water. The pitcher, usually filled, sits empty. My throat, parched from the chill, remains dry. I do not want to go outside to the well. I have had enough of darkness and frozen air in the cell I inhabited with my grandmother.

Whatever plan the inquisitors had did not come to fruition. But I still do not understand why she is still there. My parents say I am foolish to anguish over this question. They do not need to give us reason to hold an innocent woman, they repeat to me. I grab a knitted shawl near the door, a shiver crawling through my body. The well in our courtyard might be frozen in the dawning light of grey-blue, but mi madre will be pleased I have accomplished this chore for our morning coffee.

While I lower the wooden bucket with a long rope, my fingers numb with cold, it bangs its way up the side. Hooves break my reverie. I pull hard with all my strength to set the bucket down and abandon my spot to hide behind the wall near the street. Who can be out at this hour? A tradesman? The clip-clop comes closer with the sound of a donkey's bray.

I am crouched low so I cannot be seen. First, I am not presentable and secondly, I have trepidation of strangers. The sounds halt in front of our gate with snorts and cooing words. A man ties up reins, dressed as a Mexican peasant, a faded serape across his chest covering his chin, a hat low on his brow. I do not know this man.

He opens the gate to enter our courtyard. Is he a robber? A beggar? A spy? None of my father's business compatriots would come to our home. I am not spotted crouched against the wall quaking with cold. He reaches our solid oak door, his hands hidden in his serape. I stop him with my words.

Sir, may I help you?

He whirls toward me. I am defenseless if he wants to do me harm, but I am braver since I have faced the inquisitors. I recognize a vague familiarity in his eyes.

I know you, he says.

I jerk myself to my full height despite my thin nightclothes and shawl. I am not familiar with you. Please leave our property at once.

He looks me up and down and I am ashamed. You are the eldest daughter of the Crespins, the one who was arrested and smoldered in an Inquisition cell.

Insulted by his informality, I am determined to find out his purpose for intruding on our privacy.

What do you want? Why are you here? I raise my chin in defiance, crossing my arms.

His eyes bore through me. Celendaria.

My head wrenches in surprise. How does he know my name? This must be a trick, another trap. I am vulnerable in the semidarkness, dressed for sleep.

I am Father Lopez. Only I am no longer a priest.

I do not understand, I say, shaking my head in confusion. This is not the elegant, defiant priest I have seen strutting through our square. This is a slump-shouldered Mexican with tarnished skin, lips chapped by the sun.

I am here to ask your father for a favor.

Mi padre? Why? We have nothing and are without influence. Suddenly, I speak with fury. What do you want from us? Everything has been taken away including mi abuela. You cast us aside when we needed help.

With an unusual humility, he speaks in a subdued voice. I must leave. Rumors abound that I am to be arrested for priestly improprieties.

And why should we care? What do you think you can get from us? You are the cause of Mariel Behar's pregnancy. You alone have brought shame to their family, to our community—

I am so furious I cannot place more words in my mouth.

He looks away from me. I want to speak to your father. We need supplies for our escape.

Have you not taken everything the Behars have, including their daughter's virginity? My words stop as a candle comes to the upstairs window. I do not know how I am so bold. I want him to go away, knowing my father will not help him, afraid of the taint on our family name.

My father will not help you. Go!

I cannot leave without provisions. The baby—

What made you think you could find them here? You did not assist us in our darkest hour. Your mother took bribes for you and we saw no favors granted.

I am sorry I did not respond in kind. Many forces worked against me at that time. The civil authorities who carry out the wishes of the Inquisition are not as easy to bribe.

I take a step closer to see him more clearly. He has streaked red clay on his pallid face. You must leave. If my father finds you here, there will be a scene.

Without warning, the door swings open. The priest steps back into the shadows closer to the courtyard wall.

Celendaria, is that you? What are you doing up so early? I heard voices.

Abuelo, yes, I am hauling water from the well. I know he cannot see me in the diminished darkness because of his failing eyesight and lack of spectacles, but I can see him blinking. He waits for me to join him.

It is only me. I will be right in, Abuelo. Go inside, where it's warm. He slowly closes the door.

Go, go, I motion to the priest.

I will come back for foodstuffs tomorrow at this time. For the sake of Mariel and the baby, help me. His voice is so low I can hardly hear him.

I soften at the mention of the objects of my jealousy, the sensual face of Mariel imprinted on my mind. Where are they? I ask.

At a neighbor of my mother. They are hidden in the basement once used as a secret synagogue so no one will hear the cries of the baby.

Why is it not possible she can gather what you need?

Without my influence in the local diocese, she is shunned.

And the Behars?

Mariel has been disowned. She said you might help, that you were a friend. I have no one else to ask. You must help me. I will return tomorrow morning.

As he turns away I say, Wait. How could you know I would be outside so early in the morning?

He spins around to meet my eyes. I did not know. I thought to wait for your father as he left for work. With that, he disappears through the gate as I lift the water bucket with both hands.

CHAPTER FORTY-FIVE

CLARA

15 de enero 1655
Oficina de la Inquisición

Gossip proliferates in the tedious boredom of our incarceration. At first I ignored the calls from the other inmates, but I am lonely. It is not hard to commiserate with the other women locked up, some who hang their arms through the iron bars for hours. I am afraid of the ones who have been accused of witchcraft. They make preposterous claims of visions. One insists she has seen Our Lady of Guadalupe, although these sightings are out of fashion now. Another whom I cannot view, but I know to be an African slave from what the others have said, rants about her accusations of reading cards and mixing magic potions. She is a sorceress and I fear her. But, to my other side is another woman, Luisa Abad, who whispers to me at night after the final inspection of our cells.

I do not share any personal information with Luisa because she consorts with the guard who has bad teeth. Sometimes he removes her from the cell in the middle of the night, returning her in the early hours. After the assignation, she sleeps. Perhaps she tastes wine and earns some clean underclothes. Or a piece of fruit. I salivate tasting the sweet, juicy meat of a pear. Maybe she enjoys a bath of cool, clear water. Oh, to feel truly clean. Thank God no one is interested in an old woman.

Tonight she rolls an apple toward my cell that I grab as it passes by me. A kindness appreciated with suspicion. Eve and the apple. I remember all the stories of the Bible—Moses and the Ten Commandments, Noah and his ark, the parting of the Red Sea, our exodus and wanderings. I stop there. I retreat to the corner to bite into the thin, red-green skin of the fruit before it can be confiscated.

Clara, come closer to the front of your cell.

I move with caution. I do not trust anyone. So many traps. We are flies caught in a spider's web, struggling to be free.

Yes?

Father Lopez is accused of bedding a woman in the confessional.

I do not know who this is.

But you must! He is the tall, colorless man who likes young girls, one of those priests whose eyes and hands wander to sacred places.

Of course I know of whom she is speaking. Señora Lopez's son was a source of pride to his family. Is she speaking of my Celendaria? Oh, this would be terrible. I ask, Who is the young woman? I hold my breath.

She is of the Behar family, rumored to be with child.

This is shocking news. I do not know what else to say. Of course I know the eldest Behar daughter, an uncommon beauty with a face designed by a sculptor, the cleft in her chin distinctive.

Luisa continues. The Church has warned many before him, especially those who flaunt their rules by installing a family nearby. Do you know the daughters in the Behar family?

No. I know no one. Then I am brave enough to ask, What will they do to him?

There is silence. Maybe Luisa has gone to sleep. Then, after a time, she says, He will be tried by the tribunal. They do not need many witnesses if her belly is big.

But the Inquisition's wheels grind slowly, I offer.

Yes, they are deliberate in their decisions. Old Spain reprimands New Spain for its failings. However, he will be an example to others.

CHAPTER FORTY-SIX

CELENDARIA

16 de enero 1655

Father Lopez did not return the next day or the next days after. This day I bundle the hidden items—a jar of honey, ears of corn, a jug of water, cheese protected in cloth and tied with a string, cured olives, and a loaf of bread. It has been hidden under my bed in a basket. I offer to bring lunch to my father at the workshop, an errand I savor. I venture to the home of Señora Lopez. I know the path well.

I knock on the widow's door with my knuckles, then the side of my hand. She does not respond to my initial noise but finally, a wooden shutter opens to a sliver of light.

Go away! The door slams with finality, the iron latch sliding to seal it.

I follow the voice toward the shutter.

Señora, I have supplies for your son, I whisper in a harsh manner so as not to alert neighbors. I wait. No response.

Think of Mariel and the baby. Think of the baby, I hiss.

I do not know where they are. Go away, troublemaker!

I do not give in with ease, banging with the side of my hand balled into a fist. This woman infuriates me. I imagine her face as I continue to bang on the closed shutter until pain shoots through my hand.

Señora, open the door. If you do not want me to shout where your grandbaby is hidden, unbolt the latch. Now!

I am out of breath. Of course I would do no such thing to draw attention to myself after the Inquisition's awareness of me, but I am furious. What an arrogant woman who strutted the square with pride at her son's priesthood!

The latch on the door unfastens. Señora Lopez stands there, grey, miserable, a glum expression on her face. Instead of her black hair pulled into a chignon low at her neck, it is scrawled with grey hanging to her shoulders.

Come in.

Her gloomy home remains cheerless, musty with the smell of stale food. The odor of unwashed bed linens and clothes assaults my nose. I gag, fumbling for a handkerchief in my skirt pocket. I take a step back, adjusting to the lack of fresh air.

Your son came to me for provisions for Mariel and the baby. He said they were departing. I show her the basket covered with a cloth.

She stares at me as though I have made up a fantastical story. The expectation of trust diminishes. Am I here out of a desire to be of assistance or guilt? I am not an altruistic soul. At one time I considered indicting them all.

How do I know you are not a spy? Señora Lopez asks.

Infuriated, I respond. Because we are suffering, too. The inquisitors are not discerning. They cast a wide net. I close my eyes for a moment to see mi abuela's sweet countenance.

If you do not respond, Señora, I will leave with the goods.

She stands, frozen as a statue, without response. She appears older, her face as etiolated as a sick plant, which arouses my sympathies. But I endeavor to aid her children. I cannot remain any longer. My father waits for his lunch.

Excuse me, I am leaving. I brush past her to unbolt the latch on the door.

No.

I turn my head.

You can leave them with me, she says as she grips her skirts. Is she afraid or angry?

Ha! I refuse. They are intended for mother and child on their journey. The weather remains cold and the roads alternate from muddy to frozen according to my eldest brother who just returned from traveling.

This is not entirely true, but I am not above telling lies to complete my mission.

You must swear you will not reveal anything to the authorities.

No, I will not swear. You must take my word, the word of our ancestors. I glance to the wall where a giant crucifix once hung when I delivered spices ages ago.

Her chin drops to her chest. I will take you to them.

La señora reaches for a shawl draped on a hook. Follow me. She waits until the street is clear to slip out of her courtyard. I am on her heels. She seems to go in a circle to another courtyard around the corner, looking over her shoulder. She cuts back, retraces her steps and then steals down another street shaded with trees, then goes to another. For an older woman, she moves with grace and determination. I would never find my way again.

At our destination, a small home attached to others by way of a common wall, she raps in a rhythm. A door opens. A servant welcomes us. Ours have left us long ago. Too many of the hidden ones have been exposed by an observant housekeeper. The Inquisition tracks recipes for convictions. The ignominious chickpea or garbanzo bean, placed in a stew or salad, has sealed many fates.

Whose home is this? I ask, inspecting a fine floor made from handcrafted tiles with a well-placed table, carved chairs, an intricate cupboard and a few hand-carved chests, all in the style of colonial Spain.

Never mind, la señora snaps at me.

It must be a common routine because the servant makes no offerings. She simply opens the door to the back of the house near the hearth. Once she has left us, la señora pulls aside a drape that reveals another door. We descend the steps in darkness. I stay close to her heels, the basket swinging from my arm. As I step to the bottom, my chapines hit a dirt floor. La señora lights a candle. The glow dances across cases of wine stacked to the ceiling, dry meat hanging from hooks in the chill, shelves along the side walls with jars of preserved fruit and *pepinos encurtidos*, netted bags of potatoes, cabbages, carrots and pecans. I have not seen a larder so well stocked. Why do they need my meager supplies?

Who lives here? I ask la señora.

It does not concern you. Follow me. She clears her throat, stepping aside so I can move toward the light. La señora's breath warms my neck as she stays close behind me.

As I turn the corner, a chill courses through me. Mariel rests on a chair, her comely face illuminated by candlelight. In her arms, she holds a fat, pink baby wrapped in a blanket, nursing, the sucking sounds of satisfaction permeating the close air. I cannot speak. I drop to my knees in front of her, my finger pointed to touch the baby's cheek.

What is her name?

Serena.

She is beautiful, I whisper. I cannot breathe for a moment. She is the Madonna with child. I catch myself as I think of their liturgy.

Thank you, Celendaria. I have not seen you since the night at the mikvah. Are you and your family well?

Her calm demeanor pauses me in the awkward moment. She seems undaunted that I have appeared in her secret space. Does she comprehend the danger to herself and her child? Perhaps her sanguine nature is what brought her to these circumstances in the first place.

Are you leaving with Father Lopez? I ask.

Yes. We are leaving tomorrow. Her large eyes with caterpillar lashes embrace me, a wistful smile on her face.

What is your destination?

We are traveling north into the Southwest territories toward Nuevo Santander. Or maybe Santa Fe. Maybe a colony near the river that welcomes the displaced.

I have not heard of some of these. Are they civilized?

Miguel—Father Lopez—says there are new areas. He says the *criollos* with their Spanish descent but born in the New World have intermarried with the natives. Some live among the natives who also despise the forced conversions of the Spanish.

But they will look for you in those places. All are claimed for New Spain.

Yes, but he knows of contacts, other hidden ones, who will take us where the parish priests do not want to forge into the desert. It is a poor place but we will survive. No office of the Inquisition has established itself there.

I want to cry for her, this exquisite young woman with a baby who has given up her life. I am no longer jealous of her and her uncertain future. I do not ask about her family. I know they have declared her dead. Only the mother shamed by a son who has become a renegade priest accepts the young woman and mother of his child.

I have brought you supplies that Father Lopez asked me to gather for you. I cannot call him Miguel, the respect for the Church inbred in me. I look around half-expecting him to be there. I place the basket near her feet, separating my father's lunch.

Thank you, my friend. I was pleased when he said he saw you in the morning. I was afraid your father would deny him.

I bow my head. I want to pray. The baby stares at me, eyes wide in wonderment. What kind of life will this child have? A stronger question plagues me, one that eats at my heart. I understand the grief my family and others feel at losing another one to the Church.

Mariel, will you follow the Law of Moses in this new place?

At first her expression is one of puzzlement. Yes, this is who I am. Miguel, too, because he will no longer be a priest. We will look for the three stars in the sky and light candles. My expectations are small. I want peace. We will marry when we have settled. Mariel reaches for my hand and repeats the first line of the 133rd psalm.

How very good and pleasant it is when kindred live together in unity.

La señora taps my shoulder. Come. It is time to go. I do not want to arouse suspicion. The Inquisition is more frightening than Indians.

I stand to lean forward, brushing Mariel's cheek with my lips. *Va con pye ogurli*, I whisper in Ladino, a phrase mi abuela taught me. Go with a good-luck foot.

As I walk with haste toward our family factory, I think about Mariel and her priest. Will I find someone to love, to follow anywhere? Maybe my sisters are correct that I am too strong-willed for any man. Then I think of who possibly could have offered Mariel refuge. Who would take a substantial risk? The fear of consequences overwhelms many who turn their back on us. Then I know. Only another priest could have such an enormous cold-room filled with fruits and vegetables for the weeks ahead. Gifts of wine are common from parishioners.

Many secrets plague this Church.

CHAPTER FORTY-SEVEN

CLARA

3 de febrero 1655
Santa Oficina de la Inquisición

I have forgotten so much—the names of trees, the songs of birds, even my daughter's faces that fade behind a veil of memories. My grandchildren have grown up without me. We would not know one another if we passed in Santo Domingo Plaza.

Celendaria, my favorite, has emerged a woman. I think of her more than the others because I cannot imagine the way they look now. When she was in the cell with me, I spent hours looking at her features: the elongated nose, almond eyes so black they show no differentiation of color, and the curly hair of our name, tendrils draping her face like a silky vine feathering her elliptical face. With a full body, tall like her brothers and smart, I hope she does not bring trouble to herself or those around her. Her clever mind travels many passages.

It is apparent I will die in this place. My only distraction remains Luisa, the one with unique resources and nightly visits. What do you do with the guard? I ask.

What guard?

She knows of whom I am speaking. Is it against your will? I dare to ask. To me this would be worse than death, rotting in my cell or eating spoiled fruit scourged with maggots.

I do not know of what you speak. I work magic on all who encounter me.

At least she admits to being a sorceress, even if it is only with her magical, feminine wiles.

She lowers her voice from the usual bravado. I have learned something of interest. Come closer to the bars. She pauses, teasing me with her information. Father Lopez will not have a trial, she tells me, relishing her news. At least not until they catch him.

Why not?

He has disappeared.

How could that be? No one escapes from the watchful eyes of the authorities, I think to myself. Without anything else to assuage my boredom, I welcome her as a diversion. However, I never lose sight of the fact that she cannot be trusted nor can I reveal anything about myself.

With a donkey and cart, disguised as a peasant, he fooled those watching for him.

What of the Behar woman and their baby?

They have absconded with him. Luisa, triumphant with her information, squeals with joy at her revelation. A priest on trial would create a spectacle!

Where did they go? I know she does not know, but I ask the question aloud because it is a chorus to my song. Where did they go? Where do any of us go?

BOOK TWO
1655–1700

CHAPTER ONE

CELENDARIA

10 de abril 1655

I am in connubial limbo with a broken engagement. Were Francisco and his family disappointed with the meager dowry that we offered, especially now that the silver candlesticks are gone? With halfhearted interest, my father seeks another suitor because our situation has improved a bit; however, the church says if the female partner has been abandoned, then I cannot marry anyone else. My internment might have spoiled my opportunity. Francisco would have to find me. He knows where I am and has not sought me out. Or he has made another choice. Perhaps he did not care for my appearance. Yet, my attraction to him was noted. With his elevated stature, coarse hair and face with strong features, I thought we looked handsome together, a couple of note.

My mother dismisses him when I inquire with a false shyness. Bondsman is not a profession, she tells me. It is an ugly business, taking money or sheep or property to ensure the person will show up in court.

And if they do not appear?

Then the bounty hunters bring them back.

How do they find them in the desert?

They locate who they are looking for because they have large palominos and dogs that track the human smell. Sometimes the natives work with them to find who they are searching for in the dry wasteland. Their ability to find marks makes them able pursuers.

I do not perceive how there will be someone better, I say inside myself.

I pass through the market on my way back from my father's factory. We no longer import silks from the Philippines because we produce the fine fabrics here. A small enterprise has been set up to grow the worms that work with blind determination.

Much of silk production disappeared when the native dwellers who worked in the industry vanished with the small pox. My father and brothers have had some success. It was an afterthought to the serapes worn all over Mexico. My family produces lace, ribbons, thread and damask in colors from cochineal red to black, the color of mourning. Our father warned us not to wear too many ribbons in our hair to avoid notice. The guilds, however, forbid the Indians who cultivate the worms and mulberry trees to weave on floor looms. So they produce the fiber for us on backstrap looms.

All this was set up surreptitiously in a small village nearby, where the worms at the end of their cycle had to be fed the harvested leaves in great quantities. My sisters and I were allowed to visit a few times. It seems incredible to me that a small bug could produce something that could be made into an item of beauty. I am entranced by the process and the results. In our exile from Spain, the evil queen decreed we could not wear silk. It is a small rebellion to feel the gossamer fabric against my skin, the wings of a butterfly grazing my torso. The Inquisition always watches us. I use multicolored scraps to fashion dolls for my sisters and small cousins.

It is on one of these sojourns to pick up leftovers and bring my father his midday meal that I run into my former playmate, Elena, passing through the market. She greets me warmly. Although a friendship is uncommon between natives and our kind, I will always be grateful for the flowers and hummingbirds she took me to see.

I recognize her first, a rare smile crossing my lips. Elena, are you and your mother well?

Yes, Señorita Celendaria. She lowers her head to avoid my eyes before she speaks again. My mother is infirm and lives with my husband and me on the edge of the city. We have three children. She says this with pride.

I am not even married and we are close in age. A pang of envy slices through my heart because of my solitary state. It was easier for the uneducated to find a partner without so many rules. Elena, I am happy for your good fortune, is what I say. It was not what I felt. I pause to look at her shabby cottons covered with a shawl, woven shoes on her feet and an arm laden with baskets. A round one balances on her head.

Then she lifts her eyes to mine. Is your abuela still in jail? I have not heard of her release. She was always kind to me.

This stings me. It is unseemly that everyone should know our business, especially since it brings us great pain. Yes, I answer. Her fate remains suspended, sinister clouds roiling before a storm. It is our misfortune that we cannot be with her every day.

Ah, a sad circumstance. Now that I have my own children and my mother with me, I understand your family's grief. She looks to the ground. May I ask a question? What could she ask me? I realize we no longer had a servant-employer relationship. Yes, I reply.

She did not respond for a time. I waited, wondering if it would be about my inability to find a husband.

She moved closer to me and whispered, although no one was nearby. Do you know who put your abuela behind bars?

I shivered. No, we do not know. I am troubled, but ask anyway, Was it your mother?

She takes a step back, spitting on the ground. Her no is emphatic. We would not hurt you or your family. The evil ones are as much our enemy as yours. They mistreat us as well. Your mother and grandmother were generous to us.

It occurred to me she might know something. Do you have knowledge?

Her toes tapped as she looked away. I must go. The baby will be crying. She turns to leave our intimate conversation.

Wait. I held her arm. Who was it? Please tell me. You know something.

She tries to pull away from my grasp. I panic and hold firm. Tell me. Elena, who was it? You know something.

She lowers her head, moving it side to side in a negative manner.

I loosen my grip. She shifts away from me as if to run. Please. You must tell me if you know something. I feel like boiling bubbles on a flame, ready to explode.

She turns back to me. I do not know much. It is with trepidation that I tell you this. My mother and I know you and your family have secret practices, ones the church does not condone.

I am terrified and surprised. She could only be referring to our secret faith. I move closer to her face to ask, Did you tell?

No. We would not do such a thing, I told you. We knew about your special days for many years because your mother was obstinate about never having us work on a Saturday, dismissing us early on Fridays.

Please tell me. I am begging without dignity. I want to know if she has information about mi abuela dulce, the sweetest woman I have known. I dig into my basket of fabric scraps and lace and pull out a tangled handful of colors. Her eyes are wide with amazement. Here, take this. You can weave or sew with them.

She takes them from me without a word, placing them in the basket on her arm. Then she meets my gaze. She blurts out, Look within your family to find the source of your pain.

How do you know? I ask, pulsing with anxiety.

Because she is the most devout.

Who? What do you mean?

She does not wait and breaks into a run, shoes slapping cobblestones, one hand holding the head basket in place.

CHAPTER TWO

CELENDARIA

15 de septiembre 1655

Months pass before I feel compelled to share my thoughts with my mother. The family has been distracted with my grandfather's ill health, troubles at the workshop and unrest in the islands where some of our compatriots reside. We are told by travelers and in letters that the English have been defeated in Santo Domingo but have taken the island of Jamaica. My father says the English are as untrustworthy as the Spanish.

I do not know. What interests me is finding out who wanted to harm our grandmother and how to get her out of that despicable jail. And, if I am honest with myself, when someone will find me a husband so I do not die as a shriveled woman without children.

I go through the members of our tribe, searching for the person who would reveal that mi abuela was not a true Catholic. None of us were. I cannot think of who would do such a thing to our own. Maybe Elena lied. But why? She had no reason and our encounter was accidental. I have never seen her in the market before yesterday. Or maybe she misinterpreted information. Is it possible an inarticulate servant girl knows of our ways?

I have no way to find Elena and ask more questions. Not that she would give me ready answers. My grandmother has been incarcerated for more than five years. Who would do such a thing?

It cannot be anyone in our household. Neither my grandfather, father, mother, young sisters nor I would ever bring harm to my grandmother or endanger the rest of us. I look outside our family. My brothers, León and Aruh, would never harm our abuela. Their wives? Not possible. They are soft-spoken, devout women, Clodovea and Delfina, with Sephardic histories as long as my grandfather's. I doubt it was one of them. They are too busy with babies to show interest in what we are doing. Yet, all enter my suspicious mind.

My mother's sisters? My aunts are devoted to their mother who raised them. Maria, the oldest and my favorite, has a short temper, but holds it well. She is married to a stone carver who makes gargoyles and medallions for the homes of the wealthy. They have four children, all learning to read and write in secret, but too young to know the true faith.

My aunt Rosa, a calm being who often sits in silence, is known for her jams made from apricots and cherries. Once I saw her catch a fly that buzzed in our kitchen. She released it outside. Her husband, Desiderio? It is not possible. A humble soul, he works in the silver mines to the north that are rumored to have tunnels for escape, long days to take care of his family of eight.

Oliva? She is strange with her maladies, but would she harm her mother? Her husband, older and wealthier than the rest of us, owns a wood business importing hard varieties—cedar, cypress, spruce and oak—for furniture, cabinets, beams, benches and cradles. Yet, she shows the most interest in their trinity. And she urged abuela to confess. Why would she do such a thing? No, it cannot be.

If it is anyone among us, we are all in danger. Maybe it was nothing. But what could a servant's daughter gain from telling a lie? My inner nature that strikes feelings of knowing, tells me Elena revealed the truth. For many years we suspected her mother, but it did not make sense because we paid her well. Yet, other servants turned in their employers. I must find out. I must speak to my mother after the day we atone for our sins.

What draws my mind now as I chop carrots is Francisco. If there was to be an engagement, the time has passed. The only times I would be allowed to view my intended was at Passover and Sukkoth. We met once on the latter, but he did not appear again. The second meeting was for our families to compromise on details of the union. If he wanted me he would have come by now. Yet, my mind cannot release his broad shoulders and comely face.

Despite all we have been through, our family gathers to celebrate the most sacred of days, el Gran Día. We were grateful to be in our home with the preparations done by my mother, my sisters and me. It is too dangerous for the men to meet at a private prayer service as they have done in the past. The authorities watch for unusual behaviors.

The women work for two days in preparation of the fast where we do not let water or food pass our lips. What my grandfather does not know is that we have lost track of the date of Yom Kippur, the day we confess our sins to God. To insure our faith, we fast for three days instead of one as our ancestors did in Spain. It marks the cycle of our year with a devotion to the generations that came before us.

I dread the lack of food and a dry mouth, but everyone in our family participates, even Yael and Yonah, who now appear as miniature women, not fully grown, yet with mature bodies and short stature. My grandfather teaches them of our faith in the attic, taking my place. Soon a search will begin for their intended spouses as they will be married with children of their own. It seems impossible to separate them. Will I be married before them? Or am I destined to live under my parents' roof forever?

Candles smolder, evaporating into shadows on the sacred day. Our Gran Día. A time of repentance observed by our Hebrew ancestors. Yom Kippur, the holiest of holies. A day of reflection while we abstain from food or drink. It falls on the tenth of Tishrei, in septiembre or octubre. God forgives us on that day for all our sins.

A well-tended hearth, its embers dimming, softly illuminates my older brothers and their wives, children tucked away with pillows in the corners of the room or upstairs. We repent for the sin of our public display of Catholicism like crossing ourselves in church.

When my grandfather closes his eyes, I do too. He repeats a prayer for my grandmother's safekeeping. She is with us even when she is not. Then he begins the recitation of our sins. We repeat his words. He only glances a few times at the precious book that rests on his lap, squinting at the words. He has memorized almost all of it.

For the sin which we have committed before You under duress or willingly.

And for the sin which we have committed before You by hard-heartedness.

For the sin which have committed before You inadvertently.

And for the sin which we have committed before You with an utterance of the lips.

He recites these from memory and many more until all are completed, our fists touching our chest with each one, with interludes of joined voices.

For all these, God of Pardon, forgive us, atone for us.

The repetition over many years stays with me. I find it remarkable that our ancestors thought of these sins in biblical times.

When we are finally finished at sunset, we hold our glasses high to bless life. Now we can eat. It is my first year fasting. At fifteen, I am a young woman. My mother and the twins, who dozed for a bit, bring food to the table. We welcome the sumptuous meal.

We complete our supper prepared earlier so as not to arouse suspicion. We consume boiled eggs and vegetables from our garden, roasted chicken and rice made with onions, olives and pine nuts, all served with a small salad of greens. The adults drink ceremonial red wine with prayers to thank God for the fruit of the vine. Our family barters with other converso families to obtain it, trading some of the spices my mother grows with trepidation—cumin, cilantro, dried chilies, cocoa, cinnamon. Old Christians use wine as medicine or to symbolize the blood of their Savior. For us it is part of our ceremony to break the fast.

The meal is finished when we sip melted chocolate from a ceramic cup. It is my favorite part of the meal. I assisted with the preparation by adding chili powder, cinnamon and a bit of vanilla. In the market they serve it with cream, but that is forbidden to us. We do not mix milk and meat at our table. The ancient rabbis ruled that the milk of the animal slaughtered should not be part of a meal where the mother was being eaten.

My grandfather, beard damp with sweat, does not send me or my sisters into another room as he begins his story. He knows I am interested in the history of our people and our journey to this desert of prickly plants and deep silver mines. My brothers move the table to the side of the room, plates rattling, so we can gather our chairs in a circle.

He pauses to sip more wine before speaking, a small spot remaining on his lip, a diminutive berry glistening in the light. I know he must be tired. He says his bones hurt so his body shifts with protest. His advanced years often have him nodding off, chin to chest. But when he repeats the chronicle of our people, the tenor of his voice becomes resolved; his watery eyes behind glasses, determined; his hands curved in power.

I glance around the intimate room at the faces of my family. Who could have given up my grandmother? No one in this room. It is not possible. I miss her every day.

Mi abuelo holds his audience's interest by the retelling of our history that begins with the first expulsion from Spain in 1492 and the second from Portugal in 1497. He begins. Some of us stayed behind rather than establish ourselves again on foreign land. Our family went further underground, pretending to be faithful Catholics until we could no longer. Indeed, some have never found a home and wander from place to place, looking for what was lost.

I have heard this tale before, but I listen with interest, praying for a different ending as my grandfather tells the tragedy with a reedy voice. It is about Hernando Alonso who was rewarded with many hectares of land sixty miles north of Mexico City because he helped the Spanish build thirteen bridges to the interior of Mexico. He started a cattle and hog farm.

A hog farm? A Jew raising pigs? I do not say my thoughts out loud. Just as well.

He became the most prosperous man in the area by supplying meat to the hungry Spanish army.

I like this story of success. Has any of their wealth trickled to our family? I ask. It does not seem so.

It was most unfortunate that a Dominican friar remembered Señor Alonso from his son's baptism in Cuba, mi abuelo explains. The friar accused our relative of wiping away the chrism of the baptism and drinking wine as a mockery of the sacrament.

I speak out. But how could he be accused of something that happened long ago in another place? My sense of fairness is stepped on with his next comment.

My grandfather peers at me above his glasses perched on his nose. The church, steeped in hypocrisy, has power. Tomás de Torquemada, a Dominican friar and the evil queen's henchman, came up with this plot of persecution to unify Spain by sending us all away. Fools. We took all our centuries of knowledge and what we could carry with us. Queen Isabella's husband, Ferdinand, and de Torquemada both had grandmothers born to the ways of Sephardim. They became virulent in their denial, as though the blood of our ancestors could be purged with their lies.

My grandfather shows fatigue at this point by sighing. He wipes his face with a linen handkerchief. He persists with his story about Hernando Alonso, emotion drained from his voice. In 1528, Hernando Alonso, our esteemed relative, was a thirty-seven-year-old man with a corpulent belly who strode around wearing a belt with a large, gold buckle. He married a beautiful woman, Isabel de Aguilar after his dear wife Beatriz died. Beatriz was a valiant woman, one of the few women to settle the area. But then Hernando had more trouble.

No one speaks. Maybe the others know what happened, but I am vague on the details.

Hernando Alonso, our relative of blessed memory, died at the hands of the Church after torture and a confession in October of 1528, the first to be burned at the stake in this country. We must remember this brave soul. Many of us had settled here with the hope of staying out of the watchful eyes of the Church. Be grateful to God for the miracle of life that we are here!

The murmurations of *amen* invade our circle.

We know this might be his last time reviewing our past. Soon our father or León and Aruh will take over this responsibility. My grandfather pauses before he begins again. After the first auto-de-fé in October of 1540 in Portugal, it became a spectacle, an opportunity for the Catholic Church to create the splendor of the Mass with fire. It rooted out those who did not follow the strict guidelines of its orthodoxy. They eradicated people like us—the Church and public called us New Christians or conversos—to set an example. I deign to use the term *marranos*, another common term for us that means *swine*, the animal we refuse to eat.

I shiver at the mention of pigs, so forbidden that we were willing to die rather than consume their filthy meat. I am repulsed when I see them roasting the animal in the market, giving off a smell that nauseates me. Sometimes they force the penitents to eat the forbidden meat in front of a crowd, a horrific sight.

Mi abuelo begins anew, his eyes still watery.

When our kind first arrived in Mexico City in 1519 with Señor Hernán Cortes, we were ignored. We established ourselves, rising to the peaks of achievement because of commerce and trade. Our associates traveled with us, brave men and women who held the tenets of our faith close to their hearts, always searching for freedom. We thought in Nueva España we could flourish with so many from other cultures. Perhaps we would not be noticed.

It did not take long for the officials of the Church to realize we could fill their coffers once again. There were three synagogues built and the singing voices of the faithful could be heard spilling into the street. In the beginning, there were more of us than other inhabitants, except for the natives.

The viceroy of Ciudad de México had already given many of the Spanish nobility large swaths of land to settle this area, just as they did with our ancestor, Hernando Alonso, who perished in their fires when they became jealous of his success. They built more churches embellished with silver from the mines and encouraged travelers to come to this desolate area. Ach, the Spanish take what they want for free. Today their prosperity allows them to dwell in expansive haciendas and flourishing palaces, the most desired in Nueva España. It will be like this for years to come unless brave souls foment a revolution.

The Church feared us without bonds of control, that our sense of freedom would spread to others oceans away. In 1571, they established the Inquisition in Ciudad de México with Licenciado Bonilla as Inquisitor and Archbishop. By 1592, we felt the garrote twist around those of us who respect humanity.

I interrupt with a question that garners a harsh look from my father. Young women do not ask anything of their elders, but I am bold with knowledge. I want to remember these oral traditions.

How did the Spanish monarchs have control from so far away?

Abuelo has always been patient with his most interested student.

Ah, it is true the edicts from afar were slow and irregular. The Church became more autonomous here and needed more money. Once again, they turned to the Jews, and also some Protestants who did not accept their tenets. They levied fines, confiscated property, condemned and arrested those who resisted. After receiving threats, the Inquisition published letters to be read in every parish that forced the eight generations before my grandparents—good, sweet people as I remember—to hold up their right hands and swear on the cross an Oath of Obedience. This caused them great pain, as it does today.

My grandfather, the storyteller, does not rest, his spine curved in the warmth of the generations. His watchful, brown eyes survey the room over his glasses. His progeny are safe for another night. We have prayed, fasted and feasted, satiated with blessed food and divine grace and knowledge of our traditions and history.

León and Aruh stand to return to their families as a pounding interrupts our serenity. Mi abuelo's wiry, grey eyebrows rise in alarm.

Who would come at this hour?

My mother surveys the room for any hints of Judaizing. With the instincts of the ages, she gathers the remnants of our meal and the book and returns to the kitchen. I hurry after her. She pushes a rug aside with her foot uncovering a trap door. I pull the brass ring in the depression of the wood, lift the door and place the book carefully inside a hollowed out space my father has lined with metal scraps.

More pounding. On el Gran Día? Danger. A warning. My head begins to beat, a cobbler's hammer at work. What can I do to help? I am frantic with worry as to what awaits us on the other side of the door.

Who is it? Madre calls, her voice meek in the face of a threat.

Señor Crespin, let me in. It is Francisco Cordova.

The urgency of his knocks frightens me. What if Elena's slur is true? Has someone in our family turned us all in? Bile creeps up in my throat as I realize it is the man intended for me. My hand flutters toward my head to smooth hairs that have drifted to my face.

Go away! My father shouts.

The twins are sleeping! My mother shushes him.

He stands to his full height. We are always under threat, our bravery tested in unexpected moments.

My mother, her lips trembling, and my father, his resolve causing a vein across his forehead to pulse, exchange knowing looks. Maybe it is our time, she whispers.

Open the door, commands my grandfather. At these moments he appears strong, virile, the powerful man he was in his youth. At his age, his fears dissipate.

My mother's feet slide across the floor in her soft slippers like swallows in flight. She opens a window to our courtyard. The face of the bondsman appears behind the lattice of iron. She returns to the door to shift latches with her small hands, widens the space of the wooden entry and welcomes him with her arm into our space.

Francisco is dressed in a hat that fits snugly on his head, a serape over a plain cotton shirt and pants, his brown leather boots scraped on top, a gun and knife strapped to his side. He bows and addresses my family with formality, surveying the remains of our feast. My mother lights a lantern that reflects our worried faces. And his. It is obvious he has been in an altercation. His eye has blackened and he has a wound on his forehead that oozes blood.

I stand back, my hand covering my mouth. I cannot speak. My heart leaps while my stomach feels agony. Why is Francisco injured?

I am here to tell you we have recovered some of your stolen goods.

My father and brothers glance at each other.

After all this time? my father asks.

Yes. My brothers and I caught a renegade with the fabrics in his wagon. He is to be returned to the authorities near Monterrey. He was headed north.

Francisco glances at me. I feel elated and then frightened. What if he no longer wants me?

How did you know they were ours? asks León, puzzled as we all are.

Because the scoundrel admitted they came from your workshop in Ciudad de México. I apologize for the condition of a few pieces that were exposed to rain and dirt on the road. They—there were three of them—fought me and I fell to the ground. He touches his wound with care, wincing in pain.

My father's face reflects one of skepticism. Maybe this is another trap.

Come outside to see what I have in the under part of my wagon, Francisco offers.

At this late hour, we will see nothing, says my father. Besides, it was a long way to come to return damaged textiles. Why now?

I understand my father's suspicion. It has taken me a few moments to realize the possibilities of this visit. Francisco is as I remembered— tall with an imposing physique, firm in his speech and handsome to a fault. I cannot meet his eyes. I stare at his boots, dusty with travel.

Because I knew everyone would be at home for our holy day.

Why are you not with your family? asks mi abuelo. The Church has imposed tricks many times.

I am independent of my family, although we all work in the same business to capture thieves, bring them to justice and procure bonds. The days we celebrate el Gran Día vary across the territory. I did not know when you observed. I took a chance.

What do you want with us at this hour? The tension in my father's body has relaxed.

A place to sleep. The roads are unsafe. I had delays, which are not important to share now. I wanted to be here in the daylight two days ago so I would not arouse suspicion. We can go through the goods tomorrow.

My father takes charge. Pull your wagon to the back. We will give you blankets to make a bed in the barn. Gabriela, look at his injury and prepare a poultice. Celendaria, arrange a plate of food.

We set about our tasks. My grandfather settles into his chair, eyelids drifting downward.

Francisco leans forward in a chair as my mother cleans his wound. I steal peeks at him, his head tilted back, eyes closed, the candlelight illuminating his strong features. When she finishes adding a bandage, she admonishes him to finish his supper.

Thank you, Señora Crespin. I will gratefully decline your husband's offer of the barn and sleep under the stars in the safety of your yard, if that would be all right.

Celendaria, upstairs with your sisters, my father says in a harsh voice. He must be as puzzled as I am as to why this man has shown up at our door on a sacred day.

Francisco stares at me. What does it mean that he is here? Is it another form of torture that I cannot have what I desire? I move to the stairs hoping my sisters are asleep.

Wait. I have come for another reason.

We all turn to look at this rough stranger, his beard unclean with travel.

He takes a deep breath. I have come to respectfully ask for the hand of your daughter, Celendaria, in matrimony.

CHAPTER THREE

CELENDARIA

16 de septiembre 1655

I cannot sleep, while the twins slumber in exhaustion. What a strange day! I am thrilled with delight a savior has come for me, that my dreams will be fulfilled. If my family approves. A rush envelops my body, not unlike what I feel with my own explorations. I cannot resist my temptation. I turn on my side away from my innocent sisters, a vision of Francisco's face in front of me. I give myself another reason to go to the confessional.

In our living space the next morning, Francisco's large frame consumes the table and two chairs, his feet resting upon one, his scuffed boots at the door. I cannot look at him with my shame from the previous night.

Buenos días, says my mother. I return the greeting. She is preparing *almodrote*, a spicy eggplant dish that is my favorite, at a sideboard.

Francisco stares at me with a cow-eyed gaze. My mother notices this and admonishes us. We have not discussed this invitation of marriage, she says, so it is inappropriate for the two of you to speak or be alone. Your father forbids it.

Francisco stands, his head almost touching our ceiling. The bandage is soiled and needs to be changed. He asks my mother with a shy demeanor, Should I leave?

No! I cry out. I surprise my mother with my inappropriateness.

You must stay in the barn until we can discuss this matter when my husband returns tonight. Then she looks up from the spices she is spooning into a bowl. You realize that we have few goods to offer for a dowry.

That is not important to me. I follow my heart, not an opportunity for wealth. I can provide for both of us.

I am melting, like the candles we light, wax seeping down its sides to pool at the bottom of a ceramic plate. He wants me. Our eyes meet. At least she is not sending him home.

Please. You must go now. We will come for you when this matter is settled. But, I must warn you. My husband is unlikely to give permission to such an unorthodox arrangement. She gives him a chilled glance as he puts on his boots. Francisco gets up and shuts the door with a slam, his bandage unchanged.

I can see he is no fool. Will he listen to my parents' dictum? If he does not, am I prepared to leave the bosom of my family to retreat into the unknown? And, if I disobey them, will I see them again? It would break me in two. What about mi abuela? Mi abuelo? How can I leave them?

After he is gone, my mother says, This is not acceptable. We have ways that you may be betrothed. A young man arriving without family is not one of them. Your father will never consent to this. It is time to scrub the floors. Bring water from the well.

My mother is curt with me, as though I invited this stranger myself. I go through my tasks until it is time to prepare for supper.

Then my father appears, his face stern. He has nothing to say to me. I feel guilt. I have done nothing wrong, except to myself, but no one knows of this.

After the twins and I retire, I hear my parents' voices. I leave the warmth of my bed to find a place on the stairs where I can listen. They are discussing my fate.

Francisco came to our business today when we were packing shipments of trimmings and cotton velvet.

What did he want?

He returned the textiles that were recovered and a few damaged skeins. My father looks around at our space as if searching for answers.

Anything else?

Yes. He asked for Celendaria's hand in marriage.

When he says this, a thumping begins in my chest. I am taut with the realization the object of my dreams wants me. I hug my knees for comfort.

And, your response? my mother asks. Why did he not return the last time for the second matrimonial visit? She cannot leave with this stranger to go where she knows no one.

We do not do things this way, my father bellows in agreement.

Shush, you will wake the girls.

Ay, what is the difference? Either she is married here with our blessing or we will have a daughter to support the rest of our lives.

Why did he not return? My mother remains emphatic.

I creep down another two stair steps to hear the answer. I hear my father spew a sigh that expels frustration.

His grandmother died from an illness that ate away her body, a curse. His father was bereft. This time his mother passed from the same curse. Francisco stayed to insure the business would go on with

227

his brothers until his father could return to work … Gabriela, our choices are few. Celendaria is smart and strong.

I imagine my father crossing his arms across his chest.

Besides, the history of our people is to begin anew in strange places.

I am appalled my father would consider this option. I want to scream in fury. No one asks what I would prefer. I relax my back against the wall. The truth is I am not sure.

My mother pleads my case. Does not our daughter deserve happiness? She will be disconsolate if the twins marry before her. You should see the way she scrubbed the floors today after our feast. It is fine with me if she stays. She will help in our old age as others have done before us. But, I want her to be happy.

She will get over it.

I hear her try another approach. What else did he say?

He is leaving his brothers to trade in chocolate. The Catholics may have learned this cacao drink from the natives, but its distribution can be ours. A man named Jacob the Jew has opened a coffee house in England. The drink is popular in many homes. He is willing to allow Celendaria to stay here until he finds accommodations and establishes himself.

Well, does that not prove his heart is pure?

My mother is on my side.

My father releases a puff of air, a negative sound from what I can tell. A foolish idea. A wife has to be with her husband. Even if I approved, what kind of family does this man come from? Are they heathens who do not follow the Law of Moses?

My mother's voice sounds like that of a supplicant. You met them yourself when his father and brothers came for Sukkoth. They are like us, hidden ones trying to make their way in the world. Besides, you travel for long periods and I am left by myself. Celendaria is a good girl.

Yes, she is, but these men are without respect for tradition!

How do you know they do not follow the Law of Moses? It is done at great risk. Our community has not had a rabbi in many years. Are we to remember our ways without guidance?

I hear some movement. Maybe she is sitting at his knees, hoping to calm his fury. Mi *querido esposo*, be open to the new ways. Life is changing in Mexico and to the north of us. Maybe they will lead us out of the watchful eye of the Church.

My answer is no. We have no dowry and she is not prepared to run a household and live a rough, unstable life. His chair scrapes back on the floor that I worked so hard to rid of scuff marks.

CHAPTER FOUR

CELENDARIA

17 de septiembre 1655

Francisco has not left. He sleeps in his wagon under the stars and in the morning takes the food my mother leaves in a basket outside. I am forbidden to see or speak to him. His eye and head must be healing because the bandage is gone. I watch him through the upstairs window at night—unbridling his mule, placing straw and linens in the back of the wagon, washing his shirt in a bucket of water. When he is naked to the waist, a sight I have not seen before, I am entranced as I spy on him. Seeing his fine body makes me want him with unbridled longing. I return to my bed for the pleasure of a dream.

In the morning, my mother and I sip a thick mixture of coffee and chocolate at the table. I break our silence. Mama, why is Francisco still here if the answer is no? I wait for her answer as the cup touches her lips a few times.

Your father is testing his strength of character.

What does that mean?

He wants to see what this young man is willing to do to deserve our eldest and most beautiful daughter.

What is he supposed to do? I ask her. I am puzzled over why a man who wants to marry me is sleeping in the yard with his mule and our donkey. My passion grows more ardent with him so close. I have never been kissed. Would his lips taste sweet? His breath?

She sets her cup aside, a small line of dark chocolate on her lips that she licks with her tongue, savoring the flavor.

Celendaria, he needs to show that he is strong, loyal and willing to protect you in any circumstance. A man takes responsibility for a woman when her father turns her over in matrimony. He also must have a plan.

Mama, please do not be angry with me. I want to marry Francisco. Why does father object? I have no other prospects. And what kind of a plan?

Your father says he is not of a business that conveys respect. His father and brothers are a rowdy group of men who carry weapons. How will a refined young woman educated in the ways of our faith adapt to such coarseness? They deal with horse thieves, murderers and bigamists. We may have lost our wealth but our dignity remains intact.

But I thought he was changing professions. Is there nothing I can say that will change your minds?

I do my best to keep my composure, but it slips away from me. I cover my face with my hands to hide tears. When I raise my head up so she can see my unhappiness, I say, Mama, I want to be married and have children like you. I will teach them our ways.

My mother comes to me and drapes her arms over my shoulders. I will try again to persuade your father and grandfather tonight.

She lifts my chin toward her. My daughter, are you prepared to leave us? To travel to an unfamiliar place? To be a slave to a group of motherless men?

Her questions cause me to cry harder. I have never been so conflicted. I ask, Will there be no other women to befriend me? I do not know where they live.

Yes, of course, but you will be in wild territory with Indians who scalp heads and desperate, runaway slaves. There is little refinement in the territories. Your father told me he learned from a traveler that the Spanish kidnap the Navajo women to keep as slaves so they will weave them beautiful blankets. It makes the tribe very angry. The danger of this place is not for our daughter.

Oh, Mama, what will become of me? I lose control, sobbing with a honking noise of birds that fly south in the winter.

My mother holds me close until I calm myself. I have lost all the tears I can conjure. My Celendaria, she says, when you are with us, we are complete except for your grandmother. I cannot bear to lose you too. I feel her tears on my shoulder.

Is it possible for me to stay here while Francisco works to build the chocolate trade? Then I will not be in peril.

How do you know this?

I have been listening, I say with a small smile.

Ah, Celendaria. You are a clever one. Never mind. Your father does not like the idea of having a married daughter under our roof while her husband travels far and wide.

I sink into myself. The solution seems ideal to me. Then I remember. Mama, I have something to tell you. She loosens her hug and sits down on the bench next to me, her face expectant.

I have learned something.

Her expression changes to one of anxiety. Does she think I have the same message Mariel delivered to her parents? I tell her about meeting Elena in the market months ago. Mama, I do not think she would make up a story or lie to me.

My mother becomes wistful, her gaze far away. Perhaps she is thinking about when we had servants to assist with the work.

No, she was a simple, sweet girl. She would not cause us harm. But I trust no one.

What does she mean, Mama? How could someone within our family cause our grandmother such harm?

Her lips press into a thin line. I must think about this. We have searched for who might endanger our family among our acquaintances with no luck. Maybe we have to look nearer to home.

CHAPTER FIVE

CELENDARIA

20 de septiembre 1655

It has been almost a week since Francisco has been sleeping outside in the pleasant weather, but he cannot live in our backyard forever. What is to become of him? I see that he leaves the wagon and rides his donkey into the city some days. I stare at his broad back. We do not try to make contact. I am afraid of being caught doing what I am forbidden. My mother will not allow me to go out the back door. She reminds me of this as I sweep debris into the center of the room. Our people never sweep dirt past a doorway with a mezuzah affixed to it. The words of Adonai are sacred.

At dinner my father says Francisco has come to the factory again to ask for my hand in marriage. I squeeze myself. He will not give up. When he returns the empty basket to the back door in the morning, my mother invites him in for coffee, the aroma seeping through our rooms.

I am surprised when I come downstairs to find him sitting on the bench, his outsized hands wrapped around a cup. Our eyes catch before I lower my head. I am prepared for my mother to send me away or to retrieve water from the well in the front, but she does not. She senses his determination because he has not fled, even with my father's admonishments.

Sit, Celendaria, she says. I obey, turning myself away from him. Are you prepared to be on your own with this man?

I want to turn around and say *yes* with emphasis. Instead, I nod. I cannot look at him, but I stare at his fingers, tufts of hair on the top. His nails are short and spotless. Ah, he is a man who observes our rules of cleanliness.

Are you aware of your father's disapproval?

I nod yes again, wondering what Francisco must be thinking.

You will have to make sacrifices. Is this what you want, my daughter?

I nod yes. I have no thoughts as to what Francisco must be thinking. Or if he will stay. Tears overwhelm me and I run up the stairs. I cry, the humiliation of his possible rejection engulfing me. He will be my last chance. I feel it. Who else will come to my rescue?

In the meantime, a family meeting has been called for after dark at our home. My parents have not told anyone what it is for, although they think it is about my betrothal. We do not want to arouse suspicion. Any gathering may catch the attention of the church and cause havoc. My brothers wanted to offer their homes, but said we would keep the children awake.

After a hasty dinner of *calabaza* served with honey, salted fish my mother stored in a cool storage room below and a salad of greens from our garden, the adult members of our family arrive at dusk, their children in the care of grandparents or other relatives. They come with apprehension and settle on the chairs and benches in the main room after we have welcomed them. Maria, Rosa and their husbands sit near one another. My brothers León and Aruh and their wives arrive next. My grandfather occupies his chair covered with quilts, greeting each of them. My parents stand. The girls and I sit on the floor. The room seems cozy with most of us present.

When Oliva arrives with her unorganized gait, she says she cannot stay long because her littlest one, Diego, is ill. She sits on a bench near the back of the room, her husband, Berto, at her side. He is older than the other uncles, his head and beard tarnished with grey. I cannot tell which way she looks with her strange eye. A fly buzzes nearby. I wonder if Francisco is listening at the window, an eavesdropper like me. I am the only one besides my parents who knows why we have been called together.

My father's voice carries a strong resonance, especially helpful for my grandfather, whose hearing is as diminished as his eyesight. He leans forward to listen. We wait for my papa to speak. He begins after clearing his throat.

We are aware of information about our beloved grandmother.

No one in the room emits a sound. I am holding my breath. Oh, to see her kind face again. We have not been allowed to visit for a very long time. I pray every day she is well.

My father states in an emotionless voice, We have been informed a member of our family has leveled the accusation against our abuela. The room erupts. What? Impossible. Another way to sabotage our family!

My brother, León, says, That is outside our realm. Why would any of us squeal like a pig about our own abuela to the authorities? The Church is starting rumors to divide us. He is emphatic.

Maria, my clever aunt, offers that it is unlikely that any of us in this room would harm her. She took care of us from birth, her thoughtfulness a salve for each of us.

My father suggests we all speak as to her circumstance. Aruh and his wife Delfina stand. His tall frame unfolds. She is diminutive next to him, a beauty with a fine aquiline nose and a curl to her lips. My brother speaks for both of them.

It does not make sense one of us would turn her in. What would the motive be to harm her? They sit down to wait for an answer.

My grandfather speaks up. Ach, we have asked that question many times in the five years of her incarceration. The damn church has bled us dry. We have little money left. I have offered myself many times to no avail.

My grandfather closes his eyes after his outburst, his hands shaking on his lap.

My father turns to my Aunt Rosa and her husband Desiderio. They rise. She simpers with fear, clinging to his arm. He says, We are innocent of all blame. Nothing has changed since our first meetings about Clara. She is in our hearts every day. We are sorry for the circumstances, but we know nothing more than we did at the beginning. If someone here knows something, they should speak out. They sit down, perhaps a bit annoyed at the purpose of the meeting and leaving their four children at home alone.

It must be someone in this room, my father says, his voice loud. I want to know who is responsible for our pain. No one leaves until there is an answer.

I wonder why my parents believe with such fervor that Elena's statement to me was true.

I know the answer. They have suspected someone all along. My father stares at the corner of the room.

Berto, a widower at the time of the marriage to Oliva, has grown children in Veracruz. He stands and offers his hand to Oliva. She rises next to him, her hip thrust to one side. She does not look at us. The bricks made at his factory are visible throughout Mexico. He speaks in a calm manner. We are sorry also, but we know nothing. Thanks to our Creator, we have been provided for with more than we need. I have contributed a few times to the ransom fees, but your grandmother is still not free. At this time, we must leave because our smallest, Diego, is not well. I also have to travel in the morning.

Yes, in a moment, says my father. I would like to hear from Oliva.

Me? I know nothing. I have no interest in such things. She wrings her hands around one another, her shawl loosening from her shoulders.

She cannot look at us directly. Her eye wanders the room toward the ceiling made of thin branches. I notice that the cross she wears when I see her in the street is missing. Perhaps she thought better of it. We are aware of her inclination to be devout toward the Catholic faith. She is not my favorite aunt because she is often bossy with my sisters and me, criticizing our hair or dress. Or maybe there is envy on my part because she wears her finery on her back. Tonight she is dressed with modesty, but I have seen her in a hooded, blue velvet cape rushing through the market, her uneven amble drawing a few stares.

My father stares at her good eye, not an easy task. The room remains hushed, save the buzzing fly desperate to flee. I feel warm, a blush crawling from my chest to my neck. I have caused this with my suspicious mind.

What? Are you accusing me? Oliva's voice, angry and high-pitched, reveals the indignity of an indictment. Berto pats her arm to calm her. My father does not say anything. We all wait in awkward silence. The girls are at our feet, transfixed with the drama. She raises her voice again.

I have done nothing! You lay blame on me without reason. She lifts her chin in defiance, crossing her arms across her chest.

We are not making an accusation. But are you not a *reconciliada?*

I am surprised my father has asked this. The reconciliados are among our enemies, Jews who have returned to embrace the Church and all its doctrines, clutching a cross of forgiveness in gnarled hands. We know of some, but we shun them. They are proselytizers, something we do not do.

My mother opens her mouth to say something a few times and then closes it. My father is in charge.

Do you know why our abuela is being held for so long? We want the truth.

Oliva tosses her head, a defiant motion. How should I know? Her tone is sassy in her attempt to challenge my father. She continues. I have no qualms with our mother. She glances around the room. Or any of you for that matter. She says this with an air of superiority, her nose lifted in the air.

And why would you? My father asks the questions, a solicitor of sorts.

Because I have not been treated well. All of you look down on me. I hear your sniggers about my difficulties. She turns toward her husband, covering her shoulders with the wrap. Come, Berto, I want to leave. She begins to pick her way through us toward the door. Berto follows.

Wait. My father speaks this as a command. Oliva and Berto look up. My father challenges them. Are you prepared to make a statement to the authorities that you had nothing to do with our grandmother's incarceration?

Oliva begins to tremble. Her visible alarm is palpable. No, no, I cannot.

Berto makes an effort to guide her further to the exit, but she has begun to unravel, tears rolling down her face.

My father pursues her with his verbal acuity. What are your tears for? Perhaps it is time to share the truth. Do you want to admit something?

I think this is an intelligent question, especially knowing Oliva goes to confession. Transfixed with the drama unfolding above me, my expectations are low for a resolution to the confrontation. Oliva is in distress. Her face twists into a cabbage, tears streaming down her cheeks. Berto hands her a handkerchief to wipe her eyes. He seems as baffled as the rest of us. In all this time, no one has asked her, or any of us for that matter, a direct question. It seems impossible, incredible.

Without warning, Oliva breaks down from tears to sobs, sniveling and folding herself into her husband's arms. He soothes her with cooing baby sounds as he pats her back.

Come, let us go home. You are upset about your mother. It will be better in the morning, my sensitive one. He begins to guide Oliva around the jumble of chairs and benches closer to the door.

No! I can tell my father is angry by the tone of his voice. He persists.

I want to hear her speak. From her own lips, I want to hear of her innocence.

Oliva straightens herself, her teary face a light shade of scarlet. She inhales before speaking. I-I turned her in because she was Juda-izing—and I-I thought—I could save her soul from eternal damnation.

I inhale a breath that explodes when I release it. My eyes are wide with the horror of her confession.

The rest of the relatives in the room shout protests. My brothers are especially vociferous. How could you do this to your own mother? You have destroyed our family. Have you slipped into madness?

The last question from Aruh grips me because there are disenfranchised souls who slip to the other side of sanity. Their lives rebound between Christian and Jewish worlds because of the Church. It is difficult to live as two people with different names and identities. Many of our kind are locked away in convents or wander the countryside, never to find homes. Sometimes I am confused myself.

What?! It is my mother's screams of fury I hear above the dissent of the others. She tries to move past my father, her hands outstretched as if to strangle Oliva's neck. What did you tell the authorities? Tell me. What did you say?

Calm yourself, my father urges my mother, stretching his arm out to keep her from passing. She covers her eyes with her hands, as if she could block out this scene. The twins are disturbed and start to whimper at their mother's distress.

Oliva says, I meant her no harm. Why could she not leave the old ways behind? She was teaching them to our children. I thought if I turned her in, the authorities would frighten her with questions and release her. Her sadness seems genuine until she shifts her tone to say, Judaism is a burden. Why not shed it and accept the Savior into your hearts? It is an easier way to live. And survive.

Her last statement sends shudders through me. Oliva could turn in every one of us, a fear we live with that envelops us at strange times. I live with the fear especially when I read our sacred, secreted books.

What?! Aruh raises his voice louder than I have ever heard him before. Yael and Yonah finish their tears, stirring to go with our mother, eyes round with the alarm of an adult yelling. He is bombastic with his words.

You would have us forget the trials of our people from biblical times? We have been persecuted around the world for not believing in your Savior, and now you want us to shed our history and forget our ancestors? His eyes rock with rage. I turn my back on you with disgust. You are no better than the sycophants who search for favor with the priests. Whom did you tell your lies to? *Whom* did you tell your lies to? His hands become fists ready to release. Delfina reaches up to calm them.

Aruh turns away from Oliva toward the wall where my mother has a shelf of bowls. Maybe he is going to take his angry arm and sweep them all to the floor. I do not know what will happen next.

Oliva does not respond. She is crying uncontrollably.

Now León expresses himself. What did you tell them? I want to know. And why did you not say something sooner? You have put us all through horrific pain. Why? Tell us why!

His wife, Clodovea, nicknamed *the mouse* for her quick and tranquil demeanor, sits in silence next to him. My grandfather likes her because she knows her Sephardic history from Spain. Oliva's head falls forward in shame. She shakes it side to side.

Aruh asks, When the women went to visit her at the Inquisition Palace, why did you not say something then?

Because she is an idiot! My father's fury does not mince words. Oliva thinks only of herself. Look what she has done to our family, his voice crammed with grief.

Berto defends his wife. You may not call my Oliva names. We are leaving. But Oliva ignores him and sits down on the floor in front of the door, hugging her knees to her chest, adjusting her cotton skirts.

My father gains control. Why, tell us why you would do such a thing to tear the foundation of our family apart?

Oliva, isolated on the floor, speaks in a muted tone.

Because I believe in the Trinity. Because I am afflicted since birth. Perhaps I am this way because our mother remained one of the stiff-necked people who did not embrace Catholicism. Maybe if she had accepted their son of God we would all be safe by now. What is so difficult to see in their righteous ways and the beautiful liturgy of the Mass?

My grandfather begins to lift himself from his chair with great effort. Oliva, my Oliva, come to me. When he rises he is precarious, so he holds onto the arms of the chair.

Oliva scrambles to her feet and moves toward him, a sign of comfort. When they face one another, he says, I want to slap you but I will not. What you say is heresy to our people. We not do believe in a son. There is only one God, our creator. I do not know where you have adopted these ideas, but you must make the commitment to return to our ancient practices. You must leave this nonsense of the father and his ghost to others. We are Jews, proud Jews with an expansive history. Can you claim Maimonides, Spinoza, and Moses? Go, pray for guidance. You do not want to leave this earth as a Catholic. Come back to us. Forget the sacraments. Obey the Law of Moses. Remove the veil from your eyes.

I can tell he is tired after his outburst. I get up to assist him back into his chair.

Oliva has calmed herself before she speaks to us. I cannot leave until I make this right. It has been a great burden. What can I do? She glances at us, a disheveled woman confronted with an incensed group of relatives. She turns to address our angry family, dark eyes staring at her with intensity. In a small voice, she says, I confessed to my priest that I feared for my mother because she prepared special foods for the Sabbath and fasted on holidays.

Aruh yells, What did he say?

That I should pray for her soul. Oliva lowers her head. I was worried for all of you. You will die in the flames of hell.

My father, fury in his voice, asks, And when was this? His expression is one of darkness, eyebrows bound together in rage. He is not a violent man, but I am terrified of his bitterness.

Will he strike her?

Oliva says in a tiny voice, A long time ago.

Before she was arrested? He wants to know.

Yes.

My grandfather straightens himself in his chair. We must prepare another bribe. There are always some inquisitors more impoverished than others who use judicial fines to rob us with excuses and justification. What if we offer money directly into the pocket of one with influence?

Aruh says, Why must we be passive in the face of injustice? The Lord Inquisitor Juan Saenz de Mañzoca is known to be mercenary.

I have never seen my brother so angry, his fists clenched, ready to punch.

We have not always been so, abuelo responds. In 1485, Pedro de Arbués, an inquisitor in Aragon, was assassinated by Judaizers.

I am shocked. Would they be afraid of the consequences?

Are you suggesting such a scheme? León asks.

My father speaks up. Stop this nonsense. Then he repeats what we know. We have collected all we can offer. The money disappears into their secret chambers and we have no results. Or they put our valuables up for auction where the inquisitors themselves bid low prices. He moans. It is more important to seek our abuela's discharge. Let us repeat the Shema for her release. He glares at Oliva. We bow our heads, right hands covering our eyes, as we repeat the watchwords of our faith. *Hear O Israel, the Lord is our God, the Lord is One.* I peek at Oliva moving her lips without sound.

Sleep with peace, my loved ones, says mi madre as our family leaves. Oliva and Berto wait until the end. He speaks to my father.

Let us converse again of this matter.

My father looks grim.

The evening is over without resolution.

CHAPTER SIX

CELENDARIA

27 de septiembre 1655

After our gathering, a silence plunges us into an icy lake of despair. Our abuela rots in prison like forgotten fruit at the hand of her own daughter. It is too much to bear. My parents move through the days in a perfunctory silence. Only the twins distract me with their strange language and silly stunts. Most of the time I am of low spirits. How will we get her released?

Something else fills my mind too. Days pass until I can bear it no longer.

* * *

Mama, what is to become of the proposal from Francisco?

She sits down and takes my hands in hers. Her eyes search mine and she speaks with hesitation. I was going to tell you tomorrow after your father and Berto meet to devise a plan. It is difficult to function knowing the truth of who sent our abuela away. She pauses to swallow, as if to consume her words. Tomorrow Francisco will leave to return to his family.

My heart descends to my stomach. It is over. No wedding. No marriage with babies. What about me? Will I go with him?

Celendaria, you are a delight to your father and me. We have decided there is to be a wedding to unite the two of you despite our circumstances. It will have to be done twice, once in the church and once at home. Francisco will return with his father and brothers as witnesses. It will take a few months. In that time we will prepare a dress for you. Will you be agreeable to repeat vows to God and your family with Francisco?

Oh, Mama, is all I am able to say. I am incredulous. My parents have relented? I am to be a bride? I want to run out and hug my future husband, but I know it is forbidden.

My mother gets up to prepare our meal. Over her shoulder she says, Invite Francisco for supper. We want him to have a good meal before he embarks on his travels. I will arrange a basket for the road.

My limbs stir as though I am in a dream, sauntering on fluffy clouds. Finally, I can go out the back door and approach the man that I am now officially engaged to, the man of my yearning heart. I smooth my hair with my hands and take a scarf from a hook near the door to cover my head. Then I stop. Mama, does he know?

Yes, your father spoke with him last night. He is agreeable to the terms.

Terms? What terms? My heart sinks as fast as a fish swimming upstream.

You have a small dowry and he is without guidance. The agreement is that he will pursue the cacao trade using contacts from your father and brothers' routes. You will stay with us until he has established trade paths throughout Mexico and to the north.

We will not live together? I am cautious about asking too many questions, worrying about this circumstance.

No, not at the beginning. He must transition to a new enterprise and grant his bondsman business to his family. They have arrangements to pay him for his share.

Mama, what does this imply? Dampness begins under my arms and between my breasts. I am filled with apprehension about my future. My eyes fill with tears.

It means they will pay him for his portion. He will have money to purchase a home for you to start your own family. Celendaria, why are you crying?

I think for a moment. Perhaps this is the best way. I am happy, I say as I wrap my arms around her waist from behind while she stands at the hearth. I close my eyes. Thank you.

Do not stay outside for long. We must respect our traditions.

Suddenly, I part the clouds of my mind and flee with swift feet to speak to my intended.

Celendaria! Slow down. You are a lady with an intended.

The yard is messy with chicken droppings and muddy puddles. My mother's garden, close to the house and blooming with flowers of squash, eggplants, carrots and lettuce, is abundant. I have not been out here to glean the vegetables for a while.

I stop to put my finger into a small container of oil left outside for various purposes—to shine leather shoes to keep them supple after a rain, ease hinges on doors or burnish a gloss on my hair after washing. I spread a tiny amount across my bottom lip for shine.

I wind my way toward the barn in the back, past Francisco's wagon. In the semidarkness I see his mule tied up but I cannot see him. It smells terrible so I breathe through my mouth. My eyes see more shapes—farm equipment, tools to fix wagons and shoe the mule, burlap bags of chicken feed—and then without warning large hands cover my eyes. I struggle to free myself by clutching at their wrists, but I am not strong enough.

A deep voice I recognize says, Who do you think I am?

My heart flutters because I am no longer afraid. I touch the front of the hands and feel the hair near the knuckles. Francisco?

The hands disappear as he spins me around to face him. I have never been this close to him. We can feel each other's breath. I am immobile, caught in his spell, his coffee-colored eyes fastened to mine. He places one finger on my face and traces around my lips. I am aroused with his tenderness. I understand this feeling from my own exploration. My breathing increases as does his.

He asks, Are you pleased we are to be married?

I am so overwhelmed with emotion I can only nod.

Let me hear you address me. I want to hear your voice say my name.

In a whisper I utter, Francisco. I repeat it again, Francisco.

I have waited with patience for a long time to hear you speak my name.

Warmth spreads over me and I smile. Such a small request and it pleases him because he returns it. His even teeth shine through his beard. Then he places a temperate hand on the back of my neck, a gentleness reserved for a new baby, and pulls me upward to his mouth. I feel his yielding lips on mine. I pull back. I know this is wrong.

Yet, I have never felt anything like this sensation. His arms wrap around me and I blend into his body, feeling the pressure of his chest against mine. It is the most intimate moment I have ever experienced. His lips find mine once more with an intensity I return.

I am dissolved into a small pond. I have no legs, no backbone, my strength evaporating like puddles in sunshine. He ravishes my mouth until I push back on his chest so he is at arm's length.

I am breathing hard as though I have run from the market. We stare at each other.

Celendaria. He says my name with a guttural sound from the back of his throat.

Yes, I answer as I smooth my skirts. I cannot appear disheveled. My mother will expect me in a few moments.

Celendaria, I am leaving on a journey tomorrow. When I return you are to be my bride. Is that satisfactory to you?

I look at the man before me with a tide of sentiment. Yes, I want to be with you.

I feel a passion in my chest that wants to take a step forward and allow him to continue devouring my mouth. A flash of Mariel and her priest in the church swells in my mind. Now I understand. Now I know.

Our meal is at sundown when my father returns. Please join us. And then I run through the muddy yard, wiping my shoes near the door to go inside to the safety of my home.

CHAPTER SEVEN

CELENDARIA

27 de septiembre 1655

At the departure dinner, I cannot look at Francisco. The sting of his lips on mine appears when I close my eyes. It also makes me feel exposed to my family. Can my parents see my impurity? Is my indiscretion visible? My father explains to Yonah and Yael that the stranger at our table is to be their new uncle. They nod and whisper to each other. Yonah in her high-pitched voice asks, Will we have the bed to ourselves?

My mother says, Not in the beginning, but someday soon. The girls like her answer and play a game with their hands. My father admonishes them to stop. They are immature for their age. Or perhaps I now feel like a woman.

My mother has prepared a feast so leftovers can be taken on the road—roasted chicken, salted fish, squash and eggplant from the garden, a salad with plump tomatoes and garbanzos. We finish the meal with my favorite drink, a cup of warm chocolate and cinnamon that I savor as it slides down my throat with a sweet aftertaste.

I am excused to assist my mother with clearing the table and packing the basket. I am not privy to the conversation between my father and Francisco. Afterward, I am banished to bed with my sisters. Tonight I do not take the chance of sneaking to eavesdrop on the stairs, but I must see him again.

The twins sleep with the depth of a bottomless well. I toss and turn, my mind racing toward the kiss, his masculine aroma, his beard that I want to tease by burying my fingers in it, his arms encircling my body, creating warmth inside my most personal place. I have met the man who will marry me.

I cannot sleep. I wait and wait for the tinge of descent to take me farther away from my consciousness. It does not happen. I cannot sleep. I steal downstairs in my nightgown. Mi abuelo's rhythmic snoring fills the room. I tiptoe in my felt slippers toward the kitchen shutters, although I cannot see much in the total blackness. I open the latch with care so a noise will not awaken my grandfather. He continues emitting loud sounds as he turns in his chair. I pull on one side of the shutter to see if any light has appeared.

I open it with trepidation. I am grateful to my father that the hinges do not squeak. I expect it to be murky so I am surprised when a sliver of red greets me. It is almost morning and I have not slept.

I inhale as I make a decision. I will wish Francisco well on his trip and bring him the basket from the outside larder. With haste, I grab my mother's shawl near the door, wrap it over my head and shoulders and open the door with stealth, lifting the steel bar that keeps us safe.

I stand outside the door. The air is cooler and I am not dressed for a chill. Should I do this? My mother would say no. But I will not see my intended for months while he looks after his family and business in the north. My mother says it is one of my flaws that I am curious and ask too many questions.

While I contemplate, Francisco's wagon and mule emerge from the barn. I can see his silhouette high on the bench wearing a large hat. The donkey snorts and paws the ground. Francisco jerks the reins and calls to the recalcitrant animal.

I want to run and climb onto the seat next to him. I could leave with him now. I have been criticized in the past for my impulsiveness, my predilection to embrace what I want to do in the moment without regard to patience. I remember my nightclothes and my bare body underneath the soft, white cottons.

The wheels roll forward toward the exit gate. Once he is through the maw, I will not see him for a long time. What if he does not return? Maybe he will realize he does not love me or he will chastise himself for accepting such a small dowry. Or possibly he will be waylaid by bandits, evil men who take a life without regard. Robbers attacked him on his way here. Our people have a history of broken promises. Should I go?

Without hesitation I run through puddles to the wagon as Francisco is urging the donkey forward through the gate. The sun's light has lifted. I see the features of his face as I come closer.

Celendaria! What are you doing here?

I had to say goodbye. I lower my head. I could not allow you to leave without another kiss. I hoist myself onto the wagon wheel and lean forward, the shawl slipping to expose my shoulders.

Francisco inhales at the sight. You are more beautiful each time I see you.

Do not leave. I will long for you.

I must get an early start. I promised your father I would be gone by the time the family rose.

Francisco. I utter his name as I lean in toward his mouth. I am committing a sin. I know this as our lips reach each other. He kisses me with passion again. I will never tire of this, I think. And then in my impulsivity I pull myself up to the seat next to him. He shakes his head back and forth.

Celendaria, this is not right. Get down. I will be back. Someone will be out of the back door in moments to feed the chickens. It is time for me to go.

I grin at him in the daybreak. He is puzzled that I am not retreating. He is wearing leather gloves for his journey. I reach for his hand and remove his glove, dropping it to the bottom of the wagon. I move closer to him. I have something else in mind as my heart pounds in my chest. I reach for his hand, warm from its covering, and place it inside my nightgown on my chest.

Feel my heart beating, I say. I observe his stunned expression. I am afraid he will draw it away and think ill of me, leave me behind forever. What have I done? I am permeated with thoughts of their devil. What else could motivate me to do such a thing?

Instead, his fingers slide onto my breast. Strange pulses wing through my body. I am breathing hard as he explores the supple flesh. His fingers discover my nipple, working it like a baby suckling his mother. My head thrusts back in a newfound ecstasy. This cannot be happening to me. I am frightened and push his hand away. A lamp is lit in the living area that shines through the open shutter. Someone is awake!

I must leave, Francisco whispers to me. Go. I will be back in three months. He touches my nose as he reaches for the discarded glove.

Do you have the basket? I ask, climbing down.

Yes, I loaded it earlier. Now go. I will think of you every day. He pulls out of our yard, only stopping to close the gate.

I grab some seeds and call to the chickens. The back door opens and my mother stands watching me. What are you doing up so early? I can hear suspicion in her voice.

I could not sleep so I started chores.

The twins feed the chickens in the morning.

Oh.

I drop the rest of the feed to rush by my mother, leaving her shawl on the hook.

CHAPTER EIGHT

CLARA

1 de octubre 1655
Santa Oficina de la Inquisición

I am much older than when I came to this unspeakable place. I have lost some of my teeth but it does not matter. I eat little. I have not tracked my days as other prisoners do. It makes no difference. I do not understand why God has not taken me. I would be free in my spirit. I have been a good person, raised a family, and obeyed the laws that I was taught from my aunt, ones my parents believed before me and theirs before them.

Sadness bleeds into every part of me. It is the only emotion I feel. I have not been called to the inquisitors in a long time. Maybe they have disregard for an old woman obscured in the bowels of their jail.

Nor have I seen or heard from my family. Is it because they have been restricted or am I forgotten?

I am bored and sleep long hours. In my dream state I visit the faces of my family, Shabbat dinners where we glowed in the candlelight, the soft prayers we uttered together. My grandchildren must be grown.

Celendaria may be married with children, or maybe my husband has passed. I remain ignorant inside these walls. I cannot participate in life. I live in the Church's limbo—not of this world or the next.

My attention is drawn to tapping from my neighbor, the one who is removed some evenings to be with her guard. She has labored with a sewing needle to make a hole through the adobe bricks. It is large enough now that we can put our mouths over it to speak and listen when our ears are pressed against it.

I approach it with caution. It could always be an ambush. Maybe she has lost favor with her jailer. It is disguised on her side by her bedcovers. She lies down on her side to bring me news. On my wall, it is near the bucket where I leave waste. It is rarely emptied and smells. To hide the hole from detection, I have stuffed it with scraps from the bottom of my sanbenito, tinged with the dirt from the floor.

Lips appear in the hole as I bend down to put my ear to it, pushing my bucket and its stench away with my foot. Clara, I have news, says Luisa.

What can you tell me that I do not already know?

This will surprise you. Forces are gathering to release you.

What? This is not possible. My family no longer has the means for this venture. I have lost all hope. I am here to die, never to feel the fresh air of freedom. Why do you say this?

I have secrets obtained in many ways.

I do not want to think of your illicit ways. What do you know?

I stand for a moment from my crouch, my legs stiff with age. My heart is skeptical because so many lies have been told. The skullduggery of this church and the civil authorities who mete out their punishment cannot be trusted.

Clara, listen to me. Wash yourself when they bring a bucket of water. Money has been found to bribe an inquisitor! You have a benefactor.

I place my lips to the cavity. Who is it? I think to myself, She has lost her mind. Many do in here. I hear their cries day and night. Few are ever released except to watch their feet burn. I ask, Who would pay for my release after so much time has passed?

I do not know, but the bribe has reached one of your tormentors willing to relent.

I am stunned. I tell her, It is not plausible. The inquisitors are incorruptible.

Ha! She says into the abyss. Clean yourself. Pick the lice from your hair. They are coming for you.

And then she is gone.

I stuff the hole with rags again. I have had so many false hopes, especially in the beginning. How can this be possible? Where did the money, or maybe goods, come from?

I lie down to think about the likelihood it could be true. Impossible. The Church is a monolith, a mountain of secrecy and rules. Without regard, I begin to pull the nasty creatures living on my scalp through my tangled hair, crushing them between my fingernails with satisfaction.

CHAPTER NINE

CELENDARIA

9 de noviembre 1655

We celebrated Rosh Hashanah on the first of October, a Friday night, which we saw as a good omen. Of course, we could not openly celebrate the Festival of Trumpets with too much display, but we prayed together. On the tenth day of October, we met in the woods outside of town with other families for Yom Kippur, the Day of Atonement. We began with a prayer for the safe return of my grandmother. I have never prayed with so much ardent enthusiasm. The only other thing I can think of is Francisco's return.

Activity in our home accelerates with the anticipation that mi abuela might be discharged. It is the first hope of her release we have had in many years. My curiosity leads me to meddle more than usual.

My mother has warned us we must carry on our routine and appear normal. The twins study in the attic with grandfather most days. Even when his hips bother him, he climbs the ladder. Yael and Yonah are maturing and learning our history. Soon they will be able to recite our journey as I have been taught, starting with the expulsion in 1492, a scar we carry with us. I cannot imagine the pain and suffering of my ancestors leaving a home that they knew for so long to begin again in Portugal. They had to pay King John II eight cruzados to allow them passage. He thought the Spanish made a large error in banishing us. He said they lost the most accomplished and learned in their society. After all, our skills to forge muskets and textiles were desirable. Ah, well.

Would it have made a difference if we went another way in the Diaspora? My grandfather has explained our choices. Would anything have saved us from the Inquisition?

In my lessons, I learned that as soon as the Edict of Expulsion was nailed to the church doors in Spain, the Sultan Bayezid II of the Ottoman Empire sent ships for our compatriots to join him. He mocked the Spanish monarchs' lack of wisdom by stating they made their land poor and his rich. More than 150,000 Sephardim followed the sultan by settling in the wealthier cities of Istanbul, Salonika and Sarajevo. But, alas, we did not displace ourselves as some of our neighbors begged us to do, to join them on the Golden Horn waterway in the Bosporus Strait. Known for the sun's golden light that blushed the estuary, it was romanticized by poets. We chose Portugal, only to be banished five years later, just as our people were settling in to their new lives. King Manuel obeyed the Spanish queen and expelled the Jews and Moors once again so he could marry her daughter, the Princess Isabella.

My mother urges us to attend Mass more often than in the past so we appear devout to our neighbors. We approach all that we do with caution, lighting the Sabbath candles with apprehension, double-checking the lock on the shutters.

I think of Francisco and our brief parting with the anticipation I will be with him in a few months. He has written me a letter that arrived in a circuitous route through my father's tradesmen. Wrinkled and stained as though it had been stuffed into many bags, in the missive Francisco asks me to wait for him. It is my only option. I have strong feelings for him. Perhaps I am in love. He has not expressed this sentiment to me, but I long to hear those words.

I prompt my parents with questions about when mi abuela will come home. They shrug, as if to say, we do not know what the Church desires. But I have learned from visiting my Aunt Maria that Oliva's husband, Berto, has made arrangements to pay a large fee to a certain Inquisitor to absolve his wife of guilt. We know her lie is true. We are all Judaizers. We take great risks to pray in our own unorthodox way without a Torah. All were confiscated and burned in Spain. This caused agony that, although not a physical form of torture that the inquisitors favored, it embedded itself in our minds. We believe if God had a body, it would be our Torah.

But when will it happen? I ask Tia Maria. How much did he pay?

No one knows. Please do not tell anyone what I have disclosed.

Is she in good health?

We will know that when we see her. Most released from that palace of evil are not as they entered.

So I spend my days as I have done in the past, pretending all is the same, knowing it is not. Tension fills the air. We jump at every knock. My father and brothers proceed with the textile business, although the silkworms have died of a disease from eating contaminated Mulberry leaves. It is a source of discussion and regret. My father declares he will not start again.

261

We receive a visit from Berto one evening. We have not seen Oliva since her shocking confession that almost destroyed our family. I answer the door to allow him entrance. His expression is one of sad anger when he joins my parents and brothers at the table. I do not want to be sent upstairs like the twins so I stay busy scrubbing a pot in a tub of water. I am positioned to hear what is said.

I have bad news, says Berto with a groan. I have made all the payments requested for the release but Inquisitor Adolfo Mañzoca has changed his mind. What I have negotiated and paid is not acceptable.

What?! My father blows his words out like the geyser I once saw spurting toward the sky at a hot springs we visited to aid my grandfather's aching bones. The church cannot do this! Those inquisitors will burn in their own hell. If only I could put them in the dungeon to experience the pain they have inflicted on my family. And they do all this in the name of their hanging one—a Jew!

My father is rightly furious, but my mother manages to soothe him momentarily by stroking his arm. Esteban, Esteban, calm yourself. You are creating more heresy. Someone will hear you and we will all be arrested.

She may be right. Our neighbor, a weasel-like man with the humped shoulders of a black crow, sits outside most days on a carved chair, rocking to and fro, smoking a pipe. His countenance when I see him portrays mistrust, his eyes squinting into the sun, mustache and beard twitching. He lives in a household of women: his widowed mother, his wordless wife and five daughters. No wonder he spends his days outside. I am afraid of him and his family of harridans. Anyone can hurt us in our vulnerability.

I have never heard my father express rage in this manner. My father stands, tipping over the chair. Aruh picks it up. My father says, This is the end. No more.

Yes, I understand your frustration, says Berto. I have made the donation in a most devout manner. I cannot say who I have found to be the emissary, but they are sympathetic to our plight. Alas, the answer is no. He wants more. I have come to tell you this because I do not have more to give. My family must also be provided for.

My father, still angry, paces around us to ask Berto, How much did you pay?

Berto hesitates. I gave a large sum of money, a goat, and an offer to provide bricks to build a new home for the inquisitor.

And he refused? My father is surprised.

Yes. I have nothing else.

I know we too are drained of resources, especially with the silkworms' demise. I turn to look at Berto, a man of confidence and esteem. His face lacks its usual robust color and appears more as grey sky, jowls hanging with distress and age. I have sympathy for him that his wife has caused him so much grief. He is not a bad person, just rich. Or he was. Besides, he loves her.

My wife is distraught and consumed with guilt, Berto says, so much so that she cannot perform her wifely duties. I would like to have Oliva back the way she was—cooking, cleaning and caring for the children.

Berto does not have to explain wifely duties. Now that I know— and look forward to—what transpires in the marital bed, I am clear about what he means.

My father says, Aruh and León travel north tomorrow toward San Miguel to trade. We have work to do. He dismisses the group and retires, his feet dragging up the stairs. Buenas noches, he calls back to us.

It is an unsatisfactory ending to our evening. My parents' slouched spines declare another disappointment. I dry the pot I washed and place it on a hook above the hearth.

CHAPTER TEN

CELENDARIA

20 de diciembre 1655

León and Aruh return from their trip a week later with extraordinary news. They share it with us, their wives and children at a dinner at León's home on Shabbat.

I like my Aunt Clodovea very much. An excellent cook and a reader, she often wears glasses on her nose. Her family fled to Mexico via Veracruz from the islands near Florida, a Spanish stronghold. We sit at their table in anticipation after prayers and our meal, a leg of lamb stew with garbanzos and greens, the glow of candles illuminating faces. The children have wandered to sleeping places on pillows around the room. I look at their sweet faces, some dozing. I think about my unborn babies.

León speaks first. Our travel went well. We reached San Miguel with ease.

Did you find Señor Riboso's cattle ranch? My father interrupts, ever worried about his goods. His daughter is marrying soon and they made a request for textiles, lace and ribbons.

Yes, Padre, answers León. We delivered all the orders. I have coins in my leather pouch and bottles of wine in the cellar. He pauses as a few of us exclaim at their good fortune. On the way out of town on the River of Silver road, we avoided Puebla and Rio Frio through the mountains because of bandits. We headed where the desert blooms toward the south until we were stopped.

My mother's hand flutters to her mouth. The other women release small gasps. I know the story has to turn out well because my brothers are here.

A man on a horse wearing a black hat galloped next to us, a bandanna covering his face. I admit we both felt fear that we were to be robbed. I noticed a knife strapped to his leg and reached between the wooden seats for mine.

Halt, the stranger said, León continues. I knew we could not escape on a wagon with a mule so I slowed to a steady pace. It was a day of clouds and intermittent rain and I was anxious to continue our journey.

Where are you going? The stranger asked us.

Ciudad de México. Are you hindering our passage? We are tradesmen with little to share, I lied. I was relieved we had taken the time to wrap the wine well and hide it underneath the wagon in blankets.

Then, an amazing thing happened. He pulled down the rag covering his face and it was Francisco!

My Francisco? I ask, incredulous.

Exactly. The man who intends to marry you escorted us through the roughest part of the mountains. He knows them well. He was on his way to make contact with mestizos who are grinding beans for the chocolate he hopes to sell.

I am astounded and thrilled with pleasure that Francisco was still going to be my husband. I did not expect this affirmation. I smile with joy.

But, that is not the whole story, says Aruh. We told him of our grandmother's recent plight when we stopped to build a small fire and share a pot of coffee.

What else did Francisco say? My father leans forward, eager to know more.

Aruh continues. We told him of Berto's bribe being rejected and that no one had any more money to contribute. He said he might have a solution.

What? What did he say? My grandfather has perked up with great interest.

Aruh says, His brothers caught a man who was wanted by the Church.

So?

There is a big bounty on his head, more than all the other rewards Francisco's father and brothers have ever collected for one man. We followed him to a nunnery where his family was waiting for him in an annex nearby.

I feel sad hearing about people entrapped in the snare of the church, never to be free, although I know some are wicked. I do not understand how this information can serve us. Neither do my father or grandfather, who pepper him with questions.

What happened? Who was he? Do we know him? Their questions are incessant.

My mother sits in silence probably thinking this was another hoax, a fool's errand.

León picks up the story. The fugitive is wanted by the Church and they are willing to pay a large fee to have him returned.

What did he do? I ask. I feel sorry for this trapped soul.

I do not know the whole story, but when Francisco's brothers found him, he was working and tending animals for a rich ranchero. The Church says he is a renegade, an evil one who must be purged. They have been hunting for him many months.

Where is he now? My mother as well as the rest of us are enraptured by this narrative. She says, It is rare for the Church to pursue the clergy unless they have done something egregious.

He and his family are locked up in a jail waiting to be transported to the city.

Aha! Can you guess who the man is? Aruh asks.

We all look around the table. How could any of us know his identity? Perplexed faces do not utter a sound. I cannot imagine a priest from Ciudad de México. Someone we know? I am incredulous as are my parents.

Father Lopez? We say in unison.

And then my heart sinks to my stomach. He was with Mariel and their child. My friend is in danger.

León says, Yes! We said we knew of him and his wife.

They are caught? I ask.

Yes. Francisco told us they were to be turned in to the authorities.

No! More people for their torturous dungeons. What about Mariel and the baby? I ask.

Francisco said they are conversos and the baby has been circumcised.

They are doomed, I think to myself. I have gone from great joy about my intended to the depths of sorrow learning about my friend, all while sitting in the same chair where I had my dinner. How could my brothers have brought such sadness?

My mother, a close friend of Señora Behar, Mariel's mother, begins to weep.

There is more, says Aruh when he sees my mother's tears.

I cannot imagine how much worse it could be.

Francisco says that his brothers have collected the ransom in San Miguel from the Inquisition authorities where the priest and his family are being held at the jail. The inquisitor's house is across the street from the prison. Another fee is involved to bring them to Ciudad de México.

We are all crestfallen. Another sad termination. I wanted Mariel to survive in peace, to raise the child with love, to be with the man she desires. I am a romantic who likes happy endings, but there are so few.

Padre, says Aruh. He lays a leather pouch on the table. This is the money for the merchandise. I brought the wine earlier. Then he stands to dig inside his shirt. A leather string reveals another small bag that he places on the table. We all stare at the cowhide purses, soiled with sweat and stains.

My father speaks. We cannot accept money or conduct business on the Sabbath. Remove them.

I can tell he is annoyed at this infraction. We have to break so many rules to survive, but the Sabbath is sacred. Sometimes we have to go to the market on a Saturday, but it is rare. It satisfies the nosy neighbor that we are not doing anything spurious like praying and reading.

Padre, listen. You do not have to touch them. He points to the one he took from his shirt. This one has gold coins! Francisco gave me his share of the reward to release our grandmother. He empties the coins onto the linen tablecloth.

Silently, gold eyes wink at us. I do not know what they are worth but I have never seen so many. They gleam in the diffused light. I am stunned. Francisco gave my brothers gold coins to release our beloved? I am elated and then crash like a sizzling pot to the floor. What about Mariel, my dear friend and her baby?

No one says anything. We stare at the table that holds the possibility of release.

Finally, my grandfather asks, How do you know this will be enough to release her this time? We have been tricked before. When you share wealth with the Church, they ask for more. It has happened to us. They have soaked us dry as a desert gully. We are waterless sponges.

He cannot look at us and closes his eyes. Prayer or sleep?

León, who has been chewing his bottom lip in contemplation, says, Berto knows the proper person. It a cousin related to the inquisitor who wants to retire in Spain and needs more money. His concubine is ill and the monarchy has offered him many accolades to return. He swears he will not change his mind to release our abuela if we meet his needs.

My father interrupts, Do we know what he wants?

Yes, this will satisfy him. I will contact Berto on Sunday. In the meantime, these will be hidden in a safe place inside our wall, says León.

As my family pushes chairs back from the table and the women begin to clear the dishes, I ask in a small voice, What about Mariel and the baby?

León says, Do not worry, little sister. A plan of escape has been devised by Francisco. They are to escape with his brothers who are making the move north to Nuevo León near the Rio Grande.

Captain Luis de Carvajal, a Portuguese Jew, put down roots in the area. Many of our kind are settling in an area hospitable to us, an enclave of conversos who feel safer in the Southwest territories than here, even though the Spanish have laid claim to all the area north of here. What they control is vast. They have sent their priests to search for silver and convert the natives.

Has this happened yet? Do Señoras Lopez and Behar know?

No. There is great secrecy. Do not say a word until we can collect our abuela.

CHAPTER ELEVEN

CELENDARIA

19 de diciembre 1655

It has been confirmed that we are going to leave once mi abuela is free. I am not privy to all the details of her release, but it is to take place on 24 de diciembre to demonstrate the goodness of the Church. I dream about the possibility of wrapping my arms around her frail body and kissing her papery cheeks. An epistle with an official seal arrived from the Office of the Inquisition instructing my grandfather to sign papers to release her on that day. My father will accompany him with our mule and wagon. The rest of us will wait at home.

Francisco and I are to be married in the courtyard of a merchant's home who buys my father's goods. It will take place on 6 *de enero*, a fortuitous date because it is a Leap Year and Three Kings Day. His hacienda on the outskirts of town will hold a small celebration on Día de Los Santos Reyes, the holiday that celebrates the three wise men. My father says many will be busy exchanging gifts on this day because it is the conclusion of the Christmas celebration, so we will not be noticed.

My mother directs the plans for my wedding. Seamstresses at my father's factory are sewing my long-sleeved dress of white cotton with many colored flowers embroidered across the neck. I have been measured and fitted, but with little time, they are rushing to finish. Although there is no rabbi to marry us, we try to stay as close to tradition as possible.

We are cloaked in secrecy. No one can know our plans for the wedding, mi abuela's release or our leaving. We scurry like rats building an underground nest to gather supplies for our journey as we plan the abandonment of our dwellings and my father's business. Much of the inventory has been sent north to Francisco's brothers with the intention of creating a business in our new territory. Other families of our persuasion have settled near Monterrey, a thriving community I am told, and far enough away from the offices of the Inquisition to be ignored. At least for a while.

All my aunts and their families will make the migration with us save Oliva. She and Berto will stay as devout members of the Church. I do not know where we will live, but I intend to be in a dwelling alone with Francisco. I want to feel like a married woman.

Discussion centers about the Indians and whether they will let us live in peace. Many have horses that have been stolen from the Spaniards, but over five hundred perished in a smallpox outbreak in 1647 near Monterrey while the Spanish shepherds were killed in a raid. They are unpredictable. Complete safety is not available to us.

CHAPTER TWELVE

CLARA

24 de diciembre 1655
Santa Oficina de la Inquisición

I feel a shift in the air as we approach Christmas Day to celebrate their Savior. The last few weeks I have been given smoked meat to eat, pieces of fruit and chocolate to drink. With the first cup of the delicious beverage, I asked why I was chosen for this special treat. The jailer laughed and said, Because the inquisitor likes you. Ja! I devoured all of it, even though I know the food does not follow our kashrut laws. I do not believe the rumor I will be released. Perhaps they are fattening me up to kill me. I am told fat makes the fires burn with crackling noises like the pigs they roast.

I sit on a small stool, a new addition to my confinement, and wait for nothing. I pass the time going over my children and grandchildren's births, what I was doing that day, how they looked as red, wrinkled newborns. I dismiss the ones who did not survive because it makes me gloomy. I address God directly about what I am supposed to learn in this terrible place, whether my soul will continue for eternity, and ask blessings for my family.

Without warning, the jailer opens my cell. It is late afternoon because my breakfast of bread and water appeared hours ago.

Come, he says, holding the cell door open for me. What? No chains? With caution, I step outside and look down the dank hall. My neighbor's arms hang through the bars. I told you, I told you! she shouts to me. I shuffle away in torn slippers, my filthy sanbenito swallowing my thin frame.

Walk, he says, so I do, one foot in front of the other, shuffling, not knowing what to expect. Maybe it is another inquiry about my Judaizing. Time has passed since I was last brought before the tribunal. I do not remember all that I said. The inquisitor's job is to trick me by reading back what I said in the past after I have responded to a question. I am an old, confused woman, I will plead. It will not make a difference. The flames that lap at my feet will not know the distinction.

My gait is one of dread. Whatever is waiting for me, it cannot be pleasant. The voice that speaks to me says it will be a relief to die, to be with God, to leave the physicality of this earth. My husband taught me many prayers. Why should a learned man of God's ways suffer too? I will repeat the Shema, my eyes toward heaven asking why.

Sit here, the jailer says to me, pointing to a wooden bench in the hall.

It is not the route we have taken before to the inquisitor's chambers. No matter. I feel calm. My hands push my disgusting hair away from my face. Grey, uncombed, permeated with filth, I think of how unsoiled I used to be emerging from the cool waters of the mikvah on Shabbat.

My keeper exits through a doorway. I hear voices but I do not understand what they are saying. My hands rest on my bony knees.

Maybe this will be over soon. How many others sat here wishing the same thing? I do not comprehend man's cruelty to man or how it is interpreted that Christ, a Jew, would want this fate for his people. Did he not teach tolerance? I do not understand the rigid orthodoxy of a religious organization that murders people. I recognize love and the feelings I have for my family. I decide to rehearse a final speech for the evil men who condemn me.

Señores, I am ready to die and leave your ghastly, incomprehensible jail. I have done nothing wrong, but history will judge you, your lethal ways, your lack of empathy, the wicked torture you inflict on innocents. God will judge you not as righteous men but as sinful, immoral criminals who usurped the teachings of the Church. I am ready to die.

To make it more dramatic I will lie down on the floor. They will have to carry my sack of bones to the scaffolding. Let the public see how they treat an old woman. Let them—

Stand up, I am commanded. We are going now, the jailer says at my side.

I rise with resolution. His arm points the way down a corridor. At the end of the corridor, we climb steps. I shift from one leg to another. He prods me from behind saying, I do not have all day to finish with you.

Ah, so I am going to the fires. I ask in newfound boldness, How often do they set the fires for the Christ child's birthday? He does not respond. I am nothing.

We pass through an entry into a large hallway. Guards open an elaborately carved wooden door and suddenly I am blinded by light. I thrust my arm across my eyes that begin to water in the assault of sunshine.

I cannot see, but I hear my jailer say, Your husband arrived earlier to sign your release papers. You are liberated.

I cannot believe what I am hearing. My senses lie. He pushes me farther outside the corner portal. I blink to clear my tears and grasp where I am. What have they done? It must be a mistake. I look around for a place to hide. Someone will look for me if I am not in my cell.

And, then, another surprise. Warm arms grasp me with fervor, limbs and torso enfolding me in a familiar aroma of vanilla as tears drip on my balding head. A shawl is swathed around my shoulders as my body collapses, knees crumpling beneath me toward the ground. Sturdy hands catch me and carry me to a cart where I am laid on soft, woven blankets, the perfume of familiar scents, cinnamon and thyme wafting with gentleness unknown to me. Who has rescued me in this dream? My senses are returning—I smell pleasant aromas, I hear familiar voices and then, shading my eyes, I have the vision of my husband next to me in this slow-moving wagon. Am I in Heaven? Has the Holy Father rescued me?

Clara, Clara, it is me, *tu esposo*. You are free! Speak to me. Tell me you are all right. Our son is here too. The rest of our family waits at home. Clara, do you hear me? It is Shabbat. You have been released on the Sabbath.

I hear the excitement in his voice. I am afraid to believe.

It is hard for me to comprehend all that has happened in moments. I open my mouth to speak but nothing emerges from the back of my throat. I gaze up to see my husband's wizened face, a hat shading his eyes. The smell of clean clothes wafts toward me. I reach for his hand. The warmth of his skin will let me know he is real, not an apparition. I close my eyes, drifting back to my cell, a mouse playing in the corner, as the wagon rocks me to sleep.

It is only for a short time. I am awakened with the wagon stopping, gates opening, the wagon moving forward again, shouts from the front of the wagon and the faces of Gabriela, my sweet Celendaria. I do not recognize, Yonah and Yael, so grown, and my grandsons, Aruh and León. Hands slip behind my back to lift me to a sitting position. I pull the shawl around me. I am embarrassed to be seen in this threadbare cloth, their sanbenito that stinks. I cover my lips with my aged hand to hide my toothless mouth.

Firm hands hoist me outside the wagon and carry me to what was once familiar through the back door of the home that I know. One I never thought to see again.

Inside, I am placed in a chair and given a drink of water. The clean, cool liquid slides down my throat. I can only sit and stare at the ones I love, tears flowing down my face. It will be the sweetest greeting of the Sabbath bride I have ever known.

BOOK THREE

CHAPTER ONE

CELENDARIA

5 de enero 1656

The evening before my betrothal I am required to cleanse myself in the mikvah. It is a sacred time called the *noche de novia*, the night of the sweetheart. I do not have the ritual costume worn for hundreds of years by the bride, but I follow the mitzvoth I am to perform at home—I light candles and separate dough to make a challah, the bread we braid to represent the twelve tribes of Israel. I cannot follow the custom of painting my hands with henna because it will draw the attention of the authorities.

My father and brothers have plotted our exit with military precision. To avoid having to be married in the church and endure more scrutiny, we will leave in a caravan of wagons for the north soon after an intimate wedding ceremony in a courtyard. My grandparents will travel in low chairs wrapped in blankets.

The chilled air this time of year requires layers of clothing and head coverings. My grandmother is not the same after her imprisonment. She remains quiet, eating small amounts of food and closing her eyes in prayer. If we were able to attend a synagogue, she would be treated as the holiest of the holies to have endured what she did. For now, her presence alone inspires us to thank God for her release, no matter what sacrifices have been made. She remains revered as our matriarch and the bravest of souls among us.

Mi abuela accompanies me to the mikvah with the other females in my family. She is a bit stronger since her release. We go in twos or threes to the cellar of a friend who has dug out a ritual bath in his basement and filled it from cisterns of rainwater. Orange blossoms that float on the water's surface make me swoon. I am cleansing myself for my husband, the man who will be with me into eternity.

All my aunts, save Oliva, sisters, grandmother and mother wait for me to go first while they sit on benches behind a drape. They repeat prayers with me as I climb down the stairs of the sacred pool to lower myself underwater, sinking until my head is covered, and hair floating on the cool surface. I do this three times, holding my breath, until I burst through the top, purified. I am cleansed.

The others follow two at a time until we are finished and dressed again, our heads wrapped in scarves. A basket appears with more sweet treats. My aunts have forgotten nothing. We keep the traditions alive. We leave in small groups knowing that we will see each other again soon.

On this last night of sharing a bed with my sisters, none of us sleep well. We are restless with anticipation about tomorrow's events. Yael and Yonah are birds feathering a nest, limbs twisting, bodies turning, hands touching.

I cannot sleep wondering about what it will be like to be with Francisco alone. Will he touch me first? Will I be afraid? A marital bed has been prepared at the hacienda where he, his father and brothers are staying. We are not to see each other before the ceremony. I have waited a long time for this adventure.

CHAPTER TWO

CELENDARIA

6 enero 1656

In preparation for the wedding, Yonah and Yael pass combs, brushes, ribbons back and forth, search under the bed for shoes, rub oil on their lips, pinch their cheeks and talk incessantly in their special language. I slip the white dress over my head. My hair, washed clean, is pinned high on my head with white roses added to the sides. My mother will prepare me soon to walk out to the courtyard that has been decorated with wildflowers for the ceremony.

The idea that my precious abuela will be a witness at my wedding seems a miracle to me of biblical proportions. So few are ever released. It is the only time I am grateful for the corruption of the Church and their inquisitors who accept bribes. They have been capricious with us many years as we sought her release, but now we will triumph. Not only will I be married in the tradition of our people, but we are also going to steal away in the night, far away from their wandering tortures that look for us in every cranny.

Our families have not had much time to prepare, but we have an escape. I have heard whispered plans of our exodus after the wedding, with arrangements made to disappear the night of Three Kings Day. It seems my marital bliss will be spent riding in a wagon, the dangerous plans put together by the men and my father's benefactor who has agreed to loan us not just his courtyard and rooms to sleep for a few hours, but also supplies and two horses. I can only think of Francisco and how my skin burns when he is near.

Francisco's brothers will lead the way to safety in Nuevo León near the Rio Grande and perhaps beyond. According to them, the Southwest territories hold hope for a displaced people, despite the Spanish being in charge and the pervasion of hostile Indians. My grandfather says that the people in Europe have a more equitable way of living and the colonies north of us will adopt the same philosophies. He acknowledges that he will not be here to see the changes, but believes with his heart that someday we will be safe to worship in public, our voices stretching to God in the Universe.

A goat will be roasted for the celebration at the hacienda, with other festive foods brought by my family. Only a few friends are invited, like the Behars. We do not want to draw attention to ourselves so my father, in his wisdom, picked this date: the Dia de Los Santos Reyes. It is a day that the Spanish revere by exchanging gifts. When I go to the well to fill jugs of water for our trip, well-dressed people stroll by our casita carrying packages to share. They have already left for the site with their families. My aunts Rosa and Maria have prepared a wedding cake shaped like a king's crown so as not to arouse suspicion. The Christians bake a small token inside to represent the baby Jesus, but we place a small ceramic tube inside to represent the mezuzah. It is odd to live in two worlds.

Today is a Thursday so we do not have to wait for sundown. Family members arrive at different times to share confections made from hazelnuts, almonds and candied fruits my mother and aunts have prepared. I finish dressing myself as the twins dance around me, glorious butterflies lighting on my hair, shoulders, dress. It feels magical to be preparing for the day I have anticipated for so long.

I walk downstairs and kiss my grandmother, who rests in my grandfather's rocking chair. Mi madre is sprinkling colored sugar on cookies and sweets she has baked in a small clay oven in the yard; an apron covers her velvet skirt.

Mama, I am ready.

She turns to examine her eldest daughter, eyes glistening with pride. Celendaria, you are beautiful as a bride. I have something for you.

She wipes her hands on the apron and with a swift motion presents a package.

I have had something fashioned for you of soft cow leather.

My hands shake as I untie the string and pull away a swath of white linen. Inside are white slippers that have been bleached to match my dress. They are crafted with the finest materials, the tiniest of stitches and embellished with small roses tooled into the leather.

Oh, Mama, they are exquisite.

She smiles at my pleasure. She asks, Is there anything I can share with you?

I want to ask about the wedding night, but I cannot form the words. Private thoughts about Francisco please me. Tonight we will be alone. I am afraid, but he is older and stronger, a good guide for a new bride.

Finally, I gather courage. Mama, I am fearful of what will transpire tonight in the marital bed.

Mi hija, it is a pleasurable time to be with your spouse. You will be happy. Drink wine after the signing of the ketubah, the marriage contract that binds you to each other and the Jewish people. After that, you are in God's hands. Know that we believe in procreation as the purpose of the act, but should you feel satisfaction or gratification, it is God's will.

I think back to this morning and our departure. Our household is permeated with activity. Under the guise of a celebration, our family is taking leave of Ciudad de México. We cannot bring too many belongings that will alert a neighbor or passerby. Our furniture is to be abandoned except for a chest filled with precious items. My father and brothers left in darkness in anticipation of the longer journey after the ceremony, and stocked an extra wagon with textiles and supplies. They expect to pursue business in a new area.

We will dress in layers for the chilly air, place belongings in baskets and wrap my grandfather's precious books from the attic in cloth and rope for most to be hidden under the seat of the wagon. Only a few have been gifted to friends. Some are too cautious to have them in their home. A few must be abandoned in the attic, secreted so that a cursory look will not reveal them. Mi abuelo cannot burn them even if they might cause the authorities to look for us again. I assist him as he dresses with care, fingers bent with age, binding some of his precious tomes to his torso with strips of cotton under his clothes. He covers himself with shirts and a large serape.

A disagreement erupts between my parents when my mother insists she needs space for her candlesticks made of clay, spices packed in small bags, and other valuables.

It is not possible to move all that we own! shouts my father. Many have escaped with only the clothing they wear, Gabriela.

My mother begins to sniffle. How am I to prepare food without flavor?

Francisco's brother Manuel quickly resolves the issue. He and their brother Duarte have arrived early to take my grandparents and me in a wagon pulled by two massive horses. Only the Spanish are allowed to have horses so I am surprised. I want to know where they came from, but I know better than to ask. The natives north of us steal them from settlers to ride the plains. With bondsmen, it is not prudent to ask the origins of anything.

Do not worry, Gabriela, Manuel tells her. They will be placed with care under our wagon seat and we will protect them with our lives.

His pledge seems dramatic to me, but I like Manuel. He has a strong demeanor without being threatening. He and Duarte wear knives strapped to their legs and sport handheld firearms hidden somewhere in their belongings. Born into rougher stock, they lack some of the polite refrains, customs and manners we use. The brothers have been motherless for a long time.

Suddenly a terrible apprehension courses through me. What if we are attacked by Indians? Not only could they steal everything, they might scalp us or take me and my sisters as slaves to make up for the injustices they have suffered at the hands of the Spaniards and criollos. Or what if someone from the authorities stops us?

While the men are occupied with feeding the horses and loading the wagons in the yard, I approach mi madre with a quivering chin to ask heartfelt questions.

Is it necessary for everyone to leave? Where will we stay?

My mother places her hands on my shoulders, peering into my eyes. Celendaria, it is imperative that we leave as our ancestors did before us. We cannot trust the capricious nature of the Church any longer. They have stolen almost all that is precious to us. Perhaps they think if they arrest another of our family we will find more money for their illegal ransoms. It is our duty to pass on our ways to future generations, no matter the price. She looks down, her eyes sad before she begins again. We must be resilient and survive as our forefathers did when they were driven from our ancient lands in Israel, Spain, Portugal, Brazil and Peru. Her eyes fill with tears. She turns away to hide her face in a handkerchief.

Mama, tell me. What is it?

With a trembling lip she says, I have loved the comfort of my home. It is all I have known. Our next circumstances might not offer extra rooms for sleeping, a hearth for cooking and rugs underneath our feet.

I put my arms around her. I feel elation and sadness at the same time. We cannot look back when we pull away. We can only march toward the joy of the wedding. I say, Please, Mama, do not cry on the day of my ceremony.

She wipes her eyes and gives me a cheerless smile.

I am torn between anxiety, anguish and the pleasure that awaits me tonight.

Mama, Why do they chase us? What have we done besides not believe in their messiah?

Dear one, now is not the time for this discussion. I will tell you one word to remember that explains our treatment over the centuries. She leans close to my ear and whispers, Jealousy.

The word puzzles me because I know jealousy only as the unrequited longing in some of our ancient Portuguese songs—a man loves a woman who loves another, or a woman loves a man who desires someone else. I have never considered that the sufferings of our people occur from others wanting what we have. It seems profound at this juncture in our history.

Francisco's brother Duarte approaches me.

Nothing will happen, he tells me. We will protect you from danger on our passage. We have a trail mapped out with safe houses along the way. The territory we travel belongs to us. Do not fret, little sister. Come, assist us in gathering your grandparents and sisters to go to the hacienda. This is a time of joyfulness. Our father waits to bless the first bride in our family. I am sorry our mother cannot see your beauty. She would have appreciated your tranquil manner.

I blush. Thank you, I murmur.

In a short time, their wagon is loaded with valuables, sweet cakes, small baskets of fruit and a hamper of our personal items. I have covered my wedding dress with a few skirts and blouses, placing a new long cape of dark velvet over me, a clasp at the neck. My grandparents are loaded into the back with my sisters while I sit between the men in the front. As we exit through the back gate I glance behind at our door, the empty chicken coop, my mother's vegetable garden, the barn.

I will not see this again. A lone tear slides down my cheek that I wipe away with the back of my hand. A strong morning sun spreads warmth through my shoulders, erasing my apprehension with hope.

We roll slowly to the road, the clopping of the horse's hooves noisier than our mule, past our neighbor holding watch in front of his house, pipe in his hand.

He waves and calls out, Where do you go on Día de los Santos Reyes?

I yell back, To church, my friend, to church!

CHAPTER THREE

CELENDARIA

6 de enero 1656

Commotion greets us at the hacienda of Señor Molina. A man of distinguished heritage whose family dates back to the Portugal expulsion in 1497, he has entertained great success in Nueva España through trade. My father has had many business dealings with him and his contacts throughout the ports of Mexico. It is rumored he owns a portion of the silver mines in the mountain of Potosí, but his ownership remains concealed.

Servants ready the fiesta by sweeping the courtyard, a grand expanse inside the walls with a well, a pit for roasting the goat, tables for serving and wooden chairs decorated with handcrafted flowers from paper and fabric.

As my grandparents and I are helped out of the wagon, I see the corner where the ceremony will take place. My heart leaps at the sight of four poles in the ground covered with a white cloth draped across the top. The chuppah has symbolized the marital chamber throughout time. At this moment, I feel anxious about what will take place after the ceremony this afternoon.

The sun has moved higher in the sky, sending burnished warmth through me. After my grandparents have settled in their room, I am guided to mine. Ours. I remove some of my layers and place them across a carved trunk. The bed is covered in white sheets and blankets. The carved headboard depicts a sleeping Mexican and an outsized cactus, its arms reaching toward the sky. A large, tin mirror that fills part of a wall has been embellished with small, hand-cut animals and six-petal flowers. I stare at my reflection. I am a woman who is to be married today. It is also a day of exile that will take my family and me to a new home. I try not to think of how powerless I am to create change except in my heart. Instead, I lie down on the bed to pray for guidance, dozing in His glory.

Before long I hear the clanking of wagons, a donkey's bray, shouts of joy, greetings of welcome and the squeals of my sisters. I rush to open the shutter and peek out the window. The courtyard has been transformed into a glorious site. The wagons and animals are being moved to a barn while campesinos on ladders string lanterns and decorations. Someone has covered the poles of the chuppah with vines of a flowering plant. Señora Molina and servants spread cloths across the tables while her children and my nieces and nephews play underneath them.

I count noses to make sure all have arrived, excluding Francisco who remains out of sight. Oliva and Berto were invited but declined. Just as well. They would never agree to this expedition. I am told it will take a week because we must stop often for the elderly. I see Francisco's father and his brothers in conversation with my father and brothers drinking from small clay cups, the Behars resting on a bench in the shade against a wall, my sisters examining the tables spread with sweets, and my mother bustling toward my door.

Celendaria, Let me in! she calls, knocking with excitement. I open the door and she hugs me with exuberance even though she last saw me that morning.

We are all here! My mother is ecstatic that we have all arrived after a short trip of two hours. She points through the window to a small, draped table near the chuppah. It is time to be the bride, my loved one. Your grandfather has prepared everything. You are beautiful. You are joining the family of your husband.

But, Mama, I am afraid. I gulp for air because I cannot breathe. My knees buckle and my mother holds me under the arms so I do not collapse. We sit on the bed. She turns me to her, holding my face in her warm hands.

Mi hija, this is not the time for fear but joy. Your whole family is coming with you to a new place. You will not be alone, thanks to the kind heart of Francisco's family and others who have contributed to our passage. Come, look at your reflection. She guides me to the mirror and I see a young innocent and my mother standing next to me. She smiles and I return one from my lips. She reaches up to position the white roses in my hair.

Sit, she says.

I obey, and she kneels at my feet, placing the handsome white slippers on my feet. I stare at them. I rise, squishing my toes to the front. I am ready. We close our eyes, hold hands and repeat the Shema together, the watchwords of our faith.

A bell rings to let people know it is time to gather. The sun has dropped in the sky to a hazy, afternoon light. My sisters fill up the window with good cheer, beckoning me outside.

Come and be a bride, Celendaria, come! Grandfather is waiting for you. I step over the threshold knowing that when I return I will be a married woman. Yael and Yonah prance with delight to lead the way. They have been my most annoying and loving siblings. I hug them when we stand before the table next to the chuppah. My parents stand next to me with my precious abuela, and my abuelo is behind the table with a quill and pot of ink. He wears a black skullcap or *kipá*, as are the other men, to symbolize we are in a sacred space before God.

Francisco suddenly emerges from a door to take his place next to me. He is handsome in a dark jacket and pants with a white shirt underneath. He, too, has a small woven kipá on the back of his head. Our eyes meet and I can tell he is pleased with what he sees. I am glad not to have to wear a veil, as the Church requires. We reach for each other's hands without a word. Others gather around us.

My grandfather places his glasses on his nose and in a sonorous voice, starts the ceremony with the signing of the ketubah written on parchment paper. He is not a rabbi, but he is the best we have. He says, This document represents the contract between Celendaria Mendoza Crespin and Francisco de Cordova that commands them to keep faith in God and a commitment to the Jewish people. Do you agree?

We both say, Yes.

Then the two witnesses may sign the ketubah.

Our host, Señor Molina, goes first, dipping the pen into ink to sign the certificate. His handwriting is slow and labored so I glance around to see the faces of those we love. I cannot find Francisco's brothers until I glance farther away to the entrance and see them standing guard near the massive wooden doors with iron fittings.

Then it is Señor Behar's turn. His signature flows. My grandfather blots the names with a piece of felt, holding it up for all to see. The marriage deed is complete.

Francisco exits with his father to another part of the courtyard after he squeezes my hand. My parents escort me back to our room. My mother presents me with a bouquet of wildflowers that my sisters picked in the area, an assortment of red, purple, yellow and white, with trailing, colored ribbons. My father puts his hands on my shoulders and tells me I have been a good daughter, one who has remained true to her family and faith. The bell chimes again and they put their arms through mine to guide me to the chuppah where my brothers and Francisco's brothers hold the four poles, raising them toward the sky, their religious shawls draped across the top. Francisco waits for me as he stands next to his father. We respect the traditions of our ancestors across oceans and cultures, even if some have been lost to us.

My grandfather explains that our circumstances call for the cancellation of a weeklong ceremony called the Shevah Brachot, where relatives arrive at our home with food and drink. It is not possible. Who knows where we will live?

He reads from one of his holy books in halting Hebrew: *Barukh atah Adonai Eloheinu . . .* Blessed are You, Adonai our God, sovereign of the Universe, who has created everything for your glory. Then he repeats traditional phrases in Ladino, the language of our ancestors: *Naciemiento casamiento y mortaja, del cielo baja.* I know this to mean Birth, wedding and shrouds come down from heaven. And another: *La limpieza es juno a la rikeza,* which my grandfather taught me has caused jealousy among our enemies. Cleanliness is next to wealth.

Tradition dictates that the bride accepts a token from the groom. Francisco reaches into a leather pouch attached to his belt and drops a gold coin into my palm.

Does the groom agree to the acquisition? Mi abuelo asks.

Yes, says Francisco, his voice catching.

With the consecration of these two actions, you are married.

Francisco turns to me and kisses me in front of all our family and friends. When we pull apart, I see his eyes are smiling into mine. He grabs my hand so we can turn and face everyone. Music begins from a corner of the courtyard by musicians with wooden instruments and gut strings.

Let the fiesta begin! Francisco shouts, spinning me around.

Suddenly I am hungry with the smell of goat meat sizzling on a fire. Servants appear with large tubs of cooked beans, corn piled high, potatoes mashed with onions, green salads with garden tomatoes and my favorite, *arroz de bodas*, a Sephardic wedding recipe piled high on platters made with green grapes, nuts, scallions and mint.

Our traditions dictate a serving of fish for fecundity; however, it was too difficult to obtain. My mother has assured me that I will be most fruitful.

A crush of women surrounds me to admire my dress. The men gather around Señor Molina to taste the whiskey he has promised. The celebration has begun as dusk lowers her skirts on our fiesta. I am a married woman.

CHAPTER FOUR

CELENDARIA

7 de enero 1656

Jinging, dancing, feasting accompanied by the sounds of stringed instruments and familiar songs lasted many hours into the starry night. Fires were built to warm us as the temperature dropped. My grandparents were bundled off to bed. Francisco guided me toward our room. It was the first time I was to be alone with him without fear of being caught except for a stolen kiss.

When he pulls down the latch, I become nervous. Now what? I sit on the edge of the bed, watching and waiting. He would have to take the lead. I feel sure his brothers imparted more information than my mother. Or maybe he has experience. Will I appear as an incompetent fool?

A glow from candles illuminates the room in an eerie light. He places his kipá on the dresser below the mirror and begins unbuttoning his clothes. I stare as each piece falls to the floor until he is down to a clean, white scooped undershirt and short pants. He turns and lifts me to face him. A big man with broad shoulders, I am diminutive next to him. My lips tremble. He strokes my hair, releasing it from the pins and roses, combing his fingers through my dark tresses. His soothing hands pull my dress to expose my shoulders; he kisses them. I feel naked completely clothed. I remember my mother's words—your body is a temple prepared by God. I feel the sacredness in the moment. His forefinger tilts my chin toward him.

I love you, Celendaria. I will always take care of you. His throaty voice makes me swoon.

My eyes fill with tears. I have been in anticipation of this expression for a long time. In his generosity, he has married me with a small dowry, ransomed my grandmother with gold and accepted my entire family. I say a small inner prayer to thank God for this day.

His solid hands undress me, layer by layer, peeling my wedding costume until I, too, have abandoned most of my clothes on the floor. I do not speak while emotions rattle up and down my mind. Will I feel the passion of Mariel and her priest? Is there anything that we might do that is a sin? Will it hurt? What happens next? I am frozen, my knees stiff as pine boards laid out for tables.

Francisco places my hand in his and walks us to the mirror. I hang my head in shame.

Look at us, he says.

I lift my head to see our faces illuminated, our bodies still protected with under clothing. My undergarments have been embellished by my mother and grandmother with lace and tiny seed pearls, white ribbons woven through the holes in the fabric near my neck, armholes and legs. It is vanity to admit, but we look exquisite.

I notice a long scar on his left arm that I trace with my finger.

What is this from?

Time passes before he responds. It is from a knife.

How did it happen? The scar is angry and red and reaches from his shoulder to his elbow.

My sweet one, this is not the time for such discussions. Suffice to say I survived.

But what happened to the other man?

He was taken to jail.

My expression collapses in the mirror.

Celendaria, you will learn not to ask too many questions about our family business. It is dangerous, which is why I am transitioning to cacao and chocolate, something that will be in abundance in our home.

Oh.

He reaches for me, kissing my lips with his hungry mouth. My breaths increase to a faster pace. I reach up to touch the back of his hair, his neck, sliding my fingers to his back, mapping out the sinews of his muscles. Taut and firm, he enfolds me in his arms until I wonder if I will continue to breathe. Then he spins me around to look in the mirror again as I pant lightly, a dog after a quick chase. He places me in front of him, his arms holding me in place so that we both stare at our reflections. His face nuzzles into my hair that has been washed in orange blossoms.

I have never smelled anything so delicious, he tells me.

I feel satisfaction at all our preparations. His hands wander down my sides, my arms, my neck, stroking me gently.

And then a lightning rod streaks through my body as I watch him play over the fabric on top of my breasts. He glides by them until my nipples rise through the cotton. I feel as though my mind has left me. Now I understand what it is to live in this new ecstasy.

Franscisco leads me to the bed, pulling down the bedspread to fragrant sheets. He finishes undressing me under the covers and says over and over, You are the bride I dreamed of for so long. You are my bride.

I am in a dream, one where I can be awake to feel everything. His hands roam my body at will and with each passing stroke, I climb another hill until his fingers find me. I am familiar with this part.

We are damp with sweat but I cannot stop. Why should I? This is permitted. Something tugs at me and then I grasp what is happening. He pulls me under him and hoists himself above, his arms supporting his weight.

I feel pushing that seems blocked.

Celendaria, Open your eyes. Look at me. I can stop if I am hurting you. He kisses me again, nibbling my bottom lip with care.

I open my eyes to see his face in the shadow of light. Most of the candles have expired. The planes of his face appear as if sculpted from stone. Should I stop? he whispers.

I shake my head from side to side. I reach up to play with his beard and run a finger over his lips. I trust this man to provide for me and lead me to safety.

When our rhythm ends in sighs of pleasure, Francisco rolls off me so I can breathe. He curls his body around mine, holding me tight until we slumber. I never imagined the intimacy of this moment. The night settles over us.

CHAPTER FIVE

CELENDARIA

7 de enero 1656

We are awakened by sharp rapping at the door. I grab the sheets to cover me. Francisco pulls on his cotton undershorts and opens the latched window. I spin off the bed to crouch on the floor and dress in my underclothes.

What is it? asks Francisco. On my wedding night?

His brother Duarte is at the window.

Lover boy, I hope you have enjoyed your first night together. The fiesta has ended. We must load the wagons and horses and start our real journey.

But it is still dark outside.

I peer over the bed to see Francisco stretching his arms and moving his shoulders to loosen his joints for a long ride.

We must get an early start before the sun rises. The air is cool, but our enemies will not be detained. It is time. We are gathering in the courtyard so we may exit together.

Yes, but I feel like Moses fleeing the Egyptians with his tribe.

My brother, it is much worse than that. Hurry. We do not want to draw attention to ourselves. A delay could cost us.

Ach, you always push me.

Because you are the youngest and the slowest.

What? I will pay you back later. You are the most difficult, Francisco says turning to me.

Francisco closes the shutter and comes to where I am sitting against the bed. He offers a hand to help me up. I face him and he kisses me on the mouth. I do not remember ever being this happy. When I spot blood on the sheets over his shoulder, warmth rushes my face. I do not cover it up.

We must get ready for the road. If you fold your dress, it will fit in my bag. You were an angelic bride last night.

It is still night, I say, stroking his hair.

We have many of our own to transfer to new surroundings. Make sure your grandparents are loaded in the wagon with their belongings. Tonight we will have more explorations of our hungry bodies.

I return a smile because I know he is pleased with me.

When we separate, I roll the sheets into a ball and leave them in a corner. Then I clothe myself in layers and decide to wear the dress again on top instead of crumpling it in his bag.

We gather in the courtyard under a clear sky and blinking stars. My grandparents rest in chairs near our wagon, eating biscuits prepared by the Molinas' staff, who also hand out hot coffee from a tray. I lean over to kiss them, wishing them a good morning. My grandfather touches my cheek, but mi abuela remains quiet as she has been since her release. Who knows what terrible memories her mind harbors? Sometimes in her silence I think her tormentors hollowed out her body and returned a shell.

The Molinas greet us in sleeping caps. I am surprised they have arisen at this hour. I thank them for their hospitality.

Señor Molina says, It was our pleasure to provide a pleasant setting for your nuptials. We respect our traditions as you do, so it is a blessing to be of service. He reaches inside his velvet jacket for a small package wrapped in paper, a string holding it together. I press it to the skin of my bosom under my dress.

Thank you for this gift. It is not necessary. You provided us with so much. We are grateful. I kiss both of them.

I meet my parents and sisters, all of us subdued after a fiesta at this early hour. My mother reminds me she has put our ketubah in a safe place so that it lies flat. The wagons are lined up, Francisco's brothers and their horses leading the cavalcade. My grandparents are settled in our wagon, this time lying on their backs for a siesta. I am seated on the front bench with Francisco as his wife.

What is the holdup? calls Francisco to León's wagon in front of us, his children lounging like lizards on packages of textiles and home goods in the back.

This old donkey is slow, León responds. Have you filled jugs with water from the well our host has offered?

I nod yes.

We have to start moving! My husband, impatient with the delay, picks up the reins and shouts to our mule, Go, let us go!

Campesinos swing open the enormous gates as our caravan rolls toward the outside world with squeaky wheels, creaky wagons, neighing horses and mules, a few mongrels barking at the children tossing them bits of food as our cluster of humanity seeks new territory to survive and flourish.

CHAPTER SIX

CELENDARIA

9 de enero 1656
En route

We have stopped near a flowing river with foliage draping the banks. Insects with sheer-veined wings land on the water while birds chirp around us. A strip of sandy beach leads to the shore of the water where the children play among the river rocks, jumping from one to another, their spindly legs searching for the next one like frogs staking territory in a pond. An idyllic setting for our Sabbath that we reached late yesterday afternoon, the families gathered after my grandfather has led prayers.

Our wagons are in a double circle, rotating who gets the outside. We have settled after the trees break so that a large fire burns near the shore for warmth and cooking. My mother and Señora Behar and her sisters chat among themselves, keeping an eye on the children splashing with their bare feet, their shoes and stockings piled nearby. When the sun drops, the women will heat water for coffee and prepare a light meal of vegetables, smoked meat and bread.

The Sabbath, a time of reflection, remains an opportunity to speak with God, to remind ourselves where we have come from on the greatest passage out of Israel toward another land that promises freedom. The men gather on a blanket nearby to discuss future plans. They are not to discuss business on this holy day but our rules have relaxed in these circumstances. I overhear plans for textiles, chocolate and building homes. I feel protected and vulnerable at the same time.

Children, out of the water. It is time for candles, call the mothers. I cannot wait to be among them with a child of my own. The men have placed hats on their heads. We gather at the back of León's wagon that has a dropped leaf where my mother has placed her candlesticks. We gather around as we begin our prayer, gathering the goodness into our arms with a circular motion. We repeat the familiar words—*Baruch atah Adonai*—the words dance in my head as I appreciate the faces around me. Blessed are you, Lord, sovereign of the Universe, who has sanctified us with His commandments and commanded us to light the lights of Shabbat.

* * *

The sun awakens us, a reminder to pack up. By now we have a routine with each family preparing themselves for a dusty ride through desert landscape, an unfriendly place filled with spiny cactus, animals that disappear into holes and little civilization. We load our wagons, fill jugs with clear, fresh water and take our places. With the first roll of the wheels, I know we are closer to our destination.

Time passes until we stop again, the sun now low in the sky, but there is no shelter from the elements, no water nearby. Francisco puts his hands around his mouth to call his brothers in the front. Why have we halted?

I turn around to check on my grandparents who have fallen asleep with sombreros over their faces to block a relentless sun. I touch my grandmother's slipper. Do you need water, abuela? She rouses herself onto an elbow.

Yes, my sweet Celendaria. I am so happy to have seen you married, but this trip is arduous for me.

I pour water from a jug balanced near my feet and pass it to her in a clay cup.

Manuel yells back, Your brother refuses to stop. He wants to continue through the night.

Why? asks Francisco.

Manuel strolls toward us. The air is cooler at night and we can reach our destination by morning.

You expect me to push this mule all night without sleep?

Perhaps your new bride will take the reins while you nap. Manuel looks at me and grins.

Ach, you are leading this expedition. Whatever you say. Francisco is disgusted, but agrees. My head drops to his shoulder as our group of wagons and horses treks along a path in the desert evening. Coyotes howl, an eerie sound that echoes through a canyon. The outlines of cactus arms, the men of the desert, point the way.

I never take the reins because Francisco refuses to sleep. Finally, we reach a small village where we take respite under shade trees near a square. Native peoples gather around our wagons as we are a curiosity. Few travel these back trails when they can move swiftly on a major road built for silver trade from Zacatecas.

Women sit with goods spread out on cloths in the shade—knitted hats in many colors, baby shoes made from scraps of leather, cactus pads used for jelly, silver trinkets, pictures made with ink from desert plants, and an assortment of used clothing.

Duarte and Manuel come to confer with Francisco after getting water for their horses. What is the plan? asks my husband. His brothers have differing ideas.

Manuel says, Duarte wants us to take everyone to San Miguel, but I believe it is better for us to go alone. We can have everyone wait at another hacienda nearby and meet up on the trail later. The possibility of danger awaits us in this scheme.

Danger? I am on alert and curious. What does he mean?

My husband, agitated, asks, Why do we have to go to San Miguel? That is not our direction. Besides, we will draw attention to ourselves. The city is filled with soldiers. You must know an important Spanish military site dominates the area. He shakes his head no. Too many attacks by natives. A stupid idea.

Manuel leans into the front of the wagon to address Francisco in a lower voice. We must release the Behar woman and her baby held in a small jail outside the city. The Inquisition guards will come for them any day and move them to Mexico City to be questioned.

How do you know this? asks Francisco.

Manuel bends to the ground to cough and spit, an unpleasantness I refuse to watch. He wipes his mouth with the back of his hand. He speaks gritting his teeth.

We have information from inside the inquisitor's jail. Her priest remains there. They would not allow them to be in the same building. The authorities paid us to deliver them. Now we can seek revenge by releasing them. I want to do this with only two or three of us, but Duarte wants the entire caravan to come. He says that we will cause less suspicion if there are many of us traveling to another destination as though there is a wedding.

Manuel gives his brother a sidelong glance of annoyance.

I do not understand what is happening. My mind clicks forward. Mariel and the baby are in jail? I am shocked by this news. I knew they were gone, but not where they were. Ah, then I remember the gold coins on our table. Francisco donated his share to release mi abuela. But we never knew where they came from, only that the Church paid the brothers for capturing some people. No details were provided and with the excitement of mi abuela's release, it did not matter. What devastation I feel that she was freed because Mariel and Father Lopez were caught. I want to put my arms around my husband but I cannot with others watching.

Do the Behars know? I ask.

Yes, of course they know, says Manuel. He is the oldest and the most intimidating with his wild hair and beard. His deep-set black eyes reveal little.

And they have not revealed this to any of us? I am incredulous.

We swore them to secrecy. What we need now is to make some alterations on the document we use for transferring prisoners.

Francisco interrupts. You want to expose all these people to a perilous plan?

A rooster begins its call as Duarte walks back toward us to join the discussion, a reminder of the bright day that will greet us soon. Disheveled from the evening's festivities, his stride is off-kilter. He throws his arm around Manuel's neck.

My brother and I are in disagreement about how to proceed with our last job. I have a plan where no one will get hurt.

He squeezes harder so Manuel punches him in the stomach to escape his grasp.

Sometimes you infuriate me, says Manuel. We discussed this before. You want to take foolish chances. Better for us to storm the jail and make a hasty getaway on our horses than involve so many people. Would you have them lined up outside to applaud when we leave?

You are an idiot, says Duarte. Their jail is impenetrable.

I want to run to the Behars, but Francisco sees my agitation to get down and holds my arm.

Wait. Name-calling will not bring a solution to this dilemma, says Francisco. It is better for us to stay as a family. We are more vulnerable if we separate. Besides, you are the ones with guns and knives.

My new husband remains reasonable, but he has little influence after leaving the bondsman business to his brothers and father.

Duarte slams his fist on the wagon. Separating us even for a day will lead to trouble. I have a plan that will allow everyone to be free.

Manuel says, The two of us cannot storm a jail alone. Francisco, will you join us one last time? It is not as risky as our brother says. We have broken into territorial jails near Monterrey. We know how to protect ourselves.

Others in our caravan become restless and stroll back to see what is going on. What is the delay? I could have been sleeping. The children are impatient. When are we moving?

The rest of our group gathers around our wagon while my grandparents sit quietly in the back. People start to take sides. León and Aruh disagree about whether we should all go and argue with each other. My father interjects that he does not want any of his grandchildren exposed to peril.

Finally, the Behars join the confusion. We all fall silent. Mariel's mother says in a small voice, I want my daughter back. I want to help raise my grandchild. Her hand flies to her mouth as she cries into her husband's shoulder.

Señor Behar says, I do not care what you do. Get her out of confinement. She has done nothing wrong. I forgive you men for her capture. You did not know we were hidden ones too. But now we have sold all we have to bribe the officials. Those thieves. She must be released, whatever you have to do. His plea is desperate.

Tears fill my eyes for my friend who must be riddled with fear for her baby.

Enough! says Duarte. We are going to execute this today. The rest of you will wait here while Francisco and Celendaria come with us. It will not take long to reach San Miguel. All we need now is baby clothes and adjustments to the documents we carry to transfer prisoners. Who can assist with this?

The hushed crowd waits in silence. Duarte and Manuel glare at each other until Manuel capitulates with a nod. Francisco, are you in? asks Duarte.

Why do my wife and I have to be involved?

We need you for this venture. I can explain more as we ride.

Señor Behar raises his hand. I am accomplished with handwriting and words.

Duarte takes charge. Then we will proceed. He shouts out instructions to pull our wagons close together.

He goes off with Mariel's father, unrolling papers he pulls from inside his shirt. The irony that he is assisting with the release of the man who impregnated his daughter is not lost on me.

Francisco interrupts. I am not participating in this fiasco.

Manuel pats his arm. Little brother, we are committed. You can rest tonight. We have work to do. Celendaria, can you provide baby blankets and wrap them as a gift?

I am only married a day. I know nothing about rescuing babies.

CHAPTER SEVEN

CELENDARIA

9 de enero 1656

I do not like this, says Francisco as we ride. His brothers have gone ahead and arranged to meet us on the outskirts of San Miguel. I am nervous. A package for Mariel and her baby of a few small blankets, caps and cloths for diapers I put together from the ladies at the market perches on my lap. I am wearing my wedding dress to prove my story that I am to be married today in the church.

We pull up to see his brothers lounging on the ground, their horses tied nearby.

What took you so long? Manuel says with a smirk. What is this crazy plan of yours? I want to get back to the others, he teases.

Duarte looks me in the eye. We are going to gain entry when you distract the guard with gifts for the woman and her baby. And a small bribe. He hands me an envelop with coins.

No! I will not have it. My wife cannot be part of this. Francisco rises from his seat to jump down and face his brothers. We have had disagreements before but this is outrageous. How could you think we would agree to this?

Oh, so now that you have a wife you have gone soft on us? says Duarte. His tone reveals anger and envy. He pushes Francisco on the shoulder.

Francisco responds with a violent push back as Duarte stumbles backward. Fists are up as they start to swing at one another with neither making contact. Manuel places himself between his brothers. Duarte lands a fist below Manuel's eye meant for Francisco. Blood spurts from the cut, dripping onto his face and shirt. He is as angry as a bull I have seen charge when taunted. I am frozen.

Francisco climbs up next to me, cursing his brothers under his breath. I have not seen him like this before—angry, agitated, ready to strike

Do you have a rag? asks Manuel. I open the package meant for Mariel and remove two cloths meant for the baby, dipping one in a jug of water near my feet. He walks away to clean himself, returning a few minutes later with his shirt covered by a serape that covered his saddle.

Manuel says, bitterness in his voice, Listen carefully. Before we lead you to the jail where the Behar woman is held, we will stop at a spring to water our animals. It is called the River of Dogs because dogs guided the settlers to this spot. If I bark, it is a warning we are in danger. We must do this before we arrive because the horses will make a faster escape afterward.

And, what about us? asks Francisco in a tone I have not heard.

Manuel says, Pull the wagon in front. Only one man guards her. Celendaria, you must charm him with a story. Get him to lead you back to her cell to deliver the presents. We will do the rest. Francisco, when Celendaria comes out with the Behar woman and her baby, have them lie down in the back under blankets and return to the others. We will meet you back here. Proceed as though you are looking for the church that will marry you today. No one will bother a bride and groom.

I cannot believe his brothers want me to participate in their scheme. I am petrified of going back into a jail. What if I am caught and cannot leave? A one-day bride caught in the web of the authorities? I cannot bear it. But my poor friend, trapped. I have seen a desert tortoise on its back. Unless it has assistance, it will die. I cannot abandon my friend. I know the passion she has felt.

I do not like this, says Francisco to me, urging our horses forward. It is a short distance and we do not speak. I run over in my mind what I will do and say. We arrive in front of the jail. I close my eyes and say a prayer. Francisco leans over to kiss my cheek. He comes around to help me down. We hold hands for a moment. Be safe, he says.

I smooth my dress and take the package and coins under my arm. When I push through the heavy door, the smell of alcohol and urine waft by me. I feel nauseated. My eyes adjust to the darkness.

Can I help you? asks the jailer leaning back in his chair, his boots propped up on an untidy desk.

At first my voice is lost. I gulp air, straighten my shoulders and begin again.

My cousin is here with her baby. I have a gift for her.

He leers at me. And what makes you think I would allow you to see her? Give me your package and I will see that she gets it. He reaches toward me, his nails and hands grimy with dirt.

I press the package close to my chest. I am marrying today in the church and I want her to see my dress.

Amused, he says, This is a jail, not a place of fashion. Go, be gone. Leave your package. He tilts his chair forward and scrapes the floor with it. When he stands, he is as large as Francisco's brothers, leaning across the desk, imposing himself over me.

My heart pounds inside my breast. I manage a smile and lower my eyelashes, something I saw Mariel do in the past.

Please, sir, we have been so close all our lives. I know she has done wrong, but I want to see her for a moment.

Let me inspect your package. I place it on the desk and he tears apart the wrapping. He picks up the baby items with his filthy hands and drops them. He makes a noise of dissatisfaction with his mouth.

You are wasting my time.

I must be bold. Sliding the envelope of coins cross the desk to him, his eyebrows arch. And what is this? Again, he is amused a lady would come into this place. He tears it open and the coins bounce across the desk, a few falling to the floor. At first he is puzzled but then he releases a loud laugh.

I have been a fool to try this.

Get out of here. You think you can bribe me with a few coins? This will not buy me whiskey for a night. Go. He points his dirty finger toward the door.

I hesitate. Should I run?

Then I remember something important that happened earlier. I turn my back to him to reach my hand into my bosom and retrieve the small package the Molinas gave us as a wedding gift. I turn back and place it before him, meeting his eyes. His grimy fingers open it with caution. His eyes never leave mine until the glint of gold coins glimmers in the dim light. His head drops to examine them, even picking up one to bite. He ogles me. I do not know if he is angry I did not give him this before or pleased to see gold or—and this gives me chicken bumps up my spine,

315

raising the hairs on my neck. I fear—he has another nefarious scheme in mind.

What else is hidden inside your pristine wedding dress, Señorita?

Moistness invades under my arms and the back of my neck. My mother told me sometimes men do terrible things to a woman. Droplets of water drip down the sides of my face and between my breasts. A tremor causes my knees to quiver. I cannot look at him, lowering my head.

Do you have anything else you want to share? I glance up to see him rocking his chair back again, amused at my fading boldness. He stares at me for what seems like a very long time.

He is deciding what to do with me. Is it too late for me to turn and run?

Come with me, he says, rattling the keys on his belt as he stands.

My limbs become frozen in place. Will he lock me in Mariel's cell and do something terrible to us? Should I run now? I want to escape to the safety of my husband waiting outside.

I grab the baby items from the desk to my chest and follow him down dark hallways permeated with nauseating odors. I gag at the back of my throat. As I pass, a drunken man calls out, reaching through the bars to touch me. I twist away from a foul hand missing a finger and the man's raucous laugh.

We stop before an empty cell at the end. I see nothing. The jailer searches for his keys and opens the door. Is he incarcerating me? Panic courses through me. I am ready to pick up my dress and run back down the hall.

You have a visitor, says the jailer smirking at me. Who is he talking to?

My eyes perceive a dark cavern until Mariel's angelic face appears before me, her hair wild. Her clothes are sullied and she holds the precious baby in her arms. She blinks at me, an apparition before her.

Mariel? It is Celendaria. I have brought you a few things.

The jailer says, Enter. I do not have time to waste. He holds up five fingers to let me know I do not have long. The door clangs shut behind me, a chilling, final sound I remember from visiting my grandmother in her inquisition cell. Bile crawls up the back of my throat. A shudder of terror brings back the incomprehensible fear I felt in their prison.

Mariel does not speak. I come closer to her ear and whisper, my lips touching her untamed hair.

We are here to get you out. Follow what I tell you to do. Put these clothes on the baby. She fingers the wool caps and soft napkins. She is in a dream and I cannot awaken her.

Please. We are at great risk. Hurry.

She must realize what I am saying. She changes the baby and dresses him, wrapping the clean blanket around him with a flourish, tucking in the ends. Natives swathe their newborns this way. He makes gurgling sounds at her attention and she smiles at him.

Suddenly, we hear the clanking of chains, scrapings of furniture and a commotion of yells that echoes down the hall. The jailer spews curses I have been taught never to use; something crashes to the floor and keys clatter. I go to the bars but my view is blocked. The stride of wooden heels comes toward us.

Please let it be my rescuers, I pray.

Duarte appears before me, the keys grasped in his hand. He tries a few as the jailer makes grunting sounds.

Do not worry, says Duarte, as he tries different keys in the lock. My brother has him chained to his desk with a gag in his mouth and we have his gun. Finally, the right key fits in the lock. The door swings open and we pass through—a woman in a wedding dress and another holding a baby.

The other prisoner screams epithets as we pass. The jailer is a bastard. I am only a drunk, he shouts. Let me out too. You are cursed if you do not release me!

Manuel calls out to us. Move with haste. Mariel rushes by me with the baby clutched to her chest. I glance at the jailer, a handkerchief stuffed in his mouth, immobile in his chair and fettered to his desk. The fury he feels toward me can be seen in his angry eyes. Duarte opens the door to the sunlight where Francisco sits on the wagon waiting as Manuel backs out, his gun pointed at the jailer. Go!

I turn back toward the desk to stand in front of it.

What are you doing? Manuel yells at me.

I reach down and gather the gold coins with a swift motion, dropping them into my bosom. I give a fleeting glance at the ambushed man, shrug my shoulders and murmur, *Lo siento*.

CHAPTER EIGHT

CELENDARIA

9 de enero 1656

We arrive at our meeting place in the heat of the day when the sun
is high in the sky. Our hair and clothes are dusty, although Francisco
dons a hat and I wear a scarf, my dress covered with a blanket. My
parents approach our wagon with the Behars, great anticipation on
their faces that shifts to despair.

Where is my baby? Beatriz cries out. Her husband holds her arm,
appearing grim, his mouth set in a frown.

My parents greet me with puzzlement. What happened to Mariel
and the baby?

Francisco jumps out his side of the wagon as I turn around to
look behind me. He goes to the back and lifts a corner of a grey
blanket, sliding it down to the end of the wagon. Underneath, a
sleeping mother and child curl against one another. They look like
many Madonna statues I have seen, perfect in their beauty and repose.

Beatriz and Diego look over the side. Mariel's mother lets out
a wail when she sees them. They are dead! You brought back my

319

children without a breath! She clings to her husband. Her cries awaken the baby.

Mariel rubs her eyes and sits up to her parents' amazement. I can tell she is confused about where she is. When she spots her mother she says, Mama, Mama. Look what I brought you. Mariel gathers the baby in his swaddling clothes and hands him to her mother who accepts him with caution. He begins to cry and my aunts who have gathered around offer advice.

Hold him up higher. He doesn't know you yet. He needs his mother's milk. Beatriz hands him to me so she can embrace her daughter. I hold him close to calm him, placing him over my shoulder and patting his back as I saw my mother do with Yonah and Yael ages ago.

I pause for a moment to reflect on what I have done. I have participated in a criminal offense by breaking my friend out of jail. Yes, my Judaizing puts me at risk, but what I have done now can also mark me as a common criminal. I bounce the baby on my shoulder. I no longer feel brave but a fool for taking such risks. I could not say no to my husband and his brothers. What else might I have to do to survive? Will I be able to do this with my own child and feel safe?

We are enamored of the reunion as Mariel climbs down with Francisco's assistance, reaching her arms toward her parents. They hold each other, sobbing. Many of us have tears in our eyes.

What is the baby's name? asks Yael. Can I hold him?

Mariel looks at Yael. Asher. From the Bible. Father Lopez, uh, Miguel, said it is from the Pentateuch.

He is correct, says my grandfather who has joined the commotion.

Mariel asks Francisco, Will I see him again?

My husband states with authority, I do not know. My brothers have a plan to rescue him, but they have not returned. The thought dances across my mind. What if Duarte and Manuel have come to an ill fate?

Others must be thinking the same thing. Francisco's father, with thick, grey hair combed away from his face strained with worry, parts his way through the crowd. Where are my sons? His voice becomes demanding, angry. I remember that he was against this rescue attempt.

Padre, their plan was to rescue Father Lopez from the larger jail set up by the Inquisition. More men are guarding him than the one we encountered to free Mariel. The last I saw they rode off together. They said they would meet us here, but it is late. We were slow with a donkey. We are supposed to continue our journey tonight. Do not think for a moment that the authorities are not looking for us. The minute the jailer frees himself, the Spanish army will send out a search team of soldiers.

León scoffs at the notion. What can they do with so many of us? He contemplates for a minute. Perhaps we should split up and meet in a few days.

A bad idea, says my grandfather. We must stay together. Do not underestimate the Spanish. He points his bony finger at us. Their cruelty is legend. They live without conscience. How else could they have kept your grandmother locked up for so many years without charges?

He continues on a subject he is passionate about, stumbling over words in his fury. In their false cries for justice, they wiped out Luis de Carvajal, the governor and captain-general of Villa de San Luis, and his entire family in 1596, including his mother and three sisters, the first women to be burned alive for holding on to our traditions. The Spanish were ruthless in their persecution. Luis was arrested when someone heard him say, May God be with you.

He died in prison.

My grandfather has lost his energy, exhausted from his outburst. My aunt Maria helps him to a chair in the shade and scoops a cup of water for him from a jug.

If the Inquisition could do this to those related to a governor, what would they do to me?

My father takes charge and orders us to prepare ourselves. Eat and rest so we are ready when the men return. Water is available in a trough on the other side of the square. Clean yourselves as best you can and pack your wagons. Our group scatters with the new instructions. A stray dog lies down in the shade of our wagon. We will be moving on soon through the desert that churns up dust with each turn of the wagon wheels.

The evening sky slides into shadows. When the men do not appear, the decision is made to stay the night. We must stay together. Mariel and Asher go with her parents, my grandparents sleep in the back of my parents' wagon and Francisco and I climb into the back of ours, cuddling against the chill night air under serapes.

Francisco worries about his brothers and ignores my touches to his hair and shoulders. He turns on his side, his head resting on his arm.

What will we do with a priest traveling among crypto-Jews? he thinks aloud.

Maybe he will offer us protection. Perhaps someone will think we are his flock.

Francisco smiles at my naiveté. He says, If I am correct, he no longer wears his priestly collar. I expect work clothes from tending to a farm. He pauses to look at me. If we see him again.

CHAPTER NINE

CELENDARIA

10 de enero 1656

Morning greets us with sun in our eyes and the crowing of roosters. It takes a moment to remember where I am and what our circumstances are. I peek over the side of the wagon. People are stirring, the square fills with vendors cooking and selling. Children run and play. A church bell rings in the distance.

I peer at the bustling scene over the side of the wagon. Francisco, their food smells so good. Can we get something to eat?

My lovely wife, he says stroking my arm. Everything they prepare is made with lard from pigs. No.

Have you ever eaten food not prepared our way? I ask.

My brothers and I have traveled to strange places where it was not possible to follow our kashrut laws. It is better to nourish than go hungry. He considers his response. It is more important that we remember our lessons of morality, know right from wrong, follow our laws, teach our children to read. When we are educated like your grandfather, our knowledge is portable. We can begin again.

I am chastised.

He touches the end of my nose with his forefinger. Our lives are shifting. We seek a place that respects People of the Book, our book, the Torah, and others who believe in One God.

The day passes in an unhurried manner as we lounge around our wagons, the young ones searching for something to do. Always cautious, their parents have forbidden them to approach the children playing in the square. Flies buzz around us when we consume our meager rations. Mariel stays close to her parents, but I can tell by her sad expression she remains apprehensive that her lover has not appeared.

Francisco worries also. Maybe we should go to look for them, he says. We stand together at the back of the wagon taking inventory of our supplies. We did not pack enough for a protracted wait.

He says, We could take one wagon and my father's horse to track back toward the jails.

A terrible idea, I think. He notices my lack of response.

Francisco puts his hand over mine. What are our choices? How long can we wait here before a cavalry of horses with men seeking us rides by in a cloud of dust? With the elderly and the very young among us, we cannot make a swift getaway.

Maybe your brothers are waiting someplace else for us, I add. Is there a special hideaway or cave they might go to? Another destination? Where do others go to escape the watchful eyes of priests?

Yes, such a place exists. Rio Arriba, but it is farther north near an area we have ridden through many times.

I look around at our group of almost thirty people. I say, Maybe it is a miracle we have traveled this far. Can we get there in a day? I do not feel safe here exposed to the elements and the wrath of soldiers. We can be spotted easily.

My husband stares at me. I agree, but I cannot leave my brothers behind. I am angry at the Father and his sins. Is he one of us or not? Will he plead his case to us with his faith in Jesus? Or revert back to our one, true faith?

I do not know. Our undulating identities confuse many of us, not always confident of which faith to express in our circumstances. Please talk to me about Rio Arriba. Is it far?

Not so long ago the second Spanish governor founded a new city at the base of the Sangre de Cristo Mountains in the early 1600s. He called it La Villa Real de la Santa Fe de San Francisco de Asís. It is dedicated to their saint who loves animals. The natives have inhabited the region for centuries and the Spanish have built a church. They have water there. The part of the lower river, Rio Abajo, sits below what we now call Santa Fe. Many purebred Spaniards have made their way there among the peaceful, farming Indians.

My brothers and I have found fugitives in the upper part of the river, which is closer to us. Many find refuge in this isolated area—people of mixed backgrounds, natives, craftsmen, Europeans, hidden ones and independent souls who like the desolation. It is safer now than it has been.

Why? We stroll under the trees holding hands. I am happy to be with a man who knows the territory.

In the 1590s, the mayor of this region, Castaño de Sosa, tried to settle the area with about 170 Judaizers, renegades and those of mixed parentage, but the Spanish did not approve. His Portuguese birth blanketed him with suspicion. He also took Indians as slaves, a practice we do not condone. Eventually, he met the fate of his friend, Luis de Carvajal, and was tried by the Inquisition. The authorities, in their insidious ways, found him to be a Jew and shipped him in chains to the Philippines.

Is that in Nuevo España?

Francisco throws his head back to laugh. No, they are in the middle of an ocean. The Spanish settled the islands almost a hundred years ago. The tentacles of the Holy Office reach across all boundaries. Nor do they cease their maltreatment just because some are far away. If they are accused, they too are brought back to their punishment in Ciudad de México.

How do you know this story? I ask. I am impressed with Francisco's knowledge, but I am also skeptical.

My mother, Devorah, may her name be a blessing, liked to teach me as the youngest. My older brothers, uncultivated and rowdy, did not like to learn, but I did. We lost three of my little sisters to the flu epidemic in the same year. My mother's father, a scholar and a clandestine rabbi, knew all our history. His family collected books like your abuelo, but they were abandoned behind a secret wall in our home when she passed. Later, we realized the treasure left behind, but we were a family of men on the move with an unstable lifestyle.

Francisco becomes quiet with this memory. I do not ask more questions.

Francisco and I wile away the morning and early afternoon by walking to a nearby stream where the children sit with their feet in the water. We pause as he faces me.

Celendaria, I am proud of how you assisted us in freeing Mariel and Asher. You are a heroic soul. I did not know this about you—your bravery and fortitude. You think quickly, something that may save our lives in the future. Were you afraid?

Petrified. The jailer seemed to want to attack me, the way he leered and leaned into me. I had no other option once I was inside except to execute the plan as it was laid out. I could not run away without my friend. And I could not disappoint you and your brothers. I emboldened myself by thinking about Queen Esther in the Old Testament who saved the Jews. Where did she find her courage? I had to do the same.

Francisco folds me into his arms and kisses the top of my head. He tells me, We will triumph. You will see. Our strength of character has proven our survival through centuries. Our journey began thousands of years ago, but for us, it started in 1492 in Granada on the Second of Ab, 5252 when Isabella enforced her Edict of Expulsion, casting the Muslims and us to the winds of the world. On the same day she thought she could unify her country with Catholicism as Christopher Columbus sailed away to discover new territories to conquer.

CHAPTER TEN

CELENDARIA

11 de enero 1656
En route

We have become a restless group, similar to the flies that buzz around us. I wander among the wagons until siesta time. I greet Clodovea and Delfina, my brothers' wives, to trade some bread for a few eggs from our chickens. A pain grips me, seeing our home in my mind, and makes me sad. León and Aruh argue nearby about whether we should leave.

Why are we waiting for a man who turned on his people, brother? asks León.

Because now he is one of us, says Aruh.

How do you know this? A renegade. Leave him behind, says León, kicking up dust with the toe of his boot. He will bring us unwanted attention.

I hurry away, holding the bread close to me. I do not enjoy the sport of argument, something men seem to derive pleasure from. A soft voice calls my name. I whirl around, but see no one save Francisco's father and mine replacing a metal band on our wagon wheel.

Mariel rushes toward me. I have been calling your name, she says. Please, come with me. She takes my hand and pulls me to a blanket behind her wagon to sit. Her hair has been combed into a long tail that drapes down her back, wrapped with a ribbon, shiny underneath a flat hat to shield her from the sun. Her pale skin reminds me of alabaster decorations in churches, fine features sculpted with care.

How is Asher? I ask.

Sleeping next to my napping parents. Mariel hesitates. I want to thank you for assisting with my rescue. You took a great chance of losing your freedom. Or worse.

I raise my eyebrows. Did the jailer hurt you in any way? If he did, Francisco will find him and bring him harm.

No, although I was fearful. But I have come to a place where I expect to be punished for my sins.

Ah, the Catholic position. We do not believe a vengeful God will cause mischief. Our God remains one to guide us to the Promised Land. You were absolved when you gave birth to your son.

Is that true? Mariel looks at me with hope. We have not circumcised him yet. I am afraid the consorts of the Church check the pants of a small boy.

I reach over to touch her hand as she begins to cry into a hankie pulled from her bosom. Mariel, it will be all right. Your son will grow up to be a fine man, learned in the Law of Moses.

What about his father? Where is he? Without him, I am doomed to be alone the rest of my life, scorned by those around me. Her sobs render my heart crushed. She looks up at me, her comely face streaked with tears.

I hear what the others say, she says. Why are we waiting for a priest? He has not assisted us in any way. We face danger because of him. He led the girl astray. How can we trust him? She wipes her tears with the handkerchief, and then covers her face to hide sobs.

I bend forward to hold her, her once voluptuous body bony and spare. What she says is true. We are divided, some who want to leave now and others who are willing to stay and wait.

Her voice hiccups as she says, I will not leave this place. He will escape and look for me here.

How does he know of this place, a spit in the middle of a great expanse? It is not safe for you.

Mariel's cries begin anew. I am stymied as to how to make her feel better. I do not know when or if our departure is imminent. I stand and survey our group to see if there is activity.

I reach out my hand to lift her up. Come. Let me take you back to your parents and Asher.

She gazes at me, her eyes pooled with tears again. If we go, I will never see him again and my child will not know his father.

I walk her back to her family, our arms entwined.

CHAPTER ELEVEN

CELENDARIA

15 de enero 1656

When we arrive at our stopping place on Shabbat, we wait, lingering near the village square to trade with the mestizos, watching the horizon for my husband's brothers and the renegade priest. With no one in sight, we light candles and say a prayer for their safe return. Two more days pass and our impatience causes disagreements about whether we should stay or go.

Early on the morning of the third day a cavalry of Spaniards kicks up dust as they ride past us, the rhythm of hooves hitting the hard ground, alerting us to their authority. Where are they going with such haste? The soldier's feet are shoved into wooden stirrups with leather casings as their heels urge the horses to ride faster. They wear *cueras*, a leather vest to protect them from Indian arrows. I shield myself behind a tree to view them while others hurry to gather the children and stay close to their wagons. A few soldiers wear jackets, buttons gleaming in the sun, hats with expansive plumes. Swords, lances and pistols bounce against their hips. An impressive display of force, I think. I know they are looking for me, an accomplice to a crime. Cold shivers bristle up my spine. I thrust my guilt aside, but the jailer knows my face and Mariel's.

What is my wife observing now? Francisco asks, slipping his hands around my waist.

I whirl around to face him, my heart beating with exhilaration, my cheeks warm with color. Where are they going? Are they looking for your brothers?

Perhaps. They roam at will, especially the *tropas ligeras*, troops that travel with few possessions. Did you see the small boxes buckled around their waists to the back? I nod yes.

Cartridge boxes. They are well-equipped to do battle. Come, it is time to go.

But what about your brothers?

Duarte and Manuel are tough *hombres* who can care for themselves. We know the territory well. If they sense danger, they have places to hide.

How will they find us if we leave?

They will look for us until they do. In the mean time, we can settle ourselves.

But I worry about them. And Mariel's priest.

Forget the priest! It is the first time Francisco has raised his voice to me. The priest and his impulses have caused all of this. He softens as my eyes fill with tears. Come, prepare yourself.

My father, brothers, Señor Behar and Francisco's father agree that it is too dangerous for us to stay. We pack in haste to travel north, abandoning hope of his brothers finding us here, our elation of traveling subdued. My Aunt Maria and others complain about the Behar girl's wailing, her heart rupturing as we kick up our own dirt storm on the trail.

The journey is arduous through areas where nothing lives save a few bugs. Cacti, with protective spikes that warn us to stay away, are the only vegetation visible as far as I can see. Some are low to the ground, a menace through soft shoes, while others stick us with needles even if we never touch them. Others stand silent watch over us as we sleep, outlined in the desert sky.

Francisco, our people are like cactus. I tell him this while we look past the outline of tall, prickly plants to the stars and moon illuminating the desert.

Francisco spent the day riding a horse he unhooked from our wagon to scout what awaits us. His father worries about his sons as he keeps company with my grandparents.

Look, I say pointing, these spiny plants not only survive without water and stand tall in the unrelenting sun, but they also thrive, gifting us with flowers too difficult to pick. Maybe they are hidden Jews, too.

Francisco smiles at me. My wife, we have much farther to go. Please make sure everyone fills their water jugs. We will pass through San Luis Potosí in four to five days, depending on the weather. Mines have been discovered in the area and many Chichimecas, settlers and escapees of the Spanish, have taken over the area, a dangerous place. We will stop long enough to gather supplies, but we must be cautious. There is abundant water in the valley. My brothers could be hiding nearby—we have captured a few criminals in the area and they know it well. I do not want to tell the others and give false hope. When I ride off, I will look for them on the outskirts.

A fierce and sudden storm slows our journey. I am soaked to my skin and covered in mud. Oh, how I long for my Friday bath in warm, perfumed water, the prayers and intimacy of the women soothing me.

We stay off the main trails since we are traveling with fugitives. I never thought of myself that way, but I have committed a crime. More than one if you count my Judaizing. Why can we not let our faith go as others have? Life would be easier. I cannot forget the teachings of my ancestors. I find solace in my beliefs. Why are we still pursued? Most of us have little left to fill their coffers.

We travel for a few more days, only stopping in small pueblos to refresh supplies. I visit with my parents who appear so much older to me, their expressions grim. They have regrets about the journey, especially my father.

Did I leave my business, my home for this? he asks, swinging his arm out to the endless dirt and rocks. I do not have a response. My mother remains silent, a melancholia creeping over her, a darkness that invades the soul and rounds the shoulders.

I check on my grandmother in the back of the wagon, a small awning made from a pillow case and short branches to shield her, not unlike the chuppah at my wedding. Abuela, how do you feel? She looks at me, her eyes glassy. I touch her forehead. She feels hot. I call her name to see if I can arouse her. She does not respond. I ask my grandfather if she is well.

Your grandmother got a chill yesterday when we were soaked from the rain. She has slept since then.

Abuelo, I think she is ill.

No, she will get up soon.

Has she had water? I ask.

No, she sleeps.

I feel panic recoil inside me that rebounds up my spine, churning my stomach. We must get her to a doctor.

After the words leave my mouth, I realize how ridiculous the idea is in this desolation. No city nearby or a doctor to save her. I run to Francisco.

Mi abuela is not waking up. Please come, I beg, pulling on his arm. Francisco is repacking our goods, some ruined by the rain that the women have placed in a pile as garbage.

I am coming. What is wrong with her?

Francisco peers over the wagon.

See? Her eyes are open but she does not hear us.

My grandfather and parents gather around her. Francisco touches her head as I did. He stares at me, shaking his head.

We need a doctor. I tell him with urgency. Please. Then I begin to cry. Mi abuela. After all she went through in her terrible confinement and now she is taking leave of us? She must make it to our destination near the river. No justice prevails in this arid land.

My mother holds me, but she cries too.

Francisco, how far are we from a place where she could receive care? my father asks.

Francisco hangs his head and digs the toe of his boot in the dirt.

I am afraid she will not make it to our destination. No man with medical skills will ride two days to see an old, sick woman. Our only hope is to take her ourselves. He looks around. Can we prepare to leave right now?

My mother rushes over to the Behars to tell them to get ready while my father notifies my brothers and my father-in-law. Everyone can hear Mariel's sobbing. The news means we are taking her farther from her loved one, if he is even alive. My husband has told me few people who are not acclimated to the desert can survive without preparation, especially one who has spent most of his life inside the bosom of the Church.

CHAPTER TWELVE

CELENDARIA

21 de enero 1656

Late in the afternoon, after an arduous journey walking some of the time beside my grandmother's wagon, touching her, cajoling her to awaken, Francisco halts our caravan. We gather around.

Francisco holds up a shiny black stone. Does anyone know what this is? Some of the children call out.

It is from Indians, from their arrows. We are going to meet the Chichimecas when we arrive in San Luis Potosí, an outpost known for its rich silver deposits. They will not hurt us. The best archers hunt with short bows and long reed arrows with this stone called obsidian on the tips. My brother León's small boys reach out their hands to hold it. Francisco drops it in a child's palm and continues.

Conversation buzzes through our group. Most of us remain afraid of natives with their strange dress, unknown languages and fierce appearance. We share a common enemy—the Spanish, who want to convert them too. Many have been lost to our foes with their policy of *fuego y sangre*, a war of fire and blood that promises death, mutilation and enslavement. A shiver courses through me. Francisco tells me they are an angry people, nomads who live in caves or makeshift shelters. He has met them as he has searched for fugitives. They can be reasonable, but remained incensed at what the Spanish have wrought on their population.

Why are we stopping here? asks Beatriz Behar. I am afraid for the baby. For us.

Francisco responds. He is the leader. We must get help for the Crespins' grandmother. The mines in San Luis Potosí, discovered in the early 1580s, also have an abundant supply of water in a nearby valley. The Chichimecas will not bother us.

Wait, calls my father. Are they not the ones who killed fourteen people at a ranch near San Miguel?

My sisters-in-law and aunts begin to cry, falling into each other's arms, keening, aware that danger appears in many forms.

Yes, this is true, but they will not harm us. They are peaceful now that the Spanish have left them alone. Besides, it is halfway to Villa de San Luis, our next destination. Ready yourselves for a meal and the chill of evening.

The children gather cottonwood and mesquite branches for a small fire to cook our food, which is mostly vegetables and bread as we cannot eat the animals we have seen in the desert—armadillos with their strange, hard casing that amuses my nieces and nephews, speckled cats without tails, and javelina, their ugly faces and tusks reminiscent of large rats. Francisco starts a fire in the native way, rubbing cedar and mulberry sticks together. My sisters and I add dry moss to build a steady flame.

My grandmother has not awakened nor taken food or drink. I fear the worst, but Francisco comforts me as we huddle together on the front seat of our wagon. I sit close to him, a serape across our legs. His father is riding our donkey. I ask about the Chichimecas.

Are they as menacing as you say?

My wife, they are brutal, turbulent people who are angry at having their lands taken away, ardent about not wanting to be Catholic and ferocious with their enemies. If I tell you something, you must not share it with the others.

What is it?

Do you swear not to reveal what I say?

Yes. I hold him closer to me, the steady clip-clop of shoes making me sleepy.

The Chichimecas are suspected of cannibalism.

It takes a moment for me to comprehend what he has said. I have heard of cannibals, but I never considered someone eating another person. The thought of it makes me queasy.

How do you know this?

It is common knowledge among those of us who ride the plains.

But why? I feel my eyebrows and face crunch together in disgust.

Sometimes they eat parts of friends by cooking them over a fire, crushing their bones and ingesting them as a ceremonial drink. If the person was an enemy, they eat them as an act of vengeance, using the top of the skull as a bowl.

Chicken bumps raise on my arms and I want to vomit. Will they eat me?

No, I will not allow it. Besides, you are too skinny for them. They like meat.

You are playing with me. Is this true?

Unfortunately, yes. We heard an account from a priest who wanted to convert them. He asked the natives if they had tried human flesh or peyote. When they answered yes, and many did, the priest refused to convert them.

When he says *we* I know he is referring to Duarte and Manuel.

Are you worried about your brothers? I do not understand the word peyote.

Yes, but they have many survival skills including the use of harquebusiers, the guns that the Spanish carry. They are not as accurate as a bow and arrow, but easy to load with powder or bullets. We have spent weeks in the desert seeking fugitives who dissolve into shadows. If they are free, they will seek us.

But we are far from home. How will they know where to look?

We have places marked on a crude map that are safe for us to wait. I have faith in the Almighty that we will all be delivered and protected.

Amen, I utter under my breath.

We arrive to the outskirts of San Luis the next afternoon after riding through the night. Francisco dozed while I took the reins. He directs us to a place of many waterfalls where we bathe, the women in privacy and the men on the other side. The children play in the water that meets the rocks and jungle above us. Colored birds flit in and out, screeching at our intrusion. An enormous cave awaits exploration as well as a natural bridge and tunnels. A paradise similar to what Adam and Eve found, I think. I immerse myself in the refreshing, clear water, cleansing my hair and body.

Mariel is close to me. It is the first time I have seen her smile since we rescued her. This reminds me of the mikvah that we shared before the Sabbath, I tell her. That is when I realized she was with child. I cannot keep myself from glancing at her body when she rinses herself. Her breasts filled with baby milk are enormous, the nipples darkened, her stomach and hips slim. Her beauty, a blessing from God, can also be a failing.

After a time, we dry ourselves, dress, and load into our wagons. San Luis is a short distance. Surrounded by low vegetation, the small pueblo has fountains and a church. The men who work the mines and their families live in shelters, crude for my taste, while other tradesmen live in homes similar to the ones we left.

Francisco negotiates a place for us to stay at a nearby inn where we fill up all the rooms, many of us sharing space. With a bed, dresser and pitcher for water, it is not like the place I spent my wedding night, but it is sufficient and clean. I am relieved not to sleep in the bottom of a wagon. Aruh and León, my father and Francisco carry in mi abuela so she is comfortable. She still has not awakened or spoken to us.

We establish ourselves by buying supplies at the open market where a pig roasts on a spit over a fire, its skin crackling in the flames. It nauseates me and I turn away. Too many observers of Mosaic Law have been forced to eat the filthy animal under duress. Mariel has been told to stay out of sight at the inn.

Francisco and his father plan to ride to the outskirts of town to leave a message for the natives who inhabit the hills. I express my fear that he will be captured.

Before he leaves, Francisco says, I am in no danger. I know these people. Many times criminals try to hide among them, but they do not succeed. The Indians are smart in many ways we do not understand. They know remedies for ailments. They understand the plants that grow nearby. I want to obtain some for your grandmother.

I am skeptical that a plant can revive her, but I am willing to try anything that might save her.

The men return in time for my mother's stew made from corn, eggplant, peppers, green onions and potatoes purchased at the market. She has added spices from her cloth bags to enhance the flavors. I am happy to see our familiar, large iron pot in use. We say a blessing before eating as we gather with our bowls, sniffing the delicious aroma. It is not what we are used to, but the food and fresh bread satisfies our hunger.

When the night falls, Francisco and I crawl under blankets on a straw mattress. It pokes me through the covering. I remember the sinking feeling of my bed at home filled with feathers that enveloped me, often tickling. He reaches for me and I succumb to his touch and then fall asleep until morning without interruption.

CHAPTER THIRTEEN

CELENDARIA

25 de enero 1656

We gather in the morning, rested and content, the fire still warm in its last red embers. More wood is gathered from felled trees and it blooms again, flames reaching higher. The familiar smell of coffee awakens us. The children, bread in hand, are thrilled with an opportunity to run without the confinement of a wagon. Some gather a few errant blackberries from under bushes, returning to us with stained fingers and mouths. They have been warned not to eat strange things. We are a subdued group, the women sitting together on benches away from the sun, my aunts with sewing in their laps. I lounge, my eyes following a butterfly. The men discuss our final destination and whether our conditions will improve.

Mama, how is mi abuela today?

Ah, she continues in her sleep. I am afraid she will leave us in this state. Oh, how awful to survive the Inquisitor's jail and not see true freedom.

How do you know we will be free? I cannot imagine such a feeling. Will I be a bird who lifts its wings to soar near the clouds?

343

My mother smiles. Celendaria, Celendaria, you have always been a dreamer, a poet with words. Maybe we can resume studies again when you—

My aunt Maria stands, screaming, her sewing drops to the ground. Maybe a snake has crawled near her. Her eyes open in fear, lips trembling.

She points behind us unable to speak. The ground becomes wet as water rains from under her skirt. I turn as the others do and we are all on our feet at once. I drop my cup with coffee, the dark liquid staining my skirt.

Indians! Indians! A tumult of fear captures us. My mother and aunts cling to one another, terror on their faces. Yael and Yonah start to cry, holding their arms over their heads, knowledgeable about scalping, the horrific stories about people left bleeding without the tops of their heads. It is not lost on me that savages kidnap young women as slaves in retaliation for the white man's cruelties.

Francisco comes forward from shoeing a mule to greet five men, their silhouettes outlined in the sun. He speaks a few words to them I do not understand. He welcomes them to our fire with an outstretched hand toward the vacated benches. Shocked that not only are they almost naked, their faces and bodies are covered with paint and tattoos, strange designs of lines that make them appear ferocious even though no one has been aggressive toward us yet. Large blue and red feathers peek out from the backs of their heads. Even more strange, their ink-black hair flows to their shoulders and longer, not unlike mine. I have not seen men with long tresses.

Without moving a muscle, I stare as the others do. My husband says to us, Do not fear the Chichimecas. They have brought plants with medicinal properties for our Clara.

I feel my eyes open wide in amazement, but words do not form in my mouth. What could they possibly have for her? Wait. Are these the cannibals he told me about, the ones who could eat us all? I swallow hard as we watch without breathing, the air frozen inside us.

One of the men removes a plant from a small leather bag that he hands to Francisco with one word: Boil.

Francisco tells my mother to bring a pan with water. My aunts Maria and Clodovea follow her. They return to place the full pot on the fire, stoking it with twigs. After more whispered words to my husband, the men look around and leave.

We collapse in relief, tears and laughter making us joyous. What did he give you? I want to know.

Peyote. They use it in sacred ceremonies. Maybe it will help your grandmother come back to this world.

What are we supposed to do with it? my mother wants to know.

Heat it until bubbles appear and the water is almost gone. Then mush it into a powder to make a tea for her to drink.

This will help her? my grandfather asks. I cannot believe this. Maybe it is poison. No, I will not have it.

Francisco paces around the fire and benches where moments before we saw a sight that none of us could imagine.

He explains, The natives use it in a few ways. It can be softened in the mouth by chewing and placed on cuts or snake bites. Or taken for fatigue or rheumatism, which your abuela has. Peyote also relieves headaches and colds in tiny amounts.

What will it do to her? How can that be? I am filled with questions.

It will wake her up if we can get her to drink it. The natives believe it is a gift from Mother Earth that contacts their ancestral spirits.

How do you know so much?

345

Francisco meets my eyes. My brothers and I have found safety among these people. They understand that we are different than the Spanish. We are not interested in converting them. They will not harm us.

The shoulders of my mother and the other women relax into a comfortable pose.

Do not be surprised when we reach our destination, Francisco continues, that some of our kind has intermingled with natives.

I gasp. I am learning more than I want to know.

CHAPTER FOURTEEN

CELENDARIA

27 de enero 1656

Yonah and Yael slide their hands under my grandmother, holding up her back and head while my mother and I administer the tea. At first the liquid dribbles down her chin, but finally, when she tastes something she begins to swallow. Her sips are small but soon she gulps down the mixture.

My mother confesses to us from the end of the bed. I added a little sugar for sweetness. We watch as mi abuela lies back and blinks her eyes, the first sign of life we have seen in days.

Abuela, can you hear me? My sisters join me, asking the same question. She stares at us, her head turning slightly to stare at each face.

How do you feel? She still has not spoken to us, but she is awake.

Come, girls, help me to sit her up. My mother moves to the side of the bed to assist us. My grandmother looks tired but she is alert.

Are you hungry? Girls, find the melon and figs in the back of the wagon that I purchased this morning.

Yael and Yonah run out the room, yelling, Abuela is awake!

They return with the food as the others crowd into the doorway. We step aside as my grandfather enters, making his way with a stick found for walking, tap-tapping the bricks, calling her name.

Clara, Clara, can you hear me, Clara? The ordeal of travel has made him frail, his delicate hand reaching toward hers with a slight tremor. She lifts a few fingers as we make space for him. The recognition in her eyes as he leans forward to kiss her translucent cheek speaks volumes about what she must feel.

My mother clears the room and cuts the soft flesh of a melon and a few figs into small bites. She places them between mi abuela's lips. My grandmother eats a few while other pieces fall to her chest.

She is not strong, my mother says as Francisco and my father enter. They approach the bed to stand at the end, admonishing her to eat more.

Abuela, says Francisco, we must leave now that you are awake. Can you travel in the back of a wagon? She nods.

I heave a sigh of relief. She can see and hear us. My father turns to wipe a tear from the corner of his eye. We leave the room so she can rest.

Francisco's father approaches our wagon. I busy myself packing our pots and food in the back.

Son, why are we leaving? Your brothers must be looking for us. The longer we stay in one place, the better chance we have they will spot us. I do not want to go.

I peek around the wagon to see he has folded his arms across his chest.

Father, I am worried too, although I do not appear so. He glances toward where he thinks I am. Anything could have happened to them—Indians, the Spanish military, ordinary robbers—but I have to take my family to safety.

What makes you think there is safety ahead? Battles have been waged against the Cocaxtle natives by the military. The area is crawling with Spanish. The Spanish will not seek us there.

His angry tone is not familiar to me as he badgers Francisco.

Father, my husband says, his voice dripping with frustration, I know of a community where we can blend in with others. Word will get out and they will find us.

No! You are abandoning your brothers. I refuse to leave here.

I crouch down as his anger escalates. I have not heard Francisco argue with his father before, but he shouts in a hoarse whisper, I do not dispose of my brothers. I have others to concern myself with. You cannot stay by yourself. You must come with us.

Ach, that damn priest has caused this, his father says. I doubt he can still be alive after sharing a horse and enduring the burning sun. Wait another day, my son. I want to see all my children again.

My head peeks above the wagon as Francisco approaches his father to give him a kiss of peace, a gesture associated with our people. It is a sign of respect from the Bible my grandfather taught me. Joseph refused to kiss a priestess while she was a pagan, but when she became a Jew, he pressed his lips to her cheek. I like this story, but to our detriment, only people of our faith do this. The Church claims it is heresy, the same as Judas' kiss at the Last Supper. We are cautious because it can give us away. Observers at the auto-de-fé of 1649 told us some of the doomed gave their tormentors a kiss of peace as they placed garrotes around their necks, brave and defiant to the end.

I cannot stay, Francisco tells his father, who moves away with haste, fists clenched. We have ninety leagues to travel. That will take us two weeks without stopping, he calls after him.

Once we find a shallow place to cross the Rio Grande, our procession rolls forward on an endless journey. Mi abuela has begun to eat again; the others remain resolute. Francisco allows me to manage the reins, our wagon in front. One of my nephews dozes as he rides our mule. We follow a trail many settlers have taken. At one point, my husband was prepared to follow an ancient trade route the Caddo natives tracked toward villages along the Red River heading east, marked with rock carvings from their ancestors. Others in our party felt we should stay traveling north from Mexico, including his father who has not spoken to him directly.

On this expedition, our caravan pursues the path north, using the stars as guidance. I do not know what lies ahead, but for now, we are safe. Francisco tells me we will not cross the Río Bravo del Norte. The word *bravo* lets me know the water is agitated and not safe to cross. We will stay in a familiar area established as Villa de San Luis, named by Luis de Carvajal in the 1580s. He and his family met a sad end at the end of 1596 because they were conversos like us.

When we arrive at a settlement near the lower part of *el río*, my eyes scan the area to see fields of cotton, grain, corn, a small plot of sugar cane and other flatland cleared of brush where other food is growing. Later I learn the tilled soil grows cabbage, carrots, potatoes, beets and onions, everything we need to survive. Fertile soil is a blessing.

We stop to observe a young man leaned over a hand-dug well called a *noria*, pulling up a pail of water on a rope that he pours into a trough nearby for horses. In the distance, we see a ranch protected by walls with defensive openings, surrounded by dozens of skeletal homes built from wooden poles known as jacales. Some are covered with mud and branches for the roof; others remain unfinished.

Young man, calls Francisco. He lifts his head from the noria to take in our caravan. Who owns this land? He points to a hacienda in the distance.

Señor Guzman and his family.

We approach with caution, the wagons of our family and friends behind us. An exhausting pilgrimage has taken its toll. We wait near our wagons while Francisco goes inside through strong oak doors. Long slits built into double walls for guns protect them from invaders—and there had been many.

We grow impatient. We wash ourselves at another noria nearby, cleaning the children's faces as they line up with tin cups. Mariel and I huddle together to watch native women carrying babies on their backs.

Have you noticed the children cry less when they can look out feeling their mothers' body close to them? Mariel asks.

Yes, have you tried it?

I have, but the sadness inside me will not leave until I see my priest, and I think Asher senses it, so he still cries. Look how round the baby grows. Ah, Celendaria. If he never returns, at least I know he loved me.

I cannot respond, my throat caught, unable to form words.

My mother and I visit my grandparents, exhausted from traveling for so many days. Mi abuelo searches at the bottom of a basket for his book, *Espejo de Consolacion de tristes*. It is his favorite because, although written by Fray Juan de Dueñas, it has the Old Testament stories of our heroes who triumphed over adversity. I must know it is safe, he says.

Cómo está, Abuela? I ask.

She is napping in the back of the wagon. My grandfather constructed a cover from sheets of white linen so that she was not in the sun. We peek underneath and see her chest rise with steady breaths.

My mother touches my arm. Do not wake her.

Finally, Francisco emerges from the hacienda gates with a smile. We are welcomed in this settlement. Any of the jacales that are not inhabited may be used. The children can help us unpack. Sounds of joy and laughter inspire hugs. We have found a home away from the Office of the Inquisition.

Francisco holds my hand and kisses the back of it. We watch in silence as trunks, baskets, blankets, textiles and food are unloaded in front of us. How did you know it would be safe for us here? I ask.

When I saw the animals fenced near the main house—horses, cattle, chickens, goats and a few sheep.

I shrug my shoulders. I do not understand.

No pigs. The people here believe as we do.

CHAPTER FIFTEEN

CELENDARIA

7 de febrero 1656

Our cheerful beginning turns heartrending when it is time to move my grandparents into their jacal.

Francisco tells my grandfather, You will be here only for a short time until we can negotiate better space for you.

His arms are filled with baskets of linens and books. I am carrying bedding to be placed on a frame my brothers constructed from loose lumber abandoned on the property. Mi abuelo glances around the small space and the dirt floor. Even with his weak eyes he can see a snake curled around itself in the corner of the room.

Clara will not come inside if this creature is not removed, he says.

Do not worry, Abuelo. I will take care of it. Francisco picks up the serpent with a stick and takes it outside into the fields. I watch through a small window as it hisses, scuttling away into the brush. I hope the children are careful.

After I make the bed, even placing a cup of water on a basket nearby, we stroll outside to bring mi abuela to her new space. She has made passage from the secret cells of our enemies to the open space of the desert. My grandfather calls to her as he lifts the shade linen.

Clara, Clara. We are here. Clara?

I lean into the wagon to see her sleeping. My fingers stroke her face. Abuela, you can come now. We have made a bed for you. But she does not respond to my touch or my grandfather calling her name.

Francisco crawls into the wagon and presses his lips to her forehead. He climbs down and places his arms around us.

She is gone, he says.

My grandfather begins a wail that brings the others. I sob into my mother's shoulder while Francisco picks her up and takes her inside to the bed meant for a vibrant soul. At least she did not perish in their prisons. Perhaps her spirit is soaring, flying, sailing, gliding with the joy of freedom. I pray this is so.

According to our laws, the funeral must take place with haste. By law, someone must stay with her overnight so she is never alone. My grandfather, father and brothers take turns sitting on a low stool, candles flickering in the darkness. Behind the walls of the hacienda, our hosts have offered a small burial plot in a shady corner where others have been buried. We do not have time to build a simple pine box. León and Aruh use shovels to dig her grave deep so animals or others will not disinter her body. Afterward, all the men render a small cut on their clothing over the heart, a sanctioned destruction to express grief.

My mother, aunts and I prepare our abuela by removing her clothes to burn, washing the body according to the tenets of our faith that we must be unsoiled when we meet our Adonai. We swath her in the white linen that had protected her from the sun. As a married woman, I participate by cleaning under her nails with a sliver of wood and combing her hair. Silent as we work, we send the twins to gather the men to bring her body inside the compound walls, carrying her feet first.

Her body is placed in the grave with her head at the top, facing to the east toward Jerusalem.

My grandfather, disconsolate, rises to read from his sacred book, the *Espejo de Consolacion de tristes.* Psalms 16 and 23 are recited. When the grave is filled, he reads *Tziduk Hadin,* a prayer of our faith in God and the divinity of his justice. He recites the memorial prayer with tears coursing down his cheeks. He is the most learned among us. Who will carry on these traditions when he leaves us?

He recites the memorial prayer, an affirmation of God's compassion and mercy, and says at the end, Clara Mendoza Crespin is among the righteous.

My father uses a shofar, a ram's horn, tied to his belt, which he blows with the ancient sounds of the Israelites.

Usually a benevolent society exists to bury the dead. We make do. Mi abuela is interred in the small cemetery. May her life be a blessing. My mother and sisters leave a stone behind, something that will not wilt, die or blow away.

The children have gathered small rocks that they place at the top of the grave. So, before we have settled ourselves, we put mi abuela, my heart, into her final resting place. I wish her peace in the next life. She was the bravest person I have ever known, who never whispered a name during her confinement. I know this because none others were ever arrested from our circle, except for my brief incarceration staged to get her to reveal names. Our seven days of mourning begin when we sit on low stools on the floor. We do not last the entire week save for my grandfather who cannot abandon his grief.

We have much work to do.

CHAPTER SIXTEEN

CELENDARIA

23 de mayo 1656

Compared to Ciudad de México, the Nuevo León that Luis Carvajal founded, also known by the names Villa de San Luis and Monterrey, exists as a place of contradictions, a disorganized hub of jacales, some houses made of stone, spacious haciendas behind walls, wandering livestock, cornstalks in gardens, natives working the land, and a few public buildings including a courthouse.

I feel safer here because the Indians have made a distinction between us and the Spanish, who raid them for slaves. Our community no longer participates in this trade—we remember we were captives in Egypt. I am sad that others of our persuasion took advantage of those brought here against their will. We have an uneasy truce that we will not intrude on the other's lives.

Sometimes an itinerant Franciscan arrives with a portable altar to say mass. We participate to avoid suspicion until the men hustle the priest along to the next village, fearful of the tentacles of the Holy Office. I regret my grandmother's passing. She could have said the rosary with him so he would have left sooner.

Religiosity pervades this small place, but after shopping in the market and meeting neighbors, I feel a current of tolerance and tenacity with other conversos. Although no synagogue has been built, we know about informal meetings inside one of the haciendas established by those from the Canary Islands.

While some take their leave to travel north from this primitive area into more of the unknown, others are added to our group when more conversos find us, arriving here after travel from the Indies. Even some Asians find this area. Protestants escape the watchful eye of the Spanish, *criollo* nobility of questionable parentage look for safety in their silks, farmers come to grow crops in the fertile soil not far from the Rio Bravo and still others set up small stalls to buy and sell goods. My father has sold or traded many of his textiles, and knows a short route to more business where Indian women weave. He also purchases buttons, ribbons and lace that are all in demand. Francisco imports chocolate, bitter but enhanced with sugar, that becomes a delightful treat. He buys it from others who market the cacao beans but has plans to process them himself. And, I am with child, a blessing.

In the late afternoon after I have shoed the mules, when the full moon relaxes into a new one, I rest on our porch. Clouds roll toward us. A storm gathers dust while I search the horizon for rain, always welcome for our crops. Out of the monsoon, two men ride with haste, horse hooves stirring up dust. As they approach, I become fearful of trouble. Hats shield their eyes as droplets of water let loose. Many more horsemen approach the hacienda for shelter, but the Guzmans, our hosts, cannot welcome everyone. We are grateful they allow our family to build and farm nearby. We do not own this land, but a rumor that property can be purchased on the other side of the river for little money intrigues Francisco. He speaks to me of it often when we hold each other close at night.

The stampede of hooves comes closer. Fear crawls up my throat. I call out to my sisters nearby who are gathering vegetables from our garden.

Get Francisco! I yell.

They look at me, the cloud of dust quickly approaching, and run, their skirts lifted with anxiety. The horses draw closer, snorting and prancing. I want to run inside and close the latch, but I know it will offer little protection. Instead, I stand to face whoever has come. They circle around a few times and I see a large package behind one of the men.

Celendaria, we have arrived!

I recognize the voices under unkempt beards—Manuel and Duarte have returned!

I am thrilled to see them, but where is Father Lopez? I should not call him this anymore. It could give him away. I stand and wave.

Francisco arrives breathless. What is it?

My brother! shouts Manuel, climbing down from his horse. The two brothers hug and slap each other on the back.

Where have you been all this time? asks Francisco.

It is a long story to share later.

A face peeks around from behind Duarte who has not dismounted. It looks like a young boy until I realize it is Miguel Lopez, thinner, more drawn, less imposing without his cassock. I cannot believe my eyes. They are all alive! They get down from Duarte's horse and tie it and Manuel's to the post across our porch. I hug my brothers-in-law.

I send my sisters to fetch Mariel. Seconds later, she runs toward us from the home where she and her parents stay with the baby.

Mariel, He is here! I shout, running to greet her. She runs past me and leaps into Miguel's arms, crying, a reunion that brings tears to my eyes. Whatever I think of him, she is in love and they have made a baby together. Perhaps my grandfather will perform another wedding. It is never too late for love.

Beatriz and Diego Behar are not pleased that he is among us. Will he remain a priest or will he join us to live as Jews, albeit hidden ones? At first he is tongue-tied; a man that we know has done wrong, sheepish that we are the ones to save him. But who are we to judge?

Later, after the men have cleansed themselves at the nearby spring, Los Ojos de Agua de Santa Lucia, we feast on a dinner of roasted chicken donated by the Behars, potatoes and salad from our gardens and listen to the story of why the men have been delayed for so long. We gather near our fire that the children have fed with small branches and twigs.

Miguel begins before the brothers speak. Contrite, he shares in a low voice, unlike his priestly one. Thank you for welcoming me into your community. I have been on an extraordinary journey. I am grateful to these men for bringing me to safety, he says as he gestures toward Francisco's brothers. He pauses before he speaks again, swallowing hard and lifting his eyes. He drinks from a cup we have filled with whiskey before he continues.

At the beginning, three soldiers and a guard watched over me. I thought no escape was possible. I have sinned, so my punishment of losing my freedom was expected. I knew that if my superiors had the opportunity, they would send me to the gallows where no survival is possible and death is a relief. I have been schooled in the ways of the Church, but my family still follows the Law of Moses. My mother encouraged me to join the priesthood because it would be protection from the authorities. I have lived in two worlds for a long time.

My guard at the jail appreciated my dilemma. He expressed concerns that he had sinned so I taught him the sacraments—baptism, confirmation and Holy Communion, which he needed to be initiated into the Church. I established a friendship with him. A man of thirty years, he asked if I could take his confession, although he knew my religiosity was in question. He remained afraid of consequences that he brought into his life because he had two wives, one in Mexico City of high birth and another in San Miguel, a peasant woman he adored. He fathered children with both and was in terrible anguish. He wanted me to relieve his conflict, as bigamy was punishable by death. He trusted me to guide him through a confession and wanted ablution for his sins.

Did he love both of them? I ask.

Francisco gives me a harsh look. My wife asks many questions.

Yes, he appreciated both, but could not support them and his children as a guard. Miguel stops. He is too emotional to go on. Perhaps he is consumed with guilt for fooling the guard or maybe he thinks he had to survive for his own family. Mariel sits next to him at the fire, her head dipping to his shoulder, the baby sleeping in his lap. Her beatific face reminds me of Madonna paintings I have seen.

Manuel takes over. Freeing Mariel was not exactly easy, but getting past a guard and soldiers was a bigger challenge. We had difficulty finding the jail, a small structure the Spanish enhanced with a battalion. Eight or nine leagues from here, a terrible massacre occurred between the natives and settlers in '61 and '62. One hundred twenty-five warriors, women and children were captured. After a five-month battle, people are cautious and angry. No one would attempt to break out a prisoner with so many armed men. Except us. He smiled.

He continues his story.

Duarte and I rode up to the front. He waited outside with the horses while I strolled into a reception area, so if there was trouble, at least one of us could escape. A soldier in uniform asked my business. I removed the paper for Miguel's release from the bag inside my clothes and handed it to him. He put on eyeglasses and read it carefully. The silence made my heartbeat sound like the pounding of an anvil. The Father is a valuable prisoner, he said. The officials of the Inquisition are very interested in him. He sniggered, a Judaizer no doubt.

I do not care about those people, I told him. I make no judgments. He read the paper again, running his thumb over the seals. I did my best not to appear nervous, folding my arms across my chest. I looked around for another exit. He handed it back to me, his eyes drilling into me. Perhaps this was the moment I was going to shoot my way out of there, my duty incomplete.

Manuel lowers his voice to imitate the soldier. It appears in order. You are familiar to me. Have I seen you before?

I said, No, with emphasis. Wary of reprisals, I took a harsh tone. We are bondsmen who do the work of the courts and the Church. My duty is to return this man to Mexico City.

Guard, take this man to the prisoner.

He led me down a hallway, keys rattling against his hip, the soldier behind us. I prayed our priest would not give me away. Color faded from his face when we were led to his cell.

Miguel interjects, I thought I was doomed. Once I was returned to the Inquisition offices in Mexico City, there would be no mercy. I have sinned. He hangs his head in shame.

Manuel continues. I walked into his cell with the guard, who was not anxious for his prisoner to leave.

Father, may I have one more confession, he asked.

The soldier said, No more. He is not qualified to give anyone the sacraments. Get him out of here. They wait for him in Ciudad de México. He will get what he deserves there.

When I turned Miguel around to restrain his arms, I whispered in his ear to follow my orders. Then, in a louder voice, I said, we will make sure this renegade is brought to justice. Then I told Miguel, we do not expect any trouble from you. I cannot truss your legs so if you try to escape, we will shoot you.

With red eyes cast downward and loose flesh, he shuffled down the hall in front of us.

I left with him, my fingers embracing my gun as though he would bolt, his hands restricted behind his back. The guard thanked him for his counsel and we hoisted Miguel onto my horse.

Prisoners slide off the back if you are not careful, the soldier called out to me.

I tipped my hat to him and climbed on behind Miguel.

CHAPTER SEVENTEEN

CELENDARIA

1 de junio 1656

I want to know why it took so many months to find us. Francisco heard the story from his brothers, but was reluctant to share it with me before the baby arrived. At first he resisted my questions, but finally, one evening after our meal as we all sat together on benches and chairs, the older members drifting away to their spaces for sleep, Manuel told me the story with Francisco's urging.

Duarte, Miguel and I were chased by Indians who wanted our horses. We managed to escape the first time and found refuge in a village that had been destroyed by an attack the day before by other hostile natives. We were alarmed to see homes hollowed by fire, bodies left in the square and a few settlers who were injured, petrified, hiding in a basement. All their goats, sheep and rams were taken—900 in all. I felt such sadness to see their tears at what was destroyed. I am sure it was braves from the Cocaxtle tribe who I knew to fear.

I could not keep quiet. I said, I cannot imagine such horror. They were people like us with families, children.

I stroke my belly.

Francisco breathed a sigh. I see no hope of peace in this region in the north of Mexico between those who reside here and others who want to come. The natives do not want a peaceful coexistence. They want their land. Some of them have been baptized, but none that I have observed follow the Church. The Spanish efforts have been in vain. He shook his head in sorrow.

Manuel continues, Our priest said last rites with those from the destroyed village, although I warned him it could be a marker for us. We did the best we could for the people and continued on our trip, but alas, we were ambushed by more natives who hailed us with arrows. One shot Duarte in the arm. Others bounced off our leather cueras. I hunched over the priest who was riding in front of me, his head bent between his legs.

Manuel looks around to see who is listening. In a less boisterous voice he says, I resented risking our lives for him, but we had no choice. We kept riding until we reached a crevice we knew that led to a deep cave.

I interrupt. How did you know more Indians would not be secreted in the rocks?

Francisco smiled at my naiveté. We are experienced at survival. The natives do not know every cave, every hole in the rocks.

We had to rest to pull the arrow, Manuel explains. Sometimes they are tipped with poison from ugly gila monsters that roam the desert. The natives tease the large lizards to bite into a piece of tainted meat and stick the tip into it. Duarte, stoic, was in terrible pain, the wound weeping blood and pus.

Manuel paused and with a knowing face said, Many have lost a limb in the aftermath of an unhealed wound. Or died an excruciating death.

I put my hand over my mouth at Manuel's description. My stomach turned over and then I began to burp. It made me giggle in the middle of his story that I knew ended well.

Francisco hugs me close to him, stroking my hair. I am pleased you are my wife, he says, before kissing me on the cheek. We linger, our breaths bathing our faces, our eyes searching for solace in an incomprehensible world. I place his hand on my belly as the baby shifts. His eyes, round with pleasure, speak to me. He whispers, A miracle.

Continue the story, I tell Manuel when my burps subside.

Duarte drank all the whiskey I carried in a goat's bladder, Manuel continues. The priest—uh, Miguel—held him down while I pulled the arrow from him. Duarte groaned, delirious with pain. The blood was profuse. I knew I needed to get help. I left Duarte with the priest and rode to another town where a herbolario lived, bunches of dried herbs hanging near his hearth. He instructed me to keep the wound clean and gave me comfrey to enhance healing, valerian to assist Duarte with his restless sleep and muslin to make a poultice that was supposed to draw away the poison. When I returned, I ground the herbs and heated them in water over a fire. I followed all the instructions but my brother became very ill. He muttered words we could not understand. Miguel was kind not to offer last rites. Duarte's skin was cold yet his brow sweated. It became necessary to transfer him to a settled outpost and rent a room in a ranchero's home so he could have a proper bed.

But were you afraid to be discovered? I ask.

Yes, we were always in danger. We said little and refused to answer questions. I gave the man's wife, a mestiza, coins for food and Duarte's bed so they became less curious. Our host prepared a poultice of thyme and sage to counter the poison. Duarte's fevers raged for weeks and I thought he would die. We even used tobacco like some tribes do to draw the poison, but he became sicker. How could I leave my brother? Our father would never forgive me. At one point I thought he would die, but I still had to bring him back. I could not abandon him to the coyotes without a proper burial. Manuel glances to the floor, leaning forward. Francisco reflects by closing his eyes.

Duarte speaks to us. I am grateful to my brother but I remember little. Look at what I wear around my neck. I leaned forward to view the tip of the arrow hanging from a leather strip. It was large and sharp at the end.

I can see how this caused damage, I say.

Francisco addresses Manuel. My brother, please continue the story so I may retire with my lovely wife. He squeezes my hand.

Manuel continues, promising to be more succinct. When authorities came to the door looking for three men, the woman hid us in a root cellar but then told us we had to leave. I convinced Miguel to dress as a woman to attract less notice. We borrowed a skirt for him to wear over his pants and he donned a scarf as we rode off.

From there we went to Cadereyta, a presidio filled with soldiers who were probably looking for three men, not two men and a woman. Although it was only seven leagues from here, a day's ride, it was not safe for us to draw attention to ourselves, nor mix with the Spanish. We heard that natives from the Tetecuara nation made an appearance near the foothills, waged a few attacks and then disappeared, so we waited, idle and impatient. We obtained hardtack, meat and other provisions, but we could not leave.

Where did you sleep? I want to know.

Duarte says, I was still in pain, my arm strapped to my chest. Our brother wrapped it well, he says to Francisco with a smile. We could not stay inside the presidio, which would have been the safest place.

What happened? I want to know, raising myself to a better position. My baby is giving me discomfort.

Manuel continues. Duarte and I sought assistance from a stout woman in the market who had more herbs to relieve pain. She agreed to house us for a few days, but we stayed longer. She had five daughters. One of them took a liking to the stranger in their midst with the injury and sad eyes.

Manuel kicks his brother's leg.

It is time to tell them.

Before I tell my father? says Duarte.

I am suspicious. What is he concealing? Manuel urges him to confess.

I am married.

Married? To whom? I cannot conceive of this news.

Catalina.

Who is she? I ask, incredulous.

You will meet her soon. There are plans to bring her here.

I turn to Francisco. Has he told you this? Francisco shakes his head, but a guilty closing of his eyes lets me know his answer. Ah, he has withheld information. Not a lie, but still an untruth.

Duarte addresses me. Celendaria, my father does not know this yet. Please do not tell.

Francisco understands this will not satisfy me. I tap his shoulder so he will turn to face me. I search his face for more, but this is the way in our lives. The men do not tell the women everything. Nor do the women tell the men everything.

Would you like some mint tea?

No, says Francisco. Let my brothers finish their story so we can go to bed.

Duarte clears his throat. It was not my intention to involve myself, but Catalina, a kind, beautiful, young woman of sixteen with glossy black hair trailing down her back, took care of me. My brother and the priest went out with caution to gather information, supplies, re-shoe the horses. I could not leave her. The way she troubled herself for me—bringing me clean bandages, feeding me, making tea from bee balm—I could not leave without her. I was not able to make the trip alone with the priest at my back and no other protection. So we waited.

Why did you not bring her with you?

She could not be on a horse and we had no wagon. Besides, Manuel thought I should clean myself to speak to our father first.

Why? When will you tell him? I want to know about Catalina.

Soon. I want to be holy when I tell him. Duarte pauses. She is with child, my first. I want our father to know she is a *mulata*, the color of chocolate with milk.

What? This shocks me, but I understand the circumstances. I am surprised because we do not mix with other faiths. What is her parentage?

Duarte hesitates again. Her mother, a mestiza from the south, stayed with the son of a Negro slave owned by Portuguese explorers who freed him after good deeds. In the settlements, all people work together to survive.

Will she understand our ways?

I think so. She told me she was not enamored of the Church. But, I do not know. I did not speak of our purity of blood or the Mosaic Law we follow. But one odd thing about her family—they did not have any crucifixes in the adobe. Instead, her mother draped sausages she made across the hearth. At first I shunned them because of the pork, but when Catalina urged me to try one, I learned they were made from chicken and bread. I think they are not fully aware of what their heritage might be.

I look forward to meeting Catalina. When will she come?

After the baby. Her sisters will bring her with guards.

What about you, Manuel? There were five girls. Did you pick one too? I touch my belly. It will be good for our child to have more cousins.

No, not yet, he answers. I would like a wife. He smiles.

Francisco stands. It is time to rest. He holds my elbow.

When we return to our space and lay next to each other on our sides, I rub my husband's bottom lip with my forefinger. He pulls it in with his mouth to suck like a baby.

CHAPTER EIGHTEEN

CELENDARIA

26 de septiembre 1656

My labor was a short one with the assistance of my mother and my aunts Maria and Rosa urging me to push. I wished my grandmother could have soothed my brow. I felt her presence as my mind rolled over into a white light of pain, thunder colliding in my belly. After a cataclysmic rupture where I screamed curse words that had never been uttered from my lips before, I opened my eyes to a pink treasure resting on my chest. My hands wandered over him until I felt a bump.

A boy, I said, to the happy faces of my female relatives and Francisco, who leaned over to kiss me. Our eyes met and we knew we had created another being to learn our prayers. I will forever acknowledge the birth of our son on the 18th day of Elul on the eve of Rosh Hashanah, our New Year. Let the Feast of Trumpets herald a birth in the year 5417 in the Hebrew calendar.

Our son, Aron, named after his paternal grandfather according to the traditions of Spain, has brought more joy than I have ever known. Although he is small, his eyes follow me, tiny hands reaching out.

Before the eighth day when his brit milá would be performed by my grandfather, an argument ensued between Francisco and his brothers.

When you take the end, you mark him for life as a Jew, says Manuel. Duarte said if the authorities find him, he is doomed. We have not been circumcised. Why would you make him different from his father?

Mi abuelo makes his point: Circumcision is the oldest covenant between Abraham and God. We had to break it during dangerous times, but we must resume this tradition as our community grows. Our Prophet, Elijah, appears at miraculous times.

I am confused. I know of the tradition, even that some have been circumcised later in life, but I do not want to endanger my baby.

I ask Francisco, Are your brothers right about this? What if at some point he is with other men or the evil ones want to see his member?

Francisco sides with his father and my grandfather who hold fast to tradition. I am afraid for my baby on the eighth day of his life, but my mother encourages me. It is healthier for the baby. He will survive through storms or fevers.

But what if he is caught and persecuted because of it? I ask.

My mother hugs me. He will tell them it is the folly of women that made it shaped like a mushroom.

What? Women have nothing to do with the ritual. I cannot teach my son another lie. We repeat so many.

Ah, Celendaria, do you not know that some believe this to be true? That is why lonely women wait in Inquisition secret cells as witches.

But, how could a woman influence the outcome?

My mother shakes her head at me. My daughter, some unenlightened souls think that coupling with certain women can shift a body part.

I stutter, B-but that is ludicrous.

She shrugs her shoulders at me. The uneducated live in simplistic bliss.

Unhappiness clouds my vision, my ability to gaze forward. Mama, what do you think we should do?

My mother considers my question. Since this is the first child born in our new village, I encourage you to follow your grandfather's ways.

The disagreement with Duarte and Manuel, who refuse to attend, lasts the entire week. Francisco, annoyed with his siblings, makes a decision that he announces to us: Our brit milá is tomorrow on the eighth day of Tishrei, known as Yom Kippur, the Day of Atonement. We must fast this day but I am exempt as a nursing mother.

Please join us in prayer for our son, a celebration of joy for a new life, says Francisco as he invites others. He spends the rest of the day gathering wine from neighbors and searching baskets of my father's textiles for purple and gold fabric to drape over a chair that represents a throne for the prophet Elijah.

Elijah dwells with us at our Passover Seder where we offer a glass of wine, opening the door to beckon his entrance. He also attends every brit milá as a witness observing from his chair.

Some think superstitions like knocking on wood to represent the slain one's cross foolish, but in this case I feel the presence of the spiritual guide. After all, we cannot see Adonai yet we know He is there.

When the men stand together, Elijah's seat remains empty with a book on it so no one will sit on the patriarch's chair. Manuel and Duarte emerge at the last moment to join us, donning skullcaps on the crowns of their heads. Francisco takes Aron from my arms and brings him to my grandfather on a pillow my aunts have covered with colorful shawls. I cannot see as all the men in our family, Señor Behar and a few neighbors gather around the newborn, including the former priest. The latter does not meet our eyes, still remorseful at the trouble he has caused.

Mariel stands next to me with her son, a happy boy, so she can grab my hand when we hear a cry. Arrows burn through my stomach at the thought of anyone putting a knife near my precious child, but I understand the importance of tradition. Our neighbors have told us this is only the second brit performed in our area because fear has been so great.

After prayers that urge Francisco to fulfill his obligation of educating our son and raising him with kindness, my grandfather dribbles a few drops of red wine on Aron's lips.

My mother whispers to me. He will feel nothing. We watch from the other side of the room.

Mi abuelo's voice wavers as he says, *Bereshut moirei verabota* in Ladino, our ancient language. He explains that he is asking permission of his teachers and the community to perform this covenant. A small squeal is heard and then nothing. My heart flutters. I want to run across the room and break through the men when suddenly my son is lifted above their heads on his pillow.

Welcome Aron Cordova Crespin Trevez to this new life, says my grandfather.

I cannot wait to take Aron to my breast again, where he suckles and then sleeps. We sip wine and pass cinnamon and nutmeg on a plate to smell the fragrant spices for a sweet life. According to Mosaic Law, a soul is now infused into my son.

It is the first time since leaving Ciudad de México we have given a collective sigh away from the nightmare of the Inquisition. The

Spanish are too busy with their Indian wars, a failing economy and criticisms from others who observe their inhumanity to bother us at the moment. Francisco, Aron and I are a family.

BOOK FOUR

CHAPTER ONE

CLARA CELENDARIA CRESPIN MENDOZA

8 de octubre 1810
10 Tishrei 5571
Yom Kippur, Day of Atonement, el dia grande
San Miguel, México

Hardly a month ago on the 15 de septiembre, bells rang out in Dolores Hidalgo encouraging the people of Mexico to rise up against their Spanish oppressors. Some have responded but few have committed, so feared are our inquisitors who still reign with their hierarchal power that some of the ruling elite, the benefactors of the Spanish king's largesse of cattle and land, refuse to oppose the ecclesiastical tribunal. It is said they believe the papal government is seen as a benign institution, one that protects society. No one wants fomenters of social revolution. Except the Jews. We are their only opposition.

Our revenge, repeated in stories transported by survivors, tell of Jewish pirates—yes, some so gripped with anger, infuriated at the capture of their assets, especially gold, silver and firearms, that they attacked the Spanish ships, retrieved their goods and murdered the emissaries of the Inquisition, sinking galleons in the glittering harbors of the Caribbean. But alas, there were not enough of them. Most of the booty disappeared into the monarchy's accumulated debt and the coffers of the Catholic Church after passing through Cuba.

I am the descendant of these brave peoples known as master traders who explored North Africa, the Ottoman Empire and the Middle East until we reached South America and continued north. We trusted one another, passing our routes of commerce down to each other's families, a source of revenue in luxury goods, textiles and spices that left the women alone for long periods of time to make decisions. They are the keepers of the faith to this day.

What do I know of them? Unfortunately, some of our generations faded into the infinite depth of the seas on the long journey, but not before our memory of fear, the sensation to flee, the importance of our children to survive forced us to recapitulate the rituals that replay in our souls after thousands of years. We used clay pots to burn our candles to welcome the Sabbath bride instead of the glorious silver candlesticks passed down from generations, long ago confiscated to gain freedom. We washed the bodies of the dead for immediate burial, the prayers memorized by our mothers after most of the books were destroyed, only later to be accused, tried and executed more than men. We shared the beliefs with our children, prepared food to remind us of our ancestors in Egypt, often confessing on our deathbeds to protect our progeny from harm. The inheritance of anxiety, the scent of agitation, the foreboding of all evil made us suspicious of others outside our circle.

And some, born into our generations of remembrance, carried melancholia for the damage done; loves and possessions cast aside, the sighing grief of an unsafe future met with headaches, insomnia, palpitations of the heart. The distress of uncertainty, restlessness that twitched our souls, created pale and wan mortals with slow fevers lacking the strength to move to another land. And, always, our constant fear.

The migrations of over hundreds of years as we were hounded across seas to unexpected continents with their own native peoples took their toll, the sacred promises dissipated in fogs of faith, a love of one God above all else. Through assimilation into other cultures, we lost many to a solid belief in their Father, Son and Holy Ghost whom we called meshumadin, the ones who converted willingly. Others went underground, like my family, and some were defiant, our martyrs who held ground and spoke for those of us who remained silent in the face of overwhelming institutionalized hate, sanctioned by Pope Sixtus IV who launched the Inquisition at the bequest of the evil monarchs in 1478.

The monarchs thought they could increase their political authority by suppressing us even more, confiscating our property and arresting us with suspicion of heresy. However, our spirits were not dampened by these squalls. For those of us who never let go, we disappeared further into secrecy or took flight like my ancestors, departing for foreign shores.

Why did they hate us so? Jealousy. Our respect for education, our love of The Book, the interest in a vocation or trade, a pursuit of the highest levels acknowledged by royal courts, an accumulation of assets through hard work and diligence, a respect for God and the cleanliness ordered by our Sabbath. It did not assist our cause that the Old Christians who followed the Church with rigor were not permitted to loan money so we accepted that responsibility. The motivation to cast us out meant our neighbors and the evil monarchs did not have to pay their debts, a simple way to clear the evil queen's financial obligations to those who financed her desire to unite Spain. We were fools to trust, and trust again.

After Brazil lost their tolerant Dutch colony of Recife where we once prospered through the import of sugar cane, plantations and slaves brought from Africa—yes, we owned people—the governor, John Maurits, who invited scientists and artists to increase the population, yielded to the Portuguese in 1661.

Once again, we boarded ships that scattered us deeper into the Diaspora of the unknown, some evacuating back to Holland. Most fled, some to New Amsterdam to the north of us, where they were robbed by diabolical Spanish pirates who looted us of our meager belongings, only to have our compatriot's ships rescued by the French, who were too stingy to return the families on board to the Old World. Peter Stuyvesant, the governor of New Amsterdam, did not allow them to enter at first, but finally, he capitulated. So the French escorted and deposited twenty-three refugee men, women and children on the shores of New Amsterdam in 1654.

Others found homes in Peru and Columbia after leaving the islands off the coast of Florida, where the Inquisition built their courts and jails. Some even explored the Philippines.

Some of the loneliest conversos stayed behind, abandoned in jungles to mingle with the darker-skinned natives who knew how to survive in the forest. Many of us no longer bear the snowy, blanched skin and pitch-black straight hair of the elite in Spain. Instead, some of us have a tawny countenance and crisp curls. I am among them.

Those who remained in Recife were forced to convert, still following the commandments of their faith in secret while others fled to the Dutch West Indies, especially to Jamaica, Curaçao or Cuba where Luis de Torres who accompanied Christopher Columbus made his home. As late as 1783, the Inquisition, fueled by the hostility of the Jesuits, searched out the hidden Jews who had fled to the New World, making their way north looking for peace not prosecution.

This is where my story begins. On that endless journey through cities and states, past Peru and its Inquisition sanctioned by the Church and state, dependent on the Crown's approval, established on 5 de febrero 1570 in Lima to not only root out heretics who deigned to follow their original faith but also indigenous peoples—those of African descent, mestizos, women and European Protestants accused of heresy, witchcraft and superstitions, those poor souls seeking refuge from religious persecution.

Our stories have been passed down as we whispered among ourselves in the privacy of the Sabbath. Where does such bravery come from? Such determination? An ability to destroy one's life? After the largest auto-de-fé in the New World held in Peru in 1639, we continued to move north, avoiding Cartagena in Columbia, known for its Palace of Inquisition established in 1570.

I am still afraid, a melancholy gripping me in the night, sadness from all the fleeing. What have I done wrong? Once, my great-grandmother grabbed my arm when I peppered her with questions about why we were chased for so long. Stop it. The answers do not matter. We are the same as them. When she loosened her grip, I saw pearls of tears.

Today is the holiest day where we confess our sins and ask others for forgiveness. I am fasting. We do not have a synagogue but I will not forget our obligations and prayers to the Almighty.

CHAPTER TWO

CLARA CELENDARIA CRESPIN MENDOZA

10 de julio 1820, ten o'clock in the morning
Santa Oficina de la Inquisición
Ciudad de México

I watch as seventy armed soldiers with two cannons appear in front of the doors at the Palace of the Holy Inquisition that overlooks Santo Domingo Plaza. A tall, thin notary with many spots on his face reads a proclamation and edict that orders the Holy Office extinct. Afterward, he affixes it to the imposing wooden doors built into the corner of the building.

What will the inquisitors do without their jobs of torturing the populace? Time stops. Not even a dog barks. I huddle under the shade of a tree, a witness for all those who never saw the light of day. Even the leaves cease to rustle in the wind. I recognize the Captain Pedro Llop as he bangs on the door with fury, his fists and sword creating a racket. Still, the doors do not open. Many of us are scattered on the plaza, waiting, yearning in silence.

Blow them up! shouts the captain to his troops. The cannons roll into place. I cannot run away from the finale of almost four hundred years of operatic agony and torment. I was a witness to history as I prepared for the reverberations of cannon fodder that can cause deafness from the blast by putting my fingers in my ears.

And, as if the angels from above have eavesdropped, the massive wooden doors slide open to reveal a dark cavern.

I flood inside with others who come behind the soldiers. They could not stop us since more of us had gathered than them. Mothers, fathers, children, cousins—for were we not all related in some fashion? Some have been waiting more than thirty years to embrace their loved ones, creating a deluge of bodies through the doors, shouting names, voices hoarse from needy repetitions.

I trail behind others who charge ahead of me to observe this fortress created in the name of God. I enter with caution, as though the doors could close, trapping me inside. To the right of the main stairway, a grand affair, are the three audience chambers, doors thrust open by those ahead of me, and the elaborate apartments for those guilty of this degradation. I peek into the first one lined with oil-painted portraits and shields that belong to the forty inquisitors who perpetrated this abomination on their brethren. Each one boasts their place of birth, year of death, sometimes listing the cause, such as consumption and how long they served the Inquisition.

I squint to read their occupations before they embraced this treachery. How could anyone who had been a priest and bookbinder accept what was perpetrated in the name of the Church? One evil-looking face draws me to step closer. His eyes are cold, hard as agate, his face long, and his countenance stern. I read his name: Lord Inquisitor Dr. Juan Saenz de Mañzoca, 1640-1685, presided over the court in Ciudad de México. What filled his heart with so much evil?

Suddenly I feel a chill. I feel as though I am completely alone in this sinful building. The story of my ancestor whose name I carry was incarcerated here. The narrative of the grandmother who was given up to the authorities by her own daughter has been told many times in our family. It's a cautionary tale we tell to the young. Be careful who you are close to; keep the family secrets; be aware of those who harbor jealousy. Memories flood over me and I run from the room with the pained face of a woman in front of me. I cannot get her out of my mind. It is a veil that only lifts when I push it aside with great effort. She stays with me as I tour the building.

I wander alone, trailing, blinking in disbelief, my mind alert to memorize details, as others charge by me, anxious to recover loved ones, touch the forbidden, bellows of joy amid wails of despair.

I enter a library with windows, the glass etched with the emblem of the Inquisition, an irony since so many books have been confiscated, conflagrated for centuries, especially the Torah, the holy book of our faith. Many believed if God had a soul, it would be the Torah. I thought all were burned, but on the shelf, I see scrolls that are still in their ragged covers.

A young priest stands inside the door, hands folded in front of him. I startle with fear. I did not expect to see you, Father. My lips tremble at his proximity; his presence frightens me. My instincts tell me to turn and run. I cannot. What difference will it make what happens now? I move toward shelves stacked with volumes, my finger straying across the bindings.

Do not fear me, he says. I mean you no harm.

My heart beats faster. Is this a trick? It has happened before. I turn to him with caution, a questioning look on my face.

I am here as an observer also. Many of us inside the Church have objected to these inquiries and their methods. More than one thousand books are stored in three collections on this floor.

I am incredulous and say, Three?

Yes, my child.

My mind skips to the mockery of me as a woman in middle age being called a child by a man the age of my grandchildren. But so it is with the Church who wants to control what people read, if they are able to read at all. Distraught many years ago, 1770 to be exact, we learned of the trials in Veracruz, a coastal city where an entrepôt from the Old World emerged. All ships that arrived in port were inspected for treacherous materials, regional commissaries inspecting all cargo. Confiscated books, pamphlets, prints, paintings, even drawings were a threat to the Church and used as evidence. All aboard including the captain were arrested. If people communicated in direct response to our one God, no one would need priests. Hah! Am I free of this travesty? We will see.

My child, he repeats.

I respond with my attention, although a racket ensues outside the door.

This room holds the completed cases of the Inquisition, all who have been arrested, tried, some executed, even a few set free. The next room holds the current investigations.

There are current investigations? I ask.

Yes, heretics have not disappeared and the Church must remain vigilant.

I do not respond. Would I find my relatives accusations in there? Women, keepers of the faith. We have been Judaizers, mystics,

Protestants, bigamists, Moriscos, heretics, astrologers, witches, mulattos, and those imbued with reason.

Follow me to see the library of forbidden volumes.

I trail after him through a hallway into a chamber with red velvet drapes hanging from iron rods, elaborate silk cords at the sides. My eyes adjust to the darkness. Two large wooden chests with brass fittings sit in the center of the room. I am struck by three padlocks on the front of them. What are these? I ask.

Perhaps tomes of a prurient nature. These trunks require three different keys from different priests. He casts his eyes downward. I have never seen the contents, he says with head bowed.

I stare at shelves of prohibited books, their leather bindings embossed with gold or silver. I reposition myself next to a shelf. The priest is watching me with interest. I read titles with the names of Constantine, Copernicus, Galileo, others I cannot read in Latin, Castilian, English, some about the Lutheran leader, Quakers, Africans. I am interrupted by a hand on my shoulder.

It is time to leave this room. Have you accepted Jesus into your heart?

I have a quick intake of breath. Does he know I am not a true believer?

If not, I want to save you from the fate of the Underworld.

The veil lifts of my ancestor's face. He cannot harm me. I gather my skirts. Goodbye, Father, I say with the finality I feel.

I exit with haste, all the books trapped in their Purgatory. I have lived this long to be free of their superstitions and hierarchy.

Word spreads throughout our community, so many gather to find the treasures taken from its citizens, to witness with their own eyes this abomination perpetrated on our populace. I head down a stairwell to the spaces underneath, staring at a winch and pulley the jailers used to distribute food to the prisoners. Suddenly, I hear the Captain yell, Open the cells!

I stand back as a noxious stench erupts in a cloud of dust. Gaunt, decrepit prisoners, some being held up by others who had waited decades to touch them, made their way by me. And then I saw her. A very ancient woman, unrecognizable as anyone I knew, with light in her eyes. She could have been one of my great-grandmothers, the one turned in by an ungrateful daughter.

EPILOGUE

3 September 1884
Santa Fe, New Mexico

I am Clara Celendaria Crespin Mendoza Trevez Laredo. The history I know has been passed down through oral traditions in my family for more than twenty-five generations. Many still fear what I am going to tell you and want me to be silent. But I harbor no threat. The inner strength of many lives blooms inside of me.

I feel the tragedies of those who came before me, their pain and suffering, the melancholy that has followed us through centuries and countries. But, ah, joy flourishes too. We are a resilient people who strive to make our way in the world. We do not proselytize but observe and teach what we know. The secret Shabbats, the candles flickering in our eyes, our lips repeating the prayers, the embrace of Adonai, one God, our God—remain in my soul. Our lives connect through generations embedded in our memories from our ancestors. The trauma of our past lingers inside us, delivered to the next generations, some not knowing where the sadness comes from in our souls.

My innocent grandbaby stares at me with the eyes of knowledge passed down, knowing he too will follow his heritage in this young country that says we can be free, own land, worship as we please. I pray with the other thirty-six families that have founded our congregation in Las Vegas, New Mexico named after the English philanthropist, Sir Moses Montefiore, without retribution, cleansing myself in a mikvah, enjoying the company of my community. My grandson will be a proud Jew.

How did we get here from Spain and Portugal, Mexico to New Mexico? Our cousins, as we are all related, sent us a letter from Texas. It is a strain of our family known for its curly hair and quick wit. One of our grandmothers was imprisoned by the Inquisition for many years. Her daughter, an infidel, notified the authorities. I do not have the details but Clara Crespin, my namesake, and her family suffered yet never lost their faith.

The terrors lasted until 1834, destroying all in its path, a tornado of fear and dread. Through cunning, hard work, prayer, loyalty, we have survived. The scars will never go away. So many were forced to attend church, come home and ask forgiveness. My grandmother, until the day she passed, remained suspicious, cautious, terrified to whisper prayers aloud, but never forgetting to light her candles on Friday night with the drapes drawn. I am among a small number who rescued the faith to speak our prayers in their language of origin without trepidation.

According to my great-great-grandmother, we stayed in the northern part of Mexico for many generations, giving birth to families and businesses that prospered. At least the Pueblo Revolt in 1680 established a universal law of religious privacy; however, many of our kind still did not trust the authorities.

After the end of the Inquisition, the War of Independence and the Civil War in 1821, 1834 and 1865 respectively, which happened a mere thirty years apart, some became restless and ventured into Spanish Texas, to escape watchful eyes.

When Mexico ceded much of its land to the United States, our family moved through the southern part of the United States as peddlers, store owners, doctors and men of law, establishing themselves in small towns until the 1870s. Still others faded into oblivion in New Mexico to escape the watchful eyes of priests observing some traditions in their homes, the fabric of our belief tattered.

I have a proud life as a married woman with four children and will soon be a grandmother again. Our community, an insulated one, picks spouses for our children from nearby cities. Our eldest has married into the Mendes family, who came to the colony of Georgia in the city of Savannah from New Amsterdam after being expelled from Recife in Brazil by the Portuguese in April of 1654. I am proud to be a Jew and express my love of God.

A letter was found in an old trunk inside a book of prayers with some old serapes and textiles yellowed with age. I will read it to you. I do not know the author, who is one of my predecessors. The edges crackle and break away in my fingers.

1836 diciembre

Now I am an abuela, my grandparents long gone. I am sorry they did not live to see the last person arrested by the Inquisition. In 1826, it caused an uproar in the press all over Europe when the master of a school, Cayetano Ripoll who taught Deist principles and did not believe in the infallibility of the Church, was executed. There was Maria de los Dolores López, a blind nun garroted in 1781, whose sentencing after a two-year trial took so long, three people read it from nine o'clock in the morning until one in the afternoon. Poor woman. She was a concubine to her confessor who served her up to the malevolence of the intolerant ones.

Some say the Inquisition was not so bad in the New World, but tens of thousands of innocent souls were murdered—relaxed is the term they use—as well as thousands in Europe, but I do not accept this. Even one human dying at the hand of the Church is a travesty of justice. May their immorality of thought and evil minds reign vengeance on them for generations to come.

With diluted power, they still pursue us in desperation. Even their Supreme in Spain has found them guilty of abuses.

It was not until María Cristina de Borbón signed a paper ending the Inquisition on 15 de julio 1834, that we grasped the end was near. Of course we heard reports that the Church's revenge continued longer, seeking out those who refused to follow their ways. Today, renegade priests pursue their prey, those with heretical beliefs, chasing them into unknown territories, far to the north. Many of us disappeared into the mission area of Nuevo México and beyond, seeking refuge away from the prying eyes of parish priests, closing their shutters to light their Shabbat candles, draping mirrors after the dead leave us and revealing their true history at the very end.

But our people are a fragment, almost destroyed by the unquenchable hatred of others. Yet, even now I have hope for a better future. All the lessons I have learned have not been for nothing. To the north blooms the United States, a land of free expression. Here is where we begin our future.

I am overwhelmed with the bravery of those who came before me. Would I have had the strength of the original Clara to endure all that she did? Today my life is lived without threats. I am compelled to tell this story as it was told to me.

I have taught my children the rituals and traditions of their ancestors to anchor them to the past. The seeds of survival are within them. We celebrate the holidays that mark the seasons: Yom Kippur, the Day of Atonement when we are closest to God, Sukkoth, the last harvest festival before the rains, Purim, celebrated in the spring where we honor Esther for saving her people as well as Passover, when the Egyptians let our people go. Shavout, 50 days after Passover, is the day God gave the Torah to the Jewish people and finally, Rosh Hashanah, the beginning of the year in the autumn.

We follow the cycles just as our ancestors did—birth, death, love, pain. We slide through the generations with haste.

My children know they are from proud people who endured more than I can imagine, especially the line of strong women who kept their integrity. The original Clara never whispered another name during her incarceration.

I believe with extended prayers the sadness that dwells in our souls will leave us. I was taught to have faith from those who repeated the stories of the past. They might have given up when loved ones perished in the fires, yet our traditions endured. We are a faith of remembrance admonished to teach our children all that we know.

I want the light to shine through all our souls for future generations.

May the breath of Goodness sweep across our lives.

AUTHOR'S NOTES

I have written this novel to show the depth and breadth of the Inquisition in the Americas. Many of the characters are real like Hernando Alonso, who was the first Jew to arrive in Mexico with Hernán Cortez in 1521; Tomas Trevino de Sobremonte, who was the only one burned alive in the auto-de-fé of 1649 who refused to reconcile with the church, and the Inquisitor Dr. Juan Saenz de Mañzoca, a very cruel man. Others are the ordinary people who survived under difficult circumstances. I want to tell their story.

When I began my Sephardic journey I was not aware there was an Inquisition in Mexico. Apparently, others weren't either. I was greeted with, "What?!" There was an Inquisition in Mexico?" Yes, it was in our backyard and according to some accounts, present in Arizona, Colorado, Texas and California. They set up offices in Mexico City, Lima, Peru and Cartegena, Columbia to search out heretics. If you examine the tenets of the church at that time, most of us would have been arrested for heresy and lasciviousness.

Further research revealed it had blanketed the New World. It was hard to grasp how pervasive this blind beauracracy was entertained by so many. There are lessons to be learned for our current times.

The auto-de-fés are accurate in time and place as well as details. They were the spectacles of their time.

Although the narrative is based on the arrest of a grandmother and the confession of her accuser during the Inquisition, I have adjusted the facts to fit my story. It was not an uncommon occurrence to be accused by those that knew you.

I envision a spectrum of beliefs within the community of crypto-Jews, the hidden ones of my novel. Some are devoted to the Catholic Church so they sacrifice a son to them as a priest; others remain Jews and pay only lip service to the church while others embrace Catholicism to be accepted with reservations, while still others accept an amalgam of both beliefs that assist in their survival as well as foster confusion, secrecy and danger.

It is not possible to write a book alone. I want to thank story editor, Anya Achtenberg whose insightful suggestions made the narrative flow; line editor, Rosa Cays whose grammatical expertise and knowledge of the Spanish language made the book more readable; and Deborah Ledford, whose familiarity with publishing standards created a polished product. I have to acknowledge the extraordinary scholarship of Gustavo Adolfo Guerra Reynoso in the area of colonial Mexico. He was smart and supportive. My beta readers, Deb Vesey, Debbie Wohl Isard, Kate Timmerman, Deborah Hilcove and Virginia Nosky offered insightful suggestions. Others, such as Susan Brooks, Katrina Shawver, Monica Unikel-Fasja who took me on a tour of The Palace of the Inquisition in Mexico City, Jose Navarro who invited me to speak at Beth Israel Community Center and Renato Huarte to Limmud in Mexico City and Lucy Lisbona who translated for me when Spanish escaped my crowded brain, were valuable in so many ways. I have a special thank you to

Christopher Benton, Ph.D. for his glossary assistance. He truly is "The Wizard of Arizona."

Also, the exhibit I viewed in Santa Fe, "Fractured Faiths: Spanish Judaism, The Inquisition, and New World Identities," reinforced my research with 175 items that documented Sephardic heritage and persecution with objects collected from museums and private collections from around the world. It had a profound impact on me.

As always, I could not have completed a project of this breadth without the encouragement of Skip, my soul mate. His willingness to travel to far away destinations, experience countless seminars and remain supportive through many frustrations encouraged me. Finally, a special acknowledgement to the academics in the Society for Crypto-Judaic Studies who research, present and write papers that are invaluable to authors who want to tell a narrative of a brave, courageous people. I thank them for welcoming me into the group and allowing me to share what I have learned on my journey.

Finally, the new science of epigenetics has enriched my study of these people. Although this was not a topic of discussion for my characters, it is of great interest today. Many who have suffered trauma realize that they carry some of it forward from the past and pass it on to future generations. Rachel Yehuda, M.D., a professor at Albert Einstein Medical School, remains the pioneer in this field after studying children of Holocaust survivors and pregnant women who experienced 9/11.

My theory that Sephardim passed on melancholy is documented in their strong oral tradition, books, poetry and music. The expulsions, forced conversions, abandoned homes and loss of religious items and synagogues had an impact on them. It requires more research.

For many these stories of Sephardim echo through generations. They remember fragments, pieces of rituals, explore dreams of those who came before them. The Jewish faith is one of remembrance. We encourage a respect for those who passed before us and are told to teach our children about history. L'dor vador means from generation to generation.

READER'S GUIDE

1. The book opens with an Auto-de-Fé. In translation it is an Act of Faith. Were these common? Why did thousands view this spectacle? Who ordered it?

2. A grandmother, Clara, and her granddaughter, Celendaria, are the female protagonists. What cements their relationship? How do their habits create suspicion and endanger them and their family? What precautions do they take?

3. What is the level of religiosity of the characters? Are the men as religious as the women? How do they make a living by traveling to other outposts of *conversos*? What purpose does the grandfather serve in the novel in terms of religion?

4. When all was taken from the Sephardim, what held them together as a people?

5. Mariel, Celendaria's friend, takes great risks by jeopardizing herself and others. Is the endangerment worth it?

6. Rabid theology destroys cultures. What is the Sephardic lesson for humanity? What is the significant message for our world? What compelled them to go on when many turned away? Are there parallels to the Holocaust?

7. The priest plays a significant role in the novel. What was his background? Did his family encourage him? How do the other characters respond to him?

8. Francisco and his brothers, Duarte and Manuel, prove their worth as bail bondmen and members of the family. At first, they are not accepted. Why?

9. Sephardim experienced incomparable trauma from the time of the expulsion to the 1700s. The ordeal of being cast out of their homes, the destruction of synagogues, the loss of books and religious items and the collapse of families for almost four hundred years damaged them. Why did they repeat these stories through generations? Why not leave them behind?

11. Identity is essential for culture to flourish. Is identity influenced by genetic memory or environment? How has it affected your family history?

12. The church and civil authorities created fear. In the past men were the scholars. Since books were forbidden, women memorized the prayers. Why were they the new keepers of the faith?

13. More women were accused, tried, convicted and burned alive than men during the Inquisition which lasted 354 years. Why? What were the reasons for this?

14. The Inquisition ended in 1834. Near the end of the novel, the descendants of Clara and Celendaria find their voices. What purpose do they serve?

15. Geography plays an important part in the development of the narrative. Where are these people headed and why? Are they welcomed? Are their ancestors still practicing rituals and traditions in the 21st century? Are we more tolerant today?

16. The expulsion from Spain in 1492 and Portugal in 1497 created a Diaspora that sent the Sephardim to the corners of the known world. Are there still Sephardic communities in Recife, Brazil, the Caribbean, the Philippines, India and South America?

17. The Inquisition had to satisfy financial needs for the crown and the church. Where else did they open offices in Nuevo España?

18. Sephardim lived as Catholics outside their homes. They attended Mass, used Gentile names and worked to be accepted as "New Christians." Inside their homes, they remained Jews to celebrate the Sabbath, eat Mediterranean foods and pray. What made them continue to follow rituals? Why did they expose themselves to the danger of committing crimes against the state?

19. What were the consequences of living a duplicitous life? How did they function with two identities? How often did they tell lies? How much catechism did Clara have to learn?

20. After many Sephardim fled or went underground, what groups did the Inquisition pursue?

GLOSSARY

adafina—slow-cooked Sephardic Sabbath stew

anusim—those forced to abandon Judaism against their will; the forced ones

auto-de-fé—literally, an act of faith; a public ceremony held during the Inquisition when convicted heretics were sentenced and executed

basura—garbage

herenjenas—eggplants

calabaza—a large winter squash

cárcel secreta—jail of secrets

chachalacas—noisy galliform birds

chayotes—an edible plant belonging to the gourd family

converso—a Jew who publicly recanted the Jewish faith and converted to Catholicism under the pressure of the Inquisition; the term also applies to a descendant of a converso

criollo—a person born in the New World of white Spanish parents

dulce—sweet

effigy—at an auto-de-fé, a dummy figure to represent a prisoner who had escaped, one who had died in the cells, or a person who had been accused but who had never been captured.

familiares—official lay collaborators of the Inquisition

fiadores—bondsmen

garrote—a cord or iron collar used for strangulation at the stake and at the mercy administered by the Inquisition if the heretic expressed the desire to return to the Christian faith

haggadah—a book that contains the liturgy for the Seder service on the Jewish festival of Passover

havdalah—a religious ceremony observed by Jews at the end of the Sabbath that includes blessings over wine, spices and the lighting of a candle; a multi-sensory ritual that defines the division and separation of Shabbat from the beginning of the week

hija—daughter

horno—mud adobe outdoor oven used by indigenous people and early settlers of North America

Kabbalah—ancient Jewish tradition of mystical interpretation of the Bible; the secret level of the Torah which teaches the deepest insights into the essence of being and a relationship with God

kashrut—Jewish religious dietary laws for slaughtering animals and prepping for consumption of all food and utensils

Kaddish—Jewish prayer recited daily at the synagogue by mourners after the death of a loved one

La Convivencia—"The Coexistence" is the period in Spanish history spanning the time from the Muslim conquest of Spain in the eighth century until the expulsion of the Jews in 1492; acknowledged as a time of peace between Muslims, Christians and Jews

limpieza de sangre—literally, purity of blood; refers to those considered "Old Christians" without Jewish or Muslim ancestors

lulav—frond of the date palm used during the Jewish holiday of Sukkoth held in autumn to celebrate the sheltering of the Israelites in the wilderness *meshumadin*—"a destroyed one," those who voluntarily converted from Judaism to Christianity

mestizo—a person of mixed European and indigenous American ancestry

mezuzah—parchment with religious texts attached in a case to the doorpost of a Jewish home as a sign of faith

mikvah—a special bath used in Judaism to return one to a state of ritual purity

moriscos—Muslims who converted to Christianity

muchacha—young woman or girl

mujadara—cooked lentils with grains and onions

nietos—grandchildren

nopales—cactus paddles, especially from the prickly pear

pan de afflición—unleavened bread used at Passover; matzo

pantines—leather shoes for girls

Pesach—Hebrew word for eight day festival to commemorate the Exodus of the Jewish people from Egypt; also known as Passover

reconciliado—a heretic and first offender, who had been brought back into the Church; his or her property was confiscated and he or she was usually required to wear a sanbenito in public

relapso—a second heretical offender; someone who falls back into criminal conduct

relajado— relaxed; a term used to mean death by being burned alive; the turning over of a heretic by the Inquisition to the secular authorities for burning at the stake

sanbenito—a penitential garment worn for periods of time fixed by the inquisitors, usually yellow

serape—a colorful woolen shawl worn over the shoulders

Shema—most important of all Jewish prayers that declares the
oneness of God
Succoth—major Jewish festival held in the autumn to celebrate the
sheltering of the Israelites in the wilderness
vaquero—cowboy whose life is about cattle and horses

BIBLIOGRAPHY FOR FURTHER READING

Chapa, Juan Bautista, *Texas & Northeastern Mexico, 1630-1690*. University of Texas Press, Austin, 1997.

Chuchiak IV, John F., *The Inquisition in New Spain, 1536-1820*. The John Hopkins University Press, Baltimore, 2012.

Elazar, Daniel J., *The Other Jews*. Basic Books,Inc., USA, 1989.

Entine, Jon, *Abraham's Children—Race, Identity, and the DNA of the Chosen People*. Grand Central Publishing, New York, Boston, 2007.

Gitlitz, David M. and Linda Kay Davidson, *A Drizzle of Honey—The Lives and Recipes of Spain's Secret Jews*. St. Martin's Griffin, New York, 1999.

Gitlitz, David M., *Secrecy and Deceit—The Religion of the Crypto-Jews*. The Jewish Publication Society, Philadelphia and Jerusalem, 1996.

Hordes, Stanley M., *To the End of the Earth: A History of the Crypto-Jews of New Mexico*. Columbia University Press, New York, 2005.

Kohut, George Alexander, *Jewish Martyrs of the Inquisition in South America*. New York, 1896.

Lerner, Ira T., *Mexican Jewry in the Land of the Aztecs*. B. Costa-Amic, Mexico, D. F., 1963.

Liebman Jacobs, Janet, *Hidden Heritage—The Legacy of the Crypto-Jews*. University of California Press, 2002.

Liebman, Seymour, *The Jews of New Spain—Faith, Flame, and the Inquisition*. University of Miami Press, 1970.

Malamed, Sandra Cumings, *The Return to Judaism—Descendants from the Inquisition Discovering Their Jewish Roots*. Fithian Press, McKinleyville, California, 2010.

Victor Perera, *The Cross and the Pear Tree—A Sephardic Journey*. University of California Press, Berkeley and Los Angeles, 1995.

Roth, Michael S., *Memory, Trauma, and History—Essays on Living with the Past*. Columbia University Press, New York, 2012.

Santos, Richard G., *Silent Heritage—The Sephardim and the colonization of the Spanish North American Frontier*, 1492-1600. New Sepharad Press, San Antonio, TX, 2000.

Stillman, Yehuda K. and Zucker, George K., *New Horizons in Sephardic Studies*. State University of New York Press, Albany, 1993.

Wadsworth, James E., *In Defense of the Faith: Joaquim Marques de Araújo, a Comissário in the Age of Inquisitional Decline*. Weidenfeld&Nicolson, 2013.

Wolynn, Mark, *It Didn't Start with You—How Inherited Family Trauma Shapes Who We Are and How to End the Cycle*. Viking, 2016.

AUTHOR INTERVIEW

1. **What does the title *HIDDEN ONES—A Veil of Memories* mean?**
   Hidden ones is another term for Sephardic Jews who felt compelled to hide their Judaism. They were also called crypto-Jews, anusim which means coerced or forced ones, *conversos* and sometimes *marranos*, a negative term that means swine. The veil of memories is a reference to the strong oral tradition Sephardim passed on in their families. They remembered their family history, the Diaspora from Spain and Portugal and the impact the Inquisition had on their lives. Hidden ones was a term they used among themselves. They had to be very secretive within their own families as well as the outside world. The Veil of Memories is the shadow of their faith they passed on to future generations. Sometimes it was only a fragment such as lighting candles on Friday night that stayed with them.

2. **The format of HIDDEN ONES is unusual in that there are no quotation marks. Why did you choose to write it that way?**
   I wanted the reader to be immersed in the story immediately. "He said" and "she said" interrupt the flow. Since the chapters are labeled with the character's names, I knew the reader would figure it out. A few people have said they were challenged in

the beginning and adapted as they read more. No one has said they put it down because it is not a traditional format. Many contemporary novels are adopting this format today.

3. **You express an interest in epigentics. What does that have to do with Sephardim?**

   I have been interested in the new science of epigenetics for a while. I find it fascinating that our DNA can be adjusted by environment and passed on to future generations, especially trauma. Rachel Yehuda, M.D. at Albert Einstein Medical School is the pioneer in this arena. She has worked with the children of Holocaust survivors and pregnant women who experienced 9/11. My theory is that Sephardic Jews who were chased around the world for almost four hundred years also suffered trauma. I wonder if some of that was passed on to their descendants. No one has studied that topic yet. For more on this, watch my video at www.ELITalks/MarciaFine.

4. **You speak at international conferences about Sephardim and Trauma. How does that figure into your story?**

   This group of people suffered in many ways. They had to abandoned their homes, sometimes trading them for a donkey; they had to live duplicitous lives and remember the lies they told to survive; and they always endured the threat of death as they broke the laws of the state by practicing Judaism in secrecy. They exhibited melancholy that we call depression today in their songs, books and poetry. They never stopped longing for their life before the Inquisition in Spain.

5. **What do you mean by duplicitous lives?**

   By definition duplicitous means deception, a necessary fact of life for people who were not allowed to practice their one true faith. For Hidden Ones, it meant living as a Catholic outside their home by attending Mass, using a Christian name and not arousing suspicion of neighbors or priests by behaving in a devout manner. In the privacy of their home at great risk, they celebrated the Sabbath, washed themselves as well as linens on Shabbat, prepared foods from their Iberian past, celebrated holidays, used Hebrew names and spoke Ladino. Living two lives caused great stress because they had to remember what they said to others in order not to reveal themselves.

6. **You used the term reconciliation and relaxed. Please explain.**

The ironic term of relaxing someone, according to the church, was actually the burning of an innocent person alive. At the last moment some reconciled themselves by offering to come back to the church. Often they were given penances, but sometimes they were garroted first before their feet were set on fire. They were burned in the nude as their sanbenitos were taken away to hang from church rafters with their name attached. They served as a warning to others they considered to be heretics.

7. **When the Inquisition ended in 1834 many Jews could not re-enter Judaism because all synagogues, books and religious items were gone. Many did not want to stay in the Catholic faith. What did they do?**

Since the Catholic Church did not encourage speaking directly to God and did not give out Bibles, the Jews turned to the Presbyterians. Why? Because they distributed Bibles to study. The Jews were thrilled to have a copy of the Old Testament so they could review the stories they knew from the Torah.

7. **Hidden Ones is a sweeping saga. What are the themes in this novel?**

   I teach tolerance wherever I go. It never goes out of style to remind people to treat each other with respect and dignity, even if they do not believe as you do. Another theme would be to remember our history and the impact it can have on those who come after us. And, finally, education is a catalyst for showing us we all have a history that stays with us.

8. **Do any of these lessons apply to current events?**

   Many radical and extreme ideologies are intolerant of other's differences. We have examples in our media almost every day of the cruelty perpetuated on others. There are migrations of immigrants happening in many countries. We need to protect innocent children who have to be taught how to hate. Live and let live is a good motto for our times.

9. **What made Sephardim go on after being thwarted in so many places? Where did their resilience come from?**

   With a strong oral tradition and the Law of Moses, they persevered. They knew what happened to their ancestors and they took great precautions. They had a strong belief that they had to teach their children about their faith so they adapted to conditions that were fraught with danger. They developed an inner strength that guided them with their belief in one God. Traditions and rituals kept them together.

10. **You write about the Rio Arriba, the "Upper River" area in the Southwest territories. Did that exist? Was there inter-marriage between the diverse groups who settled there?**

    According to historical research this was an area north of the Rio

Grande where disenfranchised people settled. Some were peddlers, Europeans, nomadic Plains Indians, others who had been enslaved, some Spanish nobility, Moslems, Protestants, people who were running from the law, creative types and Hidden Ones looking for safety. It would not be unusual for people to intermarry. Even today I read about or meet people of native or Spanish descent with Sephardic names. There is a story in their past!

11. **The interrogation of Clara was so realistic. How did you re-create those scenes?**

I did a lot of research on how the Inquisition was structured, the roles people played and searched for books by scholars on the subject. I wanted the reader to feel they were in the room with Clara. The Inquisition left detailed records of arrests and interrogations. They pursued questions about what the prisoner believed and what kind of rituals they used. It is all available today.

12. **Did it disturb you to spend so much time living with the Inquisition?**

Fortunately, I have a positive outlook on life, although sometimes I had to stop because the cruelty was more than I could bear. I believe I have been divinely guided to tell this story of what happened to people who held on to their beliefs with a strength that is hard to imagine. They could have embraced the church, which many did; yet others chose to become martyrs of their faith. I would like to think readers feel uplifted at the end. L'dor vador—from generation to generation.

www.marciafine.com

CPSIA information can be obtained
at www.ICGtesting.com
Printed in the USA
FSOW01n2333200317
31935FS